The Feet of Douglas Blouse

Matthew Frame

ISBN 978-1-915787-03-3

Printed in Great Britain by
Biddles Books Limited, King's Lynn, Norfolk

For my Mum and Dad

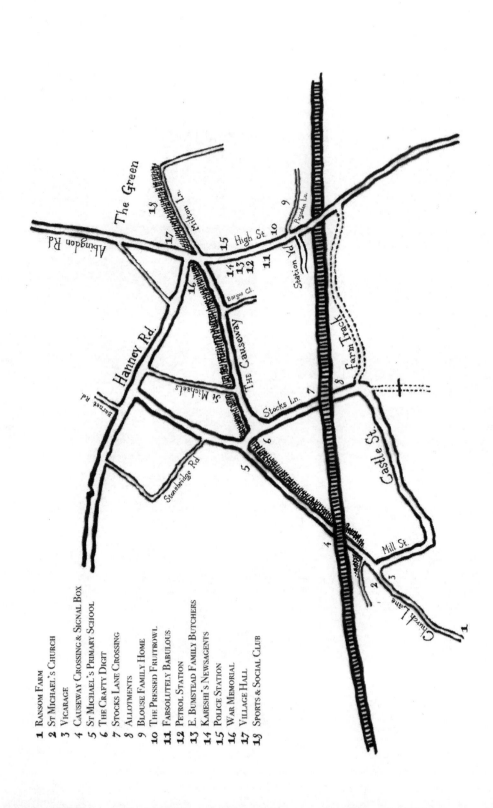

PART 1

1 *Saturday, August 14, 1993*

Bertie Blouse felt like he was on a rollercoaster, sat at the front of the lead carriage waiting for the inevitable 'Oh shit!' moment after the coaster had trundled up the chain-driven incline towards the summit and tipped into oblivion, such was the knot of anxiety in his stomach. He was in fact trundling downhill, not in a rollercoaster but a taxi, and the inevitable 'Oh shit!' moment that he was sensing would come shortly after he got out.

'It's the first turning on the left after the bridge, Butt,' Bertie said from the rear of the taxi as it finished its descent down Steventon Hill and crested the modest hump of the railway bridge. 'Just here,' Bertie said, pointing to the turning up ahead.

The taxi driver crumpled his brow at the strange pronunciation of the word 'here' which Bertie pronounced 'yur', and also at his use of the word 'Butt'. Nevertheless, the driver did as he was instructed, turning into Station Yard and pulling up beside two impressive large stone houses.

Bertie spied the meter and dug his hand into the pocket of his black Levis, more than a little conscious of his limited finances and hoping its contents would be enough to cover the fare.

'How much is that then, Butt?' he said, looking into the driver's eyes in the taxi's rear-view mirror.

'That'll be £4.80 please ... Butt,' the driver said, turning round and facing Bertie with a wry smile, which he returned.

'Guess I must've picked up some bad habits in the old language department. That's what living in Bridgend for a few years'll do to you though, I suppose,' he said, pronouncing years 'yurs'. 'Sorry, years,' he said, changing his diction. 'Don't worry, though, Bu.. err, mate,' Bertie said,

7

adjusting to the more parochial dialect. 'Butt's a nice word, despite how it sounds.'

The driver frowned, but his grin remained. 'You're not from round yur then?' he said, mimicking Bertie's accent.

Bertie gazed out the windows of the taxi, taking in the view of his new but oh so familiar surroundings. 'Yes and no,' he said.

'£4.80,' the driver repeated.

Bertie pulled a crumpled five pound note from his pocket, relieved at dodging the potential embarrassment of not being able to cover the fare. He had to be extremely careful with what money he did have. If he'd been stuck on the train any longer, he probably would've spent half of it in the buffet car, trying to submerge the nerves he was feeling at being back in his old village.

'Keep the change,' Bertie said, reaching for the door handle.

'You're too kind,' the driver said with a sniff of a laugh.

'And don't spend it all on sweets,' Bertie said, grabbing his bag and leaving the taxi with a little smile on his face.

It might only be twenty pence, but Bertie was not exactly in any position to be flash with his money. Not with the way things had gone back home. Back home? That sounded strange, given where he was standing. He was home. Despite living in Bridgend for the best part of the last six years, it had never really felt like home to him. Not like Steventon did. Even now, nervous as he was about what might lie ahead, the old place still had that old familiar feeling.

The taxi pulled away, leaving Bertie standing in the warm sunshine of a mid-August Saturday afternoon. He put the black and red Head sports bag containing his meagre belongings down on the pavement and gazed over at the impressive stone buildings that once served as Isambard Kingdom Brunel's headquarters during the building of the Great Western Railway, his old village's equidistant location between London and Bristol being ideal for the famous engineer's needs.

Bertie removed his denim jacket and slung it over his shoulder, enjoying the fresh air. After being stuck on a train for what turned out to be nearer three and a half hours rather than the scheduled two, it was good to finally stretch his legs. His modest beer gut, that was actually more like a paunch, pressed gently against the tucked-in grey and blue of his Status Quo, 'End of the Road' baseball shirt. Bertie pulled the shirt free from his waistband and wafted some fresh air against his clammy upper torso and back.

Picking his bag up, he walked to the top of Station Yard, looking left down the High Street of the village that still felt so familiar to him. He could see his old local down on the right, the Pressed Fruitbowl. Its exterior resembled his own boozer back in Bridgend; though he doubted the Fruitbowl was facing the same financial problems that the Red Dragon was. Bertie let out a small chuckle at the ridiculously stereotypical name of the pub he had left behind, feeling no sense of loyalty to the place whatsoever, nor of regret at doing so; nor for the woman he had left Steventon for nearly six years ago, who had turned into something more resembling the pub sign's fierce mythical creature than the vivacious and flirtatious woman he had met on Bullseye back in 1987.

A wave of nostalgia came over him as he gazed down at the Fruitbowl, recalling many a jovial evening spent in his old local. He wondered if his old darts partner, Graham Glass, was still in the village with his wife Edna and their son Peter. Unlike him, Graham hadn't run off with the other contestant on Bullseye, much as Bertie thought his old mate would've liked to.

Looking beyond the pub, he could make out the tall horse chestnut trees that stood at the edge of both the big and the little green at the crossroads with the causeway, where the war memorial was; where he and Douglas had been standing when the power came back on after the big hurricane of 1987, just before he'd left for Wales.

His eyes turned slowly to the right, almost as if he was checking for something he half wished not to see. But of course it was there. As if a road was just going to disappear! His gaze was drawn inexorably towards the street sign of Pugsden Lane on the opposite side of the road: the small cul-de-sac that he had not ventured down in almost six years. Part of him wanted to run, to turn on his heels and get the hell out of there. But where could he run to? Not back to Rhonda and the nightmare of Bridgend. That was out of the question, especially after what Rhonda had put him through; her treacherous actions having an oddly Karmic feeling to them, that he thought was the universe's way of punishing him for what he had done to Alice and Douglas. What right had he to come back here? To just turn up unannounced and totally out of the blue. But this was where he wanted to be. He knew that much at least. He felt it. What he would have to do to make amends was a question yet to be answered, but one he knew he needed to tackle. Douglas would be seventeen, going on eighteen now, he calculated: no longer the boy who didn't yet come up to his shoulder who was just starting out at big school back in '87. That boy would be a man now.

A wave of anxiety washed over Bertie. He quickly patted himself down, suddenly in desperate need of a cigarette. He could feel no reassuring rectangular bulge in either the front or back pockets of his jeans. Then he remembered; popping the button on the right breast pocket of his denim jacket and extracting a ten deck of Benson and Hedges. He was trying to give up, or at least cut down, but the way he was feeling right now was going to make that particular endeavour one hell of a task. He considered nipping down the Pressed Fruitbowl for some Dutch courage. The effects of the two cans of McEwan's Export he'd had on the train had been nullified by the anxiety building in his knotted stomach, and his thoughts once again turned to the two people he had left behind here.

He lit the cigarette with a trembling hand and crossed the road, enjoying the almost immediate effects of the head rush the cigarette induced. Feeling a little dizzy, he leant up against a nearby telegraph pole, feeling the warmth of the wood and the ever so slightly sticky texture of the tar being melted by the August sun. After his head rush had fully dissipated, Bertie's eyes were drawn to a colourful piece of paper stapled to the telegraph pole. It was a brightly illustrated A4 poster advertising the village's annual fete. He squinted, reading the list of attractions, taking deep drags on his cigarette as he did so. 'Stalls, bouncy castle, judo display, Morris dancing, police dog display and much much more!' the poster read. He looked at the date, quickly checking it against the digital read out of his cheap Casio wristwatch. The fete was today. Or at least it had been, he thought, clocking the time on the poster which advertised it as taking place between 12 and 4pm. It was now almost 5pm. Presumably the festivities would be over by now.

He crushed his cigarette out under his foot, took a deep breath of clean summer air in through his nose and out through his mouth and began the trepidatious walk down Pugsden Lane, trying not to think of what he was going to say by way of an explanation. Bertie passed the rusting hulks of the derelict coal lorries in the dilapidated sheds on his right as the lane veered round to the left. The old lorries were in the same position and the same shit state of affairs as they had been on the day he'd left.

The pounding of his heart grew harder and faster as the distance to his former home decreased with every step. He saw the caravan first. At least, he saw its roof protruding above the hedge line of the bungalow and its adjacent property. The memory of hitting that winning dart on Bullseye returned and Bertie smiled, remembering how Jim Bowen had shouted at him to leave his darts in the board after Bertie had automatically gone to retrieve them. 'Leave them!' Jim had shouted as Bully's star prize had been revealed to himself, to Graham and the cheering, clapping audience, not to mention the apoplectic host himself. The prize caravan had then been towed onto the set by two men in red Bullseye polo shirts. Bertie had done exactly as Jim had instructed, and both he and Graham had gone over enthusiastically to inspect the Marauder 500, opening the door and collecting their tankards, bendy bullies and cash from the caravan's plush interior.

It had been so modern and clean that day. Quite the opposite of the sad sight that slowly revealed itself as Bertie drew closer to it, or the shabby-looking maroon Ford Orion that was parked next to it. Regardless of its poor condition, seeing his old car brought another wave of nostalgia, and at first he didn't even notice the police car, partially obscured though it was, nor the back end of the black van that was also parked on the driveway. As Bertie finally registered both unfamiliar vehicles, a ripple of unease crept over him, but he just assumed that whoever owned the vehicles must be attending to business elsewhere and that they were merely parked on his old driveway for convenience purposes only. That was until he saw the policeman standing in the shade of the bungalow's porch, just in front of the front door that was slightly ajar. Bertie thought he recognised the man: tallish and with glasses, a short almost flat-top style haircut and a short moustache.

The policeman soon noticed Bertie standing on the opposite side of the bungalow's waist-high brick wall. Removing his glasses, the officer squinted and walked towards Bertie, scrutinising him in the sunshine before replacing his glasses. Over the policeman's shoulder, Bertie saw a man in a black suit backing out of the front door of his old home. He was holding something, like he was a removal man, but one that was inappropriately well-dressed for the job. As the man backed out further, another man dressed identically to the first emerged into the sunshine, and Bertie now saw that they were carrying something about six foot long, black and horizontal. He saw the wheels on each of its corners and realised that they were carrying a stretcher. A black cover hid whatever was on it.

The policeman walked over to the wall. 'Is it Bertie Blouse?' he said, shielding his eyes from the sun with his right hand.

Bertie didn't hear him. He was watching the men in black suits walking gingerly towards the back end of the black van. He could now make out that it had the words 'Private Ambulance' printed on the back in dull silver lettering. The rear was now being opened with one hand by the man closest to it as he balanced the weight of the stretcher on his thigh. Then the black stretcher was loaded into it.

'Bertie?' the policeman asked again.

Bertie silently nodded.

'Bertie, I'm Sergeant Frisk,' the policeman said, as Bertie at last met the policeman's gaze.

Bertie vaguely remembered him, as the gravity of what was unfolding around him started to sink in. 'Is it? ... It's not?' Bertie said, softly shaking his head and raising a tentative hand to his mouth.

'Bertie, I'm so sorry,' Frisk said, 'it's Alice.'

Bertie dropped his sports bag on the warm, dusty ground, standing motionless save for the gentle nodding of his head as he struggled to take in the tragedy playing out before him.

'I'm so sorry,' Sergeant Frisk said again.

Bertie and Frisk watched in silence as one of the men in black brought the back end of the van down, hiding the shrouded form of his wife and eliminating any hope of reconciliation that Bertie might have harboured. 'How? How did she...?' Bertie said, trailing off.

'We're not sure,' Frisk said. 'We think it might've been the electrics, but I wouldn't want to speculate at this stage.'

The words floated around Bertie's head like a swarm of softly buzzing bees, but they did not register at any point between his ears.

'Listen, Bertie,' Frisk said, removing his glasses and pinching the bridge of his nose, 'I'm not quite sure how to say this but ...'

'What?' Bertie said, redirecting his gaze from the van back to the policeman.

'Well, it's just ...' Frisk drew in a deep breath and exhaled. 'You picked one hell of a day to come back here.'

Bertie and Frisk stood in silence as the funeral director's black van slowly crunched its way off the driveway and up Pugsden Lane. Bertie's dulled senses gradually returned to him as it all started to sink in. He had thought that by now he would be conversing with his wife; perhaps grovelling and apologising before sloping off to find a Bed and Breakfast for the night, somewhere where he might be able to strategise a better plan of action for winning his family back. Instead he was watching his wife being taken away on a stretcher in the back of a van, like an old sideboard. He still could not find his voice as the van finally disappeared up the lane and out of sight. It was Sergeant Frisk who broke the silence.

'Listen, Bertie, I need to talk to you about all this,' he said. 'The truth is that we've had a bit of trouble today, and that's putting it mildly, to say the least.'

'What's happened?' Bertie said.

'Bertie, Alice isn't the only member of your family that's been taken to the hospital today.'

Bertie's head turned quickly on his shoulders, sharp focus reasserting itself. 'Douglas!?' he said. 'Oh Jesus no, not him as well. Not Douglas,' he said, as all hope of reconciliation felt as if it was fast flying out of the window, and the realisation that he had left it all too late gripped him in a sudden and urgent panic.

'No, Bertie, he's OK,' Frisk said, holding up a placatory hand. 'Well, not OK. He was unconscious when the ambulance came to get him from the railway, but he was alive.'

'The railway?' Bertie repeated. 'Unconscious? ... What the hell's happened to him?'

'He had an accident on the level crossing,' Frisk said. 'He fell. The train went over his legs. He's extraordinarily lucky to be alive is the truth of it,' Frisk said, shaking his head. 'If it hadn't been for those sheep...'

'Sheep!?' Bertie said, perplexed. 'What the bloody hell have sheep got to do with it?'

'Like I said,' Frisk sighed, '... it's been a hell of a day.'

'That's why my train was stopped, wasn't it?' Bertie said, more to himself than to anyone else. 'Christ, I must have been on the train that hit him. The driver was blaring his horn as we came into the village and then he slammed on the brakes. I caught a glimpse of the crossing out of the train window as I came through, and I could have sworn I saw a police van, but I didn't make the connection... Oh Jesus.'

'I've got one of mine up at the hospital as well,' Frisk said. 'A young constable who was injured during the dog display at the fete. It's been a rare old day.'

Frisk ran his hand over his head, took off his glasses and rubbed the bridge of his nose with his thumb and index finger.

'Listen, Bertie, I need to get back to the station and make a few phone calls,' he said, putting his glasses back on. 'I think it would be good if you popped down and saw me, in an hour or so perhaps. I can bring you up to speed on everything that's been happening. Douglas has been a bit of a handful these past few days, and it's only now, obviously, that I'm beginning to understand why.'

'This is all bloody bonkers,' Bertie said. 'Alice dead. Douglas...' Bertie didn't finish the sentence. He just shook his head in total incomprehension, staring at the bungalow. Beyond the black metal gate at the side of the

14

house, Bertie could just make out the back end of Alice's purple Raleigh Shopper bicycle leaning up against the wall: the bike that Alice had owned and proudly maintained for so many years, still with its matching purple holdall on the rack of the bike's rear wheel. Fresh tears filled his eyes. 'Bloody bonkers,' he repeated.

'I know,' Frisk said. 'I really am very sorry, Bertie. Where do you intend to stay? I'm afraid this place is going to be off limits for the time being until we establish what's happened. If you do intend to stay local, I will obviously keep you fully informed of any developments, if that's what you want? For what it's worth, I don't think Alice's death is suspicious, but we'll have to wait for the coroner's report to have that confirmed.'

'Yeah,' Bertie said, picking up his sports bag. 'Thanks. I'll go and knock up an old pal. Is Graham still in the village?'

'Graham Glass?' Frisk asked.

'Yeah. He used to live down Bargus Close.'

'Yeah, they're still there.'

'Tidy,' Bertie said absently, turning away from the bungalow.

'Come down and see me in an hour. I can fill you in a bit better on what's been going on around here,' Frisk said, tying off some blue and white police tape across the driveway of number 8 Pugsden Lane and walking towards his police Ford Escort, next to where Bertie was standing. 'I'm afraid I had to break the back door in to get into the place earlier. We'll obviously pay for the damage. I'll have to ask you not to touch anything as well,' Frisk said. 'That includes the car and the caravan. Just until we hear back from the coroner. I was also going to make some phone calls to try and locate Douglas's next of kin. You've saved me the bother to a certain extent there, but...' Frisk trailed off, scratching his chin.

'Yeah, I understand,' Bertie said.

Frisk smiled sympathetically as he opened the driver's door of the police car. 'Why don't you go and get yourself something to steady your nerves,' he said, climbing in. 'You've had quite a shock.'

Sergeant Frisk pulled the door shut and wound down the window. 'Come and see me in an hour.'

Bertie was left standing alone in the sunshine. The rollercoaster had tipped into oblivion. The 'Oh shit' moment had well and truly begun, and Bertie Blouse had absolutely no idea how long it would last.

As she pulled her meaty trike onto the gravel driveway of the vicarage, Reverend Bowen found it hard to believe that after everything she and Douglas Blouse had been through over the past week, she would find herself returning from the hospital, where Douglas's condition had now thankfully been downgraded from critical to serious, genuinely concerned for his well-being and, for the first time in a long time, praying for his recovery. She'd been unable to see him, of course. The doctors had still been working hard on trying to re-attach the feet that had been severed by the train. The results of their efforts were yet to be determined.

Bowen extracted the keys from her trike's ignition, opened the gate and walked down the garden path. As she opened the front door of the vicarage, Moses, her black and caramel King Charles spaniel, was there enthusiastically welcoming his owner home. Moses had suffered as much as anybody at the hands of Douglas Blouse, having only just escaped near decapitation three days ago after being involved in an incident on the railway himself. Bowen and Sergeant Frisk had only just managed to save the dog from Douglas's maniacal clutches.

'Hello, you ... Hello, you... Come on then, my beautiful boy,' Bowen said to the dog as the pair took a walk over to the church opposite, specifically round to the building's east window where Douglas's destructive handiwork was still on display. The hole in Jesus Christ's groin was yet to be fixed: something she had to sort out. Still, it didn't seem quite so much of an insurmountable task as it had yesterday.

They walked back over to the trike, Hilda placing her helmet on the rear bench seat, catching a glimpse of her reflection in the vehicle's wing mirror. The red welts that Douglas had inflicted upon her with the bamboo cane following the incident with Moses on the railway were receding; in fact they had almost disappeared entirely. Yesterday they had been red and livid; today they were a soft pink, blending in almost seamlessly with her natural skin tone. She smiled at her reflection in the mirror, feeling a sense of contentment that had for so long been totally alien to her. Even here, standing on the driveway of the vicarage that she was soon to be evicted from did nothing to dampen the feeling of serenity she had felt growing inside her after seeing the departed spirit of Alice Blouse standing by the railway line earlier today. After so many years in the wilderness of spiritual turmoil, she had at long last been given the clear and simple vision of the life eternal always promised to her. As she had cradled the bloodied and battered body of Douglas Blouse on the railway, she had finally understood the power of forgiveness, the importance of compassion and the absolute necessity of unconditional love.

She glanced over at the church door. The laminated 'Church open' sign hung on the chunky iron handle of the large oak doors. Only this morning had she considered altering the sign to say the complete opposite and locking the church doors indefinitely, while staying in bed on a Sunday morning for the first time in over twenty years! But that had all changed. Even though church numbers had been in sharp decline, she would get up tomorrow morning with a renewed enthusiasm and a determined will to serve the spiritual needs of her congregation.

She opened the front door of the vicarage, with Moses following on close behind, and entered the cool and shady hallway. On the side table next to the coat hooks and umbrella stand sat her telephone answering machine. One red eye was blinking at her, informing her that she had a message. The machine was relatively new and she was still getting to grips with the thing. She pressed the grey button with the white sideways triangle on its front panel and after a beep and short crackle the voice of Sergeant Frisk began talking inanimately in the hallway.

'Hilda, hi, it's Alan here. I just wanted to ring to let you know I'm starting operation clear-up and I wanted to talk to you to make sure we're all on the same page with regards to what happened today... In other news, I think you should know that an old ghost showed up earlier. Strange as it may sound, it's Bertie. Bertie Blouse, Douglas's dad. He turned up at the bungalow just as the funeral directors were taking Alice away in the van. Terrible timing, poor sod. He's coming down here in about half an hour for a chat. He's going to want to know what happened earlier and I personally have got no option but to tell him as much as I know about the fete and what we had planned with Gooch and the display.' There was a short but perceptible pause. 'But that's not necessarily *all* there is to know about Gooch and the display, is it? ... Anyway I'll...'

It was at that point that the machine ran out. Hilda's heart skipped a beat as she processed Frisk's words. She took a deep breath and hesitantly picked up the phone, dialling Alan Frisk's direct line at the police station, nervously twiddling the white coiled telephone cord, not quite sure what she was going to say to him. 'An old ghost', Frisk had said of Bertie's surprise reappearance, she thought, as the telephone's ringtone chirped in her ear. So between them they now had the Blouse parental set.

Bertie could hear the noise coming from number 4 Bargus Close before he could see the property itself. As he got closer, he could also hear another dissonant sound merging with the racket of what he assumed must be the television. It was a low but very loud rumbling noise. He knocked on the glass panel of the front door. The collective noises coming from within easily absorbed the sound of Bertie's knuckles rapping modestly on the glass. He knocked again, harder this time. Still nothing. He tried the door handle. It was unlocked. Tentatively he pushed it open and stuck his head in. Graham Glass was snoring raucously in his armchair in front of the television. His feet were raised up on the armchair's built-in extendable foot rest. On the screen of the large television set in the corner of the room, a middle-aged woman wearing only khaki shorts, boots and a pair of gardening gloves was tickling the testicles of a slightly older man with a clutch of stinging nettles. Her saggy breasts dangled down towards her flabby midriff, which in turn hung limply over the waistband of her shorts. Her eyes twinkled with sadistic pleasure behind a pair of gold-rimmed spectacles. The man on the receiving end of the nettles was groaning in pain, or maybe pleasure, and was lying naked on a sun-lounger with his hands tied together behind the back of his head, while the dumpy woman armed with the stinging nettles in her gloved hand set about his privates with gleeful enthusiasm.

Graham's armchair was surrounded by discarded VHS tapes and their card sleeves, empty crumpled cans of lager and silver-foil takeaway cartons. Beside him was a large cabinet close to six feet tall crammed full of VHS tapes. Bertie smiled, looking from the bizarre image of the middle-aged perverts on the TV screen to the mountainous form of his slumbering former darts partner. Unable to resist, Bertie pinched his friend's nose and abruptly all snoring sounds ceased, in fact all breathing sounds appeared to have stopped entirely. Only the low-pitched groaning of the man on the television screen having his ball bag swished at with the stinging nettles could now be heard. Bertie thought for an irrational moment that he might have killed his old mate, until a guttural, gurgling sound began emanating from Graham's throat, then exploded with a massive intake of breath as Graham was startled awake by the lack of oxygen.

'You always were a deep sleeper,' Bertie said, smiling down at his friend.

Graham's eyes widened with incomprehension as he rubbed the sleep from them. 'Jesus Christ, Bertie, you old bastard!' Graham exclaimed. Making a bleary-eyed glance around his immediate vicinity he located the television remote control, pausing what was playing on the telly. 'What the bloody hell are you doing back here, boy!?'

Bertie took a long intake of breath. 'That, my old mate, is a long story.'

'Well, that's all right,' Graham said, beginning what looked like the extremely laborious task of extricating himself from his armchair. 'You can tell me all about it over a couple of cold ones, can't you?' Graham grunted, shifting his weight from side to side, and slowly but steadily made it to his feet. Bertie watched on with mild amusement at the sights and sounds of shifting flab and heavy breathing as Graham finally achieved verticality and toddled his way towards the fridge. It opened with the sound of clinking glass and Graham took out two green bottles of cold Stella Artois, opening them on the in-built bottle opener screwed to the side of the kitchen work surface.

'The old team, eh?' Graham said, proudly holding his bottle aloft.

'The old team,' Bertie responded, clinking bottles with his friend.

'So what's the story, partner? What's going on? What the bloody 'ell are you doing back here? Does Alice know you're back here? In the dog house, I bet, aincha? You seen 'er?'

Bertie was temporarily bamboozled by his friend's rapid-fire questioning.

'Sit down, mate, come on, sit down,' Graham said, gathering up the collection of magazines that were scattered across the sofa, two of which Bertie noticed were pornographic in nature, and tossing them to the floor.

'In a manner of speaking, pal, yeah, I've seen her. It's kind of complicated,' Bertie said, taking a long pull on his beer and making his way to the now magazine-free pink two-seater sofa that sat at a right angle to the well-worn armchair that Graham was now lowering himself back into. The unseen springs cried out for mercy under the weight as Graham flipped up the footstool again and began taking a big swig of his own beer.

'So what you doing back here after all this time then, boy?' Graham asked, absently rubbing his belly.

Bertie took another swig. 'I've run away from home,' he said with a humourless chuckle.

'What? By coming back here?' Graham said with a mirthful chuckle of his own. 'You left home six years ago, didn't you, boy?'

'Told you it was complicated, didn't I?' Bertie said.

'And I bet Alice wasn't exactly best pleased to see you turning up at her door after all this time, was she?'

Bertie looked down at the frayed pink carpet, head bowed. 'I wouldn't know, mate,' he said forlornly. 'I never got the chance to speak to her.'

'What d'you mean?' Graham said, frowning.

'She's dead,' Bertie said simply. 'Alice is dead, mate.'

'Eh?' Graham said, perplexed.

'She's dead. I saw them taking her away in the back of an undertaker's van up at the house. That copper was there, Sergeant Frisk. Alan Frisk. I've just come from the police station. He's been filling me in on everything that's been happening. Apparently Douglas went completely mental on Thursday, smashed in a load of windows, tied the vicar's dog to the railway, attacked the vicar herself. Then Frisk told me what he and the vicar and a couple of others did to Douglas... or what they were going to do.'

'Which was?' Graham said, leaning forward.

'You don't know?'

'Nah,' Graham said, settling back into the chair. 'Well, I heard there was something going down up the Fruitbowl last Friday night. I was up there, but I was a bit piddled by that point. I'd been drinking and taping videos for most of the day. I'd heard about the windows 'n' all that 'n' all, but...' Graham trailed off, leaving Bertie space to pick up the thread.

'They were going to stick Douglas in the police dog show at the fete. Apparently they all came up with the idea Friday night at some parish council meeting.'

'Oh yeah, I seem to remember popping in there on my way up to the pub,' Graham said, reaching round to scratch his arse.

'Douglas even agreed to the dog thing apparently. Frisk said that doing it would save him from going to prison, or young offenders. What this Sergeant Frisk fella didn't know though, apparently, was that the police dog was totally bat shit crazy.'

''Kin'ell!' Graham said. 'Did it get him?'

Bertie gave a little smile. 'No. The dog tore into what they all thought was Douglas, but it turned out to be some other copper: Frisk's constable.'

'Who, Binsley?' Graham asked.

'Yeah, that's him, Dennis Binsley. Apparently Douglas got his hands on a bloody pipe bomb from somewhere and made this Binsley bloke take his place. Douglas had it away on his toes and was apparently heading for the church with a petrol can in his hand. Frisk said he was gonna burn it down. They chased him up that way in the police van but Douglas didn't get past the railway line.' Bertie paused, necking the last of his Stella, shaking the empty bottle.

Graham nodded towards the fridge. 'Get me another one 'n' all, boy,' he said. 'Actually make that two,' he added, 'they're only gay little bottles, ent they?'

Bertie got up, making his way over to the fridge, extracting a trio of cold green bottles.

'Then a train came,' Bertie said, closing the fridge door and popping the tops on the bottles. 'There was an accident.'

'What sort of accident?' Graham said, taking his pair of bottles from Bertie.

'Douglas fell on the line. Lost his feet and about six inches of his shins. Frisk said it could've been a hell of a lot worse if it wasn't for the sheep. He's lucky to be alive.'

'The sheep?' Graham said. 'What bloody sheep?'

'They knocked him out the way apparently,' Bertie said. 'Then they both got creamed under the train. They saved his life but the train got his feet. He's up at the hospital now,' Bertie said, wiping away a tear. 'Him and Alice are both up there.'

'That's what them sirens were about earlier then,' Graham said, scratching his flabby chin. 'They woke me up about half three, four o'clock... Bloody Nora, what a palaver!'

'Yeah, I suppose that's one word for it,' Bertie said with an ironic chuckle. 'They found Alice back at the house. Frisk's guess is Douglas found Alice sometime around Thursday morning. That's when his crime spree started, they reckon. Must've found her and just gone into meltdown. Another tear streaked down Bertie's cheek, pattering on the magazine at his feet. 'I got here too late,' he said. 'I got here too bloody late,' he repeated, wiping his eyes.

'You gonna stick around then?'

Bertie levelled his gaze at Graham. 'Oh yeah,' he said, 'Douglas is gonna need me.'

Graham shifted a little uncomfortably in his chair. 'I wouldn't be quite so sure of that,' he said.

'What do you mean by that?'

'I mean, he was what, eleven when you buggered off to wherever it was. Where was it again?'

'Bridgend,' Bertie said.

'Yeah, that place. That must account for that silly accent you've picked up.'

'Yeah, I gotta work on that,' Bertie said... 'Issenit,' he added with a little smile.

'Yeah, you better had,' Graham said. 'Anyway, Douglas ain't a kid any more, mate. He was what, a year or two younger than my Peter. He's a man now, mate.'

'Dougie'll be 18 in November.'

'My point egfuckingzackly, boy!' Graham said.

Silence fell between them for a moment as Bertie sat in quiet contemplation. 'Well, whatever,' he said finally. 'I'm staying.'

'Suit yourself, boy, suit yourself.'

Bertie drained the last of his second beer and Graham nodded once more towards the fridge as he finished his third.

'So how is Peter then, mate?' Bertie said, glad to be changing the subject. 'Is he around or has he flown the nest?'

'He's gone 'n' all,' Graham said sombrely. 'Same way your Alice has gone.'

Bertie's head swivelled forty-five degrees. 'No, not your Peter?'

'Yep.'

'How?'

'Car crash,' Graham said matter of factly. 'Should've asked your mate Frisk about it while you were over there. They was chasing the ones that crashed into him. Some shitty old car they thought had been nicked. It made a dodgy overtake and ploughed into him.'

'When did this happen?'

'February last year. He'd not long passed his test. He was out delivering some videos for me. Edna doesn't know about that bit. I don't think it'd be wise to tell her somehow; we ain't exactly what you'd call happily married these days.'

Bertie shook his head. 'Jesus, what a mess.'

'Come on,' Graham said, chirping up, 'let's not get all doom and bloody gloom. How about we get stuck into this lot?' he said, swinging open the right-hand door of his video cabinet and stretching out to pick a tape off the shelf. 'Freddie Mercury tribute concert!' he said gleefully. 'Got all seven hours of it on here, boy!' he said, patting the tape against his leg.

'You, err, not in the middle of something already?' Bertie said, nodding at the frozen image of the middle-aged woman wielding the clutch of stinging nettles.

'What, that?' he said, looking at the television with mild revulsion. 'No, God no, that ain't for my viewing pleasure, boy. I'm doing a copy of it for a mate. 'Mingers in Stingers' it's called. Bit niche, to say the least. It's some kind of fetish, naturist, sado-masochistic sub-genre that some really weird bastards go in for. Can't say I'm one of them, mind. No, that thing there has totally transformed my business empire,' Graham said, nodding towards the twin-deck video recorder beneath the television. 'Amstrad double-decker!' Graham beamed. I can copy and record to my heart's content on that. Quite a profitable little sideline. Some blueys, some I just pirate from the garage as soon as they come out on video.'

'Gary's garage?' Bertie said. 'He still there, is he? Some things never change.'

'Yeah. It's easy bloody money, boy. He don't know what I'm up to, silly sod. Sometimes I don't even wait till the bastards are out on video. I got a mate, Ken Bevan, who goes in the cinema with a video camera under his coat; he tapes 'em straight from source and I copy 'em back here. Plus I got the dish. Did you see it? Satellite dish. I was the first one in the village to get one of them bastards back in '89. I gets allsorts off there for people. Easy bloody money, boy!' Graham proudly repeated, rubbing his thumb and index finger together. 'Oh and, err, if you 'appen to be talking with your new mate Sergeant Frisk,' Graham said, lowering his voice and leaning in to Bertie, 'I'd be grateful if you could keep that information to yourself.'

Bertie drew an invisible zip across his mouth, locking it and throwing the invisible key over his shoulder.

'Cheers, boy,' Graham said, draining another Stella, growling with satisfaction as the last of the liquid drained away down his gullet like an egg timer running out of sand. 'You still throwing then, are you, boy?' he asked.

'Hmmm, sort of,' Bertie said. 'Let's just say my average has dropped quite significantly over the past couple of years.'

'Bloody 'ell, then I'll 'ave to give you a game up the Fruitbowl sometime. Might actually stand a chance of pinching a leg off you,' Graham said, frowning a little. 'Err, no pun intended, boy,' he said.

'It's OK, I know what you mean,' Bertie said, softly nodding.

'You was bloody unplayable before you fucked off.'

'Nothing lasts forever,' Bertie said. 'Listen, Graham, Alan said it might be a few days before I'm allowed in the house. If I'm allowed back in there at all. I'll need to find out what the score is there as well. Till I do, I'm a bit stuck for somewhere to ...'

'Stay 'ere, boy!' Graham boisterously proclaimed, waving a hand in the air. 'How you off for cash?'

'OK ... for now at least anyway,' Bertie said. 'My brother's lent me a few quid to tide me over. I went up north to see him a couple of weeks ago. He sorted me out. I gotta be careful though. So yeah, I'd be grateful to take you up on the offer of staying, mate, cheers.'

'Yeah, course, no worries, boy. Be good to have a proper drink an' a catch-up. Good to have some decent company for once 'n' all.'

Bertie smiled. 'Will Edna not mind? Is she about?'

'She'll be all right. Anything for an old mate. I tell you what,' Graham said, wagging his finger, 'probably best I phone work and tell 'em I won't be in tonight. Still got the day job till I go full-time on the videos. Well, night job.'

'You still at Tesco? In their warehouse?' Bertie asked.

'Yeah, boy,' Graham said, beginning again the complicated task of extricating himself from the armchair. 'Still on that poxy forklift.'

After about fifteen seconds he had just about managed it. After thirty he had made it to the telephone. Graham theatrically mopped his brow with a nearby tea towel as he picked the phone up from its cradle. 'Think I got a fever coming on, boy!' he said, smiling as he began to dial. 'Of the Saturday night variety!'

For Edna Glass, the culmination of the village fete could not have gone any better, and though she had been tasked with her usual round of washing glasses, hoovering carpets and generally tidying up other people's mess, for once she had done it with a smile on her face. The sports club had turned in to a ghost town after the last of the emergency service vehicles had vacated the green that had borne witness to the day's unprecedented destruction. A few regulars had stayed on to try it on, but she had swiftly spurned their advances, growing increasingly bored of their drunken, lecherous tactics. After word had reached her about Douglas's accident, she had chosen to lock up the sports and social club early, closing the curtains and savouring a period of quiet reflection and a well-earned drink by herself, toasting the memory of her dear departed son, Peter, who stared down from the cricket team photograph on the wall. Edna raised a glass to his memory as she gleefully recalled the mauling of PC Dennis Binsley at the hands of their dumb, demented dog.

It was nearly dark as she walked back down the causeway towards her home. As she turned into Bargus Close she was immediately struck by the sound of thumping music. As she neared the static home, she could see that the lights were on also. 'What the hell's going on here?' she said to herself as the beat of the music intensified and the muffled melody of a song she vaguely recognised got louder and more pronounced.

Ascending the three small steps that led to her front door, Edna flung it open and was greeted by the sight of her husband, seated as he always was in his armchair, only this time with his flabby arms held aloft in an upward V and clapping enthusiastically as he joined in with the Queen song 'Radio Ga Ga' being sung on screen by Paul Young.

'Why aren't you at work?' Edna shouted over the top of the blaring television. It was then that she noticed that Graham had company, as a man slumped on the sofa raised his head above the cushions.

Edna did a double-take, not believing what she saw. 'Bertie?' she said, surprised at how easily she recognised him.

'Yes, dear, the wanderer has returned, issenit!' Graham shouted in the best Welsh accent he could muster. 'We're 'avin' a nice drink and a little catch-up.'

Bertie raised a half empty bottle above the sofa.

'Cheers,' he mumbled.

'You know your son is up the hospital, don't you?' she said.

'Yep,' Bertie said, following it with a hiccup. 'So's Alice,' he slurred, 'and only one of 'em's alive.'

'I'm gonna forward this one, boy,' Graham said, nodding towards the television as Lisa Stansfield walked onto the Wembley stage pushing a hoover. 'Always thought this track was a bit bent,' he said, hitting fast forward, sending Stansfield into a Benny Hill-type speeded-up romp around the stage.

'What do you mean, only one of them is alive?' Edna said in the now quieter lounge. 'What's happened?'

Trying to sound a little more sober than he was, Bertie gave Edna a rundown of his day so far. When he'd finished, Graham piped up.

'So I said he could stay here for a bit. That's all right, isn't it?' Graham said, starting to laugh. 'Issenit, eh, boyo!?' he repeated, this time adopting his Welsh accent, slapping Bertie on the leg. 'He can have Peter's room.'

'No he bloody well can't,' Edna shouted. Now competing with the noise being made by David Bowie and Annie Lennox who were smashing out a duet of Queen's 'Under Pressure'. 'If he has to stay here he can kip on the sofa and bloody well think himself lucky. What the hell are you doing back here anyway? Left it a bit late by the sound of it, haven't you?'

In his drunken state, Bertie offered no response.

'Anyway, whatever, I'm tired and I've got to be up early tomorrow, so you two can turn that frigging racket down!'

'It's bloody Sunday tomorrow, woman,' Graham said. 'Where are you going on a Sunday morning?'

'Church,' Edna said.

'Church?' Graham echoed, a little perplexed.

'Yeah, church. What are you, deaf as well as fat and stupid?'

'Oh sod off to bed then if you're going, woman,' Graham moaned. 'I'm not in the mood for any of your nonsense.'

Edna did just that, leaving them to it as Queen's surviving members and David Bowie went into a rousing rendition of the Bowie song 'Heroes'. She tried to process the information she had just received. Alice dead? And Douglas badly injured, lucky not to be joining his mother in the mortuary. The pieces of the puzzle started to fall into place as the last few days at last started to make sense. 'She's gone, I don't know where,' Douglas had said when she'd slipped him the pipe bomb in the changing rooms earlier this afternoon. Now at last she knew what he'd meant by that. And now Bertie was back on the scene as well. What timing!

From the lounge Edna could still make out the song playing on the TV, though thankfully it was at least a bit quieter now. She took off her shoes, rubbing her feet as the chorus to 'Heroes' repeated over and over in the living room. Though it was tinged with sadness, Edna smiled to herself nonetheless, thinking that, after her performance at the fete earlier, just for one day, a hero is exactly what she had felt like.

5 *Sunday, August 15*

Bertie woke from a thin sleep on the Glasses' sofa feeling pretty stiff and more than a little heavy-headed. He was lying under an unzipped single sleeping bag, still in the clothes he'd arrived in, but minus the double denim of his jacket and jeans that were now half folded up on the floor beside him. He was stirred by the sound of the kettle being filled and clicked on out of sight behind him.

'Edna?' he whispered.

'What?' she answered, her voice flat in the acoustically deadened confines of the static home's kitchenette.

'Are you still going to church?' Bertie said, still in a whisper.

'I said I was, didn't I? And you don't need to whisper. It'll take more than that to wake him up,' Edna said, nodding at her slumbering mass of a husband rumbling away in the armchair. She lit a cigarette and poured boiling water into a mug. Bertie raised his head above the sofa, peering over to where Edna was blowing smoke into the early morning sunshine that was pouring in through the kitchen window. She was already dressed, in tight blue jeans, a loose-fitting black top and black flat shoes. Her hair was a frizzy sphere of greying black.

'Is it OK if I come with you?' Bertie said, surreptitiously sliding into his jeans on the sofa. He stood up and walked over to the kitchen. 'Had a bit of a tidy-up before I hit the sack,' he said, nodding at the neatly assembled collection of empty Stella bottles on the side by the sink.

'Gee thanks,' Edna said, tapping ash into a triangular metal ashtray on the counter.

'Enough in there for two, is there?' he said, nodding at the kettle.

Edna said nothing but took out another mug from the cupboard, placing it by the coffee jar and sugar bowl before taking a seat at the small breakfast bar. Bertie fixed himself a coffee and, holding up his own pack of Benson and Hedges, enquired, 'May I?'

'If you want. Don't be long, mind. Service starts in half an hour.'

Bertie lit up and sipped his coffee. 'I need this after last night. I'd had a few by the time you got in; I'm sorry, I was a bit out of it. I didn't get much sleep either, thinking about everything. Kipping next to that is easier said than done 'n' all,' Bertie said, nodding at Graham.

'Why d'you think he always sleeps out here?' she said.

'I still can't believe Alice is gone, y'know,' Bertie said, finishing his cigarette and adding a splash of cold water to his coffee.

'No,' Edna said, crushing her own cigarette out. 'No, neither can I. It's proper shit. Come on then, if you're coming.'

Bertie drained his coffee as Edna made for the door. He followed on behind, closing the door behind him. They turned left out of Bargus Close, walking parallel to the causeway up on their right. The mid-August sun was warm, even for the early time of day.

'Why did you come back here, Bert?' Edna asked testily, breaking the silence between them and lighting up another cigarette. 'Life in Bridgend not quite as glamorous as you'd hoped? Must've been all right, you stuck at it this long. Your Welsh bird finally give you the boot, did she? So you thought you'd come back here, cap in hand, to try again with Alice? Left it a bit late though, haven't you? Should've come back last week.' Edna took a long drag on her cigarette. 'So come on then, what's the story?'

'You're right, Edna, I did come back here with the intention of trying to start again with Alice and Douglas. And yes, I have left it too late, I know that, so thanks for stating the bloody obvious. You can take all the satisfaction you want out of that now that it's no longer a possibility, but I genuinely wanted to make a new start.' Bertie lit up a cigarette of his own. 'I left Rhonda. That was her name. We ran a pub together in Bridgend, although I should put the words "into the ground" at the end of that sentence. At least she did. She wasn't exactly blessed with the best business brain. It was all right for the first couple of years. It was good. She was fun

32

and the pub was doing well, my darts were good.' Bertie paused. 'Then the dartitis started and everything just seemed to go downhill from there.'

'Dartitis?' Edna said. 'I thought that was just an old story that crap players told themselves when they started to play rubbish.'

'I wish it was,' Bertie said, 'but it's real enough all right. I couldn't compete any more, my average tumbled. I was playing at county level then, but that soon came to an end. At the same time the pub started losing business. Rhonda was mad about her karaoke, not letting the fact that she had a voice like a cat tied to an electric fence stop her. It was basically her own little vanity project. She absolutely loved it, it's just a shame that no one else did. When my arrows really started to fail me and I was even dropped from the pub team, Rhonda banished me to the kitchen. Funnily enough in the end it was my cooking which was the only thing keeping the place afloat. Turns out I'm actually quite a dab hand at it. Necessity being the mother of invention and all that. In the end I was happy to be there. I had my own space, not being made to feel like a darting leper. In the end, though, I just couldn't take it any more. The solitude of the kitchen gave me time to think. I couldn't stand to be around it... or her.' Bertie took a long pull on his cigarette. 'That was when I really started to realise how much I missed this place. And really felt the remorse for how I'd behaved towards the people I left behind here.'

'So you've left Rhonda in the lurch as well, have you? Classy.'

'She cheated on me, if you must know,' Bertie said, stopping to crush his cigarette out under foot. 'Are you happy to hear that? I know you'll probably say it's exactly what I deserve after what I...'

'Yep,' Edna swiftly interjected.

'... We had a kid together, me and Rhonda. At least that's what I was led to believe. A boy, called Rhyss. She chose the name, obviously. It was a couple of years ago. She had me believing that he was mine right up until his real father was released from prison. She cheated on me with one of the locals. Dai, his name was. He was a county darts player too. And one that didn't succumb to dartitis. I could see they were getting close when my game started to go downhill. Plus he was about the only other person who'd do karaoke. He was a massive Elvis fan. Always murdering 'Jailhouse Rock' or 'Suspicious Minds'. Obviously she didn't wanna be around a loser like me any more, and being English didn't help either. Rhonda found out she was pregnant not long after Dai had been arrested and charged for an ABH assault that happened at the pub. He got sent down for two years. I was duped into believing the kid was mine and I raised him as my own all the time Dai was inside.' Bertie paused, fishing another cigarette out of the gold packet. 'I'm trying to cut down, believe it or not,' he said lighting up with a half grin. 'Anyway, then Dai got released from prison and the truth about Rhyss came out with him.'

'Sounds like something out of bloody Eastenders if you ask me,' Edna said. 'Bloody carry on.'

'Yeah. Bridgenders,' Bertie said with a smile, unable to suppress his amusement. To his relief Edna smiled as well.

They walked on in silence for a while, approaching the Crafty Digit pub.

'Well, it serves you right,' Edna said. 'You've got a son, in case you'd forgotten.'

'Yeah, ironic really, isn't it? Karma's a bastard, I guess.' Bertie drew deeply on his cigarette. 'I never forgave myself for what I did to Alice, you know. How I did it. Just going like that. I'd thought about coming back before; before my other so-called kid came along.' Bertie stopped, and after a couple of paces Edna did too, as the pair of them stood opposite the village's primary school. 'I really did come back here with the honest intention of trying again with Alice and Douglas,' he said. 'I had all these ideas in my head of what it was gonna be like coming back here. What might or might not happen. Whether she would have me back. What Douglas would be like, all grown up. I knew it was gonna be tough, but I never thought for one minute it would be like this. Edna, what the bloody hell happened at the fete yesterday? Alan told me about everything that Douglas did on Thursday leading up to it and he told me what they were gonna do to him with the police dog as punishment. He said that Douglas had agreed to do it to keep him from having charges pressed against him for everything he did, is that right? To keep him out of a young offenders', or worse, prison?'

34

Edna nodded. 'Apparently,' she said, 'but Alan and his cronies had other ideas, didn't they? Especially when there was no sign of Alice. They never would have got away with it if she'd been around. Did Alan tell you about the dog being mental? About Reverend Bowen and her cosy little alliance with that police dog handler, Laurie Knox?'

'He did,' Bertie said, nodding his head. 'Alan assured me he had no idea the dog was going to behave like that though, and for what it's worth I believe him. Thank God it wasn't Douglas out on that bloody field, that's all I can say. Christ, how the hell did he get out of that? That's what I want to know. Alan was completely baffled by it. I am too. He said that Douglas got a bloody pipe bomb from somewhere. I mean where the hell did he get that from?'

As they continued on towards the church, the pair now approaching the causeway level crossing, a thin smile played at the corner of Edna's mouth which quickly developed into an uncharacteristically broad grin.

Bertie stopped and stared at her. 'You?' he said as the level crossing's warning lights began to flash and the barriers of the level crossing began to lower. 'What did you do?'

'When you're allowed back down the house, have a look at the exhaust pipe on your old car. You'll see it's missing about eight inches. Douglas and Peter made a little improvised explosive out of it one day a couple of years back. They said they got told how to make one by one of their mates' older brothers. Isn't that always the way? I found it and confiscated it. I had absolutely no idea what to do with it. When Peter died I'd thought about using it on the police station. Or on Graham. The amount of times I'd fantasised about dropping it into his big fat lap as he snored in front of that telly. In the end I did neither. It just sat in a drawer by my bed.'

'You slept with a pipe bomb in a drawer by your bed?' Bertie said, smiling and bemused.

'Handy for if Graham ever tried to come in there, I suppose.'

An HST hurtled past from the west, tearing over the level crossing. The barriers stayed down.

'I heard that dog handler and that smarmy little shit Dennis Binsley taunting Douglas in the changing rooms of the football club before the police dog show. Frisk had left them alone to attend to business elsewhere. As much as I might dislike him, I'd tend to agree with you when he says about him not knowing just how crackers that bloody dog was. Anyway Knox and Binsley knew, and they were in the changing rooms. I heard Knox telling Douglas all about Gooch, that was the dog's name. I was in the showers.'

'The showers?' Bertie said, a little perplexed.

'Yeah. The showers run the length of the changing rooms. I was in there listening to them. I wasn't in there washing my bloody hair, was I?'

Bertie smiled.

'So anyway, as luck would have it, they left Douglas on his own while they were all talking outside. I managed to sneak in and slip him the pipe bomb and a lighter before they came back in. They were none the wiser. So then Douglas makes Binsley take his place in the back of the van on the way round to the display. Binsley's a spineless little coward and he knew Douglas was probably crazy enough by that point to light the pipe bomb if he didn't swap with him.'

Another HST hurtled past, this time from the east.

'And the rest, as they say, is history,' Edna said as the barriers began to rise and the pair stepped onto the crossing. 'And oi, that information is not for public consumption,' Edna said, 'understand?'

'Yeah, of course,' Bertie said, crouching down to inspect the dry, faded blood that only yesterday had pumped from the severed legs of his son. He placed the flat of his hand on the warm, rust-red stain. 'I'm so sorry, Dougie,' he said softly.

Bertie looked up towards the church. He could see people milling around by the building's car park and rear entrance. Behind him many more villagers were heading in its direction.

'Looks like this place might have a bit of a guilty conscience,' Edna said, as they too headed for the church.

Despite sleeping better than she had done for quite some time, Hilda Bowen was still up early. It was force of habit. After so many years of Sunday services, her biological clock was by now well programmed for Sunday mornings. She was also making the most of her soon to be ex home and enjoying her restored feeling of inner peace that, despite what Bishop Rowan Trimble had got planned for her and Moses, steadfastly remained within her. She was using the time to think about what she was going to say in church, actually looking forward to addressing her congregation for once, though still feeling slightly apprehensive at the prospect of having to do so. With Moses nestled in his basket beside the Aga and the washing up from breakfast now drying on the draining board beside the sink, Bowen was seated at the kitchen table enjoying a final cup of tea before church. There was only half an hour to go before the service was due to start. Half of her wanted to share her spiritual awakening with the world, but at the same time the other half felt that such a deeply personal and revelatory experience was something she wanted to hold close to her, and not risk diluting by revealing its unspeakable wonder. Perhaps there was a happy medium to be found somewhere.

She smiled down at Moses: her second miracle. The image playing out in her mind of him yesterday walking dry-pawed through the red sea of Douglas Blouse's blood and settling down in the spot where she had witnessed the appearance and subsequent dematerialisation of Douglas's mother, Alice.

She looked up at the clock on the kitchen wall. It was time she got going. 'See you soon, sweet pea,' she said, stroking the appreciative dog under the chin. She opened her front door, agog at the sight that greeted her. Dozens of people were congregated outside her church, with many more headed in its direction. 'Well, the miracles just keep coming, don't they?' she said quietly to herself with a little smile, closing the vicarage door behind her and walking towards them.

'Come on, Reverend, let's get in there and have a good old singsong,' the lead dancer of the village's Morris men, Terence Russell, said as Bowen opened the church's large oak door. 'Me and the boys've gotta pray we don't ever have another performance like yesterday, eh boys?' Russell said, looking round at fellow dancers Bob Dobson, Colin Blunsden and Gerry Hayman, the latter standing arm in arm with his wife.

'I don't think you'll be alone in that endeavour, Terence,' Hilda said.

'Reverend,' Terence said, taking the vicar quietly to one side, 'I wonder if I might be able to have a little chat with you after the service? It's of a, uhh…' Terence searched for the right word, 'well, it's of a spiritual nature,' he said.

'Of course, Terence. I'd be happy to,' she said, at last feeling once again qualified to discuss such matters.

'Lovely stuff.' Terence stepped back. 'I must say you're looking much more prosperous today, Hilda. Them marks've all but disappeared, 'aven't they? You look positively radiant, Reverend.'

'Crawler,' Colin Blunsden said.

Terence and Hilda both looked at the squat little man in his creased, short-sleeved shirt, smiling as they did so. 'And I feel it, Terence,' she said. 'It's very kind of you to say so.' Hilda's high spirits dropped slightly as she looked down the causeway. She saw Edna Glass walking towards her, and she wasn't alone. It had been more than six years since she last laid eyes on Bertie Blouse, but she recognised him instantly. Her confidence wavered as nerves at what she was going to say to him threatened to overwhelm her. 'If you'll all excuse me,' she said, 'I must go and get prepared.' She turned to the crowd. 'Please, come on in, all of you.'

Despite her nerves, Reverend Bowen stepped into the cool confines of the church that she had been parishioner of for nearly twenty years with renewed enthusiasm, knowing exactly what she needed to do; and what she had to say. She breathed in the aroma of the aged timber pews and prayer books, heading into the vestry where she changed into her cassock and put her robes on, looking at the framed pictures on the wall of past church choirs. Smiling faces beamed from beneath the dusty glass of the picture frames that housed them, with her standing at their centre. She resolved to get some polish and have a good old clean of the place. From behind the curtain of her secluded vestry she could hear the growing chatter as more and more unseen members of her congregation filled the church. A very pleasing sound indeed. She was going over the service in her head. She didn't have anything written down, but she was confident the good word would flow from her, passed down to her by a higher force.

The nerves really started to build, though, as she thought of Bertie Blouse sitting out there somewhere in the congregation. What had he come back to? And how much of that had she been responsible for? There was no running away from it, though, and so with a restored and sincere faith once again in her heart, she parted the curtains and stepped out into the church. The scene she was met with took her breath away. The church was full. Staggered and a little overwhelmed by the turnout, she had to take a moment to compose herself. The place was silent and all eyes were on her as she walked over to the pulpit, her shoes tapping rhythmically on the cold stone floor. She ascended the small steps to where her Bible lay open. She took a deep breath and began to read.

'I am the resurrection and the life, sayeth the Lord. He that believeth in me, though he were dead, yet shall he live. And whosoever believeth in me shall never die, but have everlasting life.'

'Amen,' the congregation answered, unprompted.

Reverend Bowen surveyed the faces of her congregation. Sheep farmer Butch Ransom was seated beside Barbara Rix, owner and proprietor of Fabsolutely Babulous. Parish councillor and co-architect of Douglas Blouse's intended downfall, Petra Carr, was seated alongside her husband and daughter Daisy, whose subjection to Douglas's sexual advances in Colin Blunsden's dilapidated shed had partly precipitated the events of yesterday's doomed village fete. She saw local groundsman Fred Hillock, seated alongside the Morris men. Presumably he was here to pray that his village green would never see such hellish sights again. Sergeant Frisk, along with his wife and young daughter, were also in attendance.

'Before we start, may I just say how truly pleased I am to see so many familiar faces here on such a beautiful day.' She paused. 'That first passage, I'm afraid, is very poignant to us all today. It carries with it, of course, a true and certain hope, but what underlies it is loss. Earthly, physical loss. And I'm afraid it is my unfortunate duty to inform you all that we have lost a very dear and devoted member of our community. It is with deep sadness that I have to report that Alice Blouse of Pugsden Lane was found dead at her home yesterday afternoon.'

The congregation began to murmur. For some it came as a shocking surprise. For others it merely confirmed rumours that had already circulated around the village.

'As some of you may know, Alice's son Douglas was involved in an accident on the railway line yesterday afternoon; he is now in intensive care at the John Radcliffe hospital. I think it is no secret amongst you all that Douglas and myself have not exactly seen eye to eye recently, but I am not here to judge. For did the Lord not teach us, "Judge not, lest ye be judged yourself." "Let he who is without sin cast the first stone." A trace of a smile spread across Bowen's face. She tilted her head towards the smashed stained glass panel of the church's rear window. 'No pun intended, of course,' she said.

A ripple of laughter and levity permeated the church, many looking, some also pointing at the still broken stained glass window above and behind Reverend Bowen.

'No, we shall not judge, for none of us here is perfect. Every one of us has the potential for weakness and corruption. This, I'm afraid, is part of the human condition that sets us apart from God. But in seeking to overcome such earthly trials, we strive to move closer to God. We do this through understanding, love and forgiveness.' Reverend Bowen at last looked into the eyes of the man she had been so far avoiding, and Bertie Blouse stared straight back at her. 'That is what's at the heart of the message I want you all

40

to take away from today's sermon,' she said, still holding Bertie's gaze steady as she gently closed her Bible. 'Forgiveness.'

7

'Goodbye, God bless,' Reverend Bowen said an hour later, for what seemed like the hundredth time; and it probably was. Despite the repetition, she said each word with the same level of sincerity as if it were the first. Bidding farewell to her congregation was taking almost as long as the service itself, as Bowen warmly shook hands with each and every person vacating her church. Already Sergeant Frisk, Daisy Carr and Terence Russell, again, had asked if they could all have a private word with her when their turn had come to bid the vicar farewell, and now bringing up the rear, a few paces behind Edna Glass was Bertie Blouse, who inevitably was going to ask her that very same question himself. She held out her hand, thoroughly expecting him not to shake it. To her surprise and relief he did.

'Hilda, hi. Bertie,' he said with a disarming smile. 'Been a while.'

'Hello, Bertie,' she said, almost stumbling over the two simple words.

'I'm very sorry about your window,' Bertie said, still holding on to the vicar's hand. 'Do you know how much it will cost to repair?'

'Err, I...' Bowen stuttered, caught a little on the hop. 'I'm not entirely sure yet, Bertie. But I think whatever we raised at the fete yesterday will definitely help.'

Bertie smiled. 'Sounds like all you raised at the fete yesterday, Reverend, was merry hell,' he said, finally letting go of Bowen's hand.

'Bertie, I must tell you here and now that I knew all about Gooch,' Bowen said without hesitation. 'I knew he was dangerous. I knew the dog was dangerous and I went ahead and did it all the same. I'm utterly ashamed of myself for what I did, and I am completely at your mercy. In the presence of God I stand before you begging your forgiveness. I have no excuse for my actions.'

From among the slowly dispersing crowd, Sergeant Frisk joined Bertie, Edna and Reverend Bowen by the church door.

'What about your PC Binsley?' Edna said, addressing Sergeant Frisk. 'He knew Gooch was nuts as well. And by the end of the day he knew just how bloody nuts he was, didn't he?'

'Yes, Edna, thank you for that,' Frisk said. 'And now that young man is having reconstructive facial surgery. Does that make you happy? And as I have already stated, I had no idea what the pair of them did or didn't know,' Frisk said. 'If Laurie told him, then it was without me knowing.'

'He told him after you'd gone out to see to Tony,' Edna said.

'Well then, how could I have known?' Frisk said. 'Do you honestly think I would have let *anyone* go out there and face down that dog if I knew what Laurie had done to him?'

'They were taunting Douglas,' Edna said. 'The pair of them, in the changing rooms before the show. They were giggling like a pair of children, delighting in the fact that Douglas was going to get ripped apart. Sadistic bastards.'

'Well, I had no idea, I swear to god,' Frisk said, looking up at the church. 'And anyway, how do you know that? What were you doing in the changing rooms?' Frisk said, levelling a suspicious gaze at Edna.

'I wasn't *in* the changing rooms. I heard them talking when I came looking for you,' Edna said. 'When it was all kicking off at Tony's gazeebo. You were just leaving when I came through looking for you.'

Bertie and Edna exchanged the quickest of looks, both just about managing to suppress their knowing grins.

'Look,' Bertie said, 'I didn't come back here to wage war against the church and the police or to start personal vendettas. It sounds like there's already been enough of that type of thing to last a lifetime. I came back here looking to fix a broken marriage and re-establish a relationship with my son. Sadly now only one of those things is possible.' Bertie took in a deep breath, surveying the churchyard. 'The way I see it after everything I've heard since coming back here, it sounds like things ended up just about even.' He looked at them each in turn. 'So I think it's probably best if we all just let sleeping dogs lie, eh?'

They all managed a little smile at that.

'Like you said, Reverend,' Bertie said, 'perhaps we all need to learn to forgive? And in time, hopefully, forget.'

Reverend Bowen breathed a huge sigh of relief. 'I think that's a very good idea, Bertie,' she said, smiling. 'And again, I am truly sorry. I cannot tell you the difference a day makes. Seeing Alice by the railway yesterday just...'

'You what?' Edna said, and Bertie turned to stare at the vicar also. 'What do you mean, you saw Alice?'

'Yes, we both did. Douglas and myself. That was when I knew she was... that she had...'

Frisk was also now looking at Bowen. 'And that's why you knew to send me down to Pugsden Lane.'

Bowen nodded. '"Though she may die, yet shall she live."'

Breaking away from her mother's side a short distance away, Daisy Carr tentatively joined their group. Edna stared across the churchyard at Petra Carr, her eyes boring a hole into the head parish councillor's soul. Petra looked away.

'I saw her too, Reverend,' Daisy said timidly. 'By the railway. Me and Dan both saw her. I thought I was going mad, but she was definitely there, wasn't she? You did see her, didn't you?'

'The amount of green that you and Dan got through yesterday, I wouldn't be surprised if you saw Elvis Presley,' Frisk said.

Daisy looked over her shoulder towards her mother. Petra was thankfully now out of earshot.

'Yes, Daisy,' Bowen said. 'I saw her.'

'She was holding up a Mr Bump jumper,' Daisy said with a tear in her eye. 'I remember she used to knit them for Douglas. He used to wear them all the time as a kid when we were at primary school. She looked so beautiful. And Douglas looked so sad. Now I...' Daisy faltered, 'I... ' She didn't finish the sentence. It was cut short by the fit of sobbing that overcame her. Bowen put an arm around her and Daisy composed herself. 'The sheep came just

44

as the train came through. I saw him fall. I screamed. When I looked back, Alice was gone.' She looked up into Bowen's eyes. 'Then I saw you climbing over the barrier and going to him.'

'It was then that I knew exactly why Douglas had been behaving the way he had. All the chaos he brought to the village. He'd lost his mum and none of us understood.'

'She's gone. I don't know where,' Frisk and Edna said simultaneously, looking at each other with surprise as they did so.

'I think now we know what Douglas meant by that,' Frisk said. 'That's all he said when we asked him about Alice. The house was locked when I went down there. The curtains were closed. The place looked abandoned, and that's just what I thought it was.'

'But it wasn't,' Edna said, 'not quite.' A silence descended on the group.

'He didn't?' Bertie said, looking at Frisk. 'You don't think Douglas had anything to do with it?'

'Don't be so bloody stupid, Bertie,' Edna snapped. 'God, you really don't know your son at all, do you?'

Bertie had little to say by means of a defence.

'It's not my place to speculate,' Frisk said. 'But for what it's worth, I honestly don't believe Alice's death is going to be treated as suspicious. Not from what I saw there, and no, I don't believe that Douglas had anything to do with it.'

'When can I go up and see him?' Bertie said.

'Ha! Good luck with that!' Edna said.

'One step at a time eh, Bertie?' Frisk said, immediately frowning. 'Sorry,' he said, realising his inadvertent faux pas. 'I'm going up to see him later. If he's out of surgery and awake, I need to speak to him. Get his version of events so we can clear up once and for all what happened exactly.'

'I'd planned on going up to see him too,' Bowen said.

Bertie levelled his gaze at Reverend Bowen. 'Oh, so suddenly the woman who'd planned to have him mauled by a mad police dog,' he said, now looking at Frisk, 'is his guardian angel?'

'Bertie, I'm so sorry,' Bowen said, 'I know how you must feel, but Douglas and I shared a profound experience yesterday. I think maybe if you allow me to broach the subject of your return with him, he may just take it a little better. Particularly if you're there too?' Bowen said, looking at Frisk.

'You're not family though, are you, Reverend?' Bertie said.

'Oh, speaking of family,' Frisk interjected, 'and Alice's next of kin, other than yourself, of course, Bertie. I had a cursory look through an address book I found at the house when I went back, but I couldn't see any names in there that immediately stuck out as being family.'

'Alice had a sister,' Edna said, lighting a cigarette. 'Both her parents are gone but she had an older sister. It'll be under Mackenzie. Linda Mackenzie. That's Alice's maiden name. From what I remember Alice saying, she worked abroad. Some medical company or something.' Edna exhaled the last sentence in a cloud of smoke.

'Where are you staying, Bertie?' Bowen asked.

'At her place,' Bertie said, nodding at Edna. 'On the sofa,' he added for clarification. 'How long until I'm allowed in the bungalow?'

'Don't count your chickens just yet, eh, Bert?' Edna said.

'Oh, so can I stay at yours for a bit longer then, Edna?' Bertie said. 'Graham's happy for me to, he's already said that.'

'Yeah,' Edna said testily, 'I didn't say that either, did I?' She crushed out her cigarette on the path and strode away through the headstones towards the far end of the churchyard, leaving the others to it.

'How long d'you reckon, Alan?' Bertie asked.

'As long as everyone is satisfied that it's not suspicious, and after I've got Douglas's take on things, I'd say a couple of days. The post mortem will be carried out some time tomorrow, I imagine. We'll know for sure then. Would you like a lift up the hospital later, Reverend?'

'That's kind, Sergeant, but I think the ride will do me good. Hopefully the surgeons who worked on Douglas will have some more news with regard to his condition.'

'How bad was it?' Bertie said, looking from Bowen to Frisk. 'You were there, how badly was he hurt?'

'Pretty bad, Bert,' Frisk said. 'It was a bit of a mess. From what I saw at least, one of his feet looked very badly injured. They both came off, but I think one came off worse than the other.'

'Will he walk again, do you think?' Bertie said in a croak that bordered on a whisper. 'I mean they can work wonders these days, can't they?'

'Let's not speculate, eh?' Frisk said. 'Wait till we know for sure. In the meantime I'll try and get hold of Alice's sister. Find out where she is. Let her know what's happened. And Bertie, I don't want to be the prophet of doom any more than I have to, but when you're allowed back in the house, have a look in the caravan. Forewarned is forearmed, and all that. Have a look at the dart board. You'll see what I mean. Right,' Frisk said, 'I must be going. I've got some potatoes to peel for Sunday lunch. I'll see you up the hospital later, Reverend. three o'clock OK?'

'That's fine, Alan,' she said as Frisk walked away towards the gate.

'Be patient,' Bowen said, putting a hand on Bertie's forearm. 'It's a lot to take in, I know, but try and have faith. The Lord works in mysterious ways. I for one can certainly vouch for that.'

'I'll try,' Bertie said, wandering away the same way Edna had gone. Coming the other way was Terence Russell.

'Just been talking to Iris,' he said to Bowen with a sad little smile.

'So, Terence, what is it I can do for you?' Bowen said.

'Well,' Terence said, looking around and about him as though the answer was circling around his head somewhere. 'Well, I wanted to know...'

'Yes?' Bowen said.

'Well, it's just after everything you said in there, I wanted to know what the church thinks about, err...'

'Come on, Terence, spit it out,' Bowen said with a smile of bemusement.

'What does the church think about mediums, Reverend? I want to talk to my Iris again, contact her, I mean. I wanna know she's all right and I wanted to know what your lot thought of that kind of thing. You know, what God thinks about it. Is it wrong?'

Bowen took a deep breath, quietly appraising Terence's question and considering her own new-found spiritual enquiries. To say her experiences of the previous day had piqued her interest in the same subject was an understatement. She had her own questions regarding the life eternal and the destiny of the human soul, once it had moved beyond the physical realm.

'Strictly speaking, Terence,' she said at last, 'from my own experience, the church seem to take quite a narrow-minded view on one's own personal pursuit of the spiritual life outside organised religion. Mediumship generally is still classed as heresy among the ecclesiastical hierarchy.' She paused. 'And yet...'

'Yes?'

'Terence, if you'd asked me that question a week ago, I probably would have said you're not only wasting your own time but mine as well ... But today,' she said, frowning a little and cocking her head slightly to one side, 'today I'm not so sure.'

*

Bertie found Edna seated on a wooden bench in the churchyard. She was staring at a headstone. Bertie didn't need to look at it to know whose name was etched on its granite surface.

'I'm so sorry, Edna,' he said, taking a seat beside her but keeping his distance. 'Graham told me. I didn't really know whether to say anything to you. After Alice it just... I don't know. It's just all such a sad state of affairs, isn't it?'

'I'm surprised Graham even remembered he had a son,' Edna said distantly.

He was out delivering videos for me, Bertie thought, remembering his and Graham's conversation from the previous night. Thinking it best to keep that information to himself. 'Well, either way, I truly am very sorry, Edna. And I am thankful to you for letting me stay. It won't be for much longer.'

'Mmmm, s'all right, I suppose,' she said.

'As soon as Alan gives me the word, I'm gonna try and get back in the bungalow. Get a job. Do things right by Douglas. I mean it, that I'm here to stay, you know. Douglas is my son.' Bertie paused. 'My one and only son. And I'm not going anywhere.'

*

Bertie stayed with the Glasses on Sunday night and, despite a permanent and obvious chill between Edna and Graham, particularly after Graham had thrown another sickie, all three of them ate a Chinese takeaway and talked about old times in a fairly civilised manner. At 9 p.m. Edna answered the phone to Reverend Bowen, who was calling to request Bertie's presence at a meeting with herself and Sergeant Frisk at the vicarage at 5 p.m. the following day, to which Bertie unhesitatingly agreed.

As had happened the night before, Graham predictably fell asleep in front of the TV and Edna went to bed alone, leaving Bertie to another restless night on the sofa, struggling to sleep over the sound of Graham's incessant snoring and unable to stop his mind from racing at the prospect of what the new day would bring.

8 *Monday, August 16*

Bertie was early to the vicarage by half an hour and so was not at all surprised when nobody answered as he knocked on the door, though he could hear a dog barking inside. He chose to wait under the shade of the large oak tree on the raised bank outside the church.

At quarter to five he heard a rumble coming from down the causeway and, looking straight down the road from his position beneath the tree, soon saw Reverend Bowen astride her trike coming up and over the railway's level crossing. The noise grew louder the closer she got. Bertie got up and made his way over to the vicarage where Bowen was shutting off her engine, removing the keys and dismounting her trike.

'Hi, Bertie,' she said brightly. 'You're a little early.'

'Yeah, I know,' Bertie said, joining Bowen by the garden gate. 'Nice as it's been of Graham and Edna to let me stay, I can't help but feel a bit in the way. Plus I needed a bit of space.'

'Well, perhaps Alan may have some news for you on the domestic front shortly, hmm?' she said, removing a Tesco carrier bag from the parcel box fixed to the back of the trike.

'Bit of shopping?' Bertie said.

'Yes, something like that,' Bowen replied, walking to her front door with the bag under her arm and inserting the key. She pushed the door open and Moses came scampering out to greet her. 'Hello, my little love,' she said, fussing over the dog. 'Hello, hello. Hang on, sweet pea, Mummy must get this in the freezer, come on, shift yourself. Come on in, Bertie,' she said.

Bertie followed her down the hallway and into the vicarage's large farmhouse kitchen where Bowen was putting the carrier bag into an empty drawer in the lower half of her upright fridge freezer. 'I've got the bishop coming round for dinner tomorrow to talk about the house.'

'What house?' Bertie said. 'This house?'

'Yes.'

'What about it?' Bertie asked.

'He's selling it,' Bowen said matter of factly, closing the freezer door.

'Oh shit, err, sorry,' Bertie said. 'Sorry to hear that. And sorry for swearing.'

'It's OK. I'm getting used to the idea of moving now. They're only sending us up the road, aren't they, sweetheart?' Bowen said to Moses, who was still fussing around her feet. 'Up on Field Gardens. The new estate. They've got a new-build for us. This place will be going up for sale.'

'Bummer,' Bertie said. 'It's a lovely place. Whoever buys it will be very lucky indeed. If you can hang on ten years or so I'll have it off you.'

Bowen smiled. 'If only Bishop Trimble would let us wait that long. No, I think his mind's made up. He wants to swell the coffers as usual. Heaven knows what for, we certainly never see the money. Yet trying to get it out of them when it does come to something like fixing the roof or the stained glass window, it's like getting blood from a stone. That's the frustrating part.'

'I'm sorry again about that, Reverend,' Bertie said. 'When I get some money together I'll pay you back for the damage.'

'It's OK, Bertie,' Bowen said, filling the kettle. 'It's good leverage against the bishop. It'll be hard for him to wriggle out of it after he does sell this place. Tea?'

'Yes please. Thanks,' Bertie said as the doorbell rang.

'It's all go today, isn't it?' Bowen said, making her way back down the hall, Moses following on obediently behind her.

Bertie could hear the muffled tones of Sergeant Frisk, his voice becoming clearer as he made his way down the hall and into the kitchen.

'Bertie,' he said, holding his hand out. Bertie shook it with good grace.

'That's another for the pot,' Bowen said, impressively throwing another teabag in to the pot from a distance of about six feet. 'And one more for our guest,' she said, putting another in, this time at close range.

'Guest?' Bertie said. 'Who else are we expecting?'

51

'Yeah, look, Bertie,' Frisk said, 'I hope you don't think we're ambushing you here, but she wanted to come. We managed to get hold of her yesterday afternoon. I brought her pretty much up to speed on what's happened and she insisted on coming straight away. She's already been to see Douglas with us up at the hospital today.'

'Who has?' Bertie said.

'Linda,' Frisk said. 'Douglas's Auntie Linda. Alice's sister.'

Reverend Bowen was pouring the tea out when the sound of a car crunching on the gravel of the front drive could be heard from the kitchen. Bertie's heart rate had increased significantly following the information concerning his sister-in-law. It had been nearly six years since he'd seen Alice and Douglas, so it was probably at least a year longer since he'd last seen Linda.

Bowen was stirring Bertie's tea when the tinkling of the teaspoon was accompanied by the the bing bong of the front doorbell. 'Excuse me a moment,' she said, handing Bertie his tea and making her way back down the hall, with Moses, as usual, in hot pursuit.

'Hi, Hilda,' Bertie heard from down the hall. 'Hello! Hello, boy!' Linda said, now clearly fussing over the dog. 'Oh, you must be Moses. It's nice to meet you! I've heard so much about you, you poor little thing.'

Bertie heard the front door close.

'My naughty nephew told me to tell you how sorry he is for all the nasty things he did to you.'

'Come through, dear,' Hilda said.

'Come on then, boy,' Linda said, still talking to the dog. 'Let's go and say hello, shall we?'

'How are you bearing up, dear?' Bowen asked as she, Linda and Moses made their way into the kitchen.

'Oh, you know, so so,' Linda said. 'Obviously it was a terrible shock receiving the news about Alice. And then hearing what happened to Douglas as well. It's all rather a lot to take in. I'm not quite sure if it's all sunk in just yet.'

'Of course,' Bowen said. 'And for my part I would just like to say again how sorry I am for the role I played in it all.'

'Hilda, please, we've been through all this. I think we've got enough on our plate with the events of the present without delving back into the past.'

Upon entering the kitchen, Linda shot Bertie a cursory glance, registering his presence but not acknowledging it. Bertie thought she looked well, as he supposed most women with a sizable amount of disposable income tended to do. She wore a white cotton shirt, the sleeves of which were casually but elegantly rolled up to her elbows, and black denim clung greedily to her shapely thighs.

'Hello again, Sergeant,' she said, shaking hands with Frisk.

'Hello, Linda,' Frisk replied. 'Nice to see you again.'

'Let me take that for you, dear,' Bowen said, relieving Linda of her black leather blazer.

'Well, well, well,' Linda said, now giving Bertie her full attention, eyeing him up with a cool, appraising stare. 'Leek what the cat dragged in.'

Bertie rolled his eyes. 'Very good,' he said with a sarcastic smile. 'And how long have you been practising that little zinger for?'

'Ohh, I'd say about six years, Robert,' Linda said, using his full name like he was a naughty child, which in a way he supposed he was. He certainly felt like one. 'Since the day my sister phoned me up in tears telling me her husband and the father of her son had buggered off to Wales with some tart he met on blummin' Bullseye.'

Bertie flinched internally. He had nowhere to go with such an accurate and inescapable statement of fact. He recalled the day back in '87 when he had left the note for Alice. He'd felt he owed her that much at least. To leave without any word would have been callous. At least that's what he told himself: erroneously believing that the note would somehow cushion the blow of what he knew would be devastating news. Now with the double-edged sword of both hindsight and remorse, he dearly wished he could turn back the clock.

'I'm not proud of myself, Linda...' Bertie said.

'I should jolly well hope not,' she said, cutting in.

'I can't change what I did. God knows, I wish I could. I'm sorry. I guess this is my punishment. Coming back here to find Alice ... and Douglas...'

'Ohh, stop feeling so bloody sorry for yourself, Robert, this isn't about you.'

'I know there must be anger, Linda,' Bertie said, after a quiet pause. 'But my intentions are entirely honourable. I want to make up for what I did. Like you said, we've got enough on our plates with the present.'

'You'd better just jolly well hope that I can take my own advice then, Buster,' Linda said.

'Have you seen Douglas?' Bertie asked.

Linda took in a deep breath. 'Yes, I have. I went up there yesterday afternoon straight after Alan told me about what had happened. He's in pretty bad shape, as you can imagine. They've been unable to re-attach his feet. He was too badly injured for that. There was hope with one of them to start with, but that was short-lived. So now he's facing up to the prospect of life without his mother and without the ability to walk for what is likely to be some considerable time. Obviously there's the hope of prosthetics, eventually, but that's a long way off yet. To say he is upset about it all would be the understatement of the century.'

'Does he know about me? Bertie asked tentatively.

'Yes, he does,' Linda said, taking a cup of tea from Reverend Bowen. 'Thanks, Hilda.' She sipped the tea before placing it on the chunky oak work surface that she was leaning up against. 'Alan told me over the phone and I told Douglas up at the hospital. I thought it was best that he heard it from me. For what it's worth, I personally thought he'd take it a lot worse than he did. But after the shock of finding Alice and then the accident, well, he's...' Linda groped for an appropriate word, 'he seems rather subdued, shall we say. Plus he is on some pretty hefty painkillers. I think it might have taken the edge off it a bit. But I can see in his eyes just how devastated he is.'

'You said about him finding Alice,' Bertie said, looking at Sergeant Frisk. 'Is that what happened?'

'Yes,' Frisk said. 'After speaking to Douglas yesterday and again briefly this morning, I'm satisfied that what he is saying is true. It all adds up. He said he found Alice in the kitchen late Wednesday night. I needn't go into too much detail, but from what I saw at the house with the electrics and the markings on Alice's hand, I'd say it was an electrical fault. There were a lot of overloaded plug sockets. Something certainly short-circuited the place.' Frisk took a swig of tea. 'I also noticed some medication in Alice's bedroom, Linda. A box of Propranolol tablets, to be exact. Did she suffer with anxiety, do you know?'

Linda reached for her own mug of tea. 'It had got worse over recent years,' she said, looking at Bertie. 'She always was a bit of a worrier, especially where Douglas was concerned. Often with very good reason.'

'You kept in regular contact with Alice then, Linda?' Bowen asked.

'I spoke with her about once a month. Even while I was away. I'd been working in Brussels up until May this year. I've got a place over in Marlow that I've been letting out while I've been working away, but I was recently offered a consultancy role with a pharmaceutical company which I worked for some years ago. I've accepted the position, which means I'm mainly going to be based from home, and the hours are a lot less demanding. My property portfolio is pretty healthy and I'm thinking of adding to it with something else around here. Given everything that's happened, I think it's only right that in my role as Douglas's godmother it should be me that takes care of him.'

'How long will he be in hospital for, Linda?' Bowen asked.

'They still can't be sure at this stage,' she said. 'He's got some tough weeks and months ahead of him. Not just physically, but emotionally. I haven't even thought about Alice's funeral arrangements yet,' Linda said, sipping her tea. 'There's no way I can take my sister's place, but I think I've got no alternative but to give it a bloody good go. Douglas won't be out of hospital for some time yet, though, that's almost certain. When he is, he's going to need stability and support, and a strong infrastructure around him. He has told me he doesn't want to go back to Pugsden Lane, and I can't blame him after what happened. It's going to be tough, I'm under no illusion there, but, well, like I said, Alice was my younger sister and I am Douglas's godmother.' She downed her remaining tea. 'So there it is.'

'And I'm his father,' Bertie said, sounding a touch meeker than he intended.

'Yeah, no offence, Robert, but from what I hear regarding your prospects, we'd probably be better off leaving him in the hands of Zippy and Bungle, but thanks for your input.'

Bertie had no counterargument to make. Linda was speaking the truth. He leant up against the kitchen unit feeling decidedly out of his depth as the reality of the situation really started to hit home. Despite never really seeing eye to eye with Linda, he was actually secretly quite glad she was here. Her confident and pragmatic approach was strangely reassuring, despite her rather caustic attitude towards him.

'You said something about the electrics, Sergeant.' Linda said. 'What's that all about?'

'When I found Alice on Saturday, all the electrics were short-circuited in the house. The plugs in the kitchen were overloaded with extension lead sockets that led out to the caravan. My guess is that the whole place will probably need rewiring.'

Linda exhaled, taking out a Filofax from her bag. 'That'll cost me a pretty penny as well then, won't it?' she said with a sigh.

'You?' Bertie said. 'How do you mean?'

'I'm the landlady, Robert,' Linda said, not looking up as she scribbled in her Filofax. 'I own the place.'

'Eh?' Bertie said with obvious confusion. 'Since when?'

Linda closed her Filofax and shot Bertie a look that was half frown, half smile. 'Since you blummin' well buggered off, Buster! That's since when. You weren't exactly much help when it came to paying the rent, were you? I helped her out for over a year with the rent on that place. Then the opportunity came up to buy it. I was doing well with work and looking to start investing in property. Number 8 Pugsden Lane was my first. It also meant that Alice could pay me back at a much more reasonable rate, which helped her out significantly, considering she was only on dinner lady wages. Now, I'm pleased to say, the mortgage is fully paid off so I own the place outright.'

Bertie was feeling decidedly emasculated and rather ashamed of himself in the presence of this clearly savvy and efficient businesswoman. Any fleeting thoughts he harboured about suggesting that Douglas be handed over into his sole care had quickly evaporated as his sister-in-law calmly took control of the situation.

'So, if you intend to just waltz back in to that place, boyo,' she said, fixing her eyes on Bertie, 'then you'd better find yourself a job pretty sharpish, hadn't you?'

Surprised and relieved at Linda even broaching the subject, Bertie replied, 'You'd consider me taking the place on then? As a tenant?' he said.

'Like you said, Robert, despite your appalling timing and your equally abysmal track record ... The fact remains that you are still Douglas's father. I suppose that still has to count for something.'

'I'll do whatever it takes, Linda,' Bertie said, standing up straight. 'I'll pay you whatever you want. I'm starting the job hunt tomorrow, and if you need help with the electrics, then I hear Mike's still in the village, right, Alan?' Bertie said, looking to Sergeant Frisk.

'He is,' Frisk said. 'God, as he was known back in '87.'

This time it was Linda who looked at Sergeant Frisk. 'God?'

'The hurricane back in '87,' Frisk said, 'took out the power in the village. Took the power out in most places in the south of England, to be fair. Mike got it fixed... Here at least.'

Bertie remembered the storm only too well. It had hit just before he'd left. Another wave of guilt washed over him as he thought back to the time he'd stood with Douglas on the High Street when Mike had just turned the power back on. The electrician strode out from under the tall trees of the causeway declaring himself God. Douglas was just starting secondary school at that time.

'I'm pretty sure Mike'll do mates' rates if I have a word with him,' Bertie said, trying to shake off the clinging guilt.

'Oh, OK, good. I'll leave that to you then,' Linda said, looking appeased and for the first time in the exchange ever so slightly on the back foot.

'And I will happily get on to him first thing tomorrow morning and have the place looking shipshape for you, if you're definitely sure about me taking over the rental payments?' Bertie said, feeling that a minor piece of the bridge had just been built.

'Subject to circumstance, I don't really see it being a problem,' she said, folding her arms and looking Bertie in the eye. 'So that's my story,' she said. 'What's yours, Buster?'

*

When Bertie had finished recounting his tale, the four of them shared another pot of tea along with some stories of old, recounting memories of Alice. Bertie felt as though the ice was slowly melting between Linda and himself. After Reverend Bowen had put the mugs in the sink, they all made their way towards the front door, Bertie chatting with Frisk behind Bowen who opened the front door up ahead, with Linda being the first to step back out into the early evening sunshine.

'I just hope Edna will be OK with me staying at theirs for another couple of nights,' he said to Frisk.

'If I was a betting man, Bert, I'd say you should be allowed back in the next couple of days,' he said.

'Good to know,' Bertie said. 'And the new landlady giving me the green light should cheer Edna up a bit.' He lowered his voice. 'That's a hell of a result. Edna and Graham have been good to let me stay as long as I have.'

Up ahead, Reverend Bowen was taking Linda's leather jacket off the coat hook and handing it to her as she unlocked her smart-looking silver Mercedes convertible.

'Thanks, Hilda,' Linda said, putting the jacket on the passenger seat. 'I'll be in touch about the funeral arrangements just as soon as I'm able,' she said.

'Of course,' Bowen said with a warm smile.

'OK then,' Linda said, starting the car and putting it into reverse. 'I'll be in touch. Goodbye to you all,' she said waving to the three of them. Bowen, Bertie and Frisk all waved back.

Linda was reversing into the road when the sound of a rumbling diesel engine came quickly upon them, and a red Toyota pick-up truck came into view, blaring its horn and screeching to a halt, narrowly avoiding a collision with the rear end of Linda's Mercedes by a distance of about six inches.

'Uh oh, there goes the neighbourhood,' Sergeant Frisk said, smirking after watching the near collision.

'You wanna be a bit more careful there, sweetheart,' a toned man with an Australian-sounding accent said in a cautionary voice, stepping out of his vehicle. 'I almost slammed right into the back of you.'

'Well,' Linda said, eyeing up the stranger, 'we wouldn't want that now, would we?'

'Now she's for it,' Reverend Bowen said quietly to Frisk and Bertie, smirking.

'Butch Ransom, Linda Mackenzie; Linda Mackenzie, Butch Ransom,' Frisk said, making the introductions.

Butch smiled. 'We'd better swap numbers then, Linda, eh?' he said, making his way towards her vehicle. 'For insurance purposes.'

'I thought that was only if you had an accident,' Linda said.

'Well, it's better to be safe than sorry, isn't it?' Butch replied. 'And besides, I'm thinking I might have to claim for psychological damages. I think I'm suffering from bloody shock,' he said, dramatically shaking his head.

'A big man like you?' Linda said. 'Whatever are you in shock for?'

Wobbly-legged, Butch theatrically steadied himself, putting his hand on the driver's side door of his pick-up truck. A black and white border collie barked from the passenger seat. 'I'm shocked to see someone as good-looking as you in a place like this,' Butch said.

'Smooooth,' Linda replied with the hint of a smile as she looked Butch up and down for a second time.

Butch smiled and gave her a cheeky wink in return.

10   *Tuesday, August 17*

'Any luck at the job centre then, boy?' Graham Glass boisterously enquired from the comfort of his armchair, turning the sound down on the television as Bertie entered number 4 Bargus Close.

'A couple of bits,' he replied. 'I registered with them. Left my details. Got a couple of interviews lined up potentially. Nothing exciting, but it'll be money, I suppose. Could always try and get my old job back at the brewery if all else fails.'

'You wanna get on this, boy!' Graham exclaimed, nodding at the TV and holding up a copy of *The Bodyguard*. 'Just rented it from the garage. Gonna knock out five copies of these for some of the tarts at work. Money for old rope. Gary don't even know how much I'm mugging him off, the wally. Fuckin' priceless, I tell ya, boy!'

'They're gonna call here tomorrow, if that's OK,' Bertie said just as Edna appeared from the bedroom. 'The people at the job centre, I mean.'

'And what address did you give them, Bert?' she asked. 'Here, I suppose? You may as bloody well.'

'I put Pugsden Lane down actually,' Bertie said, just as the phone rang. Edna answered it, gave a non-committal grunt and handed the phone to Bertie.

'Call for you, sir,' she said sarcastically. 'The long arm of the law, Frisk.'

Bertie's pulse rate quickened as he put the receiver to his ear. 'Hi, Alan...'

*

Five minutes later Bertie hung up the phone. Edna came back into the lounge and Graham once again turned the sound down on the TV.

'Well?' she said.

'That was Alan,' Bertie said, his voice soft and distant. 'The results of Alice's...' he faltered, then took in a sharp breath. 'Alan said Alice suffered a major cardiac arrest following a severe electric shock,' he said, blurting it out in one go in the hope that he would not break down halfway through. 'He said I can go back to the bungalow as soon as I like.'

'Well,' Edna said, mellowing, 'at least you know now.'

Bertie locked eyes with hers. 'Will you come with me, Edna?' he said, beginning to well up. 'To the house? Can I stay one more night then go back there tomorrow? I don't want to... I ...' Bertie trailed off. 'Will you come down to the bungalow with me?'

For once Edna's hardened facade cracked just a little and she smiled. 'If it gets you out from under my feet,' she said with a look that Bertie could've sworn contained a trace of compassion, 'I suppose I could.'

'Yeah, stay here one more night, boy!' Graham said. 'We'll have ourselves one last party. You're going to work in a bit anyway, ent ya?' Graham said, craning his neck and looking over towards Edna who was still looking at Bertie.

'Yeah, I am,' she said, her voice once again set on edge. 'And I assume now that you probably aren't?'

'I gotta get this done,' he said, nodding at the TV. 'They'll be all right without me for one more night,' he said.

'You're starting to take the piss,' Edna said, lighting a cigarette.

'And you're starting to get on my bloody nerves,' Graham responded.

Caught in the middle of the game of verbal tennis, Bertie kept quiet for a moment, his mind whirring with the information he had just received. His thoughts turned to the house, and what Sergeant Frisk had said about the wiring at the bungalow. 'Is it OK if I phone Mike later? About the electrics at the house?'

'Course, boy,' Graham replied.

'I'm going,' Edna said.

'Tarrah!' Graham said from the armchair.

Bertie gently put his hand on Edna's arm just as she was about to leave. 'Thank you, Edna,' he said, locking eyes with hers. 'You will come with me

62

tomorrow, won't you? I don't want to ... I don't wanna go down there on my own. Not the first time.'

'It's not the first time though, is it?' Edna said. 'It's your bloody home, you daft sod.'

'You know what I mean though,' Bertie said.

Edna exhaled a cloud of smoke. 'Yes,' she said, 'I do.'

Bertie smiled and Edna left for her shift at the pub.

'Get the drinks in then, boy!' Graham called.

'You know what, mate, I think I'm gonna keep a clear head,' Bertie said. 'For tomorrow.'

Graham snorted. 'Suit yourself,' he said. 'Get us one anyway then.'

11 *Wednesday, August 18*

The sun was shining down on Bertie and Edna as they walked together up Steventon High Street towards the Pressed Fruitbowl where a little later Edna would be starting her shift. Beyond that was Pugsden Lane and the home that Bertie had not entered in nearly six years.

'You work a lot, don't you, Edna? At the school and in there,' Bertie said, nodding at the pub up ahead.

'Yeah, and you can probably guess why, can't you? You don't exactly need to be Einstein to work that one out, do you? And it looks like I'm gonna be on my own down the school when term starts till they find a replacement for Alice.' Edna lit a cigarette. 'Not that they'll be able to replace her,' she said. 'I'm gonna bloody miss that woman.'

Bertie detected Edna's usually forthright and direct voice wavering slightly.

'I could make a good dinner lady,' Bertie said. 'I've got experience of kitchens.'

'Kids are back in a couple of weeks. I can probably manage single-handedly for the time being. Just won't have anyone to sing along to the radio with.'

'Bit of a duo, were you?' Bertie said.

'She was always singing. Despite everything, she would always sing. When she did, she sounded like she didn't have a care in the world.'

'She was great, wasn't she?' Bertie said.

'And the kids'll miss her,' Edna continued. 'Someone'll have to explain it to them somehow, I suppose. They all knew her. It'll be a shock, that's for sure. It ain't like losing a hamster. Probably a lot of those kids' first experience of losing someone they know. She might not have been family to 'em, but she damn well felt like it.'

'Mmmm,' Bertie said.

'We're having the same problem up at the pub 'n' all,' Edna said, nodding towards the Pressed Fruitbowl looming up ahead. 'Chef problems. Bloke's a total flake and Terry's had enough. I've been picking up extra shifts to help out in the kitchen as much as I can. I don't mind so much over the holidays. Anything to get me away from that fat slob back there.'

'The pub needs a chef?' Bertie said, stopping and turning to face Edna. 'I worked in the kitchen of the Dragon for a year and a half. I might not make the best dinner lady, but I might be able to plug the gap up at the pub. The money would come in bloody handy as well, now that I've got rent to pay and Douglas to think about. Do you think you could have a word with, is it Terry you said?'

'Mmm hmm,' Edna said, leaving a pause, contemplating Bertie's proposal. 'Could do, I suppose,' she said as they passed the pub on the approach to the top of Pugsden Lane.

Bertie came to a halt. 'I'm really nervous about this, Edna,' he said. 'I didn't think for a minute that coming back here would be like this.'

'Yeah, well,' Edna said. 'Shit happens, doesn't it?'

'Yep,' Bertie replied, 'it sure does.'

They walked in silence down Pugsden Lane, rounding the bend and heading towards the house. Bertie remembered the collection of vehicles that were gathered here the last time he was down this way.

'Look at the state of that,' Bertie said, nodding at the caravan. 'I can still feel Jim Bowen dragging me off by the arm to come and look at it after we'd won it. All shiny and new it was.' Bertie paused, surveying the now shabby hulk of what he supposed was still technically his Marauder 500 caravan. Bully's star prize. 'I suppose I can go in now, can't I?' Bertie said, looking at Edna, as if almost asking permission. 'Now all the police tape's gone, I mean, I can have a proper look around.'

'I wouldn't get too excited if I was you,' Edna said.

'What time d'you have to be at work?'

'Not for another hour,' she said.

'You're sure you're OK to stay?'

'Said I was, didn't I?'

Bertie gave an appreciative little smile and walked towards the door of the caravan, opening it and sticking his head into its gloomy interior. He stepped in, unprepared for how messy it was in there. There were cassette tapes and VHS cassettes littered around the place. Bertie picked up a cassette copy of Iron Maiden's *Somewhere in Time* from off the side. There was an old television and video all unplugged and a small stereo unit. Bertie picked up an empty video box: *Night of the Giving Head* was written on its spine in black pen. Edna joined him in the caravan. 'I don't suppose I need to ask where this came from,' Bertie said, holding up the video box.

'Peter and Douglas were little sods for nicking Graham's videos,' Edna said with a smile. 'It's his own fault for leaving them lying around the place, the dirty bastard.'

'Boys will be boys, eh?' Bertie said. 'Jesus, is that what I think it is?' he said, spying a familiar looking acoustic guitar in the corner of the caravan that looked like it had seen better days. It had two strings missing and was now covered in stickers of band logos. Bertie picked it up and strummed it. 'Blimey, that could do with tuning,' he said. 'Otherwise it's not in too bad shape. I reckon I could get that fixed up. It looks like Dougie's got pretty decent taste in music at least,' he said, looking at all the stickers on the front of the guitar.

'You might want to come and have a look at this before you get too carried away,' Edna said from behind him.

Bertie placed the guitar on the seating by the back window. 'What's that?' he said, walking over to her.

Edna nodded down to a tatty dartboard on the floor.

'Bloody hell,' Bertie said, pulling the meat cleaver out of the prick-marked face of the photo he barely recognised as himself.

'Told you you were gonna have your work cut out, didn't I?'

'I guess so,' Bertie said, picking up the dartboard and placing it on the side. He folded up his tatty photo and put it in the back pocket of his jeans.

'Come on,' Edna said, 'you going in that house or what?'

Bertie felt the butterflies in his stomach as his anxiety levels increased. He made his way out of the caravan. Edna was outside, walking towards the rear end of the Ford Orion. She nodded down at the car's exhaust pipe. 'Take a look,' she said, smiling.

Bertie crouched down on all fours, inspecting the rusty exhaust that was missing about eight inches of pipe, just as Edna had said. He chuckled to himself. 'I still can't believe you two,' he said, getting back to his feet. 'Thank you,' he said with eyes that conveyed a deep sincerity, 'for looking out for Douglas. You saved him from God knows what.' Bertie took Edna's right hand in his own. 'I'll never forget that, Edna,' he said.

Edna smiled. 'Come on,' she said, 'get out those keys Auntie Linda gave you.'

Bertie did as he was instructed, fishing the bunch of keys out from the front right pocket of his Levis. Hesitating ever so slightly, he inserted the key, turned it, and for the first time in nearly six years crossed the threshold of his old home with Edna following on closely behind.

The door offered some resistance as he pushed it open, Bertie soon realised why as he gathered up some, but by no means all, of a bundle of old post, free newspapers and junk mail. He stood silently in the hall, taking it in. There was a faint background smell of what Bertie thought was pot pourri. Immediately on his right was Douglas's old room. He poked his head round the door, feeling a little like an intruder. The room was covered with the posters of many of the bands that Bertie had seen stickered on his old guitar in the caravan. The single bed was made and there were more CDs and cassettes littered around the room than in the caravan. The light bluey grey carpet was mostly obscured by old copies of *Kerrang* and *Metal Hammer* magazines.

'Looks like my son is a true metal head,' Bertie said, smiling and closing the door on the mess, conscious of time and of Edna.

Bertie made his way into the front room across the hall whose bay windows, like Douglas's, looked out over the driveway. The living room was neat and tidy. The old hi-fi was in its usual place in the corner of the room, an armchair beside it. The television and video were in the corner by the bay windows, facing out to a two-seater sofa and another armchair. Next to the television was a cabinet containing more videos: *Ghostbusters*, *Beverly Hills Cop*, *The Karate Kid*, amongst others, were behind the cabinet's glass facade. 'Nice to see that Graham's films don't seem to have made it into the house,' Bertie said. He went over to the hi-fi, opening the wooden cabinet beside it that housed a fairly substantial record collection, thumbing through the LPs. Many he recognised as his own, some released in the years of his absence. 'All my old records are still here, Edna,' Bertie said, looking surprised. 'Still all in alphabetical order.' He pulled out a copy of Slade's *Old New Borrowed Blue* album. 'You know, part of me was half expecting to find that all this had been thrown out. Or that Douglas might have burnt them all in the garden, or something.'

'She'd never let him,' Edna said. 'Believe me, I think he would've done given half a chance.'

'Edna, this all feels so familiar. It's almost like I've never been away. Everything seems to be almost just the same as before I left.'

Edna looked at him from over by the bay window. 'She was waiting for you to come back, that's why, you silly sod.'

Bertie felt himself welling up, scanning the reverse of the Slade album, his eyes drawn to track 7, 'Everyday'. It had been the song they'd chosen for the first dance at their wedding. A tear pattered the number beside the song. Bertie wiped it, making a salty glistening streak across the album sleeve.

'Look at that,' Edna said, pointing above the fireplace.

Bertie followed her gaze. 'Bob Geldof?' Bertie said, at first only noticing the picture of the Live Aid architect and Boomtown Rats frontman on the mantlepiece. Then he saw the picture on the wall above it, feeling heady emotion once again welling up inside him. 'God, I remember the day that was taken,' he said, looking at the framed colour photo of Alice, Douglas and himself sitting in the sunshine of the bungalow's back garden. 'We'd just bought a camera with an automatic timer on it. Douglas was about eight or nine at the time, I think. Look at that smile,' Bertie said, as another tear traced down his cheek, dispersing on his lips. 'The timer was counting down and Alice was tickling him. "Smile, Mr Tickle!" she kept saying to him as we waited for the timer to run down. By the time the camera clicked he was virtually in hysterics. So were we.' Bertie paused, silently contemplating the photo. 'God, she looks so beautiful, doesn't she?' he said, at last totally breaking down into a fit of uncontrollable sobs. Edna came to his side and put an arm around him. 'I left it too late, Edna,' he said, wiping his eyes on the shoulder of his T-shirt. 'Why didn't I come back here sooner? Why did I wait so bloody long?'

In an uncharacteristic display of affection, Edna rubbed his arm as Bertie's tears began to subside. 'Maybe better late than never though, eh?' she said.

'Alan said he found Alice in bed. Apparently Douglas had put her there after he found her, poor sod. Will you...' Bertie said, nodding towards the hall. 'I feel weird about going in there.' He let out a nervous laugh. 'I feel a bit weird about being back here, full stop, let alone going in there.'

'Come on,' Edna said, leading the way to the bungalow's main bedroom. She stood by the bedroom door, pushing it open. Bertie stood in front of it, took in a deep breath and entered. The curtains were partially drawn, letting in a chunk of afternoon sunshine.

'Look at that,' Bertie said, his gaze pointing in the direction of the framed photo on Alice's dressing table. There were in fact two of them. 'Douglas,' he said, smiling. 'Doesn't he look cute? Must've been just after he started big school... Just before I...' Bertie trailed off, shaking his head. 'Is that who I think it is?' Bertie said, now looking at the other framed photo on the dresser. 'Marti Pellow!' he said, smiling. 'Blimey, she really did have a crush on that man, didn't she?'

'She loved Wet Wet Wet,' Edna said. 'Any time they came on the radio up the school when we were making lunch, she'd belt it out. Like I said, she'd sing along to most things, but she'd sing louder and with a bigger smile on her face when that lot came on.'

Bertie went over to the wardrobe in the corner of the room, opening the left-hand door. Alice's clothes were hanging neat and tidy: tops, T-shirts, some dresses. He opened the right-hand door, the sight that greeted him leaving him a little stunned. 'Edna, all my clothes are still here aswell,' he said, flicking through the hangers of old band T-shirts, jeans and jumpers.

'I told you,' Edna said, 'she was waiting for you to come back.'

Bertie stood, looking at the wardrobe and its contents, shaking his head. 'She was waiting and I never came. And when I did, it was too bloody late,' he said, slapping the side of the wardrobe with the flat of his palm.

A knock on the front door of the bungalow broke the silence in the bedroom.

'That'll be Mike,' Bertie said, turning towards the noise. 'Or God, as he was known back in the day. Blimey, look at the time,' he said, checking his watch, 'you'd better get off to work.'

'You gonna be all right?' Edna said.

'I think so,' Bertie said, as they both walked towards the front door. 'Thank you for coming down here, Edna. I don't think I could've faced it alone. But it feels ... well, it feels like home, doesn't it?' Bertie opened the front door.

'I am God,' the man in blue overalls said, standing on the front step with an enormous grin on his face which spread contagiously to both Bertie and Edna.

'God, am I pleased to see you,' Bertie said, welcoming in the electrician.

'See you later then,' Edna said, leaving to start her shift at the pub.

'Thank you,' Bertie mouthed silently to her before she turned and departed up the lane.

12

Bertie showed Mike where the fusebox was located in a cupboard in the hall, amazed at how easily he found navigating his former home. On a solitary clothes peg on the back of the cupboard door hung what Bertie assumed was Alice's coat, though with a strange and guilty sadness he didn't recognise it. On the floor of the cupboard in front of the hoover were two pairs of trainers: a pair of plain but well-worn black trainers, and a smaller, newer-looking pair of white Puma trainers with a faded pink and grey trim. The sight of the four shoes lined up next to one another broke Bertie's heart just that little bit more as he thought about how both pairs of trainers would, for different but equally just as tragic reasons, never be worn again.

Confident in the electrician's abilities, but feeling more and more emotionally overwhelmed, Bertie left him to it and went outside to get some air and take another look at the car. He hadn't realised that he'd taken the car keys with him when he'd left for Bridgend. By the time he'd realised, he knew it would be too late to return them. Not that it would have made much difference, as Alice didn't drive and Douglas was still at that time six years off being able to learn.

The driver's door was unlocked. It yawned open with creaking protestation as Bertie pulled on the handle. The driver's seat was further forward than he would ever have had it. He inserted the key into the ignition. The car tried but failed to start. The same could not be said for the stereo, however, as the sound of Iron Maiden's *No Prayer For the Dying* obliterated his hearing. Bertie noticing that the volume knob had been turned up full blast. He turned the volume down and inspected the glove box's contents: Metallica's *And Justice for All* and Slayer's *Seasons in the Abyss* were also stowed there. The needle on the petrol gauge was showing empty, though there was clearly nothing wrong with the battery, and other than needing some air in the tyres and a bloody good clean, the car didn't look in too bad shape. He'd fix it up. It would give him something to occupy both his mind and his time.

Bertie went back into the house where Mike was busy working away. 'It's not actually as bad as I thought, Bert,' he called out from the kitchen. Bertie still hadn't ventured into the room where Alice had drawn her last earthly breath. Steeling himself, he drew in a deep breath of his own and went in the kitchen.

'That's good,' he said, trying not to sound as shaky as he felt.

'Your fuses have all blown in this one,' Mike said, pointing to the blackened sockets in the corner of the kitchen. 'That knocked out all the others. I should have it done in about an hour.'

'OK,' Bertie said. 'Well, I think I'll leave you to it. I'm gonna go and take a walk. It's still a bit weird being back here.'

'Yeah, terrible, mate. Absolutely terrible. Must've been a dreadful shock,' Mike said, quickly putting a hand to his mouth and looking embarrassed. 'Shit, sorry, Bert. I didn't mean...'

'It's OK,' Bertie said.

'I'll crack on then,' Mike said, going back to the fusebox. 'Hey, have you seen the flowers?' he called out from the cupboard.

'Flowers?'

'Yeah, up by the school gates. Some people have laid flowers up there. Alice was a very well-liked lady up there, y'know.'

'Maybe I'll take a stroll up there then,' Bertie said.

'Give me an hour,' Mike said. 'Should have it all shipshape by then.'

Appreciative of the fresh air, Bertie strolled back the way he'd come with Edna, back past the Pressed Fruitbowl. Through the window he could see Edna behind the bar. He gave her a wave and a smile. She waved back. He continued on down the High Street, turning left at the war memorial and stepping up onto the ancient cobbles of the causeway. He walked on, taking in the view of the village from his raised position and thinking of Alice, before stepping down and out of the shady canopy of the horse chestnuts that lined the village's ancient walkway. A few drinkers were in the beer garden of the Crafty Digit, enjoying an afternoon pint. Across from it was the school.

Bertie could see the flowers laid up against the blue gates. He crossed over to the school and with creaking knees crouched down to inspect the bouquets. The messages were sweet, heartfelt and sincere, and Bertie could once again feel the tears building behind his eyes.

The one that finally caused the dam to burst was one written in what was clearly the hand of a child that read, 'Dinners will be better in heaven now'. With that Bertie lost control of his emotions, thinking about his wife. She loved the kids, and they loved her. Edna was right. How were they ever going to replace her?

With a little effort Bertie got back to his feet and turned, making to leave the school, but hesitated at the sight of a woman holding a bunch of flowers of her own walking towards him. Bertie stood aside as she reached the gates.

'It's terribly sad, don't you think?' she said, placing her bouquet gently down beside the others.

'Yes,' Bertie said, trying to hide the fact that he was wiping away his tears.

'I'm sorry,' the lady said, tumbling him immediately. 'I didn't mean to intrude.'

'It's OK,' Bertie said, 'I was just leaving.'

'I'm Trudy. Trudy Ryan,' the woman said, holding out her hand.

'Bertie,' he said, shaking it.

Trudy gave him an inquisitive look. 'Did you say Bertie?'

Bertie nodded his head. 'Mmm hmm.'

'Not ... Bertie Blouse?'

Bertie smiled, sniffling and wiping his eyes again, feeling a little more composed now. 'That's right,' he said. 'Do I know you?'

'No,' Trudy said, 'but I feel like I know you. I mean, I've heard about you. Gosh, you poor thing, Alice was your wife.'

'Yes,' Bertie said, 'she was.'

'And you're Douglas's father. The boy who had the accident on the railway.'

'That's right. Looks like this place hasn't changed much when it comes to a good gossip.'

'I'm sorry,' Trudy said, putting her hand on her heart. 'I didn't mean it like that, honestly. Forgive me. I live in the house next to the level crossing, you see. I was there just after it happened. It was horrendous.'

'I'm sure it was,' Bertie said.

'When I said I feel like I know you, what I mean is, my husband, he got a bit involved down the pub trying to ingratiate himself into the area with some of the locals. We're still pretty new here, you see, and he got talking to a man who was talking about you. It was last Friday, after the meeting. The one where they all decided to put Douglas in the police dog show. Do you know about all that?'

'I know enough,' Bertie said.

'I believe the man Jeremy was talking to, Jeremy is my husband, I believe the man he was talking to was your old darts partner? The man you went on Bullseye with?'

'Blimey, Trudy, you really have done your homework on me, haven't you?'

'Gosh, I'm so sorry, Bertie. You must think I'm a complete weirdo coming out with all this.'

'Nah, you're all right, Trudy. Graham did always like a good chinwag after a few drinks.'

'Please don't think this is idle gossip, I'm really not that kind of person. It's just that Douglas's story and what happened to him has had a real impact on me. I knew all along that there must have been something more to it, something that made him act the way he did. When Reverend Bowen announced in church on Sunday that his mum, your wife, had died, well, it really got to me, I don't know why. Maybe it's because I'm a mother myself. I felt so sorry for him, and what with him not having a father ... I mean, sorry, that sounded so stupid. God, I'm not exactly covering myself in glory here, am I?'

'I think I know what you mean,' Bertie said.

'No, what I mean is, I thought you went away?'

'I did,' Bertie said. 'Now I'm back. How long have you been here?'

'Only since May. My two girls are starting school here in September. It's so sad. How long have you been back? If you don't mind me asking.'

'I came back on Saturday,' Bertie said. 'Late afternoon.'

Trudy's eyes widened in realisation at the significance of the date. 'I'm so sorry,' she said again. 'I think it was terrible what they were going to do to him. It was barbaric. When I think about everything that happened. And then when I heard about...' Trudy nodded at the flowers, 'your poor wife, and how he'd lost her...' Trudy trailed off. Now it was she who was wiping away a tear.

'Sounds like Dougie gave as good as he got though,' Bertie said. 'One hell of a mess.'

'How is he?' Trudy asked.

'I don't really know. Bad would be my guess. I've been told that he knows I'm back, but I'm not exactly his favourite person, if you know what I mean? I can't blame him for that. I knew I was going to have my work cut out, but I never imagined it would be anything like this.'

'It's awful,' Trudy said. 'You know it's strange, even though I've not been here long, I almost feel as though I knew her. Alice, I mean. I read the cards on the flowers yesterday on my way into the village. I wanted to get some of my own.'

'I intend to do that very same thing myself,' Bertie said.

'It's sad that my two will never get to meet her.'

'It is,' Bertie said. 'She was a wicked cook.'

'Bertie, I hope it's not an imposition, and please tell me if I'm intruding, but would it be OK for me to come to the funeral? I'd like to pay my respects in person.'

'To be honest, Trudy, I'm not sure when that's going to be just yet. The date has yet to be finalised. But whenever it is, you will be most welcome.'

'Thank you,' Trudy said.

'So what is it that you do?' Bertie asked, wanting to get away from the subject of his wife's funeral.

'I'm setting up shop back at the house. I'm a holistic therapy practitioner.'

'I see,' Bertie said. 'And that is ...?'

'Aroma therapy, Reiki healing, that sort of thing. 'Woo woo hippy stuff,' as my husband calls it. He doesn't really get it. He works in the city.'

Bertie smiled. 'I see.'

'He's a banker.'

'Yeah, he sounds it,' Bertie said, succeeding in making Trudy laugh.

'I'm considering retraining again, though, as well as doing the holistic stuff. This whole business with Douglas has really caused me to take stock. I'm thinking about becoming a psychotherapist, specialising in bereavement counselling. I just want to help people, you know?'

'Yeah, I do,' Bertie said. 'I think I could do with a bit of that myself right now, you know. Give me a shout when you're up and running, won't you?'

'I'll do that,' Trudy said. 'Well, I'd better be going. I've got to get down to Fabsolutely Babulous to pick up some bits before they close.'

'Good old Barbara,' Bertie said. 'I'll be sure to let you know when the funeral is. I think the details will be in the local paper once it's all finalised, so keep an eye out for that. Anyway, knowing this place, it'll be round the village in half an hour once it's sorted out. Just pop in there,' Bertie said, nodding over at the Crafty Digit pub.

'I shall keep my eyes peeled,' Trudy said. 'Goodbye then, Bertie. Take care.'

'Yes, you too. See you, Trudy. Nice to meet you,' Bertie said as the two parted ways.

Bertie decided to walk the long way back to Pugsden Lane, over the now infamous level crossing. In the opening to the causeway on the opposite side of the road there was a candle in a jar. It had burnt down and gone out, but its proximity Bertie now knew was to the spot where Alice had supposedly been seen on the day of the accident. Bertie picked up the jar.

'*To Alice. Love from Daisy X*'

The words were written in black marker pen on the glass. Bertie put it back where he had found it and carried on walking down the rest of the causeway, into Mill Street and round onto Castle Street. He walked up the farm track that ran parallel with the railway, cresting the incline that brought him out at the top of the High Street and made his way back home.

'All done, Bert, mate,' Mike said, loading some stuff into his van as Bertie approached the bungalow.

'Thanks, Mike, I really appreciate it. How much do I owe you?'

'Don't worry about that for now, mate. I'll drop an invoice round in a day or two. I think you'll find it quite reasonable,' the electrician said with a cheery wink.

'Great, thanks. With any luck I shall be a man of means before long. I bloody need to be if Auntie Linda's going to let me stay on here.'

'Auntie Linda?'

'The landlady, Linda Mackenzie. She's Alice's sister. She owns the place.'

'Keeping it in the family, eh?'

'Something like that, pal,' Bertie said.

'Well, I'll leave you to get settled back in then,' Mike said. 'Give me a shout if you need anything else. Maybe go for a drink sometime. You can give me a good hiding on the dartboard down the Fruitbowl.'

'I'd like that,' Bertie said with a smile. 'But my form's taken a bit of a dip in recent times. The average isn't quite what it used to be. It's, well...' Bertie smiled, 'average.'

'So I might actually stand a chance of pinching a couple off you then?'

'Oh, easily. I'm in need of some serious practice.'

'Well, don't practice too hard just yet, eh?' Mike said, making his way round to the driver's side of his white van.

'I'll try not to,' Bertie said, waving Mike off. 'See you, mate.'

Mike raised his thumb above the van roof and got in his vehicle. Bertie walked up the garden path and went back inside the house. Standing in the silence of the hallway, he suddenly felt very alone. He went into the living room in need of sound. He pressed the power button on the hi-fi, excited to see the front panel illuminate. 'Houston, we have lift off,' he said. Bertie went to the small shelving unit next to the h-ifi and pulled out Wet Wet Wet's *Popped in Souled Out* LP. The record had come out in 1987, and Bertie recalled how much Alice had played it just before he left. He put the record on the turntable, lifted the turntable arm and delicately placed the needle on the record's outer groove. There was a faint crackle as the record revolved before the opening chimes of 'Wishing I Was Lucky' filled the room. Bertie turned the volume down a couple of notches, looking again at the photo of himself, Douglas and Alice above the fireplace. All smiles. He was smiling back when the sound of three sharp raps on the bungalow's front door startled him out of his reminiscence. He walked back down the hall towards the door.

'God got a bit of a mad memory?' he said as he opened the door, fully expecting to see the electrician standing there. Instead he was left perplexed by the sight that greeted him. The doorstep was empty, as was the garden path beyond it. Mike's van had gone. There was nobody there, and all of a sudden Bertie didn't feel quite so alone any more.

13 *Friday, August 20*

Reverend Bowen showed Bertie through the vicarage's now familiar hallway and kitchen and out into the property's substantial back garden, where Linda was seated at a small table and chairs. She was wearing white jeans and a slightly psychedelic-looking paisley silk shirt. In front of her was a glass of fizzing clear liquid, standing beside her open Filofax. Bertie half hoped it was a gin and tonic the way his nerves were feeling after what had happened on Wednesday. She turned towards him, taking her tortoiseshell sunglasses down to eye him as he approached. 'Ahh, Robert,' she said, 'good afternoon.'

'Hi, Linda,' Bertie said. 'Electrics are all fixed at the house,' he said, trying to earn himself some immediate brownie points.

'Oh good. Thank you for that,' Linda said. 'What's the damage?'

'It's taken care of.'

'How d'you mean?'

'I mean it's taken care of. I've sorted it.' Or at least he would, once Mike had dropped the bill round.

'OK, well, thanks then, I guess. But make sure you drop me round a copy of the invoice. I'll still need it for my records.'

Reverend Bowen was making her way back over towards them with two more glasses identical to the one in front of Linda. Moses followed on behind her. 'This weather is certainly holding on, isn't it?' she said, placing the glasses down on the table and taking a seat. 'Lemonade?' she offered.

Feeling only marginally deflated, Bertie accepted it with good grace. 'Thank you, Reverend.'

'Hilda, please.'

'OK, thank you, Hilda,' Bertie smiled. 'I see that bishop of yours hasn't wasted much time in getting the For Sale sign up. He doesn't hang about, does he?'

'He certainly does not,' Bowen said, sipping her drink. 'Yes, I must say that sign going up has made it all feel suddenly very real. But change is a constant in life. Like the changing of the seasons. We must learn to adapt, mustn't we sweetie?' she said, stroking Moses under the chin. 'It's another little adventure for us, isn't it,' she said to the appreciative dog. 'And besides, it turns out that the old place might not necessarily be falling into the hands of strangers,' Bowen said, smiling at Linda.

'Oh really?' Bertie said, a little surprised.

'Well, I told you I was going to be on the lookout for somewhere local, didn't I? Where better than here? It's a beautiful house with a great location. I'm fairly confident that I could kit out the ground floor to suit Douglas's needs for when they finally release him from hospital. Hilda has given me the sneak preview tour. My new consultancy role is going to be based mainly from home, and the company itself is based in Slough, so that's an easy train journey for when I do have to go in and kick some butt. It seems the ideal fit,' Linda said, sipping her lemonade.

'And I'd be happy for you to have it,' Bowen said. 'It's to your eternal credit, what you're doing for Douglas. And how understanding you've been about ... well, everything,'

'What was I going to do?' Linda said, letting out a little laugh. 'Call the police?'

'And it means that Douglas will be just around the corner, Bertie,' Bowen said with a smile.

'Yes. Speaking of which, how's the job hunt going, Buster?' Linda said.

'I'm working on it,' Bertie said. 'And, for what it's worth, I think it's a great idea you buying this place. I told you, Linda, I'm in this for the long haul. And I mean it about the job. There's definitely something in the pipeline, but I don't want to get too ahead of myself just yet. Hopefully I can make the last of my brother's loan last until I get something sorted. No, when Douglas is released from hospital, or whenever he wants to see me ... If he wants to see me, I'll be here,' Bertie said with a determined nod of the head.

'We all will,' Bowen said. 'Well ... not quite everyone unfortunately,' she said.

'No,' Linda said sombrely. 'So, to bring you up to speed on what's happening, I have contacted the funeral directors and had an initial chat with...' she opened her Filofax, scanning one of its lined pages, 'Pollard, Mr Roland Pollard, of R Pollard and Sons. I'm assuming you've probably had dealings with them in your line of work, Hilda?'

'Yes, I know Roland. 'Roly Poly' as he likes to call himself. The jolly undertaker. He's a good man. Friendly and sensitive, but also thorough and extremely professional. They're a good firm with an excellent reputation.'

'Good to know,' Linda said. 'So as I see it, it will be held over the road,' Linda said, nodding to the church that was partially obscured by the vicarage. 'Alice had expressed to me in the past the desire to be buried in the churchyard where she was married,' Linda said, now casting an eye Bertie's way.

The comment stung and Bertie could no longer contain his emotion. 'I feel terrible,' he said. 'It's all too surreal, this. It only feels like yesterday that we tied the knot there, and now we're talking about burying her.'

'Yes, well,' Linda said, raising an eyebrow and looking again at her Filofax, 'that's too bad, isn't it? You've got plenty of time to sit around feeling sorry for yourself. Right now we need to do what's right for Alice and for Douglas. It's going to be an extremely distressing and emotional time for him. Not that it isn't already, taking into consideration everything else he's up against. So maybe we can have your pity party another time, hmm?'

Bowen gave Bertie a smile of compassion in the silence that followed, putting her hand on his as a tear streaked down his cheek.

'Did you tell him we were meeting up today?' Bowen asked.

'Yes. I went up to see him earlier,' Linda said.

'How is he?' Bertie asked, wiping his eyes.

Linda drew in a breath, closing her Filofax and placing it back down on the table. 'Under the circumstances, I'd say he's doing OK. They're all so nice up at the hospital, and they're doing their very best for him. Mobility is obviously a massive problem for him now, but they're on hand at all times to help him. He's quiet and withdrawn a lot of the time, and he asks about Alice a lot. He blames himself for what happened to her. Says it's his fault for having all those extension cables plugged in. I've told him it was all just a tragic accident, but he's determined to give himself a hard time about it. I know he's been asking you a lot of, how shall we say, spiritual questions regarding Alice as well, hasn't he, Reverend?'

'Yes. I think after we saw her by the railway, he's looking to me for answers. I'm not sure I have them,' Bowen said contemplatively, 'but I think I might at least be starting to understand the question.'

'One other development that they're also keeping a close eye on up at the hospital,' Linda said, 'is the knock Douglas sustained to the back of his head when he fell on the crossing. They think he might be concussed. Hopefully it's nothing to worry about too much. Taking into account his other injuries, I think it's the least of his worries quite frankly, but it is something we need to keep an eye on.'

'There's no chance they can...' Bertie said. 'His feet, I mean. They couldn't ... they couldn't put them back on?'

Linda chuckled. 'I'm sure the surgeons up at the hospital would all enjoy hearing such an extremely complex surgical procedure summarised so succinctly, Robert,' she said. 'But no, they couldn't "put them back on"', she said, wiggling a set of invisible speech marks in the air.

'I didn't mean... oh, forget it,' Bertie said with a dismissive wave of his hand.

Bowen gave Linda a look of compassionate appeal.

'He was too badly injured,' Linda said, taking a deep breath. 'It just wasn't possible ... I'm sorry, Robert,' she added.

A quiet descended on the peaceful surroundings of Reverend Bowen's garden.

'We did manage a little chat,' Linda said, 'about the funeral. I asked him if there was anything he might want to suggest about the service. He was pretty dosed up, but he did say something about some music he knew his mum would like to have played. A couple of songs actually,' she said, referring back to her Filofax, flipping through a few pages. "Goodnight Girl" by ...'

'Wet Wet Wet,' Bertie said with a little smile.

'Yes,' Linda replied. 'And another one which was ...' She drew her thumb down the page. '"Stay" by Shakespears sister.'

Bertie nodded his head, silently contemplating another song he hoped but didn't yet have the courage to suggest be added to the service.

'Mr Pollard said that Alice would be with them to view on Monday,' Linda said, looking up at Bertie. 'If you'd like to? Douglas has already expressed his firm desire not to. He said that seeing her like that once was more than enough for him. I haven't made my mind up yet myself ... Robert?'

'I owe her an apology,' Bertie said, following a contemplative pause. 'More than that, I owe her an explanation. I just never thought that I'd be giving her that apology with her lying in a coffin.' Bertie turned to Reverend Bowen. 'What do you think, Hilda?' he said.

Bowen took a moment to consider. 'I think you clearly need to make your peace with her, Bertie. One way or another. But you also need to make peace with yourself. That's just as important. If there's one thing I have learned lately, it's that we all need to try to learn to be at peace with ourselves just as much, perhaps even more, than we do with other people. Compassion and forgiveness I believe are the two most important things that we as human beings possess. I think that Alice loved you, Bertie. Despite what you did in the past. And let's remember that is where it is, the past. The past is something none of us can change, no matter how much we want to.' Bowen again put her hand on Bertie's arm. 'What happened to Alice is a tragedy,' she said, 'but it wasn't your fault. Just like it wasn't Douglas's. I truly believe that and so should you. One thing I also believe is...' Bowen stopped herself. 'One thing I *know*, is that we go on. We don't die with our bodies. Something survives. I am in no doubt that Alice's gentle nature, her spirit, her love, I believe that that is what she has taken with her. I believe that that is what survives, and why it is so important for us to develop those traits while we are here on earth.' Bowen took a sip of her drink.

She continued, 'There's a lovely saying I came across the other day in a book I recently purchased and I've become very fond of it. It goes like this: "Life is eternal, love is immortal, and death is only a horizon. And a horizon is nothing more than the limit of our sight." I believe that Alice is just beyond the horizon, Bertie, that's all,' she said, putting a tender hand on top of his. 'Find a way to make your peace with Alice, Bertie. But find a way to make peace with yourself also.'

Bertie sipped his drink, quietly considering Bowen's words, remembering the knocking on the front door, and thinking that Alice might be a little closer to him than the horizon.

14

As Bertie walked home from the meeting at the vicarage, the overall feeling he had was one of relief. He opened the front door to the bungalow, noticing a small white envelope on the doormat with his name written on it in blue biro. He opened it. It was the invoice for the electrics which was again, to his relief, as reasonable as Mike said it would be. He walked down the hallway and went through to the kitchen to boil the kettle. He fancied something stronger, but he had nothing in. He flicked the switch on the wall before he even registered the significance of doing so, thinking of Alice doing the exact same thing but with tragic results just over a week ago. From the hallway came the sound of a door creaking open. Bertie felt his insides constrict and, despite feeling strong hesitation, reluctantly went to investigate. When he had come home all the doors in the hallway were shut. They still were, all except one. Douglas's bedroom door was standing wide open. Tentatively he gripped the handle, pulling the door closed and then opening it again, hearing the same identical creak he had just heard. He almost screamed when there was a loud knock on the front door: not the three sharp raps he had heard the other day, but three hefty thumps. He could also see that the porch light had come on, and whoever was standing in its illumination was as wide as the door itself. He opened it to the sight of Graham Glass, smiling and holding a carrier bag of cans.

'Fancy your chances down the Fruitbowl then, old partner?' he said, clearly a little out of breath. 'After we get warmed up of course,' Graham said, proudly holding the blue carrier bag of cans aloft.

'That, my friend, is the best idea I've heard all day,' Bertie said. 'Come on in. You want a glass for that?'

'Nah, bugger that, boy, I'm all right skulling it,' Graham said, opening the can with a loud tsshht, the can spraying a light fizz onto a navy blue polo shirt struggling to hold back the sizable girth pressing against it.

'So how you settling in then, boy? Feel like home again yet, does it? Few years now, uh?' Graham said, taking in his surroundings. 'Here, get your gob round one of these,' he continued, handing Bertie a can of Carlsberg Export.

'Cheers,' Bertie said, opening the can and considering the question. 'Yes and no, I suppose, but I think I'm starting to get used to the old place again.' He paused. 'Sort of.'

'Yeah, bound to be a bit weird, ennit, I s'pose,' Graham said, plonking himself down in the armchair next to the hi-fi and rifling through Bertie's record collection which, luckily for Graham, was within arm's reach. 'It's a bit weird being back here myself,' he said.

'Mmmm,' Bertie said, thinking that Graham was doing quite a good job of making himself feel at home.

'Bloody 'ell, I forgot about some of these gems you got here, boy!' he said, pulling out a copy of Status Quo's *Blue For You*. 'Stick that fucker on, boy!'

Bertie did as he was explicitly instructed and the opening track kicked in, Graham immediately starting to air guitar. 'How's Auntie Linda treating you?' he asked, working the imaginary fretboard.

Bertie winced, nodding at the hi-fi, turning down an invisible volume control. Graham, following instruction, leaned over and turned the music down. 'You're getting old, boy,' he said.

'I feel it,' Bertie said. 'But yeah, to answer your question, Linda is being pretty reasonable about everything, all things considered. I've not long come back from seeing her, actually, up at the vicarage with Hilda Bowen. Sorting out some of the funeral arrangements. She's a bit clinical and comes across as a bit cold, but I guess that's just her business side coming through. Perhaps it's her way of dealing with it. She'll be hurting too, regardless of how it looks on the surface. It was a bit of a surprise when I found out she owned this place, though. I didn't see that one coming. But she's let me stay under the proviso that I get on the job hunt as soon as, and if all goes to plan on that front you might soon be looking at the Pressed Fruitbowl's new chef,' Bertie said with a grin.

'You? A chef down the Fruitbowl? Bloody 'ell, I've heard it all now, boy,' Graham said, chuckling as he took a swig of beer. 'Mind you, Edna'll be happy.'

'Oh?' Bertie asked.

'Yeah, she's been having to pick up the slack from that useless twat they got up there at the minute for a while. Always leaving 'em in the lurch.'

Bertie laughed inwardly, thinking of the multiple sickies that Graham had thrown since his return.

'Yeah, Edna said the landlord – Terry, is it? – said he's been having problems with this bloke and he's on the verge of giving him the bullet. Be handy for me, though, and it sounds like there'll be plenty of shifts going, which means money to pay the rent on this place,' he said, swigging from his own can as the telephone rang in the hall. Taking his drink with him, Bertie went to answer it, looking over warily at Douglas's bedroom door next to it, which to his relief was still closed, just as he'd left it. Bertie detected the volume in the lounge increase ever so slightly in his absence.

'Hello ... oh hi, Linda, I was just talking about you ... Yes, all good.' He paused. 'Oh right... Yeah, OK sure. Yes, fine... Yes, three o'clock is fine. I've also got that invoice for the electrics... Yes, OK, will do. Yep, OK, speak soon, 'bye.'

He hung up the phone and rejoined Graham in the living room, who now had a sweaty forehead and was breathing heavily. He was no longer air-guitaring.

'That was the landlady herself,' Bertie said. 'She's fixed a time for me to go and see Alice,' he said sombrely.

'Really?' Graham said, leaning over to get himself another can. 'You sure about that, boy?'

Bertie took his time contemplating the question. 'No, not really,' he eventually said.

'I went to see Peter, after the accident,' Graham said. 'Well, I didn't actually see him, but I took Edna up and she said it was 'orrible. I waited in the car. Not my cup of tea, y'know? Still, bit of moral support for her, wan' it?'

'Yeah, I suppose so,' Bertie said with a slight shake of the head, a little bewildered. Graham, however, was once again ensconced in his air-guitaring, having got up a sufficient second wind to resume. Graham finished his can of lager in one final aggressive, upturned swallow, complete with growl as the remaining liquid slipped down his throat. He crushed the can. 'Right!' he said. 'We going down there or what?'

*

Despite the Pressed Fruitbowl only being a 200-yard walk that could usually be completed by any normal human being in under two minutes, in Graham's company it took nearer five. Bertie opened the door of the pub for his breathless friend lagging behind. As the pair made their way towards the bar, they were met with Edna's chilly gaze. The pub itself was fairly quiet for a Friday night.

'Don't look at me like that, woman,' Graham said, extracting his wallet from the back pocket of his elasticated denim jeans. 'Pint of lager for a grieving man and one for his thirsty companion if you please.'

'You're not going to work again then, I take it?' Edna asked testily.

'Oh don't start all that again, I think looking out for your mates is a bit more important, don't you?' he said. 'Now do something useful and pull us a pair of pints. Oh and pass us them darts, will you?' he said, pointing to a set of faded brass darts in an empty pint pot behind the bar. 'Can't find my fuckers,' he said, shaking his head. 'Fuck knows where they've gone.'

Hiding the almost imperceptible smile with her left hand, Edna handed the darts over to her husband with her right. Graham took them with a grunt and Edna pulled the pints, placing them on the bar in front of Bertie.

'Stick it on the tab,' Graham said, starting to throw over at the dartboard.

'Cheers,' Bertie said, taking a sip from his pint. 'Any news on the job front, Edna?'

'Terry's not in tonight,' she said, 'but I spoke to him yesterday. He's definitely given Karl the bullet, though; that's why we aren't doing food tonight. So as far as I'm aware, the job's pretty much yours if you want it.'

Bertie smiled. 'Brilliant.'

'He just wants you to come in and have a chat with him. Make sure you're not an idiot as well.'

'You told him I was, of course,' Bertie said, grinning a little.

Edna gave him an appraising stare. 'I probably should have,' she said, with a little smile of her own. 'But I didn't. Any joy with Douglas yet?' she asked.

'Nope,' Bertie said, swigging his pint, taking his darts case out of his back pocket. 'I saw Linda earlier, though. We went over some of the arrangements for Alice's funeral. Mainly music. Douglas has a couple of songs he wants played: Shakespears Sister and Wet Wet Wet.'

'That figures,' Edna said.

'Oh yeah,' Bertie said, smiling. 'Good old Marti.'

'We both used to sing the Shakespears Sister song when that one got big,' Edna said with a smile. 'Well, I didn't exactly sing. That song was on all the time when it came out. That was last year some time. Alice used to do the short-haired one's bit, Alice had a much better voice than me, see. I suppose because she wasn't on twenty a day like me. Anyway, then I'd come in and do that creepy long-haired one's part.' Edna put a small glass to the Smirnoff Vodka optic behind her, pouring herself a single measure. 'I miss her,' she said, downing it.

Yeah,' Bertie replied. 'Me too.'

'Douglas'll come round,' she said, 'in time. You've still got him and that's what matters. There's still hope. I wish I could say the same thing.'

Bertie put his hand on top of Edna's, feeling its warmth and the faint, gentle beat of her pulse. Graham kept obliviously throwing darts. Bertie quickly pulled his hand away as Graham extracted his arrows from the dartboard and turned to face them. 'They're shit, these things,' he said, waving the darts at Bertie and Edna, before turning round to throw again. 'Hurry up, Bert,' he added, now with his massive back to them both.

89

'When you do get to see Douglas, ask him where Graham's own darts are. That should get a laugh out of him.'

Bertie's face was a mask of bemusement, but Edna did not give him any more information; just smiled coyly as a grinning Bertie went over to join her husband at the board.

*

Three and a bit hours later, Bertie and Graham made the return journey back to Pugsden Lane, this time the short amble taking them more than ten minutes, such was the level of their joint intoxication.

'I know you said your darts had got a bit ropey, Bert, but I never thought they'd be that bad. And I was playing with them shitty pub arrows,' Graham slurred between puffs and pants. 'I always thought dartitis was just an old wives' tale, y'know. Something for people to tell themselves to make up for them being shit. How long you been like that?'

'About two years now,' Bertie said, slowing his pace down to match his friend. 'But it's got worse this past six months. When it all came to a head back in Bridgend, I couldn't think straight, let alone throw straight. I'll be fucked if I'll be able any good in that tournament now,' Bertie said.

'Tournament?'

'Oh, err, just some mickey mouse thing up north,' Bertie said, feeling he had already said too much. 'I heard about it while I was staying up there with my brother. Cash prize. Thought I'd have a pop.'

'Maybe I'll have a crack at that Rhonda bird myself if she's back on the market now then. Little holiday down to Wales,' Graham said with bravado. 'Or her mate, that Sheila bird. She was tidy enough 'n' all.'

'It was Shirley, not Sheila,' Bertie corrected.

'Yeah well, whatever. I should've done what you did, Bert, and had it away with her.'

'No, you shouldn't have,' Bertie said.

'Well, there ain't much love lost between me and Edna, that's for sure.'

'She's a good woman,' Bertie said, a little more defiantly than he had intended to in his inebriated state.

'Oh yeah?' Graham said, eyebrows raised.

'Well, yeah,' Bertie said, climbing down a notch or two. 'No, I mean you're lucky to have someone like that in your life. Someone to come home to.' *Even though you never go out,* Bertie thought. 'I'd give anything to have one last conversation with Alice.'

'Can't remember the last time me and Edna had one of them,' Graham said as Bertie fished his keys out of his jeans pocket, the pair having at long last reached their destination.

Bertie keyed the front door, pushing it open. His intoxication evaporated almost immediately at the sound of muffled music coming from inside the darkened house. Anxiety sobered him up as he listened in the dark to the music.

'What the bloody 'ell's that?' Graham said, following on behind.

Bertie turned on the light in the hallway, then gently swung open the living room door. The partial light now coming in from the hallway cast a half light on the front room and the hi-fi in the corner, whose red power light shone brightly in the semi-darkness, as did the blue LED lights on the front panel which displayed the word TUNER. In the half-lit gloom of the Blouses' front room Marti Pellow was crooning away, singing about angel eyes.

15 *Monday, August 23*

Bertie had spent the weekend attending to the various needs of the Ford Orion in order to try and make the old girl roadworthy again. It ate into his dwindling finances, but it kept him out of the house, and by Monday afternoon the car had tax, insurance and an MOT certificate. All had been without incident at the bungalow, and so Bertie once again tried to make himself feel comfortable back in his old home, trying to put all thoughts of creaking doors and banging on windows out of his mind.

After demolishing a much-needed plate of egg and chips, Bertie decided to put the first of two home-recorded videos of Live Aid on that he'd borrowed from Graham. The music put into his mind the idea of going through the record collection in the lounge, to begin compiling a list of songs that Alice had been fond of. Bertie was writing the words 'Deacon Blue – *Dignity*' on a page of lined notepaper when there was a knock on the door. He felt his egg and chips flip in his stomach, and thought to himself that it was about time he got himself a doorbell. He walked down the hallway, half expecting for there to be nobody there, but was pleasantly surprised when he opened the door to see Edna Glass standing on his doorstep puffing on a cigarette.

'Edna, hi. What brings you round here?'

'Had to get out of the house,' she said. 'Graham's at it again in the lounge, taping frigging films, isn't he? That bloke is doing my bloody head in. I don't know about the kids, but I can't bloody wait for term to start.'

'Come on in,' Bertie said.

Edna held up her half-smoked cigarette with raised eyebrows.

'Don't worry about it,' Bertie said. 'I've been having the odd crafty one myself. Giving up's proving to be a little harder than I thought. Are you working today?'

92

'Yeah. Shift starts at seven. Graham said he's going to work tonight, but I seriously doubt that's true somehow. *If* he does, he'll be gone by the time I get back later, but I'm not holding out much hope.'

Bertie showed Edna through to the lounge. On the TV screen, Spandau Ballet were basking in the blazing sunshine on the big white stage at Wembley stadium, soaking up the adoration of the 80,000 plus crowd that included somewhere among them, Edna and Graham, Alice and himself.

'Live Aid,' Bertie said, nodding at the TV. 'Borrowed it from your other half.'

'My other five and a halfs, more like,' Edna said, not missing a beat.

Bertie smiled. 'Graham said he taped this whole concert on his new double-decker video from a mate who taped it all live on the day. Four three-hour videos. He lent me the first two to get through. I've gotta say it's bringing back some memories. I feel hot just watching it. Look at Tony Hadley in that massive black trenchcoat of his,' Bertie said, smiling at the screen. 'That was some day, wasn't it?'

'Mmm, it was bloody boiling,' Edna said. 'I think I would have dehydrated if it wasn't for Alice and her big bottle of squash.'

'Oh yeah,' Bertie said with a chuckle. 'The big Ki Ora bottle with the handle.'

'She made that last all day, bless her,' Edna said. 'Remember how she got it watered down after half of it went? It tasted like the stuff we dish out down at the school, but on that day it was a bloody life-saver.'

Bertie smiled, thinking back to that balmy July day in 1985. 'I started making this,' he said, holding up the notepad of songs he had so far compiled. 'Watching that got me thinking of all the music she liked. Thought I'd have a little look through the records. My list only goes up to '87, obviously...' Bertie said, trailing off.

'Obviously,' Edna echoed. 'By the way, Terry's in later down the pub. He said for you to pop down and see him, to talk through your credentials.'

'Oh that's great, thanks, Edna. I'll be there for sure. This job's come just in time. Any longer and I'll be doing a Geldof myself,' Bertie said, smiling. '"Give me the fucking money!"' he said, in his best southern Irish accent.

'Even though he never actually said that,' Edna said.

'Yeah, I know he didn't, but "Fuck the address" doesn't quite have the same impact, does it? He did say "Give me the money" though.'

Edna smiled and drew another cigarette from her gold 20-pack of Benson and Hedges. 'Graham said you made him stay over here the other night?' she said. 'After he told me about how he mopped the floor with you on the dartboard. God, he was crowing about that something rotten. Probably the closest thing to a conversation we've had in months. The way he was going on about it, anyone would've thought he'd just won the world championships.'

'Yeah well, I'm not exactly hard to beat at the moment. My form on the board has fallen away pretty sharply,' Bertie said. 'Hence,' he nodded at the newly erected dartboard on the wall. 'It's the one out of the caravan. I put it up over the weekend,' Bertie said. 'Seemed a shame to leave it to rot in there and I sure need the practice. Had to rotate it round a bit so the cleaver gash is more out of the way. It's in the eleven section now,' he said, nodding up at the board.

The smell of Edna's cigarette set Bertie's senses and cravings off. He patted himself down but came up empty. 'I couldn't?' he said, nodding at Edna's cigarettes. She pushed them across the coffee table towards him and Bertie lit up. 'So come on then, what else did Graham say about the other night?'

Edna looked a little pensive. 'He told me what happened,' she said finally. 'Well, he said you left the record player on and it was still on when you got back from the pub and that you freaked out, so you made him stay over the night.'

Bertie smiled, exhaling smoke, his cloudy skeins hanging in the air and mingling with those of Edna's own cigarette. 'That's a variation on the truth, I suppose,' he said. 'The first thing I'd say in response to that is that I *know* I didn't leave the record player on. We were listening to Quo before we came down to the pub, and I remember very clearly putting the record back before we went out. Secondly, how likely is it, do you think that me and Graham would sit around drinking, listening to Wet Wet Wet?'

Edna smiled. 'Not very likely,' she said. 'But I know someone who would.' Edna was now looking at the family photo above the fireplace. 'She's still here, isn't she?' Edna said, now turning her gaze back to Bertie.

Bertie said nothing but gently stared straight ahead, nodding his head. 'That's what I'm beginning to think. I'm also starting to think that maybe I shouldn't have come back here. What if this is her way of saying she wants me out? That I'm not welcome here?'

'By putting Wet Wet Wet on?' Edna said with a laugh.

Bertie smiled. 'That's one way of doing it, I suppose.'

On the TV screen Bob Geldof and his Boomtown Rats were launching into 'I Don't Like Mondays', the scruffy Irishman in double denim prowling around the huge Wembley stage.

'She loved you, Bert,' Edna said. 'Her being gone doesn't change that.'

In a quirk of synchronicity, on the screen at Wembley Geldof delivered to the enraptured crowd the prophetic line from his band's most famous song: the one that stopped everyone there that day in their tracks. 'The lesson today is how to die', he proclaimed, holding his arm aloft to screams from the massive crowd, the band behind him falling silent as the cheers of the enormous crowd filled the vast stadium.

'I can almost feel her holding onto my arm,' Bertie said, as he began to well up. 'She cheered so loud when he did that. We could see his face up on the big screen. His eyes were so wild and alive and we all suddenly understood why we were there.' Bertie wiped his eyes. 'You know she bought five copies of the Band Aid single in '84. Just to do her bit. Two of them are still over there,' he said, nodding at the record collection. 'One for her and one for Douglas. The others I think she gave away as Christmas presents.'

Edna reached for the TV remote and turned the volume down. The Boomtown Rats were now back in full flow but doing so in silence.

'I think you need to get what you did off your chest, Bert. Tell Alice how you feel.'

'I'm going to see her tomorrow,' Bertie said. 'At the funeral director's. You think I should tell her?'

Out in the kitchen there was an audible click, followed by the sound of a soft rumbling as the kettle began to boil. Edna smiled at Bertie.

'Save yourself the journey, Bert,' she said. 'Why go to the funeral director's when she's just in the next room?'

Bertie gave a humourless laugh.

'You making that tea then, girl?' Edna said, perfectly naturally, cocking her head towards the sound of the kettle. There was no response. She looked at Bertie. 'I suppose I'll make the bloody tea then,' she said, getting up out of her chair. 'Some host you are.'

*

Two minutes later, Edna set two steaming mugs down on the coffee table. 'I don't know what you expect to see tomorrow, Bertie,' she said, picking one of the mugs up, 'but it won't be Alice.'

'How d'you mean?' Bertie said, sipping his tea.

'There's nothing left when they go,' she said. 'I learned that the hard way when I went to see Peter. I went there expecting to see my son. What I was confronted with was a poor, lifeless imitation. It's just a shell that's left, that's all. Like a waxwork. That spark, that energy, that life force, it all went on the night of the accident. They'd done a half-decent job trying to make Peter presentable after the accident...' Edna gave a mirthless laugh. 'He had more make-up on than me that day,' she said. 'But you could still see the cuts and...' Edna trailed off, as the tears started to well in her eyes.

'I'm so sorry, Edna,' Bertie said.

She took a deep breath. 'But it doesn't mean it all just ends. That everything they were just stops. The laugh. The love. That mischievous glint in their eye,' she said. 'Peter had that and so did Alice.'

'How d'you mean?'

'I mean we take it with us. And I think that Alice has done that very same thing. What she was, she still is. It's just harder for us to see it now she's in spirit.'

'In spirit? You mean like a ghost?' Bertie said.

'If you want to put it that way, yeah. Bert, I had some of the best laughs with Alice in the kitchen up at that school. She was so much fun. We would sing along together to the radio, all day sometimes. When I lost Peter, she was the one who helped carry me through my grief, and I'm gonna miss her like mad. Especially when term starts up again in a couple of weeks. You've seen the flowers up there, I hope?'

'Yes, they're lovely,' Bertie said, taking a swig from his mug. 'I took some down there myself over the weekend. She was very well liked, wasn't she?'

'Yes,' Edna said, 'because she was a very, very nice person. Selfless isn't the word. She was the most devoted person I ever met. She loved her son, and for some stupid reason she loved you!' Edna said with a flourish and a half-smile of bemusement. 'She still does! What she was, she still is. It doesn't just stop. I talk to Peter all the time around the house, when Graham's not around, that is. He thinks it's all stupid. I think he's stupid. I talk to Peter just as I would have done when he was still around, because it keeps me feeling connected to him. Time might help to heal, though it never will entirely, I know that, but it's talking that stops you from cracking up,' she said, sipping her tea and lighting a fresh cigarette. 'When I lost Peter last year, I was crushed, inconsolable. When the first wave of grief finally started to subside, I started going to a spiritualist church I'd heard about in town.'

'I thought you sounded like you knew what you were talking about a little bit too much,' Bertie said. 'Go on...'

'It was our local judo instructor, of all people, who put me onto them. He was, and still is for that matter, a big believer in what they call spiritual science.'

Bertie silently shook his head, looking blankly at Edna.

'I know, I'd never heard of it either, but Jim Leyland is quite the expert when it comes to that sort of thing. Jim's the judo instructor but he has a lot to say about non-physical energy: out of body experience, that sort of thing. He's also big into his meditation. Some say he took it too far. He had a bit of a breakdown a couple of years ago. It coincided with him being suspended from the school after he injured a pupil. He got himself back together though, thankfully. Got reinstated. When Peter died he was back doing his judo classes. He was such a great help to me, just like Alice was. He always had time for a chat, and I'm grateful to him for putting me on that path. He had this quiet and gentle way about him. Not preachy or pushy. It was exactly what I needed just when I needed it. Jim's a lovely guy. Single too. You know I thought that if Alice was ever going to give it a go with another fella, other than Marti Pellow of course,' she said with a playful smile, 'then it would've been Jim. They got quite close,' Edna said, looking up at the framed photo of Bertie, Alice and Douglas above the fireplace, 'but not close enough. He used to come in and set up his judo mats while me and Alice were clearing up after lunch. He still does, in fact, during term time. We had some good chats, the three of us, and we experienced our fair share of ups and downs together. He's quite deep, is our Jim. I phoned him last week to tell him about Alice. He was devastated.'

Edna took a deep breath. 'Anyway, after a while the idea of making contact with Peter had become like an obsession to me. The spiritualist church had visiting mediums come every week and they also offered healing sessions. It wasn't like normal church. The spiritualists still go on about God a lot, but they tend to focus more on the survival of the individual soul after death. Life eternal, as Reverend Bowen would say. I think she's starting to come round to it as well after seeing Alice by the railway. When she and Douglas both saw her, that brought them together. It's definitely changed her.'

'Apparently Linda said Douglas had been asking Hilda lots of questions about Alice,' said Bertie. 'Looking for spiritual guidance. Asking her where Alice has gone. If she's in heaven.'

'And what does Hilda tell him?'

Bertie paused. 'I'm not sure. But she was saying a similar thing to what you're saying now the other day up at the vicarage when I went to see her and Linda. Something about death being a horizon. I forget the exact wording of it.'

'It was probably quite an eye-opener for her, seeing Alice,' Edna said. 'The Church of England and the spiritualists aren't really that different. They basically say the same thing. Peace, love and understanding, that sort of thing. It's just the spiritualists will actively help you access the afterlife, not stand guard over it and make you go through some gatekeeper in a dog collar to access it. People go to church every week and hear about everlasting life, heaven, the soul. But when they're given the opportunity to explore these things for themselves, or are simply flat-out shown it, they all but deny their so-called faith. Kowtowing to the self-elected guardians of the spirit world who claim to know best because they went to some Bible college.'

'You certainly kept quiet about this, Edna,' Bertie said with a smile and raised eyebrows.

A little laugh escaped Edna. 'It actually feels quite good to talk about it for once,' she said. 'With Graham, I've just become so used to saying nothing, about everything. I did try, once. He says it's all rubbish. I thought the same before I lost Peter. Well, to be honest, I never really thought about it. I'd never had to. And you know what, I'd give anything to go back to that blissful state of ignorance if it meant having my son back. And that's the point. I found out the hard way that death isn't just something that happens to other people. People dismiss and denounce mediumship, like it's some kind of circus freak show, but heaven forbid they ever lose someone. That's when they'll want comfort and answers. They'll be desperate for it, just like I was. Like a drug addict. I nearly walked out of the first spiritualist meeting I ever went to,' Edna said, smiling. 'It's all a bit happy-clappy to start off with, and they play some really cheesy music: pop music, not hymns, songs that have a vaguely spiritual-sounding message.' Edna laughed. 'The first time I went they played 'Heaven is a Place on Earth' by Belinda Carlisle. They've got all the words printed up in these hand-made songbooks they dish out. The woman working the stereo that night took ages to get the bloody thing to play. I was losing my patience with it all and I said, "I'll be in the bloody spirit world by the time she sorts that out". It just came out, I couldn't help it.'

'That's not like you, Edna,' Bertie said.

Edna smiled. 'Well anyway, it got a bit of a laugh and it relieved some of the tension I was feeling. I eased up a bit after that and I lip-synced to Belinda Carlisle after she finally got it going, wishing I'd asked Alice to come along with me. She'd have sung along to every word,' Edna said, smiling. 'I'm not gonna say too much about what I got from it, because it's too personal to me,' Edna said. 'But what I will say is I know it's real. All you need to do is ask. Be open to it. "Knock and the door shall be opened" Edna said. "Ask and it shall be given". I'd quite like to develop my own mediumship. They show you how to and there's workshops for it. I've been told it's possible. It's there for everyone if they want it, and that's just the point. It's in all of us, we just need to look for it.'

'"Seek and ye shall find" eh?' Bertie said.

'Precisely,' Edna said, sipping her tea. 'Personally speaking, I think I'm still too angry about losing Peter. Anger gets in the way and it's hard to overcome. I shouldn't have delighted in seeing Binsley mauled by that dog at the fete the way I did. Spiritualism teaches all the same basic stuff. Love, compassion, forgiveness. But I thought yeah, maybe I'll do that *after* I see that bastard get what's coming to him, and that's no way to go. I delighted in it because I was angry, and I think I still am. Maybe not as much, which is good, I suppose. But yeah, I still think I'm too pissed off with God to fully heal.'

Edna took a deep breath.

'I probably wouldn't have come today if Graham hadn't told me about the record player,' she said. 'But if Alice *is* still around,' Edna paused, 'well then I want to help,' she said finally. 'Like she helped me. Because ultimately I want to be like she was. She was the best example of how to live your life. She kept on loving and being selfless through it all. Through all the ups and downs. Through all the shit she kept on smiling, even if it was only to mask her own pain and to try and protect Douglas as best she could from the harsh reality of it all. She was the yardstick and I want to help because I don't want to be pissed off and angry any more. If she is still around, Bert, then you've got to be open to it, not fear it. She is not here to harm you, I guarantee you that. You've seen it for yourself all around you,' Edna said, casting an arm across the living room. 'She was waiting for you to come home, and here you are. And I think she wants that,' Edna said, pointing to the family photo on the wall, 'just as much as you do.'

Bertie was silent for some time. Edna did not seek to fill the silence. 'I don't want to see her like you saw Peter, Edna,' he said at last, 'up at the funeral director's. I don't want to see her like that. I want...' Bertie stumbled. 'I want to remember her like that,' he said, pointing at the family photo.

'It always will be like that, up here,' Edna said, pointing to her head. 'And in here,' she said, now pointing to her heart. 'Don't do the wrong thing because you think you're doing it for the right reasons,' she said. 'You wanna make your peace with her, then you make it with her here.' Edna was now pointing at the floor.

Edna walked over to the hi-fi as Phil Collins walked on to the Wembley stage. 'I know what we need to do,' she said, examining the list of songs Bertie had made. 'Go and make us another cup of tea and I'll help you fill in the blanks.'

*

Five minutes later, Bertie came back into the living room with two fresh mugs of tea. Edna was perched on the arm of the chair beside the hi-fi, scribbling on the notepad. 'I first had the idea when I went up to see Peter at the funeral director's. When I went in to see him, they had this soppy classical music playing in the "chapel of rest", as they call it,' she said, 'I thought how he'd much prefer to have some Guns N' Roses on in there. Why don't we give this to Auntie Linda or to Hilda to take up there for her? She'd love it.'

Bertie considered this suggestion. 'Why don't we make up another copy for Douglas?' he said. 'Something to listen to up at the hospital. His Walkman's in his bedroom. Truth be told, that's where I've been sleeping; that or in here,' he said, nodding at the sofa. 'It still feels weird going in our old bedroom.'

Bertie went quiet. After a moment of contemplation he said, 'I don't want to say the tape is from me, though, Edna. If we give it to Douglas, I mean. We can just say that you made it up for him. If he knows I had anything to do with it, he'll more than likely stick it in the bin.'

'I know what else we need to do,' Edna said, looking up at the family photo above the fireplace.

*

Fifteen minutes later, Bertie and Edna were walking back down the High Street towards the bungalow holding a colour photocopy of the Blouse family photo.

'So that was the infamous photocopier then?' Bertie said, smiling at Edna.

'Yep. That's what started it all off, pretty much; your son befouling Mr Kareshi's newest piece of hi-tech equipment. I remember Alice telling me about it after he'd done it. She was angry with Douglas, of course, but she couldn't stop smiling while she was telling me about it, and neither could I: old Mr Kareshi chasing him up the High Street with his broom, Douglas with his arse still hanging out of his jeans.'

'Would you take the tape up to Douglas, Edna?' Bertie said as they paused on the High Street. 'I know he'd be pleased to see you. Tell him you made it up for him. Tell him about you and Alice, how you used to sing in the kitchens. It might cheer him up a little to hear those stories again. Maybe you could tell him about the spiritualist church as well? Pass on a bit of your wisdom. But please don't mention anything about what's been happening back at the house. I don't want to upset him. I'll take the other cassette round to Reverend Bowen tomorrow to pass on to the funeral directors. I'll leave instruction with her.'

'Ok,' Edna said, 'it'll have to be tomorrow, though.'

'That's fine,' Bertie said, relieved. 'If you're feeling extra nice, maybe you could put in a good word for me when you see Douglas?'

Edna gave Bertie a little smile. 'Yeah, I suppose I could,' she said.

'Thank you, Edna. I don't know why you're being so nice to me.'

'Well, like I said, I'm trying to change my ways, aren't I?' she said, lighting a cigarette. 'Maybe being nice isn't as hard as I thought it was.'

'You know what I think?' Bertie said, grinning. 'I think you're a bit of a soppy old cow on the quiet.'

102

'Don't you tell anyanybody,' Edna said, holding back a grin and pointing two fingers at Bertie like a gun, her smouldering cigarette held at a right angle between them.

'Alice was lucky to have a friend like you,' Bertie said, giving Edna's hand a gentle squeeze.

Edna smiled, crushed out her cigarette and walked towards the door of the pub to start her shift. 'I was the lucky one,' she said, turning away and entering the pub, disappearing from view.

16 *Tuesday, August 24*

It had just gone midday when Bertie pulled the Ford Orion on to Reverend Bowen's driveway. He grabbed the carrier bag from off the passenger seat, stepped out and rang the vicar's doorbell. Bowen answered the door, dressed casually in black jeans and a thin blue jumper whose neckline allowed her dog collar to poke through.

'Bertie, hi. How are you? I thought I was meeting you up there later?'

'Yeah, so did I,' Bertie said a little cryptically. 'There's been a slight change of plan. Can I talk to you for a minute?'

'Of course, come on through to the kitchen,' Bowen said, stepping to one side.

Bertie walked down the familiar hallway and into the kitchen. 'Has Linda said anything more to you about buying this place?'

'She came round over the weekend and had a good old look around,' Bowen said, putting the kettle to boil on the Aga. 'She had her tape measure with her,' she said with a grin.

'Filofax?'

'Oh yes.'

They both smiled.

'I think she means business,' Bowen said. 'She's had a meeting with the bank, and if that all goes to plan, as I understand it will, then I think she has every intention of taking the old place on.'

'It'll be nice if she does,' Bertie said. 'For her and for Douglas. She phoned me this morning actually, about the funeral. The first of September.'

'Yes, I got a call from Mr Pollard this morning confirming the date,' Bowen said. 'There're still a couple of things I need to discuss with him myself regarding the service which I'll sort out when I see him this afternoon.' Bowen took two mugs out of the cupboard. 'So, what can I do for you?' she asked as the kettle began to whistle on the Aga.

Bertie explained about seeing Alice. Or not wanting to see her, as was now the case. He also told her about what Edna had said. Bowen listened intently whilst making the tea, and was kind and understanding about Bertie's change of heart.

'I wondered if you might give this to the funeral fella,' Bertie said, reaching into the bag and pulling out the compilation tape. 'Edna and me put it together. I stayed up last night recording them all on the stereo. We were wondering if he might put it on for Alice, while she's with them. Edna said they've got a room where people go to see them.'

'Yes, that's correct: the chapel of rest,' Bowen said.

'Yeah. She said they put music on in there. Usually classical or something fairly inoffensive. We wondered if they wouldn't mind putting this on for her.'

Bertie handed her the cassette. Bowen scanned the track listing, written in black biro in Bertie's neatest handwriting.

'I'm sure they'll be more than happy to, Bertie. I think it's a lovely idea.'

'There's something in it as well,' Bertie said, nodding at the tape.

Bowen opened the plastic cassette case and took out the folded piece of paper tucked inside. She unfolded it to see the colour photocopy of Bertie, Alice and Douglas. She smiled. 'It's lovely, what a nice thought.'

'I was thinking,' Bertie said, 'if the funeral director could put the cassette and that photo in with...' Bertie faltered. 'You know, in with her before they... You know, before the funeral.'

'I'm sure that will be absolutely fine,' Bowen said.

Bertie reached back into the bag, taking out a framed A4 picture of Alice, cropped from the photo of the three of them in the garden. 'I had it done at the printer's in town this morning. I thought... well, me and Edna thought it might be nice to have on the day. For Douglas maybe? Or to go on top of the coffin perhaps? I mentioned it to Linda on the phone this morning. She's OK'd it...'

Bertie faltered as he began welling up. Then he broke down in tears. Hilda put her hand on his arm, rubbing it soothingly.

'I think it's a lovely idea, Bertie. And I'm sure Douglas will too.'

'Don't tell him I had anything to do with it,' Bertie said, wiping his eyes. 'Just say it was Edna or Linda's idea. He won't like it if he knows I'm involved.'

'I'm sure that won't be the case,' Bowen said. 'But just as you wish, I shan't say anything to him about it.'

'Thank you, Reverend,' Bertie said. 'Is the church open? I think I might go and have a word with the boss.'

'We never close,' Bowen said. 'And he's a good listener. Bertie, before you go, I'd be interested to hear what Edna has to say about this spiritualist church of hers. I had a parishioner asking me about something along those very same lines recently, but to be honest I wasn't sure what to say to him, bearing in mind the church's official view on mediumship. Perhaps Edna might have time for a little chat sometime?'

'I'm sure she would,' Bertie said, heading back down the hallway. 'I think you might have more in common than you think.'

Bertie left the vicarage and walked across to the church. He clasped the large black iron door handle, pushed open the big oak door and entered the cool, quiet of the church. He took a pew near the front and began to pray. Praying for Alice, for Douglas, Edna, everyone. He was surprised at how easy and unforced his thoughts of compassion were for the people he loved ... and had lost. When he'd finished, he took a short walk around the churchyard, stopping by Peter Glass's grave and wondering whereabouts in the churchyard Alice's final resting place would be. As he meandered back through the headstones towards the vicarage, he saw Reverend Bowen heading towards her trike. She was carrying two bags: one was the carrier bag he'd just given her containing the picture and the cassette; the other was a Tesco bag, similar if not identical to the one she had been holding on the day he had come round for their first meeting together.

17 *Wednesday, September 1*

The big black Daimler hearse carrying Alice Blouse came into view down the causeway at twenty to twelve. Behind it was a matching limousine that was just as big as the hearse. Douglas, wearing a black V-neck jumper, white shirt and black tie was seated in his wheelchair with his Auntie Linda and Reverend Bowen, waiting beside the railway line close to the spot where he had last seen his mother. Not her physical self but her spirit, as Bowen had later told him with gentle reassurance. The Mr Bump jumper she had been holding that day was on his lap, the jumper's hemline covering the hidden stumps that only filled two-thirds of the black trousers he was wearing. Their bottom third hung limply, hardly moving in the almost imperceptible breeze that barely troubled the rusting foliage on the trees of the causeway. Down beside him in a glass jar, near to where he had seen his mum, a candle was burning in a jar.

'Why have they stopped?' Douglas said, lifting himself up off his chair and craning his neck to see over the level crossing and down the causeway to where the hearse was currently stationary.

'I asked them to pick up the flowers from outside the school, dear,' Linda said, 'so we can put them with all the others at the church and to keep all the lovely cards that people have written.'

The hearse had once again set off at a crawl, and both vehicles were now heading in their direction.

Douglas's heart rate increased when for the first time in nearly six years he saw his father walking a short distance behind the limousine with Edna Glass. Given the distance between himself and his father, Douglas could not make him out properly. But he knew it was him.

Douglas knew this moment had been coming. He'd been told about his father coming back, but actually seeing the man who walked out on them, now walking towards him behind the vehicle carrying his mum, made his head spin and his guts churn.

'How are you doing, Mr Bump?' Linda said, stroking Douglas's head, lightly touching the prominent lump on the back of it.

Douglas bit down on his bottom lip, nodding his head. 'All right,' he croaked, looking at the spot on the tracks where he'd fallen, causing the injury to his head. The first of the day's many tears traced their way down his cheek, spotting the Mr Bump jumper in his lap.

The hearse was about twenty feet short of the level crossing when the warning lights began to flash and the alarm sounded. A man opened the door at the top of the signal box and stepped out onto the top step. 'I'm so sorry,' he said with obvious embarrassment, 'it'll only be the one. I'm really sorry.'

Linda gave him a little smile and called up to him, 'I suppose it can't be helped, dear; it's not your fault.' Then turning to Reverend Bowen, she said, 'I guess this is something that we shall have to start getting used to if we're going to be living on the wrong side of the tracks.'

'I'm afraid so, dear,' Bowen replied. 'A constant source of joy.'

The hearse came to a halt a short distance from the barriers, and for the first time Douglas looked straight into the eyes of his father. He'd half expected his dad to look completely different to the man who walked out on them back in '87. He was surprised to see that he looked almost exactly the same.

Bertie gave Douglas a smile and a little wave, which Douglas did not return. Beside Bertie, Edna did the same. Douglas gave her a half smile and a fleeting wave but soon turned his head away from them.

'Are you really buying Hilda's house, Linda?' Douglas asked, looking up at his auntie. 'Is that where we're going to be living when they let me out?'

'Yes, love,' she replied. 'But don't you worry about...'

Linda was cut off by the sudden appearance of the Intercity 125 screaming into view from the west, obliterating all conversation. Instinct almost overcame Douglas as the desire to leap out of his chair and moon the speeding train filled his mind. His hands gripped tightly to the wheelchair's arm rests and he remained seated, a prisoner of his new-found condition. He knew those days were well and truly behind him. Instead he just sat and watched like everyone else, waiting for the barriers to lift which, a few seconds after the train disappeared, they soon did.

'OK then, Douglas?' Linda said as the hearse began to crest the incline of the level crossing and make its way slowly over the tracks.

Douglas gave a juddery nod and Linda wheeled him out from under the causeway's rusting canopy and onto the road next to the hearse. He could see the floral tributes close up now: the big spray of yellow roses on top of the coffin that ran almost its entire length. On one side of the car's big windows the large floral letters of yellow and white spelt out the name ALICE. On the other side they said MUM. The flowers collected from the school were on the roof of the hearse. Three elderly gentlemen dressed in matching black suits occupied the vehicle: two in the front and one in the back, sitting close to the foot end of Alice's coffin behind the driver.

Douglas watched as Edna went to the passenger door of the limousine that was following on behind.

'Come on, get out,' she said in a stern whisper. 'You can walk the rest of the way like everybody else, you lazy sod.'

Douglas couldn't help but smile as he watched Graham Glass slowly extricate himself from the plush cream leather seat of the Daimler limousine. 'Seems a shame to waste it, dunnit,' he said, getting out and joining his wife and Bertie behind the car.

The cortège carried on towards the church, with Douglas being pushed by Linda, and Reverend Bowen walking the last hundred yards or so out in front of the crawling hearse. Douglas looked over his shoulder. His father was still there following on behind with Edna and now also a lumbering Graham Glass.

As they approached the church, they could see the rotund figure of Roland Pollard, the funeral director. He was wearing a sympathetic smile and holding an order of service. 'Morning, everyone. There's an awful lot of people in there,' he said as they all exchanged polite pleasantries. 'And how are you doing, young man?' the undertaker said, crouching down beside Douglas in his chair. 'Are you staying strong for your Auntie Linda?'

Douglas nodded but said nothing as Pollard went to speak to his pall bearers as they got out of the hearse. The driver of the limousine now joined them also. From behind the hearse Douglas saw his father coming towards him. Squirming in his seat, he literally had nowhere to run as his dad crouched down beside him.

'Son,' Bertie said, a tear running down his cheek. 'Son, I'm so sorry. I left it too late. Dougie, I'm so sorry.'

Douglas remained silent.

'Better late than never though maybe, hmm?' Linda said, gently rubbing Douglas's arm.

Douglas's knuckles were white as he gripped the arm rests of his wheelchair. He couldn't bring himself to look at his father. He hadn't taken his eyes off his mother's coffin in the back of the hearse. 'Better never in your case,' he said finally. 'You're as much to blame for this as anyone.'

'Douglas,' Linda said, putting a hand on his shoulder. 'Not here, love. Not today.'

Bertie rose, making his way towards the church. Edna bent down to give Douglas a kiss on the cheek.

'We're all here for you, darling,' she said, softly caressing his cheek as she got back to her feet and headed for the church.

Graham patted Douglas on the arm. 'You'll be all right, boy,' he said, before slowly making his way to catch up with Edna and Bertie who were now at the church door.

Linda wheeled Douglas round to the back of the hearse where, through the large back window, he saw for the first time the framed photo of his mum. The sight of her smiling face brought fresh tears to his eyes as his mind went back to the day it was taken: how she'd tickled him, how both his mum and his dad were all laughing by the time the camera's automatic timer went off.

'Everything in order?' Reverend Bowen said to funeral director Roland Pollard in a hushed and sombre tone. Douglas, teary-eyed, looked away from his mum's photo and over at them both.

'Yes, Hilda,' Pollard said. 'All present and correct.'

Pollard opened the boot of the hearse, reverently taking out the photo of Alice and handing it to Douglas who held it close to him. Pollard then unscrewed the stopper at the back of the coffin that, along with the other three strategically placed pins, kept the coffin safely in place while the vehicle was in motion. He reached in and took out the two pins either side of the coffin.

'Do you still want to do this, young man?' Pollard said to Douglas, who in return gave a soft, teary-eyed nod.

The funeral director beckoned his pall bearers to join them at the back of the hearse. Pollard pulled the coffin out a couple of feet, and two of his colleagues gripped the side handles at the box's head end and rolled the remainder of the coffin out so that just the last foot or so was perched on the rear of the vehicle. His other two men took the side handles at the foot end and the four men held the coffin at waist height (shoulder height for Douglas). The pall bearer standing holding the handle at the back left of the coffin moved strategically to the back of the coffin's head end, continuing to hold the weight, allowing Douglas to get into position, taking a quarter of the weight of his mother on his right shoulder in the space vacated by the pall bearer who remained at the rear of the coffin.

Led by Roland Pollard, Linda gently pushed Douglas along as the four of them carried Alice into the packed out church to the sound of Wet Wet Wet's 'Goodnight Girl', which was coming from a small but powerful stereo plugged in close to the door.

Douglas's eyes were misty with tears as they moved down the aisle towards two sets of wooden trestles that stood up ahead in front of the altar between the choir stalls. On reaching them, the pall bearer following behind once again took the weight that Douglas had been carrying, and the team of pall bearers lifted the coffin onto the trestles. The four suited men remained standing with their heads bowed around the coffin. Douglas passed the photo of Alice to Roland Pollard, who gently placed it on top of the coffin. Alice's lustrous auburn hair and ageless smile beamed out at the teary-eyed faces of all of those who had gathered there to mourn her. Linda filed into the reserved front pew beside Edna and Graham. Bertie was at the far end, furthest from Douglas who was seated in his chair in the aisle next to Linda.

Marti Pellow's voice gently faded away and silence descended on the church, save for the sound of a few sniffles and clearing of throats as Reverend Bowen took her place next to Alice's coffin.

'We meet in the name of Jesus Christ, who died and was raised to the glory of God the father.'

'Grace and mercy be with you,' the congregation responded with their eyes on their service sheets.

'We look not to the things that are seen, but to the things that are unseen,' Bowen continued; 'for the things that are seen are transient, but the things that are unseen are eternal. Today we come together to remember before God our sister Alice, to give thanks for her life and to comfort one another in our grief.' Bowen surveyed the congregation with a serene but sympathetic smile. 'Let us pray. Father in heaven, we thank you because you made us in your own image and gave us gifts in body, mind and spirit. We thank you now for Alice and what she meant to each of us and for all she did in her life. As we honour Alice's memory, fill our hearts with praise and thanksgiving, for the sake of our risen lord, Jesus Christ.'

'Amen,' came the collective response.

'Dear God, in your mercy, turn the darkness of death into the dawn of new life, and the sorrow of parting into the joy of heaven, through our saviour, Jesus Christ.'

'Amen.'

Reverend Bowen went on to deliver a heartfelt sermon filled with insight, humour and joy, succeeding in painting a beautiful picture of the kind of person Alice was. Most of it was lost on Douglas, who was lost in his own private hell of grief. He just stared at the photograph of his mum on top of the box that contained her earthly remains, wondering how it had all come to this.

'We are now going to hear another piece of music that was particularly special to Alice,' Reverend Bowen said, as Douglas looked over his shoulder to where Roland Pollard was once again pressing buttons on the small stereo. Moments later the opening chords to Slade's 'Everyday' filled the church. Caught unawares by this, Douglas leaned forward in his chair, looking down the pew to where his father was seated. Teary-eyed, Bertie looked back at him as Noddy Holder's gruff but soulful voice reverberated off the church's cold white walls, the Brummie tearing full-throated into the song's emotive chorus. Douglas was painfully familiar with the song that he had heard his mum play so many times over the years. Often he would see her red-eyed after playing it, though she would always try to explain that away. If Douglas had been told about the song that was clearly of his dad's choosing, then he couldn't remember that happening. The grief and the painkillers had made the past few weeks pass him by in a strange, numb blur.

'What's he trying to do to us?' Douglas said in a croaky voice to Linda beside him. 'What does he think he's doing?'

'Sweetheart, he's still your father, and he's hurting too,' Linda whispered, rubbing Douglas's hand, which was once again gripping hard onto the handle of his wheelchair. 'Don't be angry with him today. He's upset as well.'

The tears started to flow and the pain in his head began to increase. Douglas could feel the bump on the back of his head throbbing as the song continued to play. Then his hitching sobs turned slowly into a soft giggle, before a helpless laugh sent the tears streaking down his cheeks. He stared at the photo of his mum, giggling uncontrollably. Linda rubbed his arm but it did nothing to stop the giggling fit he was experiencing. Beneath the Mr Bump jumper, his upper thighs twitched and the empty material of his lower trouser legs flapped as he fidgeted in his wheelchair. People were starting to stare at Douglas as the tears began to subside along with the music and fortunately his giggling. The church returning to hushed tones save for the sound of Douglas's, and others', residual sniffling.

At Bowen's behest, Linda rose to her feet to deliver her own reading. She recounted tales of growing up, of sisterhood, of a loving and devoted mother and a world-class dinner lady, which drew smiles and yet more tears from the seated congregation.

Linda returned to her pew where she remained standing, the congregation getting to its feet to join in a rousing rendition of 'Abide With Me'. Reverend Bowen invited the congregation to remain standing for the closing address and final prayers, after which the church once again descended into complete silence until the opening bars of Shakespears Sisters' 'Stay' swelled up to the church's high vaulted roof, and Marcella Detroit's soft, pleading voice filled the church. From the congregation came the sounds of yet more staccato sniffing as many of the mourners began to weep, Douglas included, whose shoulders hitched up and down with his sobbing as the haunting ballad that his mum had loved so much filled the church. Linda put her arm around her nephew, tears now streaming down her face also, in what was for her an uncharacteristic display of emotion.

'No no no no no no no,' Douglas said, his voice rising in panic and thick with tears as he watched Roland Pollard, accompanied by his four pall bearers, approaching his mother's coffin. His words beat in time with his right hand as it anxiously slapped the armrest of his wheelchair. On the stereo, Siobhan Fahey had taken over vocal duties. Her dark unsettling tones were somehow in tune with the atmosphere in the church.

Roland Pollard took the photo of Alice from the top of the coffin and handed it back to Douglas, before returning to his men who were once again standing around the coffin with heads bowed. The four men lifted the box and Pollard removed the two sets of wooden trestles, the pall bearers turning the coffin around so that the foot end now faced the congregation. With the plangent song filling the church, they lifted Alice onto their shoulders and began the slow walk down the aisle, past Douglas who was waiting to follow on, while Linda gripped the handles of his wheelchair in readiness.

The music built and built before lead singer Marcella Detroit let out an ear-piercing scream that threatened to inflict the same kind of damage to the church's stained glass windows that Douglas had delivered just over two weeks ago. Detroit then launched full-blooded into the song's final chorus. Her scream was still reverberating off the walls when Douglas let out one of his own. His guttural, anguished cry momentarily eclipsed all other sounds as his mother was carried away from him on the shoulders of four elderly strangers. Douglas lifted himself off the seat of his chair, as if he was about to get up and go after her, the tears streaming down his face. Linda was only just quick-witted enough to stop him in time and prevent him from potentially launching himself out of the chair. From a nearby pew up ahead of him, a girl with long blonde hair came to Douglas's side. Through eyes filled with tears, Douglas saw that it was Daisy Carr.

'I'm so sorry, Douglas,' she said, through tears of her own. 'I'm so...' She didn't finish the sentence. Her own grief and tears cut it short as she broke down, hugging Douglas, who could manage no verbal response of his own. Only more tears.

The song began to fade away, and as Douglas watched his mum being carried through the church door and out of his life, he only wished he had the legs to go running after her.

*

Bertie watched Alice's burial from a distance, respecting Linda's wishes. Douglas had asked her to warn him to keep his distance. In the bright but slightly chilly sunshine of the churchyard, Bertie stood next to Graham Glass surveying the colourful floral tributes in between the gaps in the mourners at the graveside. He could see the yellow and white letters that spelt out his wife's name, though he could only make out the first three letters of it.

With a trembling hand Bertie lit a cigarette, looking over at Edna standing beside Douglas and Linda at the graveside. Reverend Bowen's murmurings as Alice was lowered into the ground were only just audible over the sound of Douglas's weeping, though he was not the only one.

'Ere, Bert, what are they doing now?' Graham said, looking over at the mourners who had started to pick yellow roses from the spray that had until recently sat on top of Alice's coffin.

'They're throwing flowers into the grave,' Bertie said, as over at the graveside Linda kissed the petals of her vibrant rose and threw it into the grave. 'Yellow roses were Alice's favourite, and they thought it would be a nice idea.'

Graham craned his neck to look. 'Bit of a waste of money, ennit? I mean them flowers can't've been cheap.'

Bertie looked straight ahead. 'It's not about the money though, is it?' he said.

'Mmm, I dunno. Just seems a bit daft to me,' Graham said.

This time Bertie stayed quiet, not wanting to get drawn into another futile exchange. He watched as more and more mourners threw their roses into his wife's grave. 'She's pretty close to your Peter,' Bertie said eventually.

'Where?' Graham asked, frowning.

Bertie turned to face his friend. 'What do you mean, where?' he said. 'Over there. Alice's grave is just over from your Peter's.'

'Not been up here in a while, truth be told, pal,' Graham said. 'Why ain't you over there with 'em anyway?' Graham asked.

'Thought it best to keep my distance,' Bertie said. 'Give Douglas a bit of space. He's gonna be all over the place today. I don't wanna keep popping up in his face, not when he's so upset.'

'Fair play,' Graham said. 'You get all the grub done down the pub, then? I'm looking forward to a bit of scran and a good drink. Best thing about a funeral, ennit?'

Yeah, I bet you are, Bertie thought. 'Yeah, I got all the buffet food done yesterday. Part of my probationary requirements. Showing Terry I can put on a good spread. Think I just about pulled it off.'

'Still can't believe you're a bloody chef,' Graham said, chuckling away to himself and drawing glances of disapproval. 'I mean, it's a bit poofy, ain't it? Thought it was only birds 'n' gays 'n' that worked in kitchens. You may as well take over where your old lady left off, making grub for the kids down the school with Edna.'

'It suits me,' Bertie said, choosing to ignore the various levels of offence marinating in Graham's remarks. 'And it shows Linda I mean business as well. Plenty of shifts means I can pay the rent. And I can start putting a bit of money by for Douglas. That's the most important thing.'

'Well, I'll let you know if your grub's any good when we get down there, boy!' Graham said with another inappropriately loud chuckle and a rub of his prodigious gut, drawing yet more withering looks from some of the villagers standing nearby. 'If your darts are anything to go by, I'm not surprised you've been hiding in kitchens,' Graham said with a smug smile.

'Yeah, Edna mentioned that you seemed pretty happy about that.'

'Oh, did she? About the only thing I am happy about as far as me and her are concerned, daft old cow.'

'She's a good woman,' Bertie said. 'You're lucky to have her.'

'Yeah? Well I don't feel like I am,' Graham said. 'We should have a game down the pub later, when this all finishes. Or have you got a French fancy to finger?'

'I don't think so,' Bertie said. 'I don't think it's exactly the right time or place.'

'Scared you'll lose again, are ya?'

Bertie kept quiet, growing increasingly tired of Graham's company. Over at the graveside the crowd was beginning to thin, and Linda was wheeling Douglas back through the churchyard towards the path. Butch Ransom was by her side, and Edna was following on behind him.

'I'm gonna walk it back to the pub and make sure everything's all right for when this lot get down there,' he said over the lump in his throat.

'Fair dos, chief. I think I'll hang about for a lift in the limo, if it's all right with Auntie Linda. Be a shame to waste it,' Graham said, nodding over at the big black car parked up beside the church next to Douglas's hospital transportation vehicle.

'Well yeah, check with her first, eh, make sure there's space,' Bertie croaked.

'Yeah yeah, will do,' Graham said, still eyeing up the big black car. 'Yeah, sod walking it back from here, boy.'

Bertie turned away and left the churchyard, unable to bear the sight of his son's grief any more, and knowing that if he had stayed Graham would only have started taking the piss out of the fact that he himself had begun to cry again.

18

'I must say you've done an excellent job with all this,' Linda said to Bertie in the crowded bar of the Pressed Fruitbowl as she surveyed the tables of silver trays laden with the cold buffet Bertie had prepared. The chatter was low but constant as mourners shared stories over drinks and vol-au-vents.

'And the booze is definitely free, you say?' Graham asked, scoffing down three sausage rolls.

Linda appeared not to have heard him.

'Don't take the piss, eh?' Bertie said discreetly to Graham, looking through the crowd towards Douglas, who was being pushed towards the jukebox in the corner of the pub by Daisy Carr. Bertie watched as Daisy pressed the buttons on the front of the jukebox, flipping the selection panels, stopping occasionally as Douglas lifted himself up in his chair to get a better look at the song selections before pointing and relaying instructions to the blonde-haired girl.

'He wants to put some of Alice's songs on,' Linda said, ordering drinks at the bar. 'I think he could do with something to steady his nerves after the day he's had.'

'What was all that laughing in the church about?' Bertie asked as 'Drive' by The Cars came on the jukebox.

'Not too sure,' Linda said. 'But it could well be to do with the bump on his head he sustained when he fell on the railway. The doctors think he may have been concussed, which in turn may have led to a condition called emotional lability. They're still not one hundred per cent sure. It's quite rare, but apparently it can lead to extreme mood fluctuation, causing its sufferer to laugh at inappropriate times, or, conversely burst into tears for seemingly no apparent reason. It started about a week ago. They're keeping an eye on it up at the hospital. Time will tell. Anyway, do excuse me,' Linda said, carrying a tray of drinks away from the bar.

Bertie listened to the music playing in the pub as Douglas made his last selections over at the jukebox, before being wheeled back to where Linda was placing the tray of drinks down on a nearby table.

'Remember this one?' Bertie said, looking at Edna who, though not officially on duty, was habitually polishing glasses at the end of the bar. 'This was the one that finally got the money coming in at Live Aid, wasn't it? After Bowie finished. That horrendous appeal video of all those poor kids. I remember Alice watching it beside me in tears.'

'I remember it making me feel bloody hungry!' Graham said, ramming a scotch egg into his already congested mouth. 'Nothing like a video of a bunch of starving darkies to make you wanna go and get a couple of 'ot dogs,' he said, showering Bertie in crumbs.

'Jesus Christ,' Edna said, looking disdainfully at her husband.

'Bloody ridiculous, all that anyway,' Graham said, getting into his stride. 'If all that lot had given even half the money they all spent getting coked up and pissed up at Live Aid, they'd've doubled their money straight away. Bunch of hypocrites, if you ask me. Usual story, ennit? Millionaire bloody celebs begging for money off the working man.'

'You? Working?' Edna scoffed. 'You must be joking.'

'And bloody Phil Collins pissing off to America on Concorde with that Noel friggin' Edmonds! How much must that've cost in petrol, eh? Edmonds should've done something useful and brought a few of 'em over from Africa on it to get stuck into all that posh backstage catering all them boys would've been tucking in to all day at Wembley. Not much starvation going on back there, I bet. All the while the likes of us have to pay four quid for a bloody 'ot dog!'

Graham shovelled another scotch egg into his mouth, washing it down with the last of the lager in his pint.

'You know I think I might be onto something there,' he said, waving his empty pint glass at the barmaid.

'I sincerely doubt it,' Edna said.

'That friggin' Noel Edmonds, he does all that *Noel's Christmas Presents* bollocks on Christmas Day, right? Well, it's not actually on Christmas Day, is it? That's another con they pull to try and make 'emselves look all goodie goodie. They probably film it in bloody August or something, but you know what I'm on about, right?'

'Right,' Bertie said, reluctantly.

'Edmonds was picking up all them stars and ferrying 'em to Wembley on his helicopter for Live Aid, wasn't he? He's got a licence. Why couldn't he have brought a gang of them Africans over in his helicopter when they was recording the Band Aid single? Given 'em a nice day out. Meet the stars, that sort of thing. There's a bloody Christmas present!' Graham said, a broad grin spread across his crumb-strewn face.

'Hey, remember that line about there not being snow in Africa on 'Do They Know It's Christmas', Bert? I bet there was plenty of the white stuff flying about at that Band Aid recording session, eh? Ten minutes in the company of Messrs Rossi and Parfitt, and they'd soon be enjoying a white Christmas.' Graham's laughter was now starting to drown out most other noise in the pub.

'Will you keep your voice down!' Edna hissed.

'They wouldn't be too bothered about any grub once they'd got a few lines of that stuff up their 'ooters either, that's for sure, boy,' Graham said, ignoring his wife and giving Bertie a playful slap on the arm.

Edna and Bertie both eyed Graham with a mixture of disbelief and contempt.

'Here, that gives me an idea,' Graham said, looking over at the jukebox.

*

'Here, get that down you,' Linda said, handing Douglas a double measure of brandy. 'Purely medicinal, for the shock. Don't go getting used to it. You're not eighteen yet. And that's a shandy,' she said, nodding at the pint on the table. 'Come on, down the hatch.'

Relinquishing his grip on the framed photo of his mother, Douglas set it down gently in his lap on top of his Mr Bump Jumper. Douglas necked the brandy in one, giving a shudder as the spirit warmed his throat and belly. Linda left to make chitchat with some of the locals. Douglas stayed put. Daisy Carr occupied a bar stool beside him.

'I'm really sorry for what I did, Daisy,' Douglas said, feeling the immediate soothing effects of the brandy. 'In the shed 'n' that. I was drunk and I didn't know what I was doing. I was all over the place after I found ... after...'

'It's OK, you div,' Daisy said, smiling warmly. 'I just wished you'd told me about your mum. Why didn't you say anything to anyone about her?'

'I dunno. I was in shock, I suppose. None of it felt real to me and I didn't want it to be real so badly. I lost the plot trying to pretend it didn't happen. That's why I did all that crazy shit, I suppose.'

'Crazy shit is putting it mildly,' Daisy said, sipping her glass of white wine as Fergal Sharkey's 'A Good Heart' came on the jukebox. Daisy put her wine down and picked up her paper plate that was semi-laden with buffet food. 'She doesn't like me talking to you,' Daisy said, looking over towards her mother who was nursing a sherry in the corner of the pub with a pair of middle-aged women. 'Shame I'm not a little kid any more though, isn't it?'

'I like it that you talk to me. I'm glad you don't hate me,' Douglas said. 'I bet you've got your pick of blokes at drama school now, haven't you, Daisy? Bet you're gonna marry some millionaire actor.'

'Or some bloke is gonna marry me, the millionaire actress!' Daisy said with a smile, popping a mini scotch egg in her mouth.

'Is it good there?' Douglas asked.

'Yeah, I love it,' Daisy said. 'There's so many cool people there. My new best mate's called Kelly. She's almost as crazy as you ... Nearly, but not quite. I told her about what you did. She thinks you're mad!'

'You not going out with Dan any more then?'

'Douglas, I never was going out with him. We just mucked about a bit together. And anyway he's gone now. After he got fired for the old...' Daisy discreetly held an invisible reefer to her lips, then put a vertical index finger across them, looking over at her mother. 'Is that the jumper your mum was holding?' she asked, looking down at the knitwear in his lap. 'I saw her too, you know. We both did. Me and Dan. I couldn't believe it. I still can't.'

'You saw her too?' Douglas said, looking up wide-eyed at Daisy, his eyes once again becoming glassy with tears. 'I thought I was imagining it. I still think I was but Hilda said she saw her as well. She said she saw her holding this up,' Douglas said, stroking the soft wool of the Mr Bump jumper. 'I don't remember the accident. Or what the train did to me. I remember it coming at me and I sort of remember Hilda talking to me after I saw mum. I remember hearing the train... and the sheep,' Douglas said with a slight frown, 'but then... nothing. Next thing I know I'm in hospital and my feet are gone.'

'There was no way they could have reattached them then?' Daisy asked.

'Nah. They were too mangled for that apparently. Not a clean cut in either case.'

'So what happened to your feet then? Did the hospital get rid of them? What do they do, incinerate them?'

'Something like that, yeah, I guess. They ain't much use to me anymore, that's for sure,' Douglas said, placing the framed photo of his mum on a nearby table and the Mr Bump jumper in his lap on a stool. He lifted up his right trouser leg.

'Train got me six inches above the ankles, they said up at the hospital,' he said, revealing a heavily bandaged stump about six inches below his knee. 'Right across the shins. It was a right mess apparently. They had a look at trying to put them back on, but it was pretty obvious that it wasn't gonna happen. So they tidied them up and slapped some bandages on them. I've gotta wait now for them to fully heal over. What they do is they smooth all the bone down and tidy up all the muscles and nerve endings, then they take a flap of skin and they fold it over the end of the stump.'

'Mmm, nice,' Daisy said, putting her plate of food down and picking her wine back up.

'Still, I suppose it could've been worse,' Douglas said. 'I could've been one of the sheep.'

'Oh yes, speaking of which, Douglas,' Linda said, overhearing the end of their conversation and rejoining Douglas and Daisy, 'there's someone else you owe an apology to.'

122

Butch Ransom, wearing a white short-sleeved shirt, black tie and black trousers was at Linda's side.

'Ahh, don't give the poor guy any more grief, Linda,' Butch said. 'Not today, eh?'

'That's not the point, Butch,' Linda said. 'What's right is right and what's wrong is wrong. And what you did was *very* wrong, young man, regardless of your motives. So, come on...'

Douglas looked up from his chair at Butch. 'Sorry for blowing your sheep up,' he said with a hint of a smile, which Butch returned.

Daisy placed Douglas's Mr Bump jumper over his lap and handed him back the framed photo of his mother, which he gently placed over the Mr Man's bandaged head.

'No worries, mate,' Butch said, giving Douglas a little wink. 'Ten out of ten for originality, I gotta say. And hey, I'm sorry too. For what they were gonna do to you, mate. I'm ashamed to say it, but I was prepared to go along with it all. Obviously we didn't know how bat shit that dog was, but still.' Butch took a swig of his pint. 'None of us saw that climax you put on for us coming though mate, eh?' he said with a laugh.

Douglas smiled, though it was a faltering one. 'Yeah, and look where it got me. Stuck in this poxy thing for the rest of my life.'

'Not true,' Linda said. 'There's every chance you'll walk again. Eventually. That's what they said up at the hospital.'

'That's the spirit! ... Ohh, I love this one,' Butch said, craning his ear towards the sound of Paul Young's 'Every Time You Go Away' coming out of the jukebox. 'You know your mum came up to the farm one time,' he said, 'with some of the kids from school.'

Douglas shook his head.

'Yeah, her and one of the teachers came up during lambing season to see some of the newborns. She seemed like a real nice lady, mate. Friendly, funny. All the kids loved her. So much so that when I gave them the chance to name one of the new additions, they chose to call it Alice.'

'Aww, how lovely,' Linda said.

In his chair, Douglas had begun to cry again as Paul Young sang in the background. Across the room he caught the eye of Revered Bowen, who gave him a warm smile. He started to giggle a little, but his sobbing overpowered it as he looked at the picture of his mother in his lap. He reached for his shandy and took a big gulp, trying to compose himself a little before wiping his eyes with the sleeve of his Mr Bump jumper.

'The old man's put on a decent spread here, though, eh mate?' Butch said, looking at Douglas. 'Bit of a Keith Floyd on the quiet, is he?'

'Fuck knows,' Douglas said, looking morosely over towards his father. Graham Glass was stuffing his face from a bowing paper plate laden with food as he waddled back from the jukebox towards Bertie at the bar.

'Hey, language!' Linda said.

'So are we gonna be neighbours or what then?' Butch said, now looking at Linda. 'Gonna buy the old vicarage? If you ask me I think you should snap the bishop's hand off.'

'I think Hilda would quite like that, you know,' she said with a smile. 'Literally. But we'll have to wait and see. It is a jolly beautiful house, and I'm pretty confident we can get it properly kitted out for this little rascal when they finally let him out,' she said, giving Douglas a gentle jolt in his chair.

'You need a hand with anything, you just give me a shout,' Butch said. 'I can turn my hand to most things,' he said with a wink.

'Yes,' Linda said, returning his smile, 'I'm sure you can.'

Douglas's musical selection had come to an end and once again there was just the sound of low level chatter in the pub, until the sound of a guitar struck up. Standing at the bar, Graham Glass gave Bertie a little elbow to the ribs, turning to him and smiling, giving him a thumbs up as Status Quo came on. Bertie stared back at his friend, his face a mask of concern as Francis Rossi began singing the opening lines to 'Down Down'. All over the pub, heads turned in the direction of the jukebox.

Unlike in the church when he had wanted to go after his mum during Shakespears Sister, there was no stopping Douglas this time; he slipped away from Linda and the others, wheeling himself away at speed across the pub. Mourners spilt drinks and dropped food from paper plates in a bid to get out of Douglas's way as he cut a path through the crowded pub towards his father and Graham over by the bar.

'Douglas!' Linda shouted across the pub. It was no use. Douglas had his sights set as his mind played over the scene of his mother's coffin descending down, down into the cold dark earth.

With scant regard for his condition, Douglas leapt out of his chair, the framed photo of Alice and the Mr Bump jumper in his lap jettisoned along with him. The frame smashed as it hit the floor just as a mid-air Douglas punched his father straight in the groin with the balled fist of his right hand. His left grabbed on to Graham Glass's waistband for support as gravity took over and his feetless torso helplessly struggled to maintain some kind of balance. Losing his grip on Graham's trousers, which had been pulled down to an almost extremely embarrassing level, Douglas put out his hands for stability, cutting them on the broken glass of the shattered picture frame that was scattered around his father's feet. His lacerated hands left bloody prints smudged on the blue, white and grey wool of the Mr Bump jumper.

Linda and Butch dashed over to help Douglas, who was now letting off a string of profanities at his father and Graham as he continued to scrabble about on the floor at the feet of his father. Bertie attempted to help Douglas up, but his efforts were swiftly dismissed by Douglas, who punched his dad twice in the leg. Butch and Linda helped a writhing Douglas up off the floor and somehow managed to get him back into his chair, Linda having to forcibly hold Douglas down to prevent another attack.

'Edna, can you get me a couple of towels, please,' Linda said in as calm a manner as she could muster as she looked at Douglas's lacerated palms.

Edna did as she was asked, before yanking the jukebox's plug out of the socket, bringing an abrupt end to Graham's ill-thought-out musical selection. The pub fell silent, save for Douglas, who was making aggressive, animalistic noises in his chair, occasionally punctuated by sobbing tears and anguished screams.

'Can you not be a twat for just one day?' Edna said, staring daggers at her husband.

Bertie looked on silently and helplessly as Douglas was wheeled away. 'Dougie, I'm sorry,' he called out as Douglas, who was now in near hysterics, was wheeled towards the doors and out of the pub.

PART 2

19 *Wednesday, September 22*

Bertie had just hit a score of 95 on the dartboard and was on his way back to the red strip of fabric on the living room carpet that served as his makeshift oche when he saw Linda out of the bay window making her way up the garden path. So it wasn't the usual heart in mouth moment when there was a knock on the door a few moments later. Bertie threw a steady ton on the board, left the darts grouped satisfactorily together and went to answer the door.

'What's this? Surprise inspection from the landlady,' Bertie said to a smiling Linda.

'No, nothing like that Robert, fret ye not.'

'Come on in. Tea?' Bertie asked as Linda took her shoes off in the hall.

'Love one, thank you.'

Bertie ducked into the kitchen and flicked on the kettle. When he came back out into the hall, Linda had just stuck her head into Douglas's old room.

'I'm on a mission to collect some of his things,' she said as Bertie joined her by the bedroom door. 'I thought it would be nice to make his new room feel nice and familiar for when he comes home tomorrow.'

'Tomorrow?' Bertie said, excitedly. 'He's coming home tomorrow? Fantastic.'

Linda went into Douglas's old room, eyeing up the unmade single bed and the clothes strewn about on the floor. She gave Bertie a look. 'Have you been sleeping in here?'

Bertie nodded. 'Yeah. It still feels a little bit strange, y'know? Mine and Alice's old room. Something just doesn't feel right about it. So I stay in here.'

'Well, you might at least learn to make your bed, Robert,' Linda said.

'I know. It's a habit I haven't quite managed to get into yet. You're not going to fine me for it, are you?' Bertie said, grinning.

Linda smiled. 'I'll let you off just this once,' she said.

'So Dougie's coming back tomorrow? That's great news,' Bertie said.

'Yes indeed. Butch is up at the vicarage now helping out with some last minute DIY. I must say he's been very useful to have around the place,' Linda said. 'It's all been such a whirlwind buying the vicarage and then kitting it out for Douglas. It's been like Challenge Anneka. Butch has been great, though. Very helpful indeed.'

'Ohh yeah?' Bertie said with a wry smile.

'Yes,' Linda said, trying and failing to suppress a smile of her own. 'He's very... well, he's very handy.'

They both laughed.

'Come and sit down, Linda, I'll make the tea,' Bertie said, heading back into the kitchen while Linda took a seat on the sofa in the front room.

Two minutes later Bertie came back in with two mugs of tea and a packet of custard creams on a tray, setting it all down on the coffee table in front of Linda.

'You know, it would be nice if you informed me beforehand if you're going to be putting up pieces of interior design,' Linda said, nodding at the dartboard.

'Ahh, yeah. Sorry, Linda, I didn't think. It's Dougie's old one out of the caravan. I put it up a few weeks ago. My throw has actually improved a bit since coming back here, I think. Mind you, it couldn't exactly have got much worse. In fact there might be a little tournament coming up that I'm thinking of entering if I can keep the dreaded dartitis at bay.'

'A tournament?' Linda said. 'Down the Fruitbowl, you mean?'

'No, nowhere round here,' Bertie said. 'Up north, near my brother's place. I'm gonna pay him back some of the money he lent me while I'm up there. It's been nice to get some practice in away from the Fruitbowl, actually. Now I'm working up there, I don't wanna be spending all my free time up there as well. I gotta be down there for midday today, actually,' Bertie said looking at his watch. 'Start the lunchtime shift. Trying out a new menu. Edna's back up at the school running the kitchen single-handedly, so she only really does evenings now.'

'They still haven't found a replacement for Alice yet then?' Linda asked.

'Nope. So, the vicarage is all shipshape and ready for the boy's arrival then?'

'Yes, just about. He's got his own downstairs en suite room, all kitted out specially for him. And he'll be getting home help, I've sorted that out. He's obviously been having help with everything up at the hospital, and their people will be coming by to make regular check-ups and for his physio and occupational therapy. He's had to make some massive readjustments in his life, and he still tries his best to be as independent as he can be, but still he needs help.'

'Makes sense.'

'On the recommendation of the specialists up at the hospital I've also booked some private counselling sessions for him with a psychotherapist,' Linda said. 'Whether he wants to or not he needs to open up about what he's been through. He's suffered a massive double trauma and if that's allowed to fester away unchecked then who knows what could happen down the line. It will be hard for him, I know, and probably the last thing he'll want to do but I think it's for the best in the long run. It'll probably do him good to talk to them about you too,' Linda said. 'Perhaps it'll help, who knows?'

'I doubt it could make things any worse, put it that way.'

Linda gave Bertie a little smile. 'No,' she said. 'You're probably right there. Here's to hoping then, eh?'

'And how about Hilda?' Bertie said, 'Is she all settled in up at her new place?'

'Yes, she's there. I couldn't believe how quickly and easily the sale went through in the end, to be honest. That Bishop Trimble certainly seemed in a hurry to sell the place. So much so that I got it for quite a sizable chunk under the asking price. God is very reasonable these days, it would appear,' Linda said, sipping her tea.

'In fact Hilda's coming over for dinner tomorrow night. Douglas has been asking after her quite a lot. Asking about his mum. She agreed to come over.' Linda's tone changed. 'I would've asked you as well, Bertie, but I think Douglas is still a little raw, shall we say. With what happened at the wake.'

'Linda, I swear,' Bertie said, putting his mug back down on the table, 'that had absolutely nothing to do with me. Graham had been piling into the free booze from the moment we got into the pub. Before I knew it he was over at the jukebox. As for his bloody song selection, well, I would've swung for him myself if Douglas hadn't kicked off first. Besides, the funeral was over three weeks ago now.'

'Yes, but you know what Douglas is like.'

'No, I don't actually,' Bertie said in frustration, 'that's just the point. I've been back here over a month now and I've hardly said two words to him. That punch in the bollocks he gave me is the closest we've got to each other since I've been back. I can't get near him.'

'Give him time,' Linda said. 'He's been through so much. I'm hoping that coming back home will give him a lift. He'll be glad to be out of that hospital, that's for sure. And being able to sleep in his own bed again will be nice for him.'

'His own bed is through there,' Bertie said, nodding towards the door.

'Yes, but somehow I don't think he'd planned on sharing a single bed with his father when he came out of hospital,' Linda said, smirking.

'Touché,' Bertie said.

'Anyway, who knows, once he gets settled he might start coming round to the idea a bit more. He's still quite unstable emotionally as well as physically. His mood swings have been quite severe. They're now almost certain that it's linked to the concussion he sustained on the railway. The staff up at the hospital said they've heard him laughing away to himself quite a lot. Then other times he's completely down in the dumps and in floods of tears. There's a name for it, I think I might've mentioned it to you at the wake.'

'I think you did, but I can't remember it, I'm afraid,' Bertie said, sipping his tea.

'It's called emotional lability. Or emotional liability, as Douglas calls it. The sufferer can find themselves laughing at strange or even completely inappropriate things, like his giggling fit at the funeral for one. Then next moment they can be tearful, morose and completely withdrawn. It's become more severe since the funeral, that's for sure. I don't know whether being right across the road from Alice is going to be a help or a hindrance, to be honest.'

'Douglas adored his mum,' Bertie said. 'I think it'll be nice for him to know that she's close by.'

'He keeps talking about her. About when he saw her on the day of the accident. He's asking where she's gone. Whether I believe in heaven. Frankly, I don't have the answers. I'm hoping Hilda might be able to help out a bit in that department. It's one of the reasons I asked her over to dinner. Theology was never really one of my stronger subjects. To be honest, I've never given much thought to the afterlife.'

'Well, you've been off empire building, haven't you?' Bertie said. 'I'd never given it much thought either until ...' he trailed off.

'Until what?'

Bertie hesitated, unsure exactly how to proceed. 'Well, it's just that... this place... there's been...'

'There's been what?'

'Well, there's been, I mean, things have ...'

'Ohh come on, Robert, do spit it out,' Linda said.

'Well, put it this way, when I said it'd be nice for Douglas to know that his mum is close by,' Bertie frowned, 'I think she might be closer than we think.'

'Meaning what exactly?' Linda said, scrutinising Bertie's face.

'Well, it's just there's been some funny things happening around here recently.'

'Here? In the house? What sort of funny things?'

Bertie told Linda about the record player. About the doors opening and closing. The lights. The knocking on doors. The feelings of not being alone in the house. 'It's like she's just in the other room, Linda. That's the main reason why I've been sleeping in Douglas's room. It's not scary or anything. Well, it was a bit to start with, I suppose, before I knew what was going on.'

'Robert, are you saying that Alice is haunting this house?'

Bertie shrugged. 'I honestly can't think of any other rational explanation for it all,' he said, shaking his head. 'Edna heard it too when she was round here. She says she can sense Alice's presence. She's a bit of a spiritualist on the quiet.'

'Oh yes, Douglas said something about this too. She went up to see him before the funeral.'

'Yeah. Well, she used to go to one of their churches, trying to make contact with her son Peter who died in a car crash last year.'

'Yes, I remember. He was Douglas's friend, I understand?' Linda said. 'He's talked about him quite a lot as well. Another loss he's had to bear.'

'Indeed. It almost killed Edna too. Then she found out about this spiritualist lot. As a consequence she's developed a bit of mediumship herself. She thinks Alice is still around trying to communicate from the other side. She thinks she's got unfinished business and that me being back here is part of that. Edna says it's like they can see things over there that we can't. Like they get the bigger picture. Edna says Alice has got unfinished business, and that is why she's still around.'

'Edna?' Linda said. 'That's the lady with the big hair and the big...' Linda held her hands out in front of her as if she was cupping a pair of invisible breasts twice the size of her own. 'The woman you were walking with behind the hearse at the funeral?'

'Yes, that's her. She's Graham's wife,' Bertie said, rolling his eyes. 'Although they're really just husband and wife in name only. There's no love lost between them, that's for sure. She's been good to talk to, and she helped me get the job up at the pub. I think Graham's been a bit of a bastard to her over the years, to be honest, and I'm beginning to see that myself now as well. He hasn't been particularly supportive of her either since Peter died. Whether he's done it on purpose or not I don't know. Personally, I think he's just a bit of an emotional retard and he can't do that sort of thing. He's a pretty selfish bastard too, that much is obvious. Either way I think Edna's had enough of him. To be honest with you, after what he did at the wake, I know exactly how she feels,' Bertie said. 'But I'm determined not to let that bugger things up between me and Dougie, Linda,' he continued. 'I mean it. I'm here to stay, and no matter how long it takes, I *am* going to put things right with him.'

'And I for one will not stand in your way, Robert,' Linda said. 'I'd be lying if I said I didn't still harbour some residual feelings of ill will towards you for what you did to them. But the past is the past, and I believe you when you say you want to put things right. It just might take a little time, that's all. We all need to help build a stable environment around Douglas now, so that he has every possible hope of recovery for the future. Speaking of which,' Linda said, extracting a small blue book from her handbag, 'I've set up a savings account for him. I thought you might like to start making a contribution as well, now that you're a man of means.'

'Yeah, of course,' Bertie said. 'And thank you. Y'know I thought you were gonna have me hung, drawn and quartered when they said you were coming round that day at the vicarage. I'm glad you've been... well, I'm glad you've been OK with me.' Bertie smiled. 'You've been great.'

'Part of me would have liked to see you put in the stocks, believe me,' Linda said with a smirk. 'But the fact remains that you were Alice's husband, for better or worse, and you are still Douglas's father.'

'Thanks,' Bertie said, breathing a big sigh of relief.

'Right,' Linda said, checking her watch, 'time is of the essence so how about you give me a hand taking some of those posters down in his room?' she asked, rising to her feet. 'That's if you're sure you won't miss them too much?' she said, smiling at Bertie.

'I'm sure I'll cope,' he said, following on behind her as the pair walked down the hall and towards Douglas's bedroom. Linda went in first and Bertie followed on behind. Linda stopped dead in her tracks, looking from the bed to Bertie then back to the bed again.

'Who made the bed?' she said, pointing at the neatly made single bed with a look of confusion etched across her face.

Bertie was leaning up against the door frame, smiling at Linda. 'Have a guess,' he said.

20 *Thursday, September 23*

'I must say it feels a little strange coming back here as a visitor,' Reverend Bowen said as Linda took her coat in the hallway of her former residence. Linda hung it up and led Reverend Bowen into the kitchen; Moses followed on behind, clearly still feeling on familiar territory, and immediately made himself comfortable next to Butch Ransom at the Aga where the Kiwi, in his faded All Blacks rugby shirt and cut-off denim shorts, was stirring a big pan of spaghetti bolognese.

'You've got him well trained,' Bowen said, looking from Linda to Butch.

'There's not a lot I won't do for a feed, Reverend,' Butch said, winking at the vicar.

'I take it from the noise coming from down there that Douglas is in his room?' Bowen said.

'I bought him a new hi-fi as a little housewarming present. He's been well and truly putting it through its paces. Some days the music coming out of there is actually quite pleasant. I think it's his mum's old favourites that he likes to listen to.'

'And some days it's World War Three!' Butch said with a wry smile. 'Still an ardent head banger, is young Mr B.'

'Yes, I've had to ask him to turn it down once or twice,' Linda said.

'Don't suppose you'll get many complaints from the neighbours though, eh?' Butch said, nodding in the direction of the churchyard opposite.

Linda frowned. 'Butch, really?' she said.

'Sorry, I didn't mean ...' Butch trailed off, turning his attention back to stirring the bolognese. 'Sorry.'

'Will Douglas be joining us?' Bowen said.

'I'll give him a shout when dinner's ready. Shout being the operative word. Which will be how long?' Linda asked, looking at Butch.

'Ten minutes, chef,' Butch said. 'Just gotta cook a bit of spaghetti up, eh?'

'Please take a seat, Reverend,' Linda said, beckoning the vicar towards the kitchen table. 'I must say it was awfully nice of the diocese to leave the furniture and contents, Hilda. I mean, they put a bit on the price to include all the stuff we wanted, but still, it was great not having to buy a ton of furniture and a fridge freezer and all that.'

'None of this would've fitted up at the new place anyway,' Bowen said. 'It's quite a bit smaller. But they've kitted it out for us, so it's not like I had that problem either, thankfully.'

Linda pushed the kitchen door closed but not entirely shut. 'I actually wanted to talk to you before Douglas makes an appearance, Reverend.'

'Please call me Hilda,' Bowen said, taking a seat at the table.

'OK, Hilda. Let me get you a drink first. What will you have? I've got a nice bottle of red open,' Linda said, pointing to an uncorked bottle of Côtes-du-Rhône.

'That sounds just the job.'

'I hope you don't mind me taking the direct approach,' Linda said, pouring the wine, 'it's just that I popped round to see Bertie yesterday to get some things for Douglas's new room, and we had a chat while I was there. He told me...' Linda paused, 'well, I'm not quite sure how to put it, but the long and short of it is that he thinks Alice is haunting him. Haunting the bungalow. I think I might actually own a haunted house.'

'Haunting him?' Bowen said, looking a tad perplexed.

'I know, it sounds mad, doesn't it? I thought as much myself when he was telling me about it. But then I saw...' Linda again hesitated, not quite sure how to proceed. 'Well, I saw something myself that neither of us could really explain.'

'Which was?' Bowen said, sipping her wine.

'Douglas's bed.' Linda said. 'When I first got there, I stuck my head in his old room to have a look at what I might like to bring back for him, posters and whatnot, and I noticed that his bed was unmade. It turns out that Bertie's been sleeping in there. Anyway, thinking nothing of it, Bertie and I had a chat and a cup of tea and then he told me about things that he'd been experiencing around the house. Things he can't explain: banging noises and lights going on and off, that sort of thing. Anyway, after we'd finished our little chat, I went back into Douglas's room to start getting some of his things – and the bed was made. I couldn't explain it and neither could Bertie. He only left the room briefly to make tea, and he swears he never went back in Douglas's room. I heard him all the time he was in the kitchen, and anyway to get to Douglas's room he would have had to walk past the doorway to the lounge, so I would have seen him. So anyway, it turns out that the reason Bertie's been sleeping in Douglas's old room is because he doesn't feel comfortable in his and Alice's old one.'

'Wasn't that where Alan said he'd found Alice?' Butch said, placing a generous clutch of dry spaghetti into a steaming pan of boiling water.

'Mmm hmm,' Linda said, nodding her head. 'I know it all sounds a bit mad, but he sounds genuine about what he says, and I can't deny what I saw myself. One minute it was a mess, and the next it was perfect.'

Linda took a seat at the end of the dining table, placing her own wine glass in front of her. 'Bertie also said that you saw Alice on the day of the accident. You and Douglas both, and that it somehow changed you. It has almost certainly changed Douglas, I know that much. That's why I think he asks after you so much, to keep that shared experience of Alice alive. However, Bertie's now got it in his head that Alice is unhappy with him coming back and that he shouldn't be at the bungalow. I said that's probably nonsense, given my own experience of how Alice felt towards Bertie, even after he left. Though I told her at the time he was a complete arse for doing so. And besides, all the things Bertie's said that have happened down there aren't mean or malicious. It's just like she's letting him know that she's still around. To be honest, Hilda, all this is a bit out of my area of expertise, that's why I wanted to pick your brains about it. Even if I have to bribe you with food. Sorry,' Linda said smiling. 'So, what do you think?'

Bowen took a sip of wine, followed by a deep intake of breath. 'I've been a vicar for nearly twenty years now,' she said. 'And for years I have preached about the life eternal that the Bible assures us of if we follow God's teachings, about heaven, hell and all points in between. But I'd never seen it or experienced it for myself. To me it was all just words on a page, like reading from a script. It was different when I was young and just starting out on the spiritual path. I kept telling myself that it would happen one day, that patience and faith was all that was required. Only the day never came, and the more I read about it and the more I talked about it and preached it to others, the less I saw and the less I believed. My faith had been slowly eroding. True spiritual understanding became nothing more than a confusing and frustrating mystery to me. When Douglas put my stained glass window through back in August, that was the cherry on top of the cake. And then what he tried to do to him,' Bowen said, nodding towards Moses, still dozing contentedly at Butch's feet by the Aga, 'it all just sent me over the edge. My faith had all but evaporated by that point. I had become spiteful and vengeful. I blamed everybody else for my problems. I was quick to judge others and slow to take responsibility for my own thoughts and actions.' Bowen took another sip of wine. 'This is lovely,' she said, holding up the glass appreciatively.

'So then what?' Linda said.

'I'd become a stranger to myself,' Bowen continued. 'I barely recognised the person looking back at me in the mirror in the morning. Every day I woke up and stared into the eyes of the same angry, bitter woman. I am not proud of what we had planned for Douglas on the day of the fete. I cannot restate that enough, and I will be eternally ashamed of myself for my part in it. But I realise now that my actions were a symptom of the sickness I was suffering from, a symptom of the mental and spiritual disease that had been growing unchecked and festering away inside me. It was an expression of all the negativity and anger I harboured. I felt cheated by a God I thought had abandoned me. Every Sunday I would preach his word, and every week that word would sound ever hollower, and every week there would be fewer and fewer people there to hear it. By the time the fete rolled round, I was virtually talking to myself and I simply didn't believe a word of it any more.'

Bowen took a hearty slug of wine and another deep breath.

'Then I saw Alice by the railway line,' she said with a tender little smile. 'I saw Alice staring lovingly into the eyes of her son, and in that moment I

139

understood pain. I understood loss. I understood it all. I felt it, and I knew she'd gone. It was then that I realised just how much Douglas and I had in common. Both of us were full of that same anger and abandonment, only for different reasons. Alice made us both understand that, and no words were necessary. Not a single word. What I had been waiting for had been revealed to me, just as I had reached my lowest ebb. I understood because for the first time I had been given a glimpse of the life eternal that I had talked about for so many years: Alice's soul incarnate in human form, only no longer a physical one; her spiritual body. Looking at her on that day, even a blind man could have seen the love she had for Douglas, and the pain and sorrow she felt for leaving him behind, for being taken from this world and leaving him on his own. But in that moment I knew for sure that some part of us does indeed go on. That something survives our bodies' physical death. That the afterlife is real, but most importantly that we take that love which we cultivate here on earth with us when we go. It is in fact the only thing worth taking, but in order to take it, first we need to make it and to give it freely and unconditionally. To give love is really the *only* important thing, because it is the only surefire way to receive it. I heard a saying recently that said there is no such thing as evil, only the absence of love. I think that statement sums up pretty well what Douglas and myself were both going through in the days leading up to the fete, as well as on the day itself. That's why I ran to Douglas on the railway line after he'd been hit. I knew and I understood that compassion and forgiveness were my only route to salvation; that love is the only way to conquer so-called "evil".'

Bowen drained what was left in her glass. Linda smiled, refilling it.

'That is how it changed me,' Bowen said. 'Alice showed me that and I will be forever grateful to her. And for what it's worth, if there is any truth to her spirit still being on the physical plane, then it can only be for reasons of good.'

Over at the sink, an uncharacteristically quiet Butch Ransom was draining the spaghetti and transferring it into a large ceramic bowl which, along with an equally large bowl of bolognese, he placed on the table with a bowl of grated parmesan beside them.

'That smells absolutely delicious, Butch,' Bowen said. Butch smiled, opening the top door of the Aga's oven and removing three nicely browned batons of garlic bread.

'Hilda,' Linda said, a wrinkle of concern creasing her brow, 'do you think I should tell Douglas? You know, about what Bertie said? I'm just worried it might upset him. Even more than he already is, if that's possible. He's still so up and down at the moment. This is all so out of my comfort zone, and to be honest I don't really know what to do for the best.'

Linda got up and stood behind the dining chair she had just vacated, clasping the top of it and looking Reverend Bowen in the eye. 'What do you think? Should I tell Douglas about Alice haunting the bungalow?'

The kitchen door creaked open behind them. All three heads turned towards the noise, Moses included. Douglas quietly wheeled himself into the warm kitchen that smelt of spaghetti bolognese and garlic, his bandaged hands gripping the wheels of his chair.

'Yeah,' he said, 'I think you should.'

21 *Friday, September 24*

Bertie's pulse rate quickened as he eyed the remaining space next to the two darts already in the small red treble twenty segment. Then there was a knock on the door. 'It's open,' he called out, half expecting no one to come in, but too focused on the board to really care. Bertie eyed the remaining space in the treble twenty bed, hearing the front door open as he threw. The dart hit the treble, sitting snugly beside the other two. He had now thrown six perfect darts. He pulled them out of the board, walked back to the oche and was eyeing up the first dart of his 141 finish when Linda stuck her head round the living room door.

'Hi,' she said, 'all right?'

Bertie said nothing, only raised his hand as if to say, 'I'll be with you in a minute,' as he focused on what could potentially be a nine-dart leg. The treble twenty went in, Bertie focused intently on the treble nineteen, but it missed by half a centimetre, the dart landing just beneath his intended green segment of the board. 'Ohh bollocks,' he said. 'Oh well, let's see what you could've won,' he said, taking aim at the double twelve anyway ... and hitting it. 'Shit,' he said, leaving his darts in the board and turning to face Linda for the first time.

'It's getting better,' he said, with a rueful smile. 'Might be on for this tournament after all.'

'Oh the tournament, yes. The one up north you mentioned last week?' Linda said.

'It's only a little amateur open thing, but it'll be good to have a bash. It's been a while. I think I might actually stand a chance, as it goes. The dartitis has gone. I can't believe it. I'm playing better than ever. And that was nearly a nine-dart leg,' he said, nodding at the board, though he sensed the significance of such a potential achievement was lost on Linda. 'So, how are you? And how's Douglas?'

'He knows about Alice. He overheard me talking to Hilda when I was asking her advice about it,' Linda said. 'He knows about Alice possibly haunting this place.'

'No "possibly" about it,' Bertie said, moving an acoustic guitar from off the sofa so Linda could sit down. 'I've restrung that old thing and tuned it up. I thought maybe you could give it back to Douglas? If he wants it, that is. It was in the caravan.'

'I'm sure he'd like that. It will be nice for him to have something constructive to focus on.'

'So how was dinner?'

'Well, Douglas had quite a lot of questions for Hilda as usual. I suppose that is a good thing, him talking about it and opening up to her, I mean. It's good he's talking about it, as he can still be very quiet and reticent about things when he wants to be. The counselling has definitely helped him in that respect I think. Hilda did her best to answer his questions. I'm sure she can explain it all a bit better when she gets here. Douglas asked me if I could collect some of Alice's records and CDs. I think he wants to make up a compilation of his own, like the one you and Edna made.'

'They're all over there,' Bertie said, nodding towards the storage unit beside the hi-fi. 'No real danger in me wanting to keep them. Not really my cup of tea. Unlike these,' Bertie said picking up two CDs from off the coffee table and handing them to Linda. 'Little present for him.'

'What do we have here then?' Linda said, scrutinising the first CD's front cover. '*Earth Vs The Wildhearts*. Goodness me, is that a scorpion on that man's face?' She narrowed her eyes. 'It is a man, isn't it? Sensitive stuff, I'm sure.'

'It got a great review in this,' Bertie said, picking up a copy of *Kerrang* and handing it to Linda also. 'I kept his subscription going down at Kareshi's. He used to get that and that,' Bertie said, pointing to a copy of the WWF magazine on the coffee table. 'Thought it would be nice to keep it going.'

'I think it's a lovely idea, Robert, I'm sure he'll be thrilled with it all. He could do with some reading material to help take his mind off things. He's been spending quite a lot of time in his room, which I'm not particularly thrilled about, and I'm still hearing him giggling away to himself in there. Then of course other times I hear him crying. "I'm an emotional liability, remember?" he says to me when I ask him about it.'

'I thought it was lability?' Bertie said.

'It is. Still, at least it shows that he's still got some of that old sense of humour left intact. Talking of wrestling, Butch is up there with him at the moment doing some male bonding. They're watching *Summerslam*, is it? Your friend Graham dropped it round for him the other day. He taped it off Sky for him. I'm thinking of getting a dish myself, actually. Only for the living room, though. I don't want to give Douglas any more reason to sit in his room on his own. Graham was quite apologetic about what happened at the wake. I think the tapes were his way of saying sorry. He brought quite a few round for him, actually. I suppose they'll help Douglas pass the time.'

'Not if I know Graham, they won't,' Bertie said under his breath.

'Hmmm?' Linda said absently, flicking through the pages of *Kerrang*.

'Oh, nothing.'

'So what's this other album you've got for him?' Linda asked, squinting at the cover of AC/DC's *High Volatage*. 'Ahh, now I've heard of them,' she said. 'Butch was talking about them only the other day in fact.'

'I should hope so too. Only the second best rock 'n' roll band in the world,' Bertie said proudly.

'The first being?'

Bertie frowned, a little astounded by the question. 'Status Quo, obviously,' he said.

'Obviously,' Linda repeated, smiling. 'Quite the gift giver today, aren't you, Robert?'

'Well, now that I've settled in down the pub and I'm working steady, I've actually got a bit of money coming in. Speaking of which, can you pay that into Douglas's account?' Bertie said, handing Linda a cheque for £50.

'You're sure you can afford that much?'

'Yeah, no sweat. Hopefully it should be more before much longer. A lot more with a bit of luck,' he added, speaking more to himself than to Linda.

'Oh, speaking of the pub, Douglas, Butch and I will be popping down for some dinner tomorrow night. It's my treat to Butch for all the hard work he's done around the house, helping get it ready for Douglas. Thought he deserved it. Saturday night on the town. And it will be nice to get Douglas out of the house. I think he and Douglas are actually beginning to get on quite well.'

'He's not the only one getting on with Butch, I'll wager,' Bertie said with a wry grin.

Linda blushed. 'Mind your own business,' she said, unable to suppress her own smile. 'Hey,' Linda said, 'why don't you give this little bundle to Douglas at the pub tomorrow? Will you be working?' she said, picking up the CDs and magazines off the table. 'I'm sure he'd be most grateful.'

Bertie frowned, considering the question. 'Mmmm, nah, I don't think so, Linda. I don't wanna ambush him with it all. He might feel a bit overwhelmed by it and I'm worried he'll throw it all back in my face. Best you give them to him, eh?'

Linda nodded. 'OK,' she said, 'I'll pass them on.' She placed the little bundle back on the coffee table. 'It was Douglas's idea to go to the Fruitbowl tomorrow night, you know,' she said. 'We gave him the option of where he might like to go. He said it was because Edna might be there, but deep down I think there's part of him that wants to see you.'

Bertie smiled. 'That's nice of you to say so, Linda,' he said. 'I'll be in the kitchen, but maybe I'll be able to come out and say hello, eh?'

'Yes, I think you should,' Linda said as she carried on flicking through the pages of *Kerrang*.

A knock on the front door broke the temporary silence that had descended on the living room and Bertie went to answer it, still grinning as he went. He opened the door to Reverend Bowen standing on the doorstep. 'Good afternoon, Reverend,' Bertie said. 'Come on in.'

Bowen followed Bertie into the front room.

'Hi, Hilda,' Linda said brightly.

'Hello, dear,' Bowen replied.

'Let me take that, Hilda,' Bertie said, going back out to the hall to hang up the vicar's coat. He came back in a moment later and glanced at his darts in the board. The dart that had missed the crucial treble nineteen on his nine-dart finish a few minutes ago was now sitting in the middle of the green segment. 'That's cheating, Alice,' Bertie said, shaking his head and grinning.

Linda looked at the board, at first a little flummoxed, but eventually grasping the meaning of the situation.

'Everything all right?' Bowen said, taking a seat next to Linda on the sofa.

'Yeah, fine,' Bertie said, smiling and taking a seat in the armchair beside the record player.

'Thank you again for serving up such a lovely meal last night, Linda,' Bowen said.

'You are most welcome, Hilda. I hope it wasn't too weird being back in the old place so soon. I felt a little bit like a squatter in your company, I must say.'

'It's fine, dear. Actually, Moses and I are settling into the new place quite nicely. It isn't too bad at all. And as I've said before, I'm pleased that it's you and Douglas who are in the old place. It'll be good for him, I'm sure. How is he doing after last night? Quite a lot to take in, I imagine?'

'Yes, but overall I think it was a positive thing,' Linda said. 'He actually sounded quite upbeat about it all when he finally went off to bed.'

'He certainly had a lot of questions,' Bowen said. 'Which is understandable, I suppose, given the circumstances. I'm afraid I don't have all the answers, but I have a lot more confidence and conviction in what I say than I did a month ago, that's for sure. And I've been in touch with the people at the spiritualist church that you mentioned. The one you said Edna attends,' Hilda said, looking at Bertie. 'I managed to have a little chat with her after church last week.'

'Good,' Bertie said, nodding his head.

'They in turn have put me in touch with someone else. Goodness, it sounds bizarre me saying that I've been in contact with a medium, but if the past month has taught me anything, it's that sometimes one shouldn't be afraid to look a little further afield for broader spiritual understanding. Just don't tell Bishop Trimble about it, for heaven's sake,' Bowen said with a little laugh, 'or else Moses and me could be squatting in your caravan!'

'You don't think the bishop would be too happy about outsourcing your line of enquiry then?' Linda said.

Bowen paused, contemplating the answer. 'The Church of England has some very comforting things to say regarding the life hereafter, but when it really comes to pursuing that particular avenue for oneself, well, it can often be quite obstructive, if I'm being honest. I feel a lot of the time that we are seen by many as gatekeepers of this spiritual knowledge, because we've done our time at the seminary; almost the same way that you put your faith in a plumber to fix your sink because he's trained to fix it. People look to us, but who do *we* look to if we don't feel confident ourselves in the message we give? Who's to say there are not plenty more people out there in the world who have access to this spiritual understanding? After all, "Ask, and it shall be given." Why would that not apply to every enquiring mind who asks the question? The Rowan Trimbles of this world are more of the "Put your faith in God and don't ask too many questions" school of thought. They are generally mistrusting and suspicious of mediumship. Rightly so, in some cases. I'm sure there are a lot of shameless charlatans about who have no moral compass when it comes to exploiting the grieving and the vulnerable, but I have certainly come round to the very real possibility that there are also people outside organised religion who have just as much spiritual insight as any person wearing a dog collar; people who can bring just as much comfort to the bereaved as I can reading passages from the Bible. And from speaking to Jason Rose on the phone, I believe that he is genuine and sincere in what he says; and he's given me a couple of dates when he's free for a possible meeting.'

At this piece of information, Linda whipped out her Filofax from her handbag. Bertie and Hilda exchanged a brief smile that Linda was not privy to.

'Where do you suggest as a venue?' Bowen said.

From the kitchen came the sound of bubbling as the kettle came to the boil and then clicked off. They all turned towards the noise.

'Why not here?' Linda said. 'I mean, it makes perfect sense, doesn't it?'

'Will Douglas be all right coming back here, do you think?' Bowen asked.

She hesitated a moment. 'I'm sure he'll be fine,' Linda said finally. 'I think last night really straightened a few things out in his head. Knowing that Alice is still around is a comfort to him, I'm sure. I don't see any reason why he wouldn't want to come back here. And we'll all be here to support him.'

'Edna said it brought her great comfort after Peter died,' Bertie said. 'From what she's told me, this spiritual lot sound like a nice enough bunch, and Edna is one of the most cynical people I know. It would take a lot to impress her. She might have a tough exterior, but she's quite a sensitive soul on the quiet.'

'Yes, I've noticed you've been spending quite a lot of time together,' Linda said, closing her Filofax.

'She's been a good friend to me since coming back here,' Bertie said. 'God knows why, but she has. She was a little frosty to begin with, but she thawed out eventually.'

'So it wasn't just me then?' Linda said.

Bertie smiled. 'And Edna sorted me out with the job at the pub. I can't thank her enough for that. Us working together up there has helped us get,' Bertie paused, 'reacquainted. I thought she'd be another one wanting to see me put in the stocks and have rotten fruit thrown at me, but she's been OK. She's been great, in fact.'

Linda smiled at Bertie with the merest hint of a raised eyebrow.

'So when have you potentially got this chap lined up for then, Hilda?' Bertie asked.

Bowen flicked through her own little black notebook. 'He's got the tenth or the seventeenth of October free. He's attending a conference and also the spiritualist centre itself over that time, so he can potentially do either of those dates.'

'To be honest, I think it's probably best if I'm not here when he comes,' Bertie said. 'It's going to be hard enough for Douglas to come back here as it is, and I think it might be easier if I was out the way for it. Which is quite fortuitous actually, because there is the chance I'll be going up north on the weekend of the seventeenth to see my brother and have a go in that darts tournament. But I'd rather you didn't mention it to Douglas, though, about me going up north. I don't want him getting the wrong idea. So, if you're sure you want to do it...?'

'You said yourself, Bertie, how it brought Edna a great deal of comfort in her time of need,' Bowen said. 'I think it might be just what Douglas needs to help him heal.'

At that moment the living room light came on and in the kitchen the kettle was heard coming to the boil once again.

'Take the hint, for goodness sake, Robert,' Linda said, nodding towards the kitchen.

22 *Saturday, September 25*

'Your old man must be one dab hand in the kitchen, mate,' Butch said, surveying the crowded dining area of the Pressed Fruitbowl. 'I've never seen it so busy in here before.'

'He never made me dinner before,' Douglas glumly said from his wheelchair. 'Now he's making it for everyone.'

Linda was studying the menu. 'Well, there's a first time for everything, isn't there?' she said, not looking up from it. 'Like your shirt, for instance, Butch.' Linda closed the menu and placed it down on the table. 'I was beginning to think that All Blacks shirt of yours was a skin graft. I'm amazed to see you looking almost half respectable in the wardrobe department for once.'

'This is my smart casual look, eh? As it's a special occasion,' Butch said, lovingly caressing the red and white check pattern of his long-sleeved shirt. 'And you don't scrub up too bad either, eh mate?' he said, looking at Douglas in his smart new navy blue sweater that Linda had bought him. A dark blue tartan blanket covered his lap, reaching almost to the floor, obscuring his dark blue jeans.

Douglas remained silent, looking at the menu. 'Can I have a pint, please?' he said.

'You can have a shandy, like we agreed. You're not eighteen yet.'

'Soon will be, though, won't you, mate, eh?' Butch said, giving Douglas a playful punch on the arm.

'Yeah, and when I am I'm gonna get totally legless!' Douglas said with an unexpected flourish and even the hint of a smile.

'Have you thought any more about it?' Linda said. 'What you might like to do?

'Get lashed up,' Douglas said. 'Properly.'

'Creative,' Linda said. 'But I suppose it's up to you. And I won't be able to stop you any more.'

'How about fancy dress!?' Butch said excitedly.

'Oh God, trust you,' Linda said, shaking her head and looking at Douglas, who appeared to be giving it some serious thought.

'Could we have it here?' Douglas said.

'It's up to you, sweetheart,' Linda said. 'If that's what you want?'

'As good a place as any, I suppose. Get Keith Floyd to knock up another buffet like he did for mum.' Douglas nodded his head in silent contemplation. 'Mmm, maybe,' he said to himself.

'Do we order at the bar?' Linda said, looking through the open double doors of the dining area towards where Edna was pulling a pint in the main bar.

'Think so,' Butch said.

'Here,' Linda said, giving Butch her credit card. 'Stick that behind the bar and ask Edna to start up a tab for us, would you, please? Oh, and be a dear and get us some drinks. Dry white wine for me, shandy for him and whatever you want.'

'Yes, m'aaam,' Butch said, sounding like one of his sheep as he undid the buttons on the cuffs of his shirt and rolled them up to the elbows.

'Well, that lasted long, didn't it?' Linda said, eyeing the Kiwi as he rose from the table to make his way towards the bar, Butch giving her a wink as he vacated the table. 'What do you fancy then, young man?' she said now to Douglas, who was eyeing his menu with quiet concentration.

'Seen this?' he said at last after some serious study. 'Big Girl's Blouse Burger. "Can you handle it? Or are you just a big girl's blouse?" he said, reading from the menu.

'I didn't see that. What exactly does a Big Girl's Blouse Burger consist of?' Linda asked.

'Two quarter pounders, bacon, cheese, fried egg and onion rings,' Douglas said. 'And it comes with chips and a salad.'

'Goodness me, all at the same time? So is that what you're going to have?'

151

'Yeah, probably,' Douglas replied as Butch approached with a tray of drinks.

'Here we are then,' he said, offloading a large glass of white wine for Linda and two pints. 'One shandy,' he said, giving Douglas a conspiratorial wink. Douglas looked over at Linda but she was busy looking at the menu again.

'Thanks, Uncle Butch,' he said with a smile and a nod, sipping his pint.

Butch shook his head and took his seat. 'What did I say about that?' Butch said. 'It just sounds weird. Uncle bloody Butch indeed.'

The doors to the kitchen opened off to the left, and Edna came out holding two plates of food. Douglas caught a glimpse of his dad busily working away in the kitchen. Bertie looked up and waved, catching his son's eye just as the swing door closed shut. Douglas just caught the last of his father's smile.

'Well then,' Linda said, putting down her menu. 'Cheers! Thank you, Uncle Butch, for all your hard work.'

'Oh don't you bloody start,' Butch said as the three of them clinked glasses.

'I dunno about you, mate, but I'm gonna have a Big Girl's Blouse Burger,' Butch said. 'Sounds like a beast!'

'Is that two then?' Linda asked.

'Yeah, may as well,' Douglas said.

'Well, you two can fill your guts up, but I'm going to have the sea bass. See how good your father is with a piece of fish.'

'Can I take your order?' Edna Glass said, appearing at the table.

'Oh, Edna, hi,' Linda said brightly. 'I thought we had to order at the bar?'

'I make exceptions for special customers,' she said. 'And they've actually got extra staff on behind the bar for once, which makes a change. How are you doing?' she said, looking down at Douglas in his chair.

'OK. Bored of this frigging thing,' he said, looking downcast at his wheelchair, 'and my stumps are sore. Apart from that, everything's great,' he added with maximum sarcasm.

'Douglas, mind your language,' Linda said.

'Frigging isn't a swearword,' Douglas said.

'Yeah, he's right,' Butch chipped in, 'it isn't.'

'What will you have?' Edna asked, suppressing a smirk.

'If you've both quite finished?' Linda said, looking from Douglas to Butch, both of whom were now grinning. 'Well,' Linda continued, opening up her menu again, 'I think it's going to be two Big Girl's Blouse Burgers for the two big girl's blouses in my life,' Linda said, smiling at Butch and Douglas. 'And I'll have the sea bass, please.'

Edna scribbled down their order and disappeared into the kitchen. She came out a few moments later holding a different piece of paper and walked back into the bar area.

Douglas hadn't registered the music coming from the now infamous jukebox until 'Young at Heart' by The Bluebells came on. He thought about his mum. It was one of her favourites.

'Hey, isn't this the one I heard you playing along to on your guitar earlier?' Linda said, registering the music playing.

'Yeah. It's well easy to play,' Douglas replied. 'Four chords.'

'Well, to you maybe,' Linda said. 'I don't think that just anybody could pick out a tune quite so easily as you can. It's a gift, you know; don't be so modest.'

'Agreed,' Butch said. 'You are quite the axe man.'

'Maybe it might be nice to thank your dad for the CDs and the magazines while we're here?' Linda said. 'And the guitar?'

'Yeah, I heard you playing along to that AC/DC album earlier, mate. Bloody shit hot!' Butch said, drawing one of Linda's looks.

'Could do, I suppose,' Douglas said.

'It's only polite,' Linda replied.

'He's busy though, isn't he?'

'I'm sure he's not *too* busy, though.'

Over at the jukebox, The Bluebells had finished and Nik Kershaw's 'I won't let the sun go down on me' started playing.

'Bit of an '80s theme going on here, eh?' Butch said.

In his wheelchair Douglas started to laugh. It increased in both volume and intensity as the song played, drawing some rather bemused looks from around the pub. Then a tear streaked down his cheek as the laughter began to subside. Linda put a hand on his arm as Douglas wiped his eyes with the sleeve of his jumper.

'Are you OK, sweetheart?' she said.

Douglas nodded, taking a deep breath followed by the swift downing of the remainder of his pint. 'Can I please have another?' he asked.

'Good job they're only shandies,' Linda said, rising to go to the bar. 'Oliver blummin' Reed. And for you, sir?' she said, addressing Butch. 'Same again?'

'Atta girl,' Butch said with a wink.

'Don't worry, mate, I'll get the next round,' Butch said as they watched Linda move off towards the bar.

'Good selection, eh?' Butch said, craning his neck towards the music. He looked at Douglas who was quietly singing along. Almost in a whisper.

'You know, mate,' Butch said, necking the last of his pint, 'I think a party could be just what you need. It'll be a good chance for you to blow away the cobwebs. Get some friends along. Invite a couple of chicks.'

'Ohh yeah, coz I've got loads of friends and I'm beating the "chicks" off with a shitty stick, aren't I? I don't want a party stuck in this poxy thing,' Douglas said, nodding down at his wheelchair.

'I think there're plenty of people round here who'd come along. And hey, a party is not only the perfect place to renew old acquaintances, it's a great place to make new ones too,' Butch said with a nod.

'You just wanna dress up again,' Douglas said, smiling.

Butch laughed but offered no resistance to the accusation as 'Everybody wants to rule the world' by Tears For Fears came on the jukebox. 'And anyway, who knows, maybe the hospital will have sorted you out with your new legs by then, eh?'

'Maybe,' Douglas said. 'They'll be some spazzy-looking plastic ones though, won't they? It'll be weird and I'll look like even more of a freak than I do already.'

'Nah, mate, that's not true. And hey, at least it'll get you back on your feet again. And besides, you can always get a new pair later on, I'm sure.'

'A new pair of what?' Linda said, returning to the table with the drinks.

'Young Douglas's new legs,' Butch said.

'Ahh yes, you never know,' Linda said, dishing the drinks out. Butch and Douglas exchanged a look of mild disappointment as the shandy was passed to him, the drink noticeably lighter in colour than his previous pint. He drank it gratefully nonetheless.

'I was just saying to young Douglas here that a good old knees-up might be just what the doctor ordered,' Butch said, taking a hefty slug of his own pint.

'You just want to get dressed up again,' Linda said. Butch and Douglas both began to laugh.

'What?' Linda said, eyeing them both with a look of mild confusion.

Douglas smiled, 'That's what I said to him.'

'Well, there you are then,' Linda said, 'we can't both be wrong, can we?'

*

A little under ten minutes later, the kitchen door swung open again and Bertie entered the dining area with three plates of food. Two plates were skilfully and strategically placed in one hand, and one plate in the other. 'One sea bass for madame,' he said, placing Linda's meal down on the table in front of her. 'Two Big Girl's Blouse Burgers for the lads,' he said, placing one mammoth burger in front of Douglas and its twin in front of Butch.

'Goodness, you'll need to dislocate your jaws to eat that,' Linda said, surveying the well-stacked burgers.

'How you doing, Dougie?' Bertie said, smiling down at Douglas.

Douglas remained silent, uncomfortable and unsure of what to say. He suddenly felt hot and his stumps began to itch and twitch beneath his tartan blanket. He started to laugh, but soon quietened down again.

'Douglas?' Linda gently said, looking from Douglas to Bertie and back to Douglas.

'Thanks for the grub,' he said, 'and...' he paused, 'and thanks for sorting the guitar out 'n' that. And for getting me those CDs and magazines.'

'You're welcome, mate. Have you had a chance to listen to them yet? That Wildhearts lot look like quite a rowdy bunch, don't they? And that album's got five Ks in *Kerrang*, so they must be good, eh?'

'Yeah, they are,' Douglas said, a little hesitantly, thinking they were more than just good.

Bertie smiled. 'Well, I won't keep you. Don't want your food to get cold.'

'Thank you, Robert, it looks lovely, if somewhat intimidating,' she said, looking at Butch and Douglas's towering burgers.

'Enjoy,' Bertie said before heading back into the kitchen with a smile on his face.

*

By nine pm Douglas, Linda and Butch had headed for home; the kitchen at the Pressed Fruitbowl was officially closed for the night. Bertie was out in the now much quieter bar area playing darts with Graham, who after a hard day's video piracy had ambled into the pub just before nine. Edna, now the only member of staff still on duty, remained behind the bar.

'So how much is this Ghostbuster gonna fleece you for then, boy?' Graham asked, waddling up to retrieve his measly 43 from out of the dartboard.

'Nothing,' Bertie said, throwing a treble twenty and two single twenties. 'He says it's a gift from God and that it would be inappropriate for him to take payment for sharing it with those who could benefit from it.' Bertie took his own darts out of the board and went back to stand behind Graham.

'Bloke sounds like a mug, if you ask me,' Graham said. 'I'd be taking the gullible suckers for all they're bloody worth.'

'Yeah, well you would, wouldn't you?' Edna said from behind the bar.

Graham gave a short snort of derisive laughter, ignoring his wife. 'What's going on with your throw, Bert?' he asked. 'You was a complete bloody shambles the last time we played in 'ere. You must be averaging at least a ton. What happened to your so-called dartitis?'

'God knows,' Bertie said. 'But whatever it is, I hope it sticks around. I'm gonna need it if I'm going to win the big tournament in a few weeks.'

'What tournament?' Edna asked.

'Yeah, what bloody tournament?' Graham echoed.

Bertie threw a tidy 97, switching seamlessy to nineteens after throwing two single twenties that blocked the treble twenty bed. 'I've been keeping quiet about it, because I didn't know if I was gonna go back for it or not. Especially after the way I've been playing. But that all seems to have changed now and I reckon I can safely hold my own in it. Maybe even win the bugger, who knows?'

'Go back where?' Graham asked, throwing two single twenties and a single five.

'Bridgend,' Bertie said after a moment's hesitation, as Graham extracted his darts and shuffled back up the oche.

'Bridgend?' Edna said. 'You're going back to Bridgend for a darts tournament?'

'I said I might be,' Bertie said, lowering his voice. 'The thing is, I've spoken to Rhonda,' he was now almost whispering, 'my ex, the one I ran the pub with back in Bridgend. I've told her I might be coming back.'

'You're going back to that tart off Bullseye that you left Alice for and then left to come back here?' Graham said chuckling. 'You sly old dog. Gonna re-enter the dragon, eh?' he said. 'Ere, I've got a bluey called that as it goes. Well, that's the sequel. The first one's just called *Enter the Dragon*, like the Bruce Lee film, but it's about this female martial arts instructor who teaches all these little Jap ninja fellas to be top shaggers and...'

'Graham,' Edna said, stony-faced, 'shut up.'

'Pfff, sorry I spoke,' Graham said, leaning on the bar and draining his pint.

'I'm not going back to be with her. No way,' Bertie said. 'Not after what she did.'

'So why are you going back there? What's so special about this tournament?' Graham said.

'Because it's one of the biggest amateur open darts tournaments in the UK, with big prize money to boot. It was one of the pub's only guaranteed money spinners. They probably would've gone elsewhere by now if it wasn't for the fact that Rhonda's uncle is one of the tournament's organisers. I've been back in touch with her, over the phone. I've told her I've been up north at my brother's trying to get my head straight. I haven't seen her since I left there to come back here the day...' Bertie stopped himself, putting a hand to his mouth as if trying to stop what was in his head from coming out of his mouth. 'Well, you know when,' he said at last. 'And that was just a flying visit to get the rest of my stuff; what there was of it. But since then Rhonda's told me she wants me back. That she's sorry. Says that she's had enough of Dai. He's the real father of the kid she told me was mine. I said that I'm playing better and that I might be prepared to come back. She said that's what she wants. I told her if I win the tournament that maybe we'll put the money towards a holiday. She's always wanted to go to Las Vegas. Typical really, given her love for all things tacky and superficial.'

'But you're not? Surely,' Edna said. 'What about Douglas? ... What about...' Edna hesitated, glancing at her husband who was standing on the oche with his back towards her, then looking at Bertie.

'I'm not going back for her,' he said. 'No chance. This is purely financial. And to see the looks on their bloody faces. I could set Douglas up with some real life-changing money if I can pull this off. Give him a real chance at a new start. I'd love to be able to do that for him. It broke my heart earlier seeing him like that. I'm glad at least I managed to talk to him tonight, even if it was only for a minute. Thanks for sticking the music on the jukebox for me,' Bertie said, smiling at Edna.

'S'all right,' Edna said, drying a pint glass with a tea towel. 'I even sneakily turned it up a little bit when they came on as well. Think I saw him having a little sing along to himself.'

'Nice,' Bertie said.

'Shame you couldn't've done that when I put Quo on the other day instead of pulling the plug out, you bloody killjoy,' Graham said. 'Come on then, Bert, 156 required.'

Bertie stepped up to the oche, choosing not to take issue with Graham's attitude towards his tasteless actions at Alice's wake, and instead focusing his attention on the two treble twenties required. He hit the first one, then the second, leaving him needing double 18 to win. He took aim, throwing the dart with no hesitation at all on release, wiring the double and missing it by mere millimetres. He strode up towards the board. 'It's getting better,' he said, walking back towards the bar with a satisfied grin on his face.

23 *Tuesday, September 28*

'Douglas, Hilda's here,' Linda shouted, knocking on her nephew's bedroom door loud enough to be heard over the wailing guitar solo coming from within. A moment later the music stopped. Douglas opened up and wheeled himself out into the hallway, pulling the door closed behind him.

'Hello, dear,' Reverend Bowen said. 'Still fancy coming out to take Moses for a walk?'

'Yeah, might as well stretch my legs, eh?' Douglas said with a rueful half-smile.

'Oi, don't forget you've got physio at one, mister,' Linda said, fetching Douglas's tartan blanket and placing it over his lap.

'Yes, Auntie, I remember,' Douglas said.

'You've got the invite?'

Douglas did not reply, but instead held up a colourfully illustrated piece of A5 paper and waved it at Linda.

'Good, good,' she said.

'We won't be too long anyway, Linda,' Bowen said, wheeling Douglas out of her old front door. 'He'll be back in plenty of time.'

'I can manage it back from Kareshi's by myself, you know,' Douglas said with a touch of defiance. 'No point you walking all the way back up here when you live down the other end of the village, now is there?'

'Only if you're sure,' Bowen said.

'Yeah, no worries,' Douglas said.

'Ok, well I'll see you shortly then,' Linda said, giving Douglas's forearm a gentle squeeze. 'See you soon, Hilda.'

Reverend Bowen pushed Douglas out the front door and down the path towards the garden gate. 'I can take it from here,' Douglas said, pushing

160

himself along. Bowen and Moses walked along beside him towards Mill Street and the causeway beyond.

'Is it weird me living in your old house, Hilda?' Douglas asked.

'No, dear, not at all. In fact I'm glad that you are. Do you like it there? Not missing your old place?'

'No,' Douglas said flatly, 'I like it at the vicarage.'

As they approached the top of Mill Street, Douglas saw a figure coming down the causeway. Almost all the trees that lined the village's ancient walkway had shed their leaves, and so Douglas could see quite clearly through the bare, sagging limbs that the man coming towards them was his father. He was also holding a bunch of flowers.

'Right turn, Clyde,' Douglas said, starting to veer away from him.

'Douglas, hang on,' Bowen said, trying to keep pace with Douglas's sudden increase in speed. 'It might be nice to say hello, don't you think?'

It was irrelevant as Bertie had already gained on them sufficiently for it to be anything other than awkward if Douglas had persevered with his getaway. Douglas slipped the template party invitation under his blanket as his father approached them.

'Dougie, Hilda, hi!' Bertie called out, stepping down from the causeway to meet them on the corner of Mill Street. 'Hello, Moses old boy,' he said bending down to stroke the chin of the appreciative King Charles spaniel.

'Hello, Bertie,' Bowen said.

'Hello, son.'

'All right,' Douglas said with minimal enthusiasm.

There was a brief moment of silence that bordered on becoming awkward.

'How did you like the grub the other night?' Bertie asked.

'S'all right, I suppose,' Douglas said. 'Pretty decent. You'll make someone a lovely wife one day.'

Bowen frowned but Bertie smiled.

'Where you off to?' he asked.

'Taking the dog for a walk,' Douglas said. 'Going down the shop.'

'I see. I'm just off to the churchyard,' Bertie said, holding up his flowers. 'Thought I'd pop these on mum's grave.'

'Bit late for all that, isn't it?' Douglas said. Bowen put a hand on his shoulder. 'Have you seen her?'

Bertie did not answer right away. 'No, son, I haven't. I've not seen her, but... I've... well, I know she's around, put it that way.'

Douglas nodded his head but remained silent. 'We've gotta go to the shop,' he said at last. 'And I've got physio later, so...'

'Oh great,' Bertie said. 'How's that all going?'

'Fine. We're gonna be doing a bit of tap dancing later actually,' Douglas said.

Bertie smiled. 'Well, don't let me keep you,' he said.

'Don't worry, we won't,' Douglas said, wheeling himself away down Mill Street.

'Nice to see you, Bertie. They're lovely by the way,' Bowen said, pointing at the flowers.

'Thanks,' he said, 'see you again.'

Bowen caught up with Douglas who was pushing himself down Mill Street at a fair pace.

'Nice flowers, weren't they?' she said, catching up with Douglas, a little out of breath.

'Mmmm,' Douglas replied.

They were approaching the waterfall, where Mill Street turned left into Castle Street. Douglas stopped himself, looking at the rushing water. 'Me and Peter caught a trout in here once,' he said.

'Oh yes?'

'Yeah. Word had gone round the village that there was one in here and me and Peter caught it. It was massive. Big rainbow trout. We took it back to his place and gutted it in the sink. Edna wasn't best pleased with us when she came home and saw the sink full of fish blood and guts.' Douglas smiled.

'You miss him still, don't you?' Bowen said as a statement rather than a question.

Douglas nodded his head. 'Yeah, I do,' he said. 'Not as much as I miss my mum, though.' With that Douglas burst into tears.

162

'It's OK, dear,' Bowen said, rubbing his shoulder. 'It's only natural that you miss them. And it's OK to cry.'

Douglas wiped his eyes with his sleeve. 'Come on, let's go,' he said, pushing himself away from the waterfall and the memory of better days.

'You know what this reminds me of?' Bowen said, walking beside Douglas along Castle Street. 'It reminds me of the day you took Moses. I was walking down here that morning. I stopped here to chat to Terence Russell and his band of not so merry men on my way to the butcher's,' she said, nodding at the neat-looking bungalow with the perfectly manicured garden on their left. 'You know they were all topless while they were rehearsing, it was that hot. You remember how hot it was that day?'

'Bloody boiling,' Douglas said. 'You mean all them old Morris men were dancing around naked? Bit weird, ennit?'

'Not entirely naked, no,' Bowen said. 'Just topless. Still rather unnecessary, though.'

'Weirdos,' Douglas said, carrying on down Castle Street.

'You think Daisy will come to my party?' Douglas said, remembering that he had stowed his template invitation under his blanket as they approached the Carrs' residence a little further down Castle Street. 'Her mum fucking hates me still... sorry,' Douglas said, looking round at Bowen who was smiling. 'She does, though. Who can blame her?'

'It's OK,' Bowen said. 'And yes, I'm sure she will come to the party. I think you and Daisy have cleared up any misunderstandings regarding what happened. The same way that you and I have. You had a good chat to her at the wake, didn't you?'

'Yeah, I did. She said it was OK. I hope it is,' Douglas said as they turned left into Stocks Lane.

'And here we are,' Douglas said, looking over towards the allotments where his rampage back in August had begun. 'D'you think Moses remembers what happened?' he said. 'I mean do dogs have good memories like that, d'you think?'

'He seems to be OK in your company, doesn't he?' Bowen said. 'I'd say he's forgiven you.'

'He probably can't remember anyway. He'd had a few.'

'How so?'

'I gave him some beer out of that crappy old fridge in that old pervo's shed. Sorry. I was wondering if dogs drank beer, so I gave him some and he seemed to like it. Maybe he was too drunk to remember what happened on the railway. I hope so. I didn't mean it. I mean ... I'm glad you and Sergeant Frisk caught me,' Douglas said, looking down at the King Charles spaniel. 'And I'm sorry for hitting you with that bamboo cane.'

'It's OK, dear, we've been over all this, haven't we? Neither of us were exactly behaving rationally, were we?' Bowen said. 'Forgive and forget, hmm?'

'Yeah,' Douglas said, pushing himself with extra exuberance up the incline of the Stocks Lane level crossing.

'Are you OK?' Bowen called out.

'Yep,' Douglas said, powering up the slope and wheeling himself over the railway line.

'Impressive,' Bowen said, catching him up as they both descended the incline on the opposite side.

'Are you going to invite your dad to the party?' Bowen asked, the pair of them now approaching the Crafty Digit pub which was looming up on their left.

'He'll be working it, I expect, won't he?' Douglas said. 'So he'll be there anyway, I suppose.'

'No, I mean are you going to properly invite him?'

Douglas shrugged his shoulders. 'Dunno yet,' he said. '... Could do, I suppose.'

Bowen and Douglas walked the remainder of the way down the causeway, sticking to the path that ran parallel to the causeway itself and on towards the High Street. Once there they turned right towards Kareshi's newsagent where by coincidence the shopkeeper was standing outside moving his swing sign.

'Ahhhh, Mr Blouse, at last I see you, huh?' he said, as Douglas and Reverend Bowen approached the shop.

Douglas did not try to evade the shopkeeper like he did his father. 'Hello, Mr Kareshi,' he said, a touch sheepishly.

'And Mrs Hilda. I am surprised to see you two together after what young bastard here did to you and your dog, huh?'

'I'm sorry for what I did to your window, Mr Kareshi,' Douglas said, getting his apology out straight away and putting the shopkeeper on the back foot a little.

Kareshi remained silent a moment before turning towards his shop window. 'I got new double-glazed pane,' he said, slapping the glass with the flat of his palm. 'Bastard window can withstand 500 pounds of pressure! Do your bloody worst, Mr Blouse, huh!?' he said, throwing back his head and laughing like a villain in a James Bond film.

Douglas remained silent for a moment. 'I won't be doing anything like that again, Mr K, don't worry,' he said. 'I was upset. It was out of order. I didn't mean it. I'm sorry.'

'Well, uhh... maybe we let bygones be bloody bygones, huh?' Kareshi said, his voice becoming slightly less animated. 'I was very sad to hear about your mother. Terrible bloody shame, huh. Lovely woman. So I am also sorry for you too.'

'Thank you,' Douglas said. 'I was wondering, Mr Kareshi...' Douglas hesitated as he began to smile, 'is it OK if I use your photocopier?'

Kareshi raised a highly suspicious eyebrow; there was a brief silence, then they all began to laugh.

*

Five minutes later Douglas and Reverend Bowen left the newsagent's, Douglas now with a clutch of twenty pieces of A4 paper, each with two invitations printed in colour on them.

'I'll chop 'em up when I get home,' Douglas said. 'After physio. Do you think everyone on the list will come? I reckon forty's a bit optimistic, don't you? But Butch said everyone loves a party and that it'll be a good place for me to get reacquainted with people.'

'I think Butch is exactly right,' Bowen said. 'I think it will do you the world of good to get yourself back out there again. Are you sure you don't need me to come back up with you? You sure you'll be OK on your own?'

'I'll be fine, thanks. Before you go, I just want to pop to the garage and get something for mum. Can you give us a push, please? Gary's got an awkward little runner across the door. I probably won't be able to get over it in this bastard thing.'

'Of course, dear.'

Bowen steered Douglas onto the garage forecourt and into the shop where Gary, the lugubrious proprietor, was sat behind the counter reading a newspaper.

'Over there,' Douglas said, nodding towards the rows of pick 'n' mix sweets. Douglas picked out a pink and white striped paper bag before trowelling in a dozen or so pink shrimps. 'They were mum's favourites,' Douglas said, wheeling himself towards the counter and digging some change out of his pocket.

Gary briefly peered over the top of his paper, looking at Douglas's purchase. 'On the 'ouse,' he said, immediately going back to his paper. 'The amount of money your mum put over this counter buying you sweets in the past, it's only fair.' Gary folded his paper in half and put it down on the counter, looking down at Douglas. 'Sorry for your loss, mate,' he said. 'I liked your Alice. Very sweet lady.'

'Thanks,' Douglas said.

'Need any vids while you're here?' Gary asked.

'Mmm, nah, I've seen most of the good ones already,' Douglas said, surveying the wall of rental tapes.

It seemed Douglas now had Gary's full attention.

'That wouldn't have anything to do with that fat bastard Graham Glass, would it by any chance?'

Not wanting to land Graham directly in the shit for his video piracy, Douglas had to think pretty quick. 'No no, it's not that. My Auntie Linda's just got Sky at our new house. Most of them are on there now.'

Gary did not look at all convinced, but he didn't push the matter any further. 'Well, if you do see Mr Glass, you just tell him I'm onto him, OK?'

Douglas smiled and nodded his head. 'OK, will do. Thanks again for the sweets.'

'No worries,' Gary said, returning to his paper.

Reverend Bowen pushed Douglas out of the garage, the sweets and invitations resting in his lap. Once outside, Douglas broke away from her.

'Douglas!' Bowen called after him as he pushed himself towards the petrol pumps. Douglas lifted the unleaded nozzle up and out of its cradle and inserted it between the spokes of his wheelchair just below the top of his right-hand wheel. 'Just gonna fill her up!' he called out, smiling at Bowen who was now starting to laugh. A crackling voice came out over the small speakers of the garage forecourt.

'I think you'll find those things run on diesel,' Gary said from within the shop. Douglas could see him through the window, smiling for once. He replaced the pump and wheeled himself back over to Reverend Bowen. 'Right, I gotta get back or Linda'll smack my arse,' Douglas said. 'Physio in a bit.'

Douglas and Reverend Bowen parted company by the war memorial on the High Street. Hilda led Moses back up towards her new vicarage on the brand new housing estate. Douglas wheeled himself back down the causeway towards her old one.

From his position in the road beside his old primary school, Douglas could see that the barriers of the causeway's level crossing were descending. The warning lights were flashing. He slowed his pace, thinking back to August when he had taken this exact route, only then he had been on foot and covered in tatty white fleece shorn earlier in the day from Butch Ransom's sheep. He had also been carrying a petrol can.

As he slowly approached the level crossing, Douglas's heart sank. His dad was waiting on the other side of the barriers. On seeing him, Bertie waved. Douglas, thinking it too late to attempt another get away, pushed himself up the incline of the crossing, applied the brake to his chair and waited, partially obscured by the wire of the barriers and the barrier itself, choosing not to wave back, instead acting like he had not seen him.

'Bloody 'ell,' he said to himself, 'mum's haunting him and he's haunting me.'

The rails began to hiss. The sound was so evocative for Douglas, reminding him of a life quite literally many moons ago. He looked at the spot on the railway where he'd lost his feet as the train approached from the left, heading towards the west. It was a class 58 diesel engine pulling a long rake of coal wagons. They clattered over the crossing, Douglas habitually counting each wagon as they went. There were 24 in all. As the last one disappeared from view and the barriers rose, Douglas again saw his father, only this time he had no head and appeared to be stumbling about on the level crossing with his arms outstretched, as if trying to locate something. Despite himself, Douglas couldn't help but laugh at his dad's recreation of the Young Ones sketch he had watched so many times over the years. His dad staggered over the rails of the crossing, heading towards him. Douglas could see the gap in between the buttons of his denim jacket where his dad was peeping through, but he went along with the charade nonetheless.

'You took your time, you bastard!' Douglas said, almost involuntarily quoting the line spoken by Vyvyan's decapitated head as his headless father loomed over him. Bertie began to unfasten the buttons of his jacket, revealing his smiling face. He pulled the jacket back down to where it should be conventionally worn.

'Hello, son,' he said. 'How are you doing?'

'All right,' Douglas said. 'It's only been about half an hour.'

Bertie laughed. 'Sorry about that, I couldn't help myself. I saw the videos in your room the other day and I had to give them a watch. "Do not lean out of the window," Bertie said, doing his best Vyvyan impression, "I wonder why?"'

Douglas gave a little smile. 'I want them back at some point,' he said, suddenly realising that his party invitations were on show in his lap. He quickly turned them over, took off the brake and wheeled himself towards the spot where he had seen his mum on the day of the fete. On the big flat stone at the mouth of the causeway's avenue of bare-limbed trees, beside the jar that Daisy had left were another two jars, each also containing a candle. All three jars now appeared to have new tea light candles burning in them.

'I got them from the church just now,' Bertie said. 'I didn't steal them,' he added with quick clarification. 'Hilda said it was OK, I asked her about it the other day. She's got a secret stash. And I put some money in the collection box.'

Bertie looked at the striped pink and white bag in Douglas's lap. 'Are they what I think they are?' he said, nodding at the bag. 'Pink shrimps?'

Douglas nodded his head as the tears began to flow once again. Bertie put a tentative hand on his shoulder.

'Get off,' Douglas said, half-heartedly shrugging away his father's gesture. He wiped his eyes and placed the bag of shrimps on the big stone beside the three jars, the flickering flames dancing inside them.

'Douglas, I'm so sorry,' Bertie said. 'Believe me, I know how angry you must be and I just want you to know that I understand. I...'

'No!' Douglas snapped, 'You don't understand. How could you possibly understand? You weren't here. You don't know what it was like for her or for me. All those nights she spent alone crying. Trying her best not to let me see her when she did. Trying to protect me. Trying to be strong. You know how much time she wasted waiting for you, thinking and hoping that you were gonna come back? Then when you do decide to show up out of nowhere, it's too fuckin' late!'

Douglas stared at the candles, their flickering flames now reflected in the bell-bottomed tears that fell from his eyes.

Bertie knelt down next to Douglas and put a hand on the arm of his wheelchair. 'And do you know how much time I wasted thinking about coming back here, but not being brave enough to do so?' he said. Bertie's eyes had now begun to glaze over also, with his own barely repressed tears. 'I know I left it too late with your mum, and there is not a single part of me that will not regret that for the rest of my days. I think about how things might've been so different if only I'd come back earlier. A year. A month. Even a week. It kills me that I left it as long as I did. Coming back that day and seeing mum...' Bertie paused, wiping his eyes. 'When Alan told me what had happened that day, I thought I'd lost you both, and it almost killed me that I'd left it too late. That I had no way of making things right.'

'Yeah, that's just it, isn't it?' Douglas said. 'You did leave it too late. You fucked up good and proper and now there's no way of putting it right. Well done you.'

Douglas stared intently at the candles' flames, not wanting to look at his father.

'I'd like to think that there might still be a way to make things right, Dougie,' he said, putting a hand on Douglas's forearm. Douglas continued to stare at the candles, as if hypnotised. 'I just wish you'd let me try and prove to you that I'm not the same person who ran out on you all those years ago. That I've changed. And Dougie, whether you like it or not, I am here to stay this time.'

'Yeah, and that's why she can't go, isn't it?!' Douglas shouted, breaking from his trance, rearing up in his chair and staring into the eyes of his father. 'You're back here now and she can't move on. She's stuck here still waiting around for you like she always was. Why can't you just leave us alone and let her go?'

'Douglas, believe me, I want to make things right. For you and for mum.'

'Yeah well, whatever,' Douglas said, releasing the brake from his wheelchair. 'I've gotta get back for physio.' Douglas reversed away from the mouth of the causeway and the candles and the bag of shrimps. So hasty was he in trying to make a swift getaway that he didn't realise the gradient of the road that fell away behind him. 'Fuck it!' he said as he began to lose control of the chair, his hands unable to get a firm grip on the wheels as he rolled backwards, gaining speed and heading towards the black metal railing out the front of nearby Rose Cottage. Bertie sprang to his feet, racing towards Douglas. In the nick of time he managed to grab hold of the chair's rear handles, halting Douglas's progress and preventing him from colliding with the railings. Douglas looked up, startled, into the eyes of his father standing behind him. Bertie was half smiling, half grimacing under the weight of the chair.

'I'm not gonna let you go this time, son,' he said. 'I'm always gonna be here for you.'

Douglas stared up and over his shoulder at his dad, frowning at first. After a moment he smiled. Then he began to laugh.

24 *Sunday, October 3*

It had been another busy service at the Pressed Fruitbowl. After dishing out nearly fifty covers for Sunday lunch, Bertie was now helping clear away glasses and enjoying a well-earned pint when Linda walked into the pub, bag under her arm and Filofax in hand. She clearly meant business. Edna was loading the dirty glasses Bertie had assembled at the end of the bar into the small dishwasher located beneath it. Linda strode purposefully towards them. 'Good afternoon to you both,' she said with a smile. 'How are we doing?'

'Hello, Linda,' Edna said.

'Linda, hi,' Bertie echoed. 'How are you doing? How's Douglas? How was physio?'

'Goodness me, questions questions, Robert,' Linda said, placing her bag on a bar stool and her Filofax on the bar. 'He's OK, Bertie, thank you. Doing well. In fact he's had a bit of good news from the hospital. He's going to be getting his new legs next week.'

'Brilliant,' Bertie said, 'that's excellent news.'

'Indeed. They've been really happy with his progress up at the hospital. The specialist in particular. He'll still be on crutches, of course, but at least it means he'll be back on his feet again,' Linda said with a smile. 'So, I think this calls for a drink. Edna, could I please have a large gin and tonic, seeing as I'm on foot?'

'Physio's been going well then, Linda?' Bertie said as Edna placed the gin and tonic in front of her. 'I saw him the other day. Couple of times actually. First with Reverend Bowen, then by himself by the railway.'

'Yes, he did mention that he saw you,' Linda said, sipping her drink. 'Oooh, lovely,' she added, smiling at Edna who gave her one in return. 'He told me all about your daft Young Ones impression. Sounds like it gave him a bit of a laugh at least.'

Bertie's grin spread across his face like butter on toast.

'For the first time he actually talked quite openly about you. He said about the candles you'd left for Alice. And the shrimps he added to the collection.'

'She used to love them,' Bertie said. 'She'd always come back with a bag of pick 'n' mix if they'd been out for a walk. Always with extra shrimps for her and flying saucers for him.'

They all smiled.

'Now, on the subject of good news and with the big day now barely a month away, it sounds like Douglas has decided what he wants to do for his eighteenth.'

'Oh?' Bertie said, eyebrows raised. 'Which is?'

Linda smiled. 'He wants a party. And he wants to have it here,' she said.

'Really?' Bertie said, sounding as surprised as he looked.

'Yep. He wants to have his first proper, *legal* drink.'

'That's great, Linda,' Bertie said. 'Is he gonna want me out the way? I mean ... how's that gonna work?'

'On the contrary, Robert,' Linda said, delving into her bag and placing a colourful piece of paper on the bar. 'He asked me to give you this.'

Bertie grinned from ear to ear, seeing the party invitation with his name written at the top in the Iron Maiden font. 'So this is what he was up to the other day,' he said. 'I saw he had them, but I didn't want to ask him about them. He was pretty quick to hide them when he noticed he'd left them on display.' Bertie laughed, reading the invite. '"Come and get completely legless at Douglas's 18th!"' They all laughed. 'And music themed fancy dress as well!?'

'Blimey, he must be on the mend,' Edna said, pouring a pint for a nearby customer.

'To be honest, I think he's been spending entirely too much time with Butch,' Linda said, rolling her eyes but smiling as she did so. 'And you giving him that AC/DC album might've helped a bit as well. He's been playing it quite a lot. I hear him playing along sometimes too, on that old guitar you gave him. He's very good at picking out a tune, you know? He's been playing a lot of guitar, and his CD collection has expanded, mostly at my expense, I might add. Still, it's worth it to see him happy, and it keeps his mind occupied. He still plays Alice's records a lot. And he still cries, but there's a lot of upbeat stuff I hear coming out of his room now too, which is encouraging.'

'That's good,' Bertie said. 'But he still has his dark days, does he?'

'Oh yes, he's by no means out of the woods yet. He still says he's an emotional liability,' Linda said wistfully, sipping her gin and tonic. 'But then I hear him giggling away in his room again for seemingly no apparent reason. Strange. Still, I suppose it's a symptom of his condition. They've always insisted as much up at the hospital, so I'm not overly worried. I ask him about it, but he can be very reticent on the subject. He locks himself away and pulls the shutter down some days. Literally and figuratively. It's an impenetrable defence system that he's developed to avoid getting hurt again, I think. Sometimes he'd rather just not open up to anyone. They think it's a pretty deep-seated psychological state. His counsellor tends to agree, though he's a lot better than he was, that's for sure. Having Butch around has been good for him, though. Another male influence. Plus Butch knows what it's like to lose someone you love. And he's been very encouraging about the party. I think it's what finally made Douglas want to go ahead with it. That and the dressing up of course,' Linda said, laughing and shaking her head. 'So much so that Butch has promised to dust off the old sewing machine for the occasion.'

'He seems like a really nice bloke,' Bertie said.

'Yes,' Linda said. 'Yes, he is.'

'I think a party is a great idea,' Bertie said. 'I can't tell you how chuffed I am with this,' he said, holding up the invite. 'And I want to make the cake,' Bertie declared assertively, 'if that's OK with you, of course?'

'A bold statement indeed, sir,' Linda said. 'I was going to buy one.'

'Save your money,' Bertie said. 'I'm on it. I've got hidden talents, haven't I, Edna?'

'Haven't you just,' she said.

'There are a lot of satisfied stomachs in this village since I started rattling them pots 'n' pans,' Bertie said. 'I'll do another buffet too, if you like? I mean if that's what Douglas would like? I'll jazz it up a bit too. Make it nice and special. Bit of posh nosh.'

'Well, if you're sure?' Linda said, sounding a little taken aback by it all.

'Absolutely,' Bertie said.

'You've got a lot to live up to in the cake department, following in Alice's footsteps,' Edna said. 'God, she could knock up a good birthday cake. Made my efforts look like a load of rubbish.'

'Well, I'm gonna give it a bloody good go!' Bertie said. 'In fact I got the idea for it when we were taking those posters down in his room. He's a big Iron Maiden fan, right?'

'If what I hear pounding out of his room is anything to go by, yes,' Linda said. 'It's Butch who mainly tells me who's who, but I'm actually starting to become a bit of an aficionado myself. Between the two of them there's not much they don't know about music, and as a natural consequence it's starting to rub off on me. Ohh, speaking of which, there needs to be music at the party, obviously. I've been given the name of a local DJ by someone in the village.' Linda opened her Filofax, scanning down the page. 'A Mr Tony Gables?'

Behind the bar Edna started laughing. Contagiously it spread to Bertie, who also started to giggle.

'Apparently he used to be on the radio, lives in the village and still does the odd private function... Sorry, have I said something funny?' Linda asked, looking at the two of them.

'No,' Edna said, 'well, sort of. It's just, well, Tony's got a bit of a reputation around here. And he didn't exactly cover himself in glory at the fete back in August either. Though he did manage to cover his turntables in sick,' Edna said, her shoulders now hitching with laughter. 'That little display came in bloody handy, actually. He'd had too much of that stuff,' she said, nodding at the gleaming row of optics behind her. 'To be fair, though, I hear he's actually sorted himself out since then. Apparently he doesn't touch the booze any more. Now attending meetings and everything. I think they were Karen's terms for taking him back. He's a changed man now he's back with her, so don't write him off just yet. Give him a call. And speak to Butch, too. Him and Tony always used to get on pretty well. He'll probably know more about it than I do.'

'Oh, OK,' Linda said. 'I'll sound him out before I make any final decision on the matter then.'

'So how many are coming to the party then?' Bertie said.

'Well, we've handed out around thirty invitations to people in the village,' Linda said. 'Most of them are Douglas's old school friends that he'd lost contact with. It'll be a good way for him to re-establish those connections. We've seen a few of them around the place when we've been out on our "walks",' Linda said. 'A lot of them were actually pretty in awe of Douglas after what he did at the fete. It would appear that he's actually seen as a bit of a local legend around here. They're all for coming to his party. Some people come by their popularity by rather unconventional means, it would seem, but personally speaking, if it makes him happy, I'll take it. Oh Edna, sorry, here's your and Graham's invitation as well.'

'Thanks,' Edna said. 'See if he can manage to drag himself away from the telly for one night.'

'Oh, and he's invited Daisy Carr,' Linda said with a little cough, raising a hand to her mouth that half covered her smile.

'Bloody hell, good on him,' Edna said. 'And Petra's gonna let her go?'

'Daisy's eighteen already, and she's living life large at a posh drama school in London, according to Douglas. I don't think Petra has that much jurisdiction over her any more. Again, it was Butch who gave him the proverbial nudge in the ribs to ask her. We thought it would be a good idea to pop round and see Petra and give her the invitation in person for her to pass on. Douglas, bless him, he apologised again for what he did. I think spending time with Hilda is rubbing off on him. All this forgiveness business.'

'Amen to that,' Bertie said, smiling down at his invitation.

176

'I went back later to see Petra by myself to have a little chat with her, woman to woman, about the fete. I made it clear to her who knows what about certain events, shall we say, that transpired that day. And how those people might be prepared to forget certain things under certain circumstances. She was a little testy at first, but I think she eventually got the message. Wouldn't want to tarnish her impeccable reputation around these here parts, would we?' Linda said, smiling.

'Yeah, she's no saint,' Edna said, 'believe me.'

'I don't doubt it,' Linda replied. 'And finally, obviously with his birthday being on November the fifth, we thought it only right that we have fireworks, so Butch is going to get on the case there and we'll have ourselves a little display out in the beer garden, if that's ok?' Linda said, looking at Edna. 'Could you maybe have a word with... is it Terry? The landlord? Make sure that it's OK with him to do so. Tell him I'll be in to see him soon with some cash to put down as a deposit for it all as well.'

'OK,' Edna said, 'I'm sure it'll be fine.'

'Well, I think that concludes our business,' Linda said, closing her Filofax and putting it in her bag. 'It looks like it's shaping up to be quite the occasion. Now,' she said, finishing her drink, 'I must be going. I'll be in touch. Cheerio for now.'

'Tarrah,' Edna said.

'Bye, Linda, speak to you soon,' Bertie said, watching her go.

The pub was now virtually empty. Bertie looked at Edna, and they both smiled. Bertie carefully folded up his invite and put it in his back pocket. He walked behind the bar towards Edna. Walking behind her, he caressed the small of her back as he made his way over to the Morland Original beer pump. 'I think this calls for a little celebration, don't you?' he said, filling a pint glass with foamy brown beer, a smile that looked like it would have to be surgically removed fixed to his face. 'That was always one of the great things about Dougie's birthday being on bonfire night,' he said, sipping his pint. 'You're always guaranteed fireworks.'

25

Bertie walked Edna back to Bargus Close as the last of the evening's daylight faded away into the black of night. After the rush of Sunday lunch, the pub kitchen was now officially closed for the evening, so neither Bertie's nor Edna's services were required; Sunday night was generally a quiet time when someone other than Edna could easily pull the pints single-handedly.

Edna opened the door to number 4 Bargus Close and Bertie followed her in. Graham was, as usual, in his armchair in front of the television. On the screen an out of focus dinosaur was roaring in what looked like some kind of smashed up leisure centre, with a banner flailing and falling around it as triumphant music played.

'*Jurassic Park!*' Graham said, turning towards Edna and Bertie. 'Pretty bloody good 'n' all. I can see why it's coining it in at the cinema. Spielberg's only gone and done it again, the beardy little fucker!' Graham turned back to the television. 'Bring any grub back, either of you?'

'Nothing left, mate. All gone,' Bertie said. 'My Sunday roasts were flying out of that kitchen.'

'Bloody starving,' Graham said, rubbing his enormous gut that was spilling out the bottom of his polo shirt.

'There's a surprise,' Edna said, taking her shoes off.

'How did you manage to get that then?' Bertie said, nodding at the screen, on which the credits had started to roll. 'Hasn't it only just come out?'

'My mate Ken Bevan up to his old tricks again, boy!' Graham said with a big smile on his face. 'He went in there with his video camera under his coat. Just sat there and filmed it right there in the cinema.'

'That makes sense,' Bertie said, watching as silhouetted film-goers were getting up from their seats and heading out of shot.

'Probably gonna have to pull an all-nighter. Got that lot to get through!' Graham said, nodding at a stack of blank video cassettes almost three feet tall beside him. He shifted his weight in the armchair, a very wet sounding fart that nobody acknowledged escaping him as he did so. 'Got a queue of customers a bloody mile long for this bugger. Gary ain't gonna 'ave it down the garage for months yet, and thanks to me by the time he does everyone round here will have seen the bastard. Should make a nice bit of wonga off this. Easy bloody money!'

Edna sighed, pouring herself a drink.

'Well, I've got some pretty good news of my own,' Bertie said, enlivened by the two pints of bitter he had quaffed in little under ten minutes before leaving the pub.

'Oh yeah?' Graham said, extricating himself from the chair with considerable effort and going over to fiddle with the video recorder. His massive rear end blocked the television, looking like the back end of a Mini wrapped in blue denim.

'Yeah, Douglas's 18th,' Bertie said with a broad grin. 'He's having it up the pub, and guess who's invited?'

'Me hopefully, if your sister-in-law's sticking another load of cash behind the bar,' Graham said, ejecting a tape from the bottom deck of his Amstrad double-decker.

'Well yeah, you and Edna are both invited as it goes ... And so am I!'

'Oh arr?' Graham said absently, still fiddling around by the television. 'Patched things up with him then, have you?'

'To be honest, mate, I'm not sure, but from what Linda was saying down the pub just now, it certainly sounds quite encouraging. I think I might have turned a corner with him. And if all goes to plan down in Bridgend, I might just have a nice little surprise for him come the big night.'

'You sticking to your plan then, are you, Bert? Bridgend 'n' all that?' Graham said, rewinding the *Jurassic Park* tape.

'Too right I am. If that lying dragon thinks for one minute that I'm going back there to play happy families, then she's got another thing coming. Mind you, after what I've been telling her, that's exactly what she's expecting to happen, and I'm more than happy to play along until that prize money is in my back pocket and I'm back on the M4 and far far away from that dump forever. I've told her that we'll spend the prize money on a once in a lifetime trip to Las Vegas and for her to pack something white,' Bertie said, beginning to laugh. 'I said the next time we make love, it's going to be as husband and wife and not a moment before. Consummate the marriage in a plush hotel room overlooking the strip.'

'Sounds like you've got it all planned out, boy,' Graham said, lowering himself back into his armchair with a grunt and a groan.

'You know, for the first time since I came back here, I actually feel like things might turn out all right. Please don't say anything to Douglas about Bridgend,' Bertie said, looking from Graham in his chair to Edna who was quietly smoking a cigarette at the breakfast bar behind him. 'I've told Linda that I'm going up to visit my brother for the weekend while this medium fella does his thing down at the bungalow.'

'I just hope you know what you're doing,' Edna said. 'What about that other fella? That kid's real dad?'

'Oh yeah, Dai. Well, I'll probably be playing him somewhere on route to becoming amateur open darts champion of South Wales. He's pretty handy and he'll be gunning for me no doubt, if he knows I'm in the tournament. I told Rhonda about how my game's been improving. But as far as them and their kid and their fucked up little lives go, I honestly couldn't care less. I feel sorry for the kid, but that's not my concern any more. Douglas is, and that's what I've got to focus on now. That and keeping my darts nice and straight.'

'You've been gone for a while now,' Edna said. 'And you're saying you're just gonna waltz back into her life? She's bound to be suspicious.'

'She thinks I'm still up at my brother's. She hasn't got a clue I've come back here. I doubt she could even spell Steventon, let alone be able to find it on a map. She's Bridgend to the core. I bet the only time she's left the place was to go on Bullseye back in '87, and even then she probably took her passport with her, the dozy cow.'

180

'Glad you got it all figured out, boy,' Graham said, the whirring of the rewinding video now ceasing as he began the recording process again. 'Chuck us a beer, woman,' he said, glancing over at Edna.

'She opened the fridge. 'There aren't any.'

'Bollocks,' Graham said, letting out a grumbling sigh and fishing around in his pocket, extracting a crumpled ten pound note.

'I thought you were skint?' Edna said.

'Emergency,' Graham replied, beginning the long-drawn-out process of getting back to his feet. 'Kareshi'll still be open. I'm not doing that lot with a thirst on,' he said, nodding at the giant stack of tapes. 'Hang about for one?' he said, looking at Bertie. 'I won't be a minute. Unless you fancy going down there for me of course?' Graham said, looking at Edna.

'No, I don't,' she said.

'There's a surprise,' Graham said, putting on his jacket, opening the door, turning sideways and heading out into the cold night air, closing the door with a soft grunt behind him.

Bertie pulled back the curtain a little, watching Graham toddle off towards the shop. 'When I get back from Bridgend, I want you to leave him, Edna,' he said, standing by the door. 'He doesn't deserve you. He's a slob and a bastard and I want you to come and live with me.'

Edna stared into Bertie's eyes, her drink now forgotten on the side.

Bertie took a seat on the sofa. 'Edna, come here,' he said, patting the faded pink cushion beside him.

Edna tentatively got to her feet and joined Bertie on the sofa. He gently took her hand in his. 'I mean it, Edna. As soon as all this Bridgend bullshit is over, I want to start again. Not just with Douglas ... with you too,' he said, holding her gaze steady. 'Over the past month or so I've really begun to understand why Alice loved you the way she did.'

Edna's eyes misted over. 'She was like a sister to me,' she said, her voice faltering slightly.

'Edna, I messed things up with Alice, and I never got the chance to make things right with her. That's a regret I've got to live with for the rest of my life. I don't want to live with any more regrets.'

For a moment neither of them spoke. Edna looked down at her trembling hand in Bertie's.

'What do you say?' Bertie said.

Edna looked up into Bertie's eyes as he moved a little closer to her, giving her a gentle kiss on the cheek that she made no attempt to refuse. She turned to face him and Bertie moved in closer and their lips met: soft and tenderly at first, but exponentially increasing in passion as their suppressed emotions rose to the surface.

As they kissed and embraced on the sofa, neither of them was aware of the little red light glowing beneath the messy pile of video cassettes beside the television.

26 *Friday, October 15*

'Do you think it will be enough?' Linda asked, surveying the roll of crushed red velvet at the end of the kitchen table where she, Butch and Douglas were eating lunch together.

'Oh yeah, easily,' Butch said. 'You got the lining as well, yes?'

'Yis,' Linda said with a little laugh. 'It's rolled up inside the roll of velvet. Are you quite sure you're up to this?'

'Are you questioning my textile abilities as well as taking the piss out of my accent?' Butch said, dipping a piece of crusty bread into his home-made leek and potato soup.

'Oh, as if I would,' Linda said.

'You saw the Little Bo Peep dress he made for the fete, didn't you?' Douglas said. 'Pervert,' he added, grinning.

'Indeed,' Linda said. 'No no, I'm quite sure you'll pull it off.'

'Nah, it'll be sweet. All I gotta do is get young Douglas's measurements there,' Butch said, winking at Douglas. 'Then it'll be pedal to the metal on the sewing machine.'

'32 inch waist, 14 inch leg,' Douglas said with a wry smile.

Linda tutted. 'Not for much longer, mister,' she said, pointing a finger at her nephew.

'The party's three weeks today, right?' Butch said. 'I'll be able to knock that out by then, easy. It's gonna be nowhere near as hard as the Little Bo Peep dress. Jacket and shorts, mate, it'll be a doddle. Another Ransom original creation come to life. We'll have you looking every inch the rock god come party time, don't you worry about that.'

'Don't forget the hat,' Douglas said.

'Oh yeah, better make sure we keep some material back for that little bugger, eh?'

'Thanks, Uncle Butch,' Douglas said. 'When are you going to learn to knit so you can make me some woolly jumpers like mum used to?'

'Hey, you might jest, but don't think that hasn't crossed my mind, mate,' Butch said with a little chuckle. 'In fact, me and Barb were having a chat and a cuppa the other week down the shop when that very subject came up. I mean, with my wool and her expertise it could be a real money-spinner. I even came up with a great name to use if we did ever want to diversify into that area. You wanna hear the name of my shop?' he said, smiling expectantly.

'Go on,' Linda said with an air of trepidation.

'Sheep and Shearful,' Butch said, leaning back in his chair, wearing a broad smile.

'Urrhh, goodness me,' Linda said, shaking her head.

'What? It's a great name!' Butch said, looking a tad perplexed. 'At least I thought so. Come on, back me up here, mate,' he said, looking at Douglas.

'It's quite clever, I suppose,' Douglas said. 'Tell me, Uncle Butch, all this sewing and knitting and all the cooking you do around here, not to mention your previous for dressing up, when exactly was it you decided you wanted to be a woman?'

'Douglas,' Linda said only half admonishingly, unable to hold back the laugh that undermined her attempted authority.

Butch laughed too. 'As I've said before, mate, it does you no harm to get in touch with your feminine side. Especially if you wanna make it with the likes of Daisy Carr. The chicks love a guy with hidden depths. It took me ages to get the hang of that bloody sewing machine when Barbara first gave it to me, but I got there in the end, and the day I finished that dress for the fete was one of the most satisfying moments of my life. Like you and that guitar of yours. Not just anybody can play as good as you do without lessons, y'know? It's a natural gift, mate, be thankful for it. You never know when you might have to serenade some lucky young lady, eh? Like I said, mate, hidden depths.'

'I'll be lucky to serenade anyone at this rate,' Douglas said gloomily.

'Ohhh dear, making you wait, is she?' Butch asked.

'Who?' Douglas replied.

'Bloody who?' Butch said, tearing off another piece of bread. 'Daisy, obviously.'

'Yeah. She still hasn't replied to my invitation,' Douglas said gloomily. 'She probably isn't coming.'

'More like too cool for school to reply, mate. She'll probably just rock up on the night and knock you off your feet.' Butch smiled. 'No pun intended, eh?'

Outside came the sound of a car pulling up. A short while later there was a knock on the door.

'Good timing,' Linda said with a sigh, getting up from the table.

From the kitchen, Douglas could hear mumbled conversation before Linda came back into the kitchen. 'It's for you, Douglas. Graham Glass. Says he's got a couple of videos for you.'

Douglas reversed away from the kitchen table and wheeled himself down the darkened hallway towards the front door, where Graham's mass was eclipsing almost everything behind it.

'All right, champ?' Graham said brightly. 'How you doing?'

'OK thanks,' Douglas said. 'Getting pretty sick of being in this thing, but at least it won't be for much longer. I'm getting my new legs next week.'

'So I hear, mate, so I hear,' Graham said, rocking back on his heels. 'That'll be good, won't it? Get you back on your feet again. Looking forward to the party then?'

'Yeah, sort of. I'm going as Angus Young,' Douglas said. 'My Auntie Linda brought a load of material for the outfit. Butch is gonna make it for me using his sewing machine. Are you and Edna coming?'

'You bet, mate. Wouldn't miss it.'

'Will you be coming with my dad?' Douglas asked, his voice taking on a slightly more cautionary tone.

'Not sure to be honest, mate,' Graham said frowning. 'I've not seen him for a while. Plus I've been pretty busy with work. Last time I saw your dad he was round ours talking about going back to Bridgend, as it goes.'

'What?' Douglas said, his face darkening.

185

'Yeah, he wasn't specific about it or anything, but I'm pretty sure that's where he said he was going.'

Douglas's eyes had taken on a vacant, faraway look. 'He's going back to Bridgend? To that Welsh tart?' he said.

'Like I said, mate, I'm not sure. But he hasn't been answering the phone at your old place. Or the door for that matter. I went round to see if he fancied a game of darts yesterday, but there was no answer. Car's gone too.'

'What did Edna say?' Douglas asked, his voice beginning to sound pained, his hand rhythmically slapping the armrest of his wheelchair. 'Has he finished at the pub or what? She'll know, won't she?'

'She said she doesn't know either, mate. But listen, maybe I've got the wrong end of the stick, eh? Maybe it's nothing. Don't worry about it, eh? And hey, look, I got you this,' Graham said, placing a video cassette in Douglas's lap. *Jurassic Park*, you'll bloody love it. And here's your mags,' he added, placing a copy each of *Kerrang* and WWF magazine on top of the video. 'I was in Kareshi's earlier and he said your dad hadn't been in to get them, so I said I'd take them for you.'

Douglas's jaw was clenched and his knuckles were white, gripping the arms of his wheelchair. 'Cheers,' he said absently through gritted teeth.

'Anyway, mate, just wanted to say thanks for the invite and to give you that little lot. Look forward to seeing you at the party, yeah?'

Douglas remained silent.

'Well, I best be going,' Graham said breezily. 'Got a lot of work to be getting on with. I thought I might stop in on Peter while I'm up this way as well,' he said, nodding towards the churchyard.

'Yeah, OK,' Douglas said blankly, reversing back into the hallway. 'Bye.'

'See you th...'

The sound of the front door slamming cut off the end of Graham's sentence. It was swiftly followed by a second door closing, this time the one to Douglas's bedroom. Outside Graham ambled down the garden path and back to his car, wearing a smile of smug satisfaction on his face. Despite what he'd said, he decided against visiting his son's grave. Instead he squeezed back into his car and drove away whistling tunelessly. He would have been hard-pushed to remember where exactly Peter was buried anyway.

27

Douglas's soup was going cold on the kitchen table as Linda and Butch continued to knock on his bedroom door. It wasn't the sound of the doors slamming shut that alarmed Linda and Butch at first; nor was it the sound of the thrash metal coming on the stereo at full blast. It was the sound of the loud crashing noise that followed shortly after that finally made them abandon their own lunch and go rushing to his door.

'Why won't it open, for God's sake?' Linda said, trying to make herself heard over the wailing guitar solo coming from inside while trying to barge the door open with her shoulder. 'The bloody thing doesn't have a lock on it, for crying out loud.'

'Come on, mate,' Butch said, giving the door a shove himself, and trying to appeal to Douglas inside. 'Whatever it is, let's have a chat about it, eh?'

'What must Graham have said to him?' Linda said, looking disconcertingly at Butch. 'God, he's been doing so well recently. What the bloody hell happened?'

'Why don't I go out front and see if I can get a look through his window,' Butch said, before leaving the house. A few moments later Butch stuck his head round the front door, nodding for Linda to come outside. She followed and went with him to Douglas's bedroom window. Inside, Douglas was sitting in his chair, parked in front of his bedroom door with tears running down his face. His acoustic guitar was broken in two pieces lying on the floor beside him. He didn't appear to register either of them, despite their persistent knocking on the window.

'Douglas, come on, sweetheart, open the door and tell us what's wrong,' Linda said, trying to maintain a level of composure that she didn't feel.

'Come on, mate, what's wrong?' Butch said. 'What did Graham say?'

Beyond the window, like a museum piece come to life, Douglas reared up in his chair. 'He's fucked off again!' he bellowed. 'All right? He's gone back to Bridgend to be with that tart and made mugs out of the lot of us... a-fucking-gain!'

'I need to get to the bottom of this,' Linda said. 'Can you please stay with him, Butch? Keep talking to him. See if you can get him to come out.'

'Sure.'

'Where does Graham live?' she asked.

'Bargus Close. Mobile home type place off the causeway, up towards the High Street. I'm pretty sure theirs is number 4.'

'I know where you mean,' Linda said, going back into the house to retrieve her keys from the bowl on the sideboard. Butch followed on behind her. 'I'll try and find out what the hell this is all about,' she said, heading for the car.

*

Linda reversed off the driveway and headed down the causeway, gaining speed as she did so. As she approached the level crossing, the red warning lights began to flash. 'Oh bugger off,' she said, hitting the accelerator, going up and over the railway line, watching the barriers descend in her rear-view mirror from the other side.

She turned into Bargus Close and pulled up next to Graham's car, got out and walked briskly towards number 4, hearing the noise coming from within before she got close. She knocked with some force on the front door. The sound of the television blaring away inside gave Douglas's music a run for its money. She knocked for a good few minutes before trying the door handle. It was locked. She spoke with a neighbour to make sure she had the right place. The neighbour assured her that she had, whilst also making a pointless complaint to her about the noise levels she often heard coming from number 4. Linda suddenly thought about Edna, remembering the second job she had in the kitchen up at the primary school. She checked her watch. It was twenty to two. With any luck Edna would still be there.

Linda got back in her car and made the short journey up the causeway to the primary school. Given the amount of children running around outside, it looked like lunchtime might be over and playtime was in full swing: the children working off the meal that Edna would have served them a short while ago. Given the pressing circumstances, Linda decided to forego the formality of reporting to reception, choosing instead to take the direct approach and walking straight round to the dinner hall itself which was situated at the rear of the school, close to the large domed steel climbing frame that dominated the playground. Through an open window she saw the unmistakable sphere of Edna's hair. Linda made her way towards the window, swathing a path through a group of giggling children. She poked her head into the steamy kitchen, greeted by the enticing smell of shepherd's pie. Edna was at the sink, her arms submerged in steaming foamy water.

'Edna!' Linda called out.

Edna turned and took her arms out of the water, revealing a pair of marigolds that almost reached her elbows. 'Linda, what are you doing here?' Edna said, sounding a little confused. 'If you're hungry, I'm afraid lunchtime's finished.'

Linda gave a thin smile in an attempt to mask the anxiety she was feeling. 'No no, it's nothing like that. I err ...' she said, unsure of how to proceed. 'We umm, well we just had a visit.'

Edna peeled off her washing up gloves, giving Linda her full attention.

'It was from your Graham,' Linda said.

Edna shook her head with a humourless chuckle. 'My Graham? That's a good one,' she said.

Linda frowned. 'Graham is your husband, though, isn't he?'

'I'm afraid so,' she said. 'Come round to the front, the doors are open. We've got judo in here later, but Jim won't be in to set up for a little while yet.'

Linda did as she was instructed and made her way round to the double doors of the dining hall. The smell of shepherd's pie was still present, only now it was mixed with the smell of anti-bacterial disinfectant. Linda strode through the hall and into the kitchen. Edna was standing next to a kettle that had just begun to boil.

'So what's this all about?' she said. 'What's he done?'

Linda took a breath. 'We're not sure exactly,' she said. 'He wasn't really there for long. He had some bits for Douglas: a video and his magazines from the shop.'

'He took Douglas his magazines?' Edna asked. 'Bertie told Kareshi yesterday to hang on to them for when he got back. He was gonna go down there and collect them and give them to you after the weekend. Bloody Graham,' Edna said with disdain. 'So then what happened?'

'Well, after he left, Douglas proceeded to barricade himself in his room with his wheelchair parked up against the door. We went round to the window and saw that he'd also smashed his guitar. He was in tears. He didn't say anything at first, then all of a sudden he started shouting about how his dad had gone back to Wales to be with that woman.'

'Shhhhit,' Edna said, slamming her balled fist down on the metallic work surface she was leaning up against.

'Why would he say that, Edna? Bertie's been trying so hard to rebuild his relationship with Douglas, and I thought he was actually starting to get somewhere. Why would he just up and leave now? It just doesn't make any sense.'

Edna said nothing at first, just quietly shook her head as the kettle came to the boil. 'The big-mouthed sod,' she said, taking two clean mugs out of a cupboard.

'Bertie's gone up to see his brother this weekend,' Linda said, 'so's to be out of the way when that medium chap comes round to the house on Sunday. And he said he might have a darts tournament up there too.' Linda levelled her gaze at Edna. 'If you know different, Edna, then now would definitely be a very good time to say so.'

Outside a bell began to ring. The screams and shouts of playtime reached a crescendo before dying down, eventually ceasing altogether as the clock struck two pm.

'He has gone back to Bridgend,' Edna said at last.

191

Linda put a hand to her mouth. 'Oh God,' she said.

'But it's not what you think,' Edna quickly cut in. 'He's got no intention of getting back together with Rhonda. He's... well...'

'Edna?' Linda said, eyebrows raised.

'Bloody Graham!' Edna said. 'Big-mouthed sod.' Edna composed herself, taking a deep breath. 'The darts tournament's not up north, it's in Bridgend. That's why he's gone. It's a big open amateur tournament held every year at the pub he used to run with that Rhonda woman. He didn't want Douglas to know about it, for obvious reasons. He went yesterday. He was hoping he could get there and back without Douglas knowing about any of it. Obviously that fat blabbermouth has well and truly put paid to that idea. But I'm telling you, honestly, Bertie's not getting back together with Rhonda. He's coming back. He's ...'

Edna trailed off.

'Edna?' Linda said, watching Edna spoon coffee into the mugs.

'You want sugar?'

'Edna?' Linda repeated. 'Bertie's coming back here to be with you, isn't he.' It wasn't a question.

Edna hovered the sugar-laden teaspoon over the mug, her hand shaking slightly. Some granules spilt over the side onto the kitchen work surface.

'Yes,' she said, finally tipping the sugar into the mug. 'Yeah, he is. No point in trying to deny it, I suppose.'

'Not really,' Linda said with a wan smile.

'I never planned for it to happen,' Edna said. 'It just ... well, it just did.'

'As is so often the case. I for one can vouch for that,' Linda said.

Edna gave a little laugh. 'You've done well there,' she said, handing Linda her coffee. 'And I was only trying to keep my promise to Alice,' Edna said, blowing her own coffee before taking a tentative sip, 'then things just happened.'

'How do you mean?' Linda said. 'What promise?'

Edna paused, taking a breath. 'I got a message,' she said eventually, 'from Alice.'

'A message?' Linda said, frowning. 'When?'

'Not long after Bertie came back. He was still kipping at ours. I wasn't happy about it, but Graham insisted. Bertie broke the news to me about Alice the first night he was there. That was the day of the fete. I was heartbroken. So was Bertie, by the looks of him, but I was still too busy thinking what an idiot he was to have too much sympathy for him. But Jesus, Linda, what he came back to that day. I think the technical term for such a situation is a cluster fuck,' Edna said.

'Sounds about right,' Linda said.

'Anyway, the following Monday I went to the spiritualist church, the one I've been going to on and off for the past year and a half, since...' Edna hesitated, taking in a deep breath, 'since I lost Peter,' she said. 'Anyway, as soon as the medium came on stage, he was looking at me. I knew something was coming. He did the opening address, and all the usual stuff; opened the circle. Then he points at me and smiles, and you know what he says?'

Linda shook her head.

'School dinners,' Edna said, grinning. 'No hanging about, eh?'

Linda laughed. 'That's weird. So what was this message Alice had for you?'

'She said she was...' Edna paused, composing herself. She swallowed, despite the lump in her throat and tried again. 'Alice said she was sorry.' Edna gave a sad smile. '"Sorry for leaving you in the lurch, Eddie" were her exact words. She often called me Eddie.' Edna took a deep breath. 'God, I miss that woman.'

Linda put a hand of reassurance on Edna's arm and smiled. 'Me too,' she said.

'Then it was more of a request really,' Edna continued. 'She said she wanted me to help Douglas and Bertie reconcile their differences. To do whatever I could to help them sort their shit out. She didn't quite put it like that, but that was the jist of it. The medium said that Alice couldn't truly be at peace until it was done. Of course to start with I thought she'll be waiting a while for them to sort themselves out. But then things started happening. You saying he could stay at the bungalow, for one.'

'That was only really possible thanks to you getting him the job down the pub.'

'Yeah, exactly. Coincidence? Our chef walks out just as Bertie walks back in.'

'So you had a word.'

'Yes. Just keeping my promise,' Edna said. 'And what about the vicarage coming up for sale when it did, huh? Another little coincidence?'

'It was pretty fortuitous, I guess,' Linda said.

'Yeah, not 'alf,' Edna said. 'Then Bertie and me started to become...closer. Obviously working together played a big part in that. But so did Graham,' Edna said, returning to her original source of displeasure.

'Does Graham know? ... About the two of you?'

Edna shook her head. 'We've been pretty discreet,' she said. 'And we haven't... y'know, we haven't done anything. We've just grown rather fond of one another, I suppose. It sounds mad, I know, and like I say I never intended for it to happen. I do honestly think Bertie's changed. He was a broken man when he turned up at ours that day. He was racked with guilt and full of remorse. He was completely broken down. Making amends for what he did to Douglas and to Alice, and winning this tournament, hopefully, is his way of starting the rebuilding process. He's doing it all for Douglas.'

'But what's this Rhonda woman going to say when he appears just as out of the blue down there as he did when he came back here?'

'She's expecting him. They've had a few chats on the phone together. He's told her that he's prepared to forget about what happened, you know, about her and that kid that she told Bertie was his. Told her that his dartitis has pretty much cleared up. She's told him that this Dai fella, he's the kid's real father, she said that he's been a bastard to her. Bertie told her they're gonna make a fresh start with the winnings and go to Las Vegas. It was the only thing he could think to do to make sure he could get down there and play and try and get everything to go according to plan.'

'This all sounds very murky, Edna. Not to mention a trifle dangerous. I mean, what's going to happen when, if, Bertie wins and then does a runner with the cash?'

'As far as Rhonda knows, Bertie's been living in Yorkshire with his brother. He told her about a phony job he's got up there and everything. She hasn't got a clue about this place. I'm not sure if Bertie ever even told her he was married, or about Douglas for that matter. Bertie admitted what a bastard he was when he left here. Meeting Rhonda was just lust at first sight, as he put it. Darts was such a big part of his life back then, and it all just snowballed. Before he knew it, he was shacked up with her and was co-owner of a failing pub. The darts tournament is one of their only real big money-spinners. Rhonda's uncle is one of the organisers or someting. She's tried wrecking the place with her karaoke nights apparently, but Bertie's grub kept them going. Now he's gone, I think they're properly in the shit; and the prospect of him going back there to potentially win a shitload of cash and get back with her was obviously too good an opportunity for her to pass up.'

Linda took a deep breath, processing all the new information. 'So what should I tell Douglas about all this? He's the one that's caught up in the middle of it, after all. And what about this medium chap on Sunday? Do you think we should go ahead with it? I don't want Douglas any more upset than he already is. He hasn't even been back to his old place since Alice died, and he's been doing really well with his physio and convalescence. I'm worried all this drama might put a big spanner in the works. Yet on the other hand, he does still talk about Alice a lot. Perhaps he does need some sort of closure on the subject.' Linda exhaled deeply. 'What do you think, Edna?'

Edna drained her coffee and put the mug in the sink. 'Linda, I've been going to that spiritualist church ever since I lost my Peter. I say since I lost him, because some days it's as if Graham hasn't even noticed that Peter's gone. Or that he existed in the first place. We've drifted so far apart it's like living with a fat, drunk stranger. The man is toxic, ignorant, selfish and narrow-minded and I can't be around that any more. Him going and telling Douglas about Bertie going away just underlines that. As far as Douglas goes, that church has brought me a level of peace I never thought imaginable. I'll never fully get over losing Peter, just as Douglas will never fully get over losing his mum, but now at least I truly believe that Peter is at peace. You know the old cliché, "Gone to a better place"? Well, I honestly believe that he has. And I believe that Alice has too, or at least she will, only she can't quite make that final leap until she's completed her mission over here. Tell Douglas where Bertie is and let him make his own mind up. He'll do what he wants to anyway. He still misses his mum terribly, and that's not going to just go away. What matters most now is the truth. Because the truth will lead to understanding, and understanding will hopefully lead to peace. And God knows we could all do with a bit of that right now.'

Linda was relieved to find the door to Douglas's bedroom door standing open when she got back to the vicarage. Looking down the hallway as she hung up her coat, she could just see the handles on the back of his wheelchair in the kitchen. Cautiously she made her way towards him.

In the kitchen Butch was picking potato peelings from off the roll of red fabric. Douglas was sitting in his chair, his eyes red and puffy, his face gloomy.

'Are you OK, sweetheart?' Linda asked tentatively.

Douglas remained silent.

'He's OK, aren't you, mate?' Butch said. 'Just needed a bit of space to let off steam, eh?'

Butch brushed the last of the detritus from the roll of fabric and placed it back on the table. 'Done a bit of a Pete Townshend on the guitar there too, but I reckon I might be able to fix it,' Butch said, eyeing the two pieces of guitar lying on the kitchen table. 'Just the neck snapped off from the body. Fairly clean break. Should be easy enough.'

'Thanks, Butch,' Linda said, taking a seat at the kitchen table beside Douglas. She put her hand on his forearm. 'Douglas, I've just spoken to Edna. Sweetheart, I'm going to be straight with you about your father, but please, don't get too upset, let me explain first.' Linda took a deep breath. 'The truth is that he has gone back to Bridgend.'

Douglas's head swivelled ninety degrees, his red eyes wide and livid meeting Linda's.

'But darling, it's not what you think. He hasn't left again. Graham got it all wrong. Your dad's going to be back in a few days. He's entered a darts tournament down there, that's all.'

Douglas's eyes softened a little. 'A darts tournament? Why did Graham say he'd left again then?' he croaked.

'I don't know,' Linda said with a little shake of the head. 'But I went to the school and spoke with Edna. She said your dad didn't want to worry you. He thought that if you knew he'd gone back there, it would upset you. That's why he said he was going up north to see your uncle, and why he told *us* the darts tournament was up there. But darling, Edna was emphatic when she said he's coming back. I think that with everything that's been happening lately, he wanted to do it with as little fuss as possible. This business with your mum, whatever that is exactly, has had him a bit worried, I think, and that's why we chose this Sunday to see the medium. Your dad thought it would be best if he wasn't around. He obviously knew that the meeting would coincide with his tournament, so instead of worrying you unduly he told us he was going up north. I knew nothing about him going back to Wales until Edna told me about it just now. And he had asked both her and Graham not to say anything, because he didn't want word getting back to you. But sweetheart, she assures me there is absolutely nothing for you to worry about,' Linda said, gripping Douglas's arm and smiling. 'And Edna's not the kind of person who'd lie to you, is she?'

'No,' Douglas said, wiping his snotty nose on the sleeve of his jumper.

'There you are then,' Linda said. 'And she's going to have a word with Graham about what he did. He clearly had the wrong end of the stick on this one.'

Linda looked over at the now crumpled and slightly damp-looking roll of red fabric. 'I think I'd better give that a wash before Uncle Butch works his magic on it, don't you think? Otherwise you'll be going to the party looking like Mr Potato Head.'

'I don't want a party,' Douglas said. 'It was a stupid idea. Who's gonna want to come to a party with a spazzy little cripple like me anyway?' he said, wheeling himself out of the kitchen and down the hallway.

'Hey, come on now, don't be daft,' Linda said, following Douglas into his room. 'Lots of people want to come. You don't mean that, I'm sure.'

'I do,' Douglas said glumly, going over to his stereo and CD collection. 'What's the point?'

'But you've sent all the invites out now. I've booked the pub. Sweetheart, everything's arranged. And lots of people have already *said* they're coming. Darling, I know you've had a miserable day, but don't let it spoil everything.'

'You're only eighteen once, mate,' Butch said, standing in the doorway. 'When you get to that boozer and ask for your first legal pint, you'll be glad you didn't cancel. No more shandies, eh?'

'Butch is right,' Linda said. 'I think this party is exactly what you need right now.'

Douglas took out a disc from a Now 1991 double CD fatbox case, placed it in his CD player and skipped tracks with the hi-fi's remote control. The opening piano bars of Beverley Craven's 'Promise Me' softly permeated the room as Douglas wheeled himself over to the window, staring forlornly across the churchyard towards his mother's grave.

'Gotta say, mate, it's not often you hear Slayer back to back with Beverley Craven,' Butch said, trying to lighten the mood. 'You've sure got an eclectic taste in music.'

'Shut up,' Douglas snapped. 'Don't take the piss out of me.'

The chatter stopped as the pleading chorus of Craven's wistful ballad filled the room. Tears filled Douglas's eyes as he stared out of the window. 'This song reminds me of her, the way it reminded her of him,' Douglas said, sniffing and wiping his nose. 'That's how much it meant to her, and that's how much of a twat he was for leaving us,' he added, his voice rising with defiance.

Butch and Linda shared a look of pained concern as Douglas continued to stare out of the window.

'Sweetheart,' Linda said, crouching down beside him, 'are you sure you still want to go home on Sunday to see this medium? I don't like the idea of you suffering any more upset.'

For the first time since Graham's unscheduled appearance, Douglas cracked a thin smile, though his eyes were still wet with tears. 'Mum'll know what to do,' he said. 'She was the only person to ever tell me the truth around here. I do want to go.'

'As long as you're sure,' Linda said, giving his arm a gentle rub.

In his chair Douglas began to giggle. Butch and Linda looked on, sharing a similar look of confusion and concern. Douglas continued to laugh, but tears were also running down his face and his smile faltered as the potent mixture of complex emotions overcame him. Linda put her arm around him, trying to soothe and calm him. In the hallway the phone began to ring. Linda looked up at Butch. 'Would you?'

Butch went out, his voice sounding loud in the hallway as he answered the phone. 'Hello,' he said. 'Linda's place.' There was a pause. 'Oh yeah, hiya, sweetheart. How are you doing?' he asked boisterously. 'Funny, we were just talking about that, yeah ... Oh yeah? ... Yeah great, hang on, I'll go and get him.' Butch stuck his head round Douglas's bedroom door. Linda and Douglas both looked up at the Kiwi's grinning face. 'Douglas,' Butch said, 'Daisy Carr's on the phone for you, mate.'

29 *Sunday, October 17*

'What time is it?' Douglas asked.

'Five past two. Don't worry, we're only five minutes late,' Linda said, pushing Douglas up the High Street towards the top of Pugsden Lane. 'That bloody level crossing, huh?' she said.

'Well it was last time I was on it,' Douglas said.

'Oh Douglas, honestly,' Linda said, giving him a gentle tap on the shoulder.

Douglas hadn't been down Pugsden Lane, nor had he even seen his old house or indeed the caravan, since the night he found his mum on the kitchen floor. But as Linda pushed him down his old road, past the rusting coal lorries and left towards the bungalow, the caravan's roof was the first thing that came into view. Unwelcome memories of that awful night back in August barged their way into the forefront of Douglas's mind: the power suddenly going off in the caravan plunging him into near darkness, save for the orange glow of the streetlight outside; going into the house and calling for his mum and wondering why he was shouting in the dark, and why she wasn't answering him, feeling an overwhelming sense of dread as he did so; then going back to the caravan for the small battery-powered torch he had in a drawer, and finding his mum on the kitchen floor in the meagre white light cast by the torch and the moonlight coming in through the kitchen window; then the total incomprehension that followed, his frazzled mind short-circuiting on the spot. The only thing he could think to do when he couldn't rouse her was to put her to bed, to try and make her comfortable. In his deranged state he had tried to kid himself that she was just tired and in need of rest. Then he had fled to the dark and oppressive confines of the caravan, where he began robotically throwing darts, trying to put the horror of his experience out of his mind; focusing instead on the tatty photograph of the man who had abandoned them six years previously, and wanting nothing more than for that man to come back and rescue him, and feeling the deflation of knowing that he wouldn't; that that man was long gone, and that he didn't care. No one did. Back then it seemed that no one cared about him, quite the opposite in fact, and the fete was the cherry on top of the cake. But things had changed since then; changed in ways he would have thought unimaginable back then. Out of the pain and the horror and the trauma of his experiences, a new life had begun to emerge. And it turned out that some people did care; and that was what mattered; and knowing that was the only thing right now that was helping him fight the urge to turn and flee.

'You OK?' Linda asked as they neared the bungalow.

'Mmmm,' Douglas said, hoping that he was. 'Just weird, isn't it?'

'Yes, love, I imagine it must be.'

Douglas's mind turned to Daisy and her unexpected phone call; thinking how he wished he could tell his mum about it, that he was returning home with good news for once. Perhaps he would anyway. If she was here, why shouldn't he just tell her, as if she was still around? That's what this was all about, after all.

'I'm amazed he got that old piece of shit going,' Douglas said, looking at the empty space next to the caravan where the Ford Orion was usually parked, before turning his attention to the path down the side of the house that led to the back garden. Through the black metal gate he saw his mum's Raleigh Shopper bicycle leaning up against the wall. Douglas felt his eyes welling up as he thought back to when the small bicycle had seemed so big; how he had sat on its saddle, which then seemed so high off the ground, with Alice gripping the bike's white handlebars as she pushed him to school; one of his earliest memories. Douglas catching sight of his mum pulling silly faces at him in the Raleigh's small chrome rear-view mirror fitted to the handlebars. Both of them laughing as she did so.

'Hello, you two,' Reverend Bowen called out from the driveway.

Douglas snapped out of his heart-wrenching reminiscence and looked over to Reverend Bowen. Beside her stood a tall man with short, thinning blond hair, wearing a navy blue suit and a three-quarter-length black winter coat. He strode towards Douglas and Linda as they approached the bungalow. Reverend Bowen followed on behind him.

'Hi, I'm Jason Rose,' he said, shaking Linda's hand as Douglas came to a halt in front of the house.

'Hello, Mr Rose,' Linda said, 'lovely to meet you.'

'Oh, please call me Jason,' he said, crouching down beside Douglas.

'Hello, Douglas, I'm Jason Rose,' he said, holding out his hand for Douglas to shake, which he did. 'Your mum said to tell you that she's absolutely delighted for you,' Rose said with a smile of sincerity that put Douglas immediately at ease. 'About your friend coming to the party. She was very insistent that I told you. She's made up for you.'

Douglas's head swivelled round to face Linda. 'Bloody hell, he's good, isn't he? How did he know that?' he said. Douglas scanned the driveway and the house, looking for someone he knew was not going to be there; at least not that he could see anyway. 'Is my mum here?' he said.

Jason Rose got to his feet, smiling down at Douglas then looking over at the house. 'She's waiting for you by the front door, Douglas,' he said.

A short burst of laughter escaped him and a tear streaked down his face as he looked towards the front door of his old house.

'Why don't we all go inside?' Linda said, taking her keys out of her handbag and unlocking the front door. 'Hilda, could you please give Douglas a push?'

'I'm all right,' Douglas said. 'Just bump me over the runner across the front door.'

Jason Rose followed Linda inside, with Douglas and Reverend Bowen behind him.

'Oh wow,' the medium said, looking around him as he stood in the hallway, then turning to face Douglas who was just coming in. 'There's a lot of love in this house, isn't there? I can feel that straight away,' Rose said, pressing his palm flat against the wallpaper in the hallway. He closed his eyes. 'There's been some sadness too, but that loving energy is always there

203

to overpower it. Oh wow. Yeah, this is going to make my job much easier,' he said, smiling at Douglas who was beside the open door to his old bedroom.

Douglas went into his old room, amazed at how familiar everything felt, looking at the blank spaces on the wall where his posters used to be, and at his depleted music collection which was also now mostly in his new room up at the vicarage. On a small bedside table was the framed school photo of himself that had always traditionally stood on his mum's dresser in her bedroom. His smiling eleven-year-old face beamed back at his now nearly eighteen-year-old one. He thought about the guitar he had smashed on Friday, remembering the times when he'd played it in here when he was younger. He sincerely hoped that Butch would be able to fix it.

Jason Rose was still in the hallway with Reverend Bowen when Douglas wheeled himself back out of his old room.

'Why don't you all go and make yourselves comfortable in the front room?' Linda said. 'I'll make us all some tea. Or would you prefer coffee, Mr Rose?'

'Tea is fine, and please call me Jason.'

Bowen entered the living room, but Rose followed Linda towards the kitchen. Douglas followed on behind him. 'Take a seat, Jason,' Linda said, filling up the kettle, 'I won't be a minute.' But Rose did not appear to hear her. He was watching intently as Linda's hand went towards the plug socket. She flicked it on and Rose, standing in the doorway, visibly flinched as he looked at the plug. Douglas was behind him. Jason Rose turned to face him.

'Oh Douglas,' he said, 'Douglas, I'm so sorry.'

Douglas remained silent.

'You found her here, didn't you? This is where your mother passed.'

Douglas still said nothing, but gently started nodding his head.

'Why don't you both go into the lounge?' Linda said softly. 'I'll bring the tea in.'

'Lead the way,' Rose said to Douglas, who manoeuvred his chair round and headed for the lounge.

Jason Rose followed Douglas into the front room, taking in the room and its contents. 'It's strong in here too,' Rose said, absorbed in his surroundings. 'It feels as if everything in here is charged with that same benevolent energy.'

Rose took a seat in the armchair beside the bay window that looked out on to the driveway. Reverend Bowen sat on the sofa. Douglas positioned himself next to the armchair by the hi-fi.

'He could've at least asked me if he could have that,' Douglas said, looking up at the dartboard on the wall behind him, then at the mantelpiece over the fireplace where Bertie's invitation to his 18th birthday party was.

'OK, so I should start by saying that no one has told me anything about you or your family history, Douglas, OK?' Jason Rose said, flashing that endearing smile of his. 'That's a lovely picture of you all,' he said, looking up at the family photo above the fireplace as Linda came in with the tea tray. 'That's mum, obviously,' Rose said. 'I recognise her. And you of course. And that must be dad,' he added, rising to his feet and moving over to the fireplace.

'Here we are then,' Linda said, placing the tray down on the coffee table and taking a seat beside Reverend Bowen on the sofa.

'How old are you in that picture, Douglas?' Rose asked.

'Dunno, seven or eight, I suppose,' he said, looking up at the picture himself. 'You tell me, you're the psychic.'

'A, B,' Rose said quietly, drawing the letters in the air with his index finger. He was silent for some moments. 'Alice and Bertie,' he said softly, 'thank you.' Rose was quiet for some moments. 'Dad went away,' Rose said, staring at the photo, 'but he's back now. Back for good.'

'Yeah, worse luck,' Douglas said.

'That's a special picture, isn't it,' Rose said with a wistful smile, 'and she took it with her.' His expression changed. 'Why is there blood there?' he said in a whisper to himself. 'Show me that again, spirit.' He turned to face them all. 'Sorry, I should just tell you I have assistance from the other side. Not just mum,' he said, smiling at Douglas. 'They help me to see things more clearly. If you hear me talking to myself, don't worry, I'm not mad.' He went

205

quiet again for a moment. 'Oh I see, yes. You cut yourself on it,' he said, looking at Douglas. 'On the glass.'

'There was a little accident,' Linda said, 'at the wake following the funeral. The picture got broken and Douglas cut his hands on the glass.'

'Don't tell him,' Douglas said. 'He's a psychic, he's meant to tell us, remember?'

Rose smiled. 'I'll certainly do my best,' he said, now turning his attention to the dartboard. 'Your dad's dart playing has been improving hasn't it?' he said. 'I sense he was having trouble before he came back here.' Rose put the flat of his palm on the board. 'Dartitis,' he said, looking down at Linda on the sofa.

'Yes,' Linda said, looking a little startled. 'Bertie said he was really struggling with it.'

'Being back here has helped him, though,' Rose said. 'With mum's helping hand to guide him, of course.'

'Where is he?' Douglas asked. 'Where's my dad?'

Rose smiled, taking a seat beside Douglas in the empty armchair. 'Mum says you've been told where he is,' he said, 'and what he's doing.' Rose pointed at the dartboard. 'And I think he might've done quite well,' he added. 'Your mum was a great lover of music, wasn't she?'

'Well, you're sat next to a hi-fi and half of her record collection, so...'

'Douglas,' Linda said.

'She says thanks for the music.'

'Is my mum here?' Douglas asked.

Jason Rose smiled, then there was a clicking noise from the hi-fi, though the machine itself was turned off. Douglas turned his head sharply on hearing it, looking past Jason Rose sitting in the armchair and at the right-hand cassette deck as it silently opened in front of them all.

'Does that answer your question?' Rose said, looking at the tape deck, then at Douglas. 'Douglas, your mum's standing right beside you,' he said. 'Hold out your hand.'

Douglas gave a shivering laugh, looking at the empty space beside him. He did as Rose said.

'She's standing by you, just like she did when she was here on the earth plane. And just like she has been many many times since she passed from it. She's holding your hand.'

Douglas smiled through the tears that had once again started to flow. Both Linda and Reverend Bowen were smiling at Douglas, who was still holding out his hand.

'I know you've felt her presence,' Rose continued. Douglas nodded, tears running down his face. 'And what are the pink shrimps I'm being shown?' the medium said, taking the tape out of the hi-fi and passing it to Douglas, who was now smiling. Linda rubbed Douglas's arm as he gazed at the tape. Written on the paper label stuck to the front of it was 'Alice's Compilation'.

'They were her favourite sweets,' Douglas said, looking at the tape. 'Hilda and me went down to the garage and I got some from the pick 'n' mix. I left them where I saw her, by the railway.'

'With the candles?' Rose said.

'Yeah,' Douglas replied, 'I put them with the candles.'

'She's very grateful,' Rose said, 'to you and your dad.' Rose took a deep breath, looking over at the hi-fi. 'And for the music at the funeral. She said she approved of the music played at the service, but says she's sorry that it made you cry. She hates to see you cry,' Rose said, looking at Douglas as the tears ran down his face. 'And there have been plenty of tears, haven't there, mate?' he said. 'She knows you've been harbouring a lot of guilt about what happened to her, but Douglas, she's adamant that it wasn't your fault.'

Douglas broke down, his shoulders hitching up and down with each stuttering intake of breath. 'Sorry, mum,' he said, wiping the tears away as more followed on in their wake.

Linda gave his arm a gentle squeeze. 'It's OK,' she said.

'No,' Douglas said, sniffing, 'it's not OK. Why did he have to come back here?' he said, straightening up in his chair and wiping his nose. 'Why couldn't he have just stayed away and let her go to heaven? He's come back here and now she's stuck. She's stuck here because he chose the worst possible time to come back.'

Rose smiled, locking eyes with Douglas. 'Or maybe it was the best possible time?' he said. 'Douglas, sometimes our biggest opportunities come disguised as our worst nightmares. It's all just a matter of perspective. I don't think mum's staying here just for your dad,' Rose said, looking at the family photo again. 'That's what she wants for you,' he said, pointing up at it. 'There hasn't been any of that for so long that you've forgotten how it feels and it's clouding your thinking. Your mum is here for both of you, Douglas, and I don't think she can move on until she sees both of you happy again.'

'Unfinished business,' Reverend Bowen said from the sofa.

'It's a common theme in the spirit world,' Rose said, looking over at Bowen. 'The spirits of those who have passed often can't fully move on until they have completed their soul mission here on the earth plane. Your mother's spirit left her physical body prematurely and so she wasn't able to see this happen. But she is still here in spirit and just as determined to see that mission through. I think seeing you and your father reconcile your differences is what is truly keeping her here. When a person leaves their physical body and returns to spirit,' Rose said, 'they experience an amazing and transformative expansion of consciousness. And whereas we here on earth have to make do with our limited sensory hardware, where often we can only see some of the pieces of the puzzle, those on the other side can see the whole picture, and how everything interconnects.'

Douglas sniffed again, wiping away another tear. 'So why did he have to lie?' he asked, looking at Linda and Reverend Bowen. 'Why did he have to bullshit about this so called tournament? If he wants to get back into my good books so badly, then why is he sneaking off to Wales behind our backs to see that old tart of his?'

'Because he didn't want to upset you; we've been over this,' Linda said. 'Douglas, I think you're wrong to think he's up to no good on this one.'

Jason Rose's face had taken on a distant expression, the medium looking as though he were deep in thought. 'There's something else though, isn't there?' he said. There was silence. 'Say that to me again, spirit,' Rose whispered, leaning in as if listening to an unseen voice. 'Who betrayed him?' the medium said, looking up.

'Who betrayed who?' Linda asked, looking a little puzzled.

'Bertie. Someone betrayed his confidence,' Rose said. 'And they will again.' Everyone stared intently at the medium.

'Well, Graham certainly put the cat among the pigeons when he told you about your father going to Bridgend in the first place, didn't he?' Linda said, looking at Douglas. 'Bertie had originally told us all he was going up north to see his brother and maybe enter a tournament up there, but he told Edna and Graham of his real intentions. And Graham wasted no time in telling Douglas about it.'

Rose nodded silently, processing the information. 'And I think Graham knows what Bertie's intentions really are,' he said.

'How do you mean?' Linda said.

'I'm not sure, but I keep seeing a red light. I don't know exactly what it's trying to tell me,' he said. Again he was quiet a moment. 'Show that to me again, spirit,' he said softly.

Linda, Hilda and Douglas exchanged bewildered looks as Rose began to nod his head. 'Warning light,' he said. 'They're warning lights, signalling danger.'

'How do you mean?' Linda asked.

'I'm not one hundred per cent sure,' he said, 'but I keep getting this red light and it's connected to Bertie and ...' he paused, 'his old partner. Graham is Bertie's old partner.' He looked at Linda, then at the dartboard. 'They play darts together? And they were on the television together.' Rose smiled, again listening in to the unseen. 'Say that again to me, spirit,' he said. Jason Rose was quiet but he was smiling. 'Oh, I see,' he said.

'You wanna let us in on the joke, or what?' Douglas said.

With a little laugh that sounded a little on edge Rose finally said, 'You can't beat a bit of bully.'

*

Jason Rose was approaching the end of his agreed two-hour slot when Douglas asked him the big question.

'So what's it all about then, Jason?' he said. 'I mean, what's the bloody point?'

Rose laughed. 'You mean, "Why are we here?", that sort of thing?'

'Yeah, if you like.'

'I'm not sure if Jason has time to go into all that now, Douglas,' Linda said, checking her watch.

'No, it's OK,' Rose said. 'There's always time. It's actually quite simple. At least I think it is.'

Douglas leaned in.

'The way I see it, Douglas, is that life is like a school: a big rough, tough often cruel school. After everything you've been through and all that we've discussed today, I think you know that as well as anyone.'

'You can say that again, pal,' Douglas said.

'The difference being that when you're young, you can leave school at say, sixteen; later also, of course, if you wish to pursue further education.'

'Or earlier if you don't,' Douglas said.

'Or earlier, sure. But you don't get to leave life, do you? Well, you could,' Rose said, 'but it won't solve your problems. You'll only take them with you. Learning to overcome the problems while you're here is part of the soul's development. You can't escape them by...'

Douglas looked away.

'You know what I'm talking about, don't you?' Rose said as Douglas met his gaze, saying nothing, only silently nodding his head. 'On the railway?' the medium added.

Douglas remained silent for a few moments more. 'I'd had enough, and I just wanted to be with her,' he said eventually.'

Rose smiled tenderly, as did Linda and Reverend Bowen who were both looking at Douglas with silent compassion. 'I know you did mate,' Rose said, now gently shaking his head. 'But it's not your time. Nowhere near it in fact. You've got so much ahead of you to look forward to. I know it might not seem like it now but it's true. Not all lessons are going to be this tough; and you've got a real tough one out the way early!' he added with a flourish.

'At soul level, the lesson goes on. And life is like one big school; a great big school for our souls.'

Douglas's face brightened and he started sniggering. Linda shot him a glance.

'It's my belief that our souls are sent to this school to grow and to develop: mentally, emotionally and spiritually. Our souls are here to learn.'

'My old school was full of arse holes,' Douglas said, 'and the teachers used to say that I was there to do anything *but* learn,' he said, laughing.

'Oi,' Linda said, 'behave yourself.'

Rose smiled, nodding his head. 'OK, questionable turn of phrase on my part there, but you get my meaning, right?'

'Yeah, I think so,' Douglas said.

'You might've dropped out of academic education, Douglas, but you haven't dropped out of life. That lesson goes on. You've had some real tough lessons for someone so young; and some hard teachers. But it's all adding to your personal growth and experience, and to your spiritual understanding and development. You are so much more than the young man in the wheelchair, Douglas. And you will have grown and learned so much more than you think. This is just a temporary experience on an infinite journey, and you're learning every step of the way.'

Douglas laughed, looking down at his chair. 'Is he taking the piss out of me, or what?'

'Sorry, Douglas,' Rose said, looking a little embarrassed. 'I didn't ... I mean...'

'Jason didn't mean it like that, and you know it,' Linda said.

'It's OK,' Douglas said, looking at the medium. 'You're all right.'

'Well, I should be going,' Rose said, looking at his watch and getting to his feet.

Everyone filed out of the living room and out of the bungalow into the front garden. Linda locked up behind them. Reverend Bowen pushed Douglas down the garden path towards the gate.

'There was one other thing, Linda,' Rose said, taking Linda briefly aside. 'I couldn't mention it in there in front of Douglas.'

'Oh?' Linda said with raised eyebrows.

'Yes. I didn't want to spoil the surprise, you see.'

'What surprise?'

'The cake,' Rose said. 'Alice said to tell Bertie not to worry about the cake.'

Linda gave a short involuntary laugh. Rose smiled back at her.

'She said she'll be around to help him with it.'

30 *Monday, October 18*

Bertie reversed the Ford Orion onto the driveway alongside the caravan. He got out, had a good stretch and took the sports bag from off the back seat, enjoying the extra weight it was carrying now compared with before he left. He walked up the path and let himself into the bungalow, noticing the red light flashing on the telephone answering machine. Before he did anything, however, he needed a beer. He went into the kitchen and immediately did a double-take.

What caught his attention was a set of kitchen scales sitting in the middle of the floor. 'OK,' he said, picking them up and putting them on the side. He opened the fridge, grateful at the sight of two cans of cold Heineken. He cracked one open and went to the telephone, playing back the message. It was from Linda, giving him a mini debrief following their meeting with the medium. She asked if he could phone her back as she had more to tell him. After he had done so, the scales on the kitchen floor made a bit more sense.

He was however more preoccupied now by the fact that Graham had told Douglas about his trip back to Bridgend. Not only that, but that he had embellished and downright lied to him about it, causing no end of trouble in the process by the sound of it. Linda also revealed to him that Edna had made her aware of the relationship that had developed between the two of them. This, however, Douglas was thankfully none the wiser about. He needed to speak to Edna, but after his chat with Linda he was a little cautious about doing so. He checked his watch, considering her potential whereabouts. It was a quarter past three, and it was Monday. He knew where she would be – where she went most days after seeing to the well-being of everyone else's children – to visit the grave of her own.

Bertie took a twenty-pound note from one of the bundles of cash in his sports bag before stowing the bag under Douglas's bed and leaving the bungalow, making doubly sure that the door was locked. Striding down the High Street, Bertie took a detour to the garage, seeing the flowers on the forecourt. It was not usually the done thing to buy flowers from the petrol station, but he didn't want to go empty-handed, plus it had been something of a running joke between him and Alice in the past. She never used to mind. 'Flowers are flowers are flowers', she used to say.

The spring in Bertie's step was marred by the nagging feeling of frustration he felt about Graham's behaviour, particularly as he walked past the top of his so-called mate's road. Bertie resisted the urge to divert down Bargus Close and tear into the treacherous bastard. Instead he crossed the road and walked beneath the depleted canopy of the semi-bare branches of the causeway. October was almost at an end and in just over two weeks' time Douglas would turn eighteen. He only hoped it hadn't all been ruined.

Bertie entered the churchyard via the gate by the large east window, the entrance not overlooked by the vicarage. He gazed up at the stained glass window, still with a makeshift piece of wood panelling covering the damage his son had committed over two months ago. He walked round the side of the church and out into the churchyard itself, keeping a low profile as he zigzagged his way through the headstones. And there was Edna sitting on the bench by Peter's grave, now not so far from Alice's grave. She was just where Bertie expected her to be, and wearing a large grey hooded parka to protect herself from what was a bright but chilly autumn day.

'You shouldn't have,' she said upon seeing Bertie approach with his bouquet. Bertie smiled and deviated off to the left, towards the grave with the mound of still relatively fresh earth, and the temporary grave marker standing at the head of it. The wooden crucifix was about eighteen inches tall and had a plastic golden plaque on the front that bore his wife's name and dates. He placed the flowers in front of it. 'I won,' he said quietly. 'I believe thanks are in order.' Bertie kissed the index and forefinger of his right hand and touched the recessed black lettering of his wife's engraved name. He got to his feet and went to sit beside Edna, placing his hand on top of her gloved one, feeling the warmth of her body heat beneath the grey wool. She gave it a little squeeze in return.

'So, how did it go?' she said.

Bertie smiled. 'Only went and won the bloody thing, didn't I?' he said quietly, still looking at Alice's grave. 'Played like a dream, hardly missed a thing. I couldn't believe it. And ... I hit a nine-darter against Dai in the final! Beat him fair and square 18-10. It felt amazing,' Bertie said with a broad grin. 'That didn't go down at all well with the locals though, as you can probably imagine.'

'I bet Rhonda was pleased for you,' Edna said.

Bertie laughed. 'Yeah, she probably was, until yesterday morning when she didn't get her breakfast in bed.'

'You didn't? ... I mean, you and her. You didn't?'

'No,' Bertie said. 'We most certainly did not. She took the bait, hook line and sinker, though. Told her about the wedding night to come in Las Vegas. We shared the same bed for two nights, but that was all we shared, I promise you that, Edna. She must be getting quite peckish by now, I imagine,' Bertie said.

'And the money?'

'Back at the house under Douglas's bed. Prize money in cash, plus a tidy little bonus for hitting the nine-darter. I also took back some fraudulent maintenance money I was owed, ' Bertie added.

'So where did you stay last night?'

'B&B in Merthyr Tydfil. Got the hell out of Bridgend early doors yesterday morning. I just wanted to hunker down somewhere out the way for a night and get my head together. You know? Process it all.'

There was a brief but not uncomfortable silence.

'Linda knows about me and you,' Edna said. 'She worked it out the other day when she came up to the school after Graham had gone shouting his mouth off. I didn't deny it. I couldn't.'

'Yeah, she told me on the phone earlier. Douglas doesn't know anything about it, though, which I think is probably for the best, given everything else that's been going on in my absence.'

'Mmmm,' Edna said. 'But I think Graham suspects something,' she said.

'How can he?' Bertie said. 'I mean we work together, we see each other a lot there, but that's no big giveaway, is it? How would he know? I mean he's not exactly the most observant of people is he?'

'Dunno, but he's been acting funny lately, and not ha ha funny either. He's dropping sarky comments about you and the tournament, and saying to me about "Your mate Bertie". Prat. He's pretty much packed in work altogether now as well. Just sits at home pirating videos all day and all night, drinking. He's been asking me about what we should go to the party as, as well. Very unlike him to show an interest in anything that involves us as a couple.' She shook her head, biting down on the corner of her bottom lip. 'Something's not right, I can feel it.'

'Apparently that medium fella picked up on something too, about Graham. He knew that Graham had betrayed my confidence about Bridgend. And he said he'd do it again. I don't know what that means, but he sounded like he was pretty sure. Do you think he's gonna blab about us? If he knows, I mean?'

'God knows,' Edna said.

'Linda said that medium bloke kept picking up on a red light. Like a warning or something. I'm not sure what to make of it all, but I think we should definitely keep things low key for a bit. Especially if Graham is thinking about making another announcement. And bearing in mind there's gonna be free booze again. The last thing I want is for there to be trouble at Douglas's party. It'll be a big day for him, and I don't want it marred by any of our drama,' Bertie said. 'And I've got a cake to make.'

'Oh yeah, you still haven't told me what you're planning,' Edna said.

'I know. I don't want to jinx it. I mean, it could turn out to be total crap, couldn't it?'

'I suppose it could,' Edna said, smirking.

'Ohh, speaking of which, guess what was on the kitchen floor when I got back earlier?'

'Go on,' Edna said.

'Kitchen scales.'

'Kitchen scales?'

'Yeah. Linda told me that was another thing that the medium picked up on. He said that Alice is gonna help me with the cake. Not sure how that's going to work,' he said, eyeing the grave of his proposed supernatural baking assistant, 'but right now I'll take all the help I can get. Dead or alive.'

31   *Wednesday, October 27*

For the first time in seventy-seven days, Douglas was out stretching his legs, though he wasn't particularly enamoured with his new so-called limbs. They looked more like a pair of silver walking sticks, but they got him out of his chair at least, and with the aid of a set of crutches he could move around pretty much independently once again. Sticking out the pocket of his black tracksuit bottoms was a rolled up copy of *Kerrang*. His destination today was Ransom Farm and a play date with Uncle Butch.

Cautiously Douglas opened the garden gate into Butch's front garden and made steady progress down the garden path towards his front door, which he rapped on using the bottom of his crutch. Inside he could hear Finn barking, and a moment later Butch opened the door.

'Bloody hell, mate, you've grown!' Butch said, eyeing Douglas up and down as Finn sped from the house to fuss over Douglas. 'Come on in,' he said, 'take the weight off your feet.'

'Ha ha,' Douglas smirked.

'Finn, come here, get inside,' Butch said, calling his faithful sheepdog, who obediently followed his master back into the house.

Douglas followed Butch into the kitchen where a chunky white sewing machine sat on the kitchen table.

'How are they then, mate?'

Douglas gingerly took a seat at the table. 'Weird,' he said. 'They feel strange and they look a bit shit, but at least it'll stop my arse going to sleep in that bloody chair.'

'Too right, mate,' Butch said. 'Let's have a look then.'

Douglas lifted up the right leg of his tracksuit bottoms to reveal the thin aluminium tubing of the false leg attached to a barely visible skin-coloured foot that was housed inside Douglas's trainer.

'Bloody RoboCop, eh mate? Nice!'

'I only got them the day before yesterday,' Douglas said, hoisting up his trouser leg a little more. 'That's what they call the post,' he said, tapping the tubular piece of metal. 'That connects the foot to the socket, there, that's where my stump goes,' he said, tapping his knuckles on a slightly tapered piece of moulded plastic. 'It's covered in an elasticated sleeve that goes from the socket and up over my thigh. That's what mostly keeps everything held together. I've got a couple of pairs of special socks on over my stumps to stop me turning into too much of a sweaty Betty. The sleeves are rubber so they're not breathable. The specialist and all the people up at the hospital ran me through how to put everything on and off and what to do to keep them comfortable. I've got some cream too to stop them getting too sore. I can only do a certain amount of time in them in one go at the moment, and it's a bit of a faff putting it all on and taking them off. I lost my rag the first couple of times, but I'm getting the hang of it. I still have to cop out in the chair after a while, but that's OK. I'm glad I'm up and about again. It feels a bit more normal. Just in a really weird way. Good, though, I suppose.'

'I should bloody say so, mate,' Butch said, going to the fridge. 'Here,' he said placing a can of cold Carlsberg on the table in front of Douglas. 'Cheers,' he said, holding his own aloft. Douglas clinked cans with Butch, then the Kiwi tapped his can against Douglas's false leg. 'As Quint would say, "I'll drink to your leg!" Butch said with a chuckle in his best Robert Shaw voice. 'Just don't tell Linda I've been plying you with booze, eh?'

'No, I won't,' Douglas said. 'Cheers, Uncle Butch.'

'No worries, mate,' Butch said with a wink. 'It'll be a different story next week though, eh? Down the boozer, eighteen years old. Standing at that bar with no one to hold you back. You must be looking forward to it, eh? Good news that Daisy can make it after all too, eh?'

'Yeah,' Douglas said, taking a long swallow of lager. 'She said her mum was a total cow for not telling her about the party. Petra's still got it in for me, obviously. I told Daisy I was sorry at mum's funeral. She said it was OK. I said I never meant to hurt her. That I was... I ...' Douglas trailed off, taking another swig of Carlsberg. 'That I was upset.'

'Mate, everyone knows you weren't in your right mind back then. Things have settled down now and people know the score. Petra's just doing what Petra always does. She's a born bloody meddler, mate. Total control freak. She can't help herself.'

'Mmmm. Daisy's bringing a mate with her from drama school too. I said for her to, so's she won't be on her own.'

'She won't be anyway, mate, there's loads going from what I hear. I think you've taken on something of a legendary status around these here parts,' Butch said. 'Just hope those Bumstead twins don't get too jealous with all these glamorous girls falling over you, eh?'

'Mandy and Donna are all right. So's Eric. He always sorted us out with a few sausages. It was nice of them to come to the funeral. They loved my mum. She always used to give them extra pudding at school. I'm glad they can all come to the party too.'

'Absolutely,' Butch said. 'And I'll personally see to it that you'll arrive at said party looking every inch the rock god... Which brings us nicely along to this,' Butch said, closing the kitchen door to reveal the red velvet school blazer hanging up on the back of it.

'Oh wow,' Douglas said. 'That looks wicked, Butch. It's been a while since I've worn anything resembling a school uniform.'

'The shorts are over there,' Butch said, nodding towards the matching red fabric on the back of the kitchen chair next to the sewing machine. 'You're gonna look quite a sight in those shorts with your skinny little legs sticking out the bottom, aren't ya?'

'It'll look funny. And anyway, like I said, I've got a pair of big sock type things that go over my stumps, so it's not like I'm gonna feel the cold in shorts, even in November. They get pretty warm pretty quick.'

'Yeah, you'll be bloody golden, mate,' Butch said laying newspaper down on the kitchen table. 'And to fully complete the outfit,' he said, picking up a piece of MDF wood cut in the shape of a Gibson SG guitar, 'that's your job.'

'Nice,' Douglas said.

Butch placed two pots of paint down in front of Douglas: one black, one cherry red.

Douglas rolled his sleeves up, placing the copy of *Kerrang* that he'd brought with him on the table and examining the picture of Angus Young he was copying from, holding the guitar he hoped to replicate.

'Oh, and while we're on the subject of guitars,' Butch said, leaving the kitchen and coming back a moment later with Douglas's acoustic guitar, 'here we are, Mr Townshend.' Butch handed Douglas the guitar. 'It was just the bolt that held the neck and body together. Wasn't too much of a problem. Next time have a tennis racket on standby if you're gonna kick off again, eh?'

'Brilliant! Yeah, I will, thanks,' Douglas said, strumming it but flinching a little at the sound.

'Sorry, mate, I could work out how to restring it, but I'm buggered if I know how to tune the bastard.'

'That's all right,' Douglas said, beginning to tune it by ear. Satisfied with its tone, he put the guitar down and turned his attention to the imitation one on the table, opening the two pots of paint with a teaspoon.

'And what about your dad?' Butch asked, sounding a little cautious.

Douglas shook his head, dipping a paintbrush into the tin of cherry red paint. 'Oh,' he said, 'that bloke. Dunno. He's back from that so-called tournament though, apparently.'

'How did he do?'

'Fuck knows,' Douglas said. 'He had dartitis when he first came back here, apparantly. Eric Bristow had it for a while. It properly messed his career up. But that medium bloke Jason said that his darts had been getting better and that mum had been helping him. Not quite sure how that works, but...'

'At least that shows that Graham was wrong about what he said, eh? And like Linda said, maybe your dad knew it'd upset you if you found out about him going back to Wales? Because it did upset you, didn't it, mate?' Butch said. 'And I don't think you'd have been so upset if you didn't care.'

'Mmmm...' Douglas said, concentrating on his painting. 'Maybe.'

'But it's up to you whether you want him at the party at the end of the day, mate,' Butch said, rising from the kitchen table and going over to the small stereo by the cooker. 'No one's gonna pressure you either way, though, so don't worry too much, eh?'

Butch retook his seat at the table as Crowded House began playing on the stereo. Butch focused on his sewing, Douglas on his painting.

'Mum loved this lot,' Douglas said, the paintbrush gliding over the cut-out guitar.

'Course she did, mate, everyone does,' Butch said automatically, staring intently at the red material going under the foot of the sewing machine. He paused, looking up at Douglas. 'Your mum had good taste, mate,' he said with a smile.

'What shall I do about Daisy, Butch?'

The Kiwi took his foot off the pedal of the sewing machine, giving Douglas his full attention. 'Ahh, matters of the hearts, eh?' he said, pulling the shorts out from under the foot of the sewing machine. 'You've liked her quite a while, eh mate?'

'Since we were at primary school,' Douglas said, putting down his paintbrush. 'She kissed me once when we were all playing kiss chase at playtime, and I suppose I fell for her then. It's about the only time any girl has ever really paid much attention to me. I've never ... I've never had a ... '

'A girlfriend?' Butch said, helping Douglas out of his verbal blockage.

'Sad or what?' he said, picking the brush back up and applying the paint again. 'She has. I know she has.'

'What? Had a girlfriend?'

'No,' Douglas said with a little smile. 'You know what I mean. And I bet she's had...' again Douglas could not finish his sentence.

'... Sex?'

Douglas frowned, 'Yeah.'

'Mate, it doesn't matter if she's done it a hundred times, that isn't gonna change anything. You and her have got, let's say, history. Some good, some not so good,' Butch said, moving his hand like a slowly flapping fish out of water. 'The bad, OK, you're obviously not particularly proud of, but that's all in the past now, mate; and unlike her snooty mum, Daisy has forgiven you, yes? I mean, she's told you that herself. So you've got a clean slate there and the future is whatever you decide to make of it. After what you've been through, there's gonna be a heap more people that will have changed their opinion on you, and I include myself in that too, by the way. When you put Barbara's window through back in August, I wanted to see you get what was coming to you just as much as anyone else around here. I was glad when I caught you by the railway after you jumped the barrier. Remember that?'

'Yeah,' Douglas said with a little smile. 'I should've gone over the other side, shouldn't I?'

'Yeah,' Butch said with a smile of his own. 'Anyway, we all jumped straight in without even questioning why you did what you did. That's all changed now, mate. Daisy, along with everyone else round here, save for maybe Petra of course, does not look at you as the person you were, but as the man you have become. And everything you've been through has helped to shape you into that. Good and bad. I've been through it myself. Most people have to one degree or another, we just never notice because we get too caught up in our own lives, which is perfectly understandable. Daisy's agreed to come to your party, she's overruled her mum, because she's an adult who knows her own mind and can make her own decisions. And so are you, mate. Just be yourself. Be a rock god,' Butch said, nodding at the guitar. 'Be who YOU want to be.'

Douglas nodded contemplatively, letting Butch's words sink in as he carried on layering on the paint. A comfortable silence descended between Butch and Douglas as they worked; now it was just Crowded House providing the soundtrack to their respective tasks, and the track now playing was 'Fall at Your Feet'. Douglas picked out the tune, at first humming, then quietly singing along, word for word and perfectly in tune. Butch looked up from his sewing machine, watching and listening to the performance. Ensconced in his work, Douglas was oblivious to the Kiwi's gaze. As the song came to an end, Douglas began to laugh. As the next song came on, Butch got up and turned the volume down on the stereo.

'I never knew you could sing,' he said.

'I can't,' Douglas said. 'Not really.'

'I beg to bloody differ, my friend,' Butch said. 'I wouldn't let just anyone impede my enjoyment of the greatest band on earth.'

'I remember mum singing along to it. I remembered the words. It was one of her favourites. She liked Crowded House almost as much as you do.'

Butch laughed. 'I'm telling you, mate, you sing something like that to young Miss Carr come the big night and she'll be the one falling at your feet. Guaranteed.'

'Yeah,' Douglas said, once again beginning to laugh. 'My brand new super spazzy plastic feet.'

32   *Wednesday, November 3*

In the kitchen of number 8 Pugsden Lane, Bertie marvelled at his Ancient Egyptian creation, though it was still at this point a work in progress. He gazed at the cake, a little amazed at how he was so far just about managing to pull off such an ambitious undertaking. After baking and shaping the twelve cut-to-shape layers of one inch sponge that made up the pyramid, each one covered with a layer of jam and buttercream icing, he was now faced with the more daunting task of laying on the exterior panels of triangular fondant icing and decorating it. The Iron Maiden *Powerslave* LP he was copying from was propped upright on the kitchen work surface. On its cover the band's mascot, Eddie, in full Egyptian headdress, stared down from his position standing guard over the entrance to the pharoah's tomb, flanked either side by giant cats and sphinxes. Bringing the full majesty of the band's famous album artwork to life in cake form was no easy task, but it was one that Bertie felt increasingly confident of doing, and it would be more than worth it just to see the look on Douglas's face when the big night finally came.

Instead of trying to sculpt each individual piece from the album cover, Bertie instead chose to draw Eddie and his accomplices onto a flat square of icing using food colouring pens and then recess it in the front of the cake. Hand-lining the pyramid's icing brickwork would be a tricky, rather laborious task, but he had a brand new plastic ruler on standby for that particular task, and he had told himself that if he was going to do it, he was going to do it properly. All or nothing. The pyramid's golden yellow capstone would literally be the icing, on top of the icing on the cake.

Bertie was just laying another triangle of icing onto the pyramid's left side when there was a knock on the door. In his state of focused concentration, the sound didn't even make Bertie jump, despite knowing full well that there might not actually be anyone at the door. With the icing safely in place he left the kitchen and walked down the hallway, scrutinising the front door's frosted glass to see if there was anybody on the other side of it. There was. He opened the door. Linda, dressed in a light pink pea coat and matching beret, was standing on the front step huddled up against the cold of the early November day.

'Hi,' she said shivering.

'Looks like someone could do with something wet and warm,' Bertie said. 'Come on in.'

'Thanks,' Linda said, following Bertie down the hallway to the kitchen. 'Oh wow!' she said, laying eyes on Bertie's baking creation. 'Did you do that all by yourself?'

'Yep,' Bertie said, smiling, flicking the kettle on. 'Well, at least I think I did, but you never know round here, do you? I gotta say, I'm pretty chuffed myself with how it's going so far. Still a bit to do, but it's getting there. I'll pop it down to the pub tomorrow when it's finished and put it in the fridge for the big night. I've gotta start prepping the buffet tomorrow anyway. I just need to get some candles from Kareshi's and we're in business!'

Linda smiled, but it was a disconcerting one that left Bertie sensing that something was coming. Something not good.

'Come on then, what is it?' he said.

Linda hesitated. 'Bertie,' she said, 'I'm not really sure how to say this.'

Bertie sighed. 'Try,' he said.

Linda reached into the inside pocket of her pea coat, revealing a crumpled, folded piece of paper. Bertie knew what it was, even before Linda unfolded the invitation, with his name written in the Iron Maiden font at the top of it.

'I found it in his room yesterday,' Linda said. 'He must have taken it from here after we saw the medium. It was on the mantelpiece over the fireplace. I remember seeing it when we came in. I asked him about it and he said he thinks it might be better if perhaps you didn't come to the party. I'm sorry, Bertie. He's still quite confused about things.'

Bertie's heart sank, and for a brief, irrational moment he thought about slamming his fist into the cake. 'I thought Alice might have moved it,' he said after a moment silently composing himself. 'I'd noticed it had gone, but I thought it might reappear somewhere... just not like this.'

'I'm sorry,' Linda repeated. 'I think it might still be too soon for him. Personally speaking, I'm also a little concerned about this business between you and Edna coming out and overshadowing everything. We don't want any unwanted theatrics again, do we?'

Bertie did not need to ask what she was referring to.

'I think he's still a little conflicted about how he feels. On the plus side, and it might not make you feel any better right now, I honestly think he's starting to mellow towards you. I know sometimes it might not seem like it, and obviously this business about the party is a blow for you, I know, but I think deep down that he genuinely does want to get over the past. I think the meeting with the medium helped. He raised some very good points and I think Douglas definitely took them on board. And Hilda's been plugging the need for forgiveness on your behalf as well.'

The kettle bubbled, boiled and clicked off and Bertie sorted the coffees.

'Bertie, he's been through so much and he's come so far. I'd hate for anything to spoil his big night.'

'I know,' Bertie sighed. 'I'm gutted, obviously, but if that's what he wants. And you're right, this whole business with Edna has taken me as much by surprise as anyone. But I'm sure Graham knows more about it than he's letting on too. Maybe it's for the best that we aren't all in the same room on Friday. I still can't believe that Graham went blabbing to Douglas about Bridgend the minute I'd gone. Some friend he's supposed to be, eh? I think it'll be best if Edna and I tell Douglas about what's happened after the party. I don't want to be seen to be keeping any more secrets from him.'

'As long as it is after Friday?' Linda said with a raised eyebrow.

'Of course,' Bertie said. 'Look, I won't pretend that I'm not gutted about him not wanting me there, but I'm still gonna be here after the party's over, and I'll be just as determined to put things right between us then as I am now. And anyway, I suppose I'll be there in spirit... Well, in buffet and cake form.'

'Of course,' Linda said. 'And I'm sure he'll love it. And I am very grateful to you for doing it. You're sure I can't give you anything towards the cost of it all?'

'Nah, it's OK, Linda. I've got it covered.'

'Oh goodness,' Linda said excitedly, 'I haven't told you, have I? Douglas has got his new legs!'

'Oh wow, good on him,' Bertie said. 'How are they? I bet he's glad to be out of that chair.'

'He's doing fine. He's still having to use his crutches, but yes, being up and about again is like a miracle for him. He took a walk up to Butch's the other day to work on their outfits for the party. Butch is quite the dab hand with a sewing machine, although his intentions for his own costume alarm me somewhat. Douglas said his legs feel a bit weird and that they can get quite uncomfortable, but the specialist and the team up at the hospital have gone through with him how to minimise discomfort and how long to use them for. He still has to resort to the chair when he starts to feel it, but it's a massive step in the right direction, literally! Once he gets used to them and his body starts to adapt properly, he should be able to dispense with the chair completely. It'll be so good for him to be up on his feet again for the party. Even if he does intend to get "completely legless", like he said.'

Bertie smiled. 'I'd like to contribute towards that particular endeavour if you'll allow it,' he said. 'And speaking of which...'

*

Undeterred by his disappointing news, Bertie headed down to Kareshi's in search of candles nonetheless, determined to spend the rest of the evening drawing the artwork onto the icing, finishing the marzipan steps that led to the pyramid's entrance, and listening to Status Quo in an attempt to keep his spirits up.

As he was leaving the shop with a pack of twenty birthday candles in his back pocket, the twenty-stone-plus reason for his darkening mood was lumbering laboriously towards it. Bertie waited by the shop doorway, a flash of rage and an almost uncontrollable desire to violently confront his so-called friend gripping him, but he resisted, taking in a series of deep breaths and trying to remain calm and in control.

Graham raised a flabby arm to salute his old friend. 'I hear congratulations are in order,' he said wheezily, closing the distance between them at a snail's pace. 'Amateur champion of South Wales, eh? I bet that went down well with the taffs, didn't it!? Bloody good on ya, boy!'

'Why did you do it, Graham?' Bertie said, struggling to control his emotions. 'Why did you tell him, huh?'

'How did I know you was gonna come back?' Graham said with a theatrical shrug of the shoulders. 'I thought you'd buggered off and left him again, so I thought he had a right to know that his dad was doing the dirty on him...again.'

'I said I was coming back, Graham! I fuckin' told you!' Bertie said. 'And you blew it for me by shouting your big bloody mouth off.'

'Temper, temper,' Graham said with a smug smile that made Bertie want to flatten him. 'You wanna watch that. We wouldn't want any trouble at the party on Friday now, would we?'

Bertie shook his head. 'Yeah well, thanks to your antics, I've been disinvited from the party, so cheers for that, mate. I hope you're happy.'

'Well,' Graham said, scratching his flabby chin, 'it was always gonna be a bit of a stretch, you and him kissing and making up after what you done, wasn't it? I mean, me and Edna, we were there for him and Alice while you was off being Mr Big Shot Darts Player. Douglas has obviously got a longer memory than you thought.'

'You were there for them, were you?' Bertie said. 'You? The man who doesn't even know where his own son is buried. The man who can't see further than the end of his TV remote. From what I hear, all you did for him was keep him well-stocked with bootlegged horror films and bargain basement bongo flicks, you dirty fuckin' bastard.'

Graham again flashed that highly punchable smile of his. 'Ohh, I see more than you think, old sport,' he said, moving past Bertie towards the shop door. 'I shouldn't be so cocky if I were you.'

Bertie eyed his so-called friend with growing suspicion. 'I don't know what's going on in that fat, demented head of yours, but you just leave my family alone, OK?' Bertie said, the two men standing by the shop doorway now, only separated by Graham's prodigious girth.

Graham snorted with laughter. 'Me leave your family alone? That's rich coming from you, boy!' Graham pushed open the shop door, shaking his head and chuckling away to himself as he entered, his sizable mass gradually being swallowed by the shop's gloomy interior.

'And oi,' Bertie said putting his foot in the doorway before the shop door closed behind him. 'Who told you that I won the tournament?'

Graham turned to face Bertie, his big grin half lit by the shop's sedate lighting. 'Like I said, boy, I see more than you think.'

Bertie narrowed his eyes, trying to read what might be going on behind that smug facial expression.

'And I hear things 'n' all,' Graham said, turning away and disappearing down an aisle and out of sight.

33   *Thursday, November 4*

Bertie was in the kitchen of the Pressed Fruitbowl preparing the buffet for the party and listening to Chris Rea on the small stereo by the window when Edna came in to start her evening shift. Bertie looked up at the clock. It was a quarter to seven. He looked back down at what he was doing, in no mood to make conversation.

'All right?' Edna said.

Bertie gave no response.

'What you making there then, chef?'

'Stuffed vine leaves,' Bertie said, not looking up from his work.

'Very posh,' Edna said.

'Something a bit different, isn't it?' Bertie replied.

An awkward silence descended. 'You OK?' Edna asked.

Bertie at last looked up from what he was doing, making eye contact with Edna. 'Oddly enough, Edna, no, not really,' he said.

'It's Graham, isn't it?' she said. 'I knew it would be him. He said he saw you up the shop yesterday. God, he sounded so full of it when he got back, I could've swung for him. And he told me about the party. Y'know, about you not coming any more. "Must've put my foot in it", he said to me when he got back. I'm sorry.'

'So you should be,' Bertie said.

Edna frowned. 'What's that supposed to mean?'

Bertie stopped what he was doing and looked deep into Edna's eyes. 'I asked you not to say anything to Graham about the tournament, and the first thing he says when he saw me down the shop was "Oh congratulations, champion of Wales!" Why did you tell him?'

Edna slowly shook her head. 'I didn't tell him anything!' she said, her voice rising with anger. 'I barely say anything to him from one day to the next as it is; you know how things are between me and him. The last thing I'm gonna do is start up a conversation with him about you, especially after what he's said to Douglas already, bloody stirring it up.'

'You're still going to the party with him though, aren't you?' Bertie said, focused once again on his stuffed vine leaves.

'That's different. That's for Douglas. And to try and keep the peace till we can get all this mess sorted out.'

'Is that what we are then?' he said. 'A mess?'

'I didn't mean it like that,' Edna said. 'You know what I mean ... And you know how I feel.'

Bertie remained silent.

'Or do you not feel the same?' Edna asked.

Bertie gave a heavy sigh, piercing his last stuffed vine leaf with a cocktail stick, securing the leaves' internal edibles. 'I don't know,' he said. 'Yes, I suppose so.'

'You suppose so?' Edna said. 'Well, that really inspires confidence, doesn't it, thanks? Glad you put my mind at rest.'

'I do, of course I do,' he said going over to her. 'But you're right, it is a mess, isn't it? Just when I think I'm getting somewhere with Douglas, I feel like I'm thrown back to the beginning. I came back here to see my wife and try to re-establish a relationship with my son. Instead I fall for you, Douglas doesn't want to see me and Alice is ...'

Edna moved closer to Bertie, gently stroking his arm as he leant against the metallic kitchen work unit.

'How the hell did he find out about me winning that sodding tournament?' Bertie said with an air of exasperation. 'You swear you haven't said anything to him?'

Edna lifted Bertie's chin with her curled index finger and looked him squarely in the eye. 'On Peter's grave,' she said.

Bertie bowed his head. 'I'm sorry,' he said, slowly shaking it. 'I'm sorry for accusing you. Christ, what's he up to? It's like he's secretly enjoying stirring things up between us, and all the while acting like he hasn't got the foggiest about what's going on. Playing it all Mr Innocent.' Bertie paused and drew in a deep breath. 'Fuck it, we're gonna have to come clean about all this, aren't we? And the sooner the better as far as I'm concerned.'

'After tomorrow,' Edna said. 'Let Douglas have the party he deserves. It looks like you're doing a great job with all this,' Edna said, surveying the food Bertie had already prepared. 'That's got to count for something, hasn't it?' Edna put a reassuring arm around Bertie and kissed him on the cheek.

'Thank you,' he said, facing Edna and kissing her on the lips, smelling perfume and tasting cigarettes. 'That's not all I've done,' he said, breaking away from her embrace. 'You wanna see it?'

'See what?'

Bertie walked over to the fridge and opened the door. Edna gasped, gazing upon the full splendour of Bertie's heavy metal inspired baking creation.

'My God, it's amazing,' Edna said, leaning closer into the fridge to examine the detail of the cake up close. 'Wow, it looks so realistic.'

'I'm pretty pleased with it myself actually.'

'So you bloody well should be! He's gonna absolutely love it, I know he will.'

Edna closed the fridge door with a nudge of her hip. 'You really have got hidden talents, haven't you?' she said, smiling and sidling back up to Bertie. She put her arms around his waist. Bertie put his around hers. 'You see,' she said, giving Bertie another peck on the cheek. 'Me? ... Douglas? You play your cards right and just be patient for that little bit longer...' She put her lips close to Bertie's ear and in a seductive whisper that made him twinge with arousal softly said, 'You might be able to have your cake and eat it.'

PART 3

34 *Friday, November 5*

In the illuminated mirror of her dressing table, Edna carefully traced the black eyeliner pencil over her top lip, generously applying the make-up and evening up the erroneous bushiness of the thick black moustache that now adorned it. Satisfied, she stood up, smoothing down her shiny black thigh-length skirt and adjusting her pink sleeveless top. The last piece of her outfit was under the stairs at the Pressed Fruitbowl. She turned off the lights in the bedroom and went into the lounge where Graham, dressed in black trousers, blue frilly shirt and braces sat in front of the television. A dark maroon blazer was draped over the top of the armchair with a pair of aviator sunglasses perched on top of it, along with a dark haired wig of considerable length. Graham barely registered Edna's presence as she entered the room.

'What's that?' Edna said, looking at the video cassette in his lap.

'What?' he said, not looking away from the television.

'That, in your lap, what is it?'

'It's a bloody chicken! What d'you think it is? It's a bloody video,' he said.

'Don't you ever stop?' Edna said.

'Nope. And anyway this one's not for sale. It's for old Billy No Mates down Pugsden Lane. Thought he could do with some entertainment, seeing as how he's not going tonight,' Graham said with a distinct air of smugness.

'Don't gloat,' Edna said, pouring herself a large gin and tonic.

'Ahhhh, are you sad that your mate isn't gonna be there?' Graham said, turning to face his wife for the first time and doing a double-take. 'God, woman, what do you look like like?' he said, starting to laugh. 'Nice tash!'

Edna stared daggers at him. 'You know, if you were gonna go as Meat Loaf you probably should've lost some weight first.'

Graham sneered at his wife. 'Very funny. And tell me, Freddie, how long have you got left to live? Not bloody long with any luck. Grab us a beer. And watch you don't get any AIDS on it.'

Edna opened the fridge and extracted a cold can of Heineken. She walked over to her husband who was again ensconced in the television. She held the can over him, like an aircraft ready to drop its payload. She let go of the can. It missed the video tape by a couple of inches and landed straight in Graham's groin. 'Ahhh, me bollocks, you clumsy bitch!' he shouted.

Edna turned away from her grunting husband and walked back to her G&T wearing a smile of sadistic satisfaction. 'Don't be daft,' she said, casually sipping her drink. 'You haven't got any bollocks, pal.'

35

Kate Bush was down the Pressed Fruitbowl for six o'clock, ensuring everything was as it should be in readiness for the party, which was now just an hour away. It was Butch who'd told Linda how much she looked like the iconic female singer, not to mention how much of a turn-on he had subsequently found it; and it was Butch who'd encouraged Linda to dress up as her for the party. So here she was now in a red flowing dress that matched the one worn by Bush in the video for 'Wuthering Heights', complete with a large red rose choker, surrounded by colourful balloons and a big HAPPY 18th BIRTHDAY DOUGLAS banner that ran above the length of the bar. Linda was busy ferrying trays of food that Bertie had prepared earlier, from the kitchen to the long row of conjoined tables in the main bar area. The cake, however, would remain in the kitchen until the big moment came.

'Everything OK, Tony?' she said, breaking away from the buffet momentarily to speak to local disc jockey Tony Gables, who after a good sounding out from Linda was in charge of the music.

'F.A.B, Linda,' Gables said, giving her a double thumbs up from behind his turntables.

'You've got Douglas's playlist and all of Alice's records, yes?'

Gables smiled, his pearly white teeth lit by the multi-coloured disco lights that framed his DJ booth. 'For the tenth time, Linda, yes, it's all in hand, don't worry, they're all here,' Gables said, nodding at a grey plastic storage box beside him that contained amongst others Alice's *Now That's what I Call Music* compilation LPs. 'All 1-25 present and accounted for,' Gables said.

'Good,' Linda said. 'The music is very important tonight, Tony. It's Douglas's way of paying tribute to his mum; his way of having her here, if you like. She was such a big music lover, and that playlist is his way of remembering her. It's going to be tough for him, this being the first one without her and everything, but she'll be here in song and in spirit.'

'It's a well-put-together playlist,' Gables said, looking at the piece of paper with the list of songs. 'Nice and upbeat. A few slower moments and one or two weepies, but that's OK. Everyone loves a slow dance, don't they? You've got nothing to worry about, Linda, I assure you. It's all under control.'

'Good,' Linda said with a sigh of relief. 'And you're sure you're going to be up to this?' she asked with a raised eyebrow, looking from the DJ to the bar.

'I've been sober since the fete, Linda,' he said. 'Nearly three months now. You can come round here and check I haven't got anything hidden if you want to, but I promise you won't find anything.'

'No, I don't think that will be necessary, Tony,' Linda said.

'Giving up drink is the best thing to happen to me in a long long time. It was the overriding factor in Karen taking me back. I tell you, being sober and having her back in my life is just the best. I made a promise to her, and I intend to keep that promise. I'd never do anything to jeopardise what we have. Not again. No, you wait, I'll show you what I'm made of tonight, Linda, and we'll give Douglas a real good party. I've been over his playlist, and it'll all run like clockwork. I'm gonna roll back the years tonight, you mark my words.'

'I'm glad to hear that,' Linda said.

'What's Little Bo Peep got up his sleeve tonight then?' Gables asked, fiddling with his mixer. 'I know what he's like.'

'Tony, you don't want to know, I assure you,' she said. 'I just hope he isn't arrested for public indecency, that's all I can say.'

*

With all the preparations completed and the time now approaching seven pm, Linda was sipping her first well-earned vodka and tonic of the evening over by the bar when the first guest came through the door. It was Reverend Bowen, dressed in black jeans and a black long-sleeved T-shirt. Her hair was parted in the middle, and around her neck hung a large silver crucifix. A pair of round, gold rimmed glasses with dark purple lenses completed the outfit.

'Oh Reverend, you look great,' Linda said, vacating her position at the bar to give Bowen a warm embrace. 'Welcome, come on in.'

'I can hardly see a thing in these,' Bowen said, moving the glasses up on top of her head. 'My gosh, Linda, you look absolutely beautiful. Or should I call you Kate?'

'Oh, you recognise me? Well that's a relief,' Linda said, heading back towards the bar arm in arm with Bowen. 'And I've seen enough copies of *Kerrang* and Metal Hammer over the past three months to know who you are.'

'Ozzyyyyy!' Reverend Bowen said in a passable Brummie accent, holding up a balled right fist and showing off the fake finger tattoos that spelt out the prince of darkness's name.

'What time is Douglas coming down?' Bowen asked.

'He'll be here soon,' Linda said, checking the clock on the wall. 'He's coming down with Butch. He looks absolutely amazing,' Linda gushed. 'Douglas that is, not Butch', she clarified. 'I'm not even going to tell you who he's coming as,' she said with a rueful shake of the head.

'Up to his old tricks again is he?'

'Times ten,' Linda said, but she was smirking as she said it. 'He's been great helping Douglas with his outfit though, I must say. They've really bonded, those two.'

'I remember his Little Bo Peep outfit at the fete,' Bowen said with a smile. 'I must say he makes a very convincing woman.'

'Oh well, you won't be disappointed tonight then,' Linda said.

'Speaking of bonding,' Bowen said, 'what about Bertie?'

'No, I'm afraid not. Not tonight,' Linda said. 'It's still a little complicated, so in the end we just thought it might be for the best. Although he's done himself proud with this spread, I must say,' she said, surveying the monstrous buffet laid out before them. 'Oh, and wait 'til you see the cake,' she added. 'And he's put £250 behind the bar. Speaking of which, let me get you a drink, Reverend? '

'£250?' Bowen said, slightly aghast.

'Yep. Let the good times roll, eh? Vodka tonic, please,' Linda said to the barmaid. 'And for you, Reverend?'

'Oh, non-alcoholic ginger beer please, dear.'

'Bertie did quite well in the darts tournament,' Linda said as the barmaid poured their drinks. 'He wasn't specific about how good exactly, but he must have done pretty OK, I'm assuming.'

The clock hit seven and Linda gave Tony the nod. Gables gave her the thumbs up in response and placed a shiny 12" record on to the turntable. Moments later, Aztec Camera's 'Somewhere In My Heart' came pumping out of the DJ's twin-tower speakers, filling the pub. Gables twiddled a few knobs and adjusted his phaser till the music was at a perfect volume. The disco lights around his booth began flashing and rotating, the pub now in multi-coloured illumination. The disco ball slowly revolving above their heads cast a galaxy of stars to all corners of the pub. Linda smiled at the DJ, giving him a double thumbs up in return. Gables, now with his headphones on, gave her a wink as he became engrossed in his night's work, taking another record from its sleeve and getting the next track lined up.

At the other end of the pub the doors opened and in came two girls dressed in black – large, but with beaming smiles that lit up the pub almost as much as Tony's disco lights.

'Gosh, it's like Stars in Their Eyes down here tonight,' Linda said, now a little louder over the top of the music. 'Hi Mandy, Donna.'

'Tonight, Matthew,' the Bumstead twins said in unison, 'We're going to be ... Shakespears Sister'

They all laughed and Linda ordered two pints of cider for the twins as per their request.

'We thought it would be nice to come like this,' Mandy said, before the twins said in unison, 'for Alice.'

'Douglas will be so pleased,' Linda said. 'I think it's a lovely idea. You look amazing, the pair of you.'

The pub steadily filled up as more and more guests arrived. Among them were Billy Idol, a Thriller era Michael Jackson and an Alladin Sane period David Bowie.

At a quarter past seven, Edna and Graham Glass came in, though it was hard to see Edna behind the enormous mass of her husband, who wasted no time in swathing a path towards the bar and the prospect of free alcohol. From out of his shadow, Edna strutted in pushing a vacuum cleaner in her husband's wake. 'God knows, I want to break free!' she sang at Graham's enormous back.

'Oh Edna, you look absolutely amazing!' Linda said. 'Or should that be Freddie? Nice tash, by the way,' Linda said as they both started to laugh.

Graham placed the video tape he had been carrying on the bar and knocked back a pint of lager in double quick time. He furtively checked his watch and quickly ordered another, oblivious to whether his wife might want one.

At twenty-five past seven the girl Douglas had been anxiously fretting would never come walked into the pub looking a million dollars. Daisy Carr was wearing a pink dress, white gloves and white faux fur cardigan around her shoulders. A diamond necklace completed the outfit. Beside her was a shorter girl who was an absolute riot of colour and costume herself. Her hair was a myriad mixture of red, green pink and purple that had been pinned in place by multi-coloured clothes pegs. One side of her colourful head had been shaved into an undercut and dyed orange. Linda gasped as she greeted them both.

'Wow!' Linda said, looking Daisy up and down. 'You look absolutely breath-taking, Daisy.'

'Thanks, Linda,' Daisy said.

'That necklace is stunning! Is it...?'

'It's just costume jewellery unfortunately,' Daisy said. 'Borrowed it from the drama school's costume department.'

'Well, you wear it very well,' Linda said.

'This is Kelly,' Daisy said, introducing the girl standing beside her. 'She's on my course.'

'Hello, Kelly,' Linda said, shaking Kelly's colourful fingerless gloved hand. 'Material girls just wanna have fun, eh?' she said, looking at the two of them. 'Madonna and Cyndi Lauper in Steventon, huh? Who'd've thought it!?'

'When is Douglas due?' Daisy said.

Linda checked the clock, which had just gone half past. 'Any minute,' she said.

The pub was now full and lively with chatter and music as guests finished their first drinks and ordered their second. As the clock hit a quarter to eight, Linda was starting to become a little concerned for the birthday boy's whereabouts. Her concerns were allayed moments later when Cher strutted into the pub in her black fishnet stockings, skimpy leather jacket and massive black wig.

'Thunderbirds are go,' Butch said, as naturally and as unselfconsciously as if he were wearing a suit and tie. Linda was shaking with laughter, but put a hand to her mouth to try to suppress her giggles.

'What do you look like?' she said.

Butch winked, kissed her on the cheek and headed back over to the pub door. Linda went over to the DJ booth and Del Amitri's 'Always the Last to Know' faded away as Gables seamlessly placed another record on the decks. As instructed he turned the volume up considerably and the raucous stomp of AC/DC's 'It's a Long Way to the Top If You Wanna Rock 'n' Roll' filled the pub. Butch opened the door. Standing in it, in his crushed red velvet school uniform, Angus Young punched his fist rhythmically in the air in time with the music, leaning on one of his crutches with his other. His head was bowed slightly, the peak of his matching red cap covering his eyes. The tips of his flesh-coloured sockets of his new false limbs protruded beneath the hemline of his red shorts. The carbon fibre poles that connected the sockets to his new feet glinted under the technicolour illumination of Tony's disco lights. On Douglas's new feet were a pair of shiny black school shoes.

The pub's assembled masses began to clap and cheer as Douglas walked into the pub, aided by his crutches and with his painted cherry red Gibson SG and brown leather satchel hanging round his neck. It was the first time that the majority of the people in the pub had seen him on his feet since before the accident, and Douglas did not disappoint them.

Taking tentative but determined steps, Douglas headed towards the bar, the crowd of cheering revellers parting as he did so. The sound of Bonn Scott's bombastic bagpipes filled the pub as Douglas looked around at all the smiling faces that had come to join him in celebrating his big day. With their sustained clapping, cheering and back slapping spurring him on, Douglas finally made it to the bar.

'Pint of lager, please!' he shouted over the top of the music.

There was another enormous cheer and the volume of the music decreased slightly. Linda and Butch went over to him, putting an arm each around him.

'Make that two!' Butch shouted, as the barmaid began to pour Douglas his first legal pint. Douglas looked around him, trying to identify people through their various musical disguises.

To his left, Graham Glass, aka Meatloaf, necked the last of his pint, picked up the video cassette and got to his feet, trying to leave the pub as inconspicuously as someone who was actually bigger than the person he was dressed as could do.

'Won't be long,' Graham shouted over the top of the music to an oblivious Edna, who was happily watching Douglas's first foray into legal intoxication.

Douglas had just taken his second big swallow of lager when his eyes fell upon Daisy Carr, looking beautiful in her Madonna 'Material Girl' outfit. He smiled, a warm sincere smile of gratitude and thanks, which Daisy returned. It was then that Douglas noticed for the first time the girl standing just to the side of Daisy. The multi-coloured girl was obviously the friend Daisy had asked to bring along with her. Douglas's first thought was that she looked like a bag of skittles; his second was that he thought he had fallen instantly in love with her.

36

Out on the High Street, Graham Glass ambled up the modest incline that marked the beginning of Steventon Hill. Thankfully for him, as the top of Pugsden Lane came into view, he did not have to go any further up it. Instead he crossed over to Station Yard on the opposite side of the road, his first intended destination. Pugsden Lane would be his second; and there, as a result of his actions, Bertie Blouse was spending the night alone.

Around the village, fireworks had started to go off as villagers began their own celebrations of the infamous date. Some from a nearby garden partially illuminated Graham's mass as he crossed the road with the videotape in his hand.

Graham could see the red Ford Sierra parked beneath the orange glow of the street light. In the passenger seat he could make out the glowing orange tip of a cigarette. He approached it and the passenger side window began to roll down, smoke escaping from the vehicle as it did so.

'Fuckin' 'ell, what 'ave you come as?' Rhonda Griffiths said in a husky Welsh accent, looking Graham up and down.

'Meatloaf,' Graham answered breathlessly, holding the right side of his chest.

'You all right?' Rhonda asked, smirking.

'Yeah ... yeah, I'm OK,' Graham said, getting his breath back. 'Just got a bit of a stitch. You all good?'

'Yeah, tidy,' Rhonda said.

'All right, Dai?' Graham said, looking in through the passenger window past Rhonda at the muscular man with the short ginger moustache in the driver's seat.

'All right,' he said, not bothering to look at Graham.

'Where's the champ then?' Rhonda said.

'At home, like I said he would be. Probably counting your money for the hundredth time.'

'You'd better show us the way then, big fella,' Dai said with an edge to his voice as he started the car.

'It's just over there,' Graham said, pointing to the opposite side of the road. 'Follow me. Don't turn your lights on, though.'

Graham could still hear the music coming from the pub, which was little more than fifty yards away, as he crossed the High Street to the top of Pugsden Lane, walking out in front of the car like a fat undertaker leading a one-vehicle cortège. The Sierra followed on a couple of car lengths behind him, creeping along with its headlights off as Graham had instructed. As they reached the left-hand bend that led to Bertie's bungalow, Graham stopped to allow the Sierra to catch him up.

'It's just over there,' Graham said to Rhonda through the passenger side window, pointing at the bungalow. 'There's the caravan, see?'

Rhonda craned her neck a little. 'Yeah, I see it. Brings back memories, that does,' she said, turning to Dai. 'What a pile of crap, huh?' she said, lighting another cigarette. 'Glad we never got lumbered with the bastard thing.'

'Wait here. I'll go on ahead. I'm sure he'll let me in. He'll want to see this,' Graham said, waving the videotape. 'Give it fifteen minutes then come and knock on the door.'

'Go on then, big boy, don't hang about,' Rhonda said. 'Let's get this party started.'

*

With the stitch still painful in his chest, Graham walked the last thirty feet or so to Bertie's front door in considerable discomfort. Despite the cold night air, sweat was dampening the hairline of his wig, and beneath his jacket dark sweat patches were forming under the armpits of his blue frilly shirt, which was in turn sticking to his massive back. He knocked on the door and waited, hearing the faint sound of music coming from behind the drawn curtains of the illuminated front room. After a few seconds, the hallway light came on and a figure walked towards the front door. Bertie opened it, wearing a Slade T-shirt and Jeans and a rather confused look as he silently appraised the man standing on his doorstep.

'What the bloody hell do you want?' Bertie said. 'Come to gloat some more have we, Mr Loaf?'

'Oh, don't be like that, Bert,' Graham said, once again struggling to catch his breath. 'I brought you something actually,' he said waving the videocassette. 'Bloody good one, this is 'n' all.'

'Oh yeah, and what's that?' Bertie said, raising his eyebrows. 'Mingers in stingers 2?'

'Ha! No. God, no. No one wants to see that,' Graham said. 'Well, a few people probably do, but that's beside the point. Come on, are you gonna leave me standing out here all night or what?'

'Come on then,' Bertie said with an air of resignation, turning and heading back into the living room where on the hi-fi's turntable Thin Lizzy's *Live and Dangerous* was revolving. Bertie turned it down and Graham, without asking, switched on the telly.

'So what is it that's so important then?' Bertie asked, sitting back down in the armchair beside the hi-fi. 'It's unlike you to turn your back on a free bar.'

'Oh, I'll be back down there soon enough, don't you worry about that, my old mate,' Graham said through grunts and heavy breathing as he prepared the video. 'It's a little home video I made. Thought you might be interested to see it.'

'How's the party going?' Bertie said. 'How's Douglas?'

Graham got back to his feet. 'It's going good, mate,' he said with a groan as he lowered himself into the armchair by the bay window. 'Douglas had just got there when I left actually. He looks good, mate. Angus Young, he's gone as. I'm looking forward to getting back down there and having a drink with him.'

'Yeah, I bet you are,' Bertie said. 'Getting good value out of my tab, I'll bet.'

'Oh, it's your money behind the bar this time, is it?' Graham said. 'Thought it was rich Auntie Linda again. Well I'll be sure to raise a glass in your honour when I get back down there, boy!'

Graham pushed a couple of buttons on the television's remote control. The picture was blank for thirty seconds or so. 'Takes a little while to get started,' Graham said, looking over at Bertie. Then a picture came on the screen. At first it was a little jerky and hard to make out, but after a moment the picture settled down, becoming clearer, though it still took Bertie a little while to realise exactly what it was that he was looking at. After what turned out to be Graham's giant mass moving out of shot, Bertie realised that it was in fact the living room of Graham and Edna's place. Then Bertie saw himself move into shot. Graham was asking him about the tournament in Bridgend. Bertie heard himself onscreen boasting about his plans. He realised it was from the night he'd had a few drinks up at the pub after Linda had visited to tell them about the party. Bertie then remembered what also happened that night, and his pulse rate quickened as a result of it.

'Good so far, ennit?' Graham said, grinning. 'You ain't got a beer have you, mate?'

'No,' came Bertie's curt response.

On screen Graham left the mobile home. Bertie remembered he was going to Kareshi's for more beer, leaving Edna and himself alone. On the screen he watched himself go to sit on the sofa. A moment later Edna joined him there. He heard himself telling her about how he felt for her; and how he felt about Graham.

Graham looked over at Bertie with a knowing grin. 'Ken Bevan lent me his video camera.'

Bertie remained impassive. 'I knew you were up to something,' he said.

Graham turned towards Bertie again and sneered. 'That makes two of us then doesn't it, partner.'

Bertie watched himself kissing Edna on screen.

'Ahhhhh,' Graham said in a syrupy voice watching on. 'Don't you two make such a lovely couple? I think I'm gonna need a tissue,' he added, dabbing at his eyes.

'What's the point in all this, Graham?' Bertie said. 'Why are you showing me this? So you know about me and Edna, what of it? I suspected as much, I just didn't know how, so thanks for clearing that up.'

Graham stayed silent for some moments. 'You told Dougie about it yet?' he finally said, not taking his eyes off the screen. 'That you're 'avin' a pop on my missus?'

Now it was Bertie's turn to remain silent for a moment. 'Why? Gonna do what you do best are you, Graham?' he said. 'Gonna go shouting your mouth off again?'

'Probably for the best he knows that he's got a new stepmum in the pipeline though, ennit? Maybe I should be the one to let him know.'

'Oh piss off, you silly fat bastard.' Bertie said, finally losing his cool. 'Do what you like. You've fucked things up between me and Douglas enough already anyway.'

Graham had a little chuckle to himself, pausing the video and freezing Bertie and Edna's onscreen embrace. 'Always was a bit of a wally in your eyes, wasn't I, Bert?' he said, pulling back the curtain and peeping out the window. 'Just a big fat idiot with shit for brains, eh?'

'You said that, not me.'

Graham settled himself back in the armchair. 'You know, that double-decker video recorder of mine has totally revolutionised what I do. I can make as many copies of films as I want. Licence to print money, boy! It's what's finally made me able to pack in work altogether and go full-time at it. There's not much of a market for this type of thing, though,' he said, nodding at the screen, 'but I did find one or two other people who were interested in it. I nearly didn't bother, to be fair, but when I saw that smug smile of yours after you come back from Bridgend, well, I just couldn't help myself.'

Graham looked at his watch. A quarter of an hour had passed since he'd arrived.

There was a knock on the door.

37

'This is...' Daisy said, but did not finish.

'Bloody hell, all right, tin man!' said the multi-coloured girl with the clothes pegs in her hair and the beaming smile on her face, giving Douglas's new left leg a playful little kick. 'Cool outfit, Angus!'

'... Kelly,' Daisy said.

Douglas could hardly speak. He'd come to the party thinking about one person and one person only, possibly with the intention of declaring his undying love for her. That girl was here in a beautiful pink dress and diamond necklace, but Douglas could not see past the multi-coloured friend that Daisy had alongside her. His heart was pounding as he gazed upon the fluorescent pink, green and yellow clothes pegs dotted about Kelly's hair, and marvelled at the casual manner in which she removed her blue polyester baseball jacket with the big orange letter K on its left breast and slung it over her shoulder.

'I gotta say, you wear those skinny little legs pretty well in those shorts,' Kelly said. 'Daisy told me about your accident ... and the rest. Jesus, man, what was it like getting your legs chopped off by a train!?'

'Kelly!' Daisy said, shooting her friend a scolding glance. 'Sorry, Douglas, but Kelly here doesn't have a filter between her brain and her mouth.'

'S'all right,' Douglas said, at last finding his voice, 'I don't even have a brain.'

Kelly laughed. 'No, sweetheart, it's the scarecrow who doesn't have a brain. You're the tin man, remember?' she said, giving his leg another playful kick. 'Sorry about your mum, by the way,' she said, now in more sombre tones. 'That must really suck.'

Douglas nodded. 'Yeah,' he said with a sad little smile. 'Yeah, it really does.'

'Who made your outfit?' Kelly said. 'It's awesome.'

'My Uncle Butch. He's the one over there dressed as Cher,' Douglas said, nodding at his cross-dressing step uncle standing at the end of the bar. The Kiwi turned round at the sound of his name.

'Stop calling me Uncle Butch, you big girl's blouse!' the Kiwi shouted across the bar. Douglas smiled, as did Daisy and Kelly.

'He's pretty handy with a sewing machine, as it goes. He cut out my guitar too,' Douglas said, showing off his MDF Gibson SG. 'I painted it though. I'm gonna save up for a real one soon.'

'You play guitar?' Kelly asked eagerly. 'Very cool.'

'A bit, yeah. Mind you, I've had plenty of time to practise, sitting in that bastard chair of mine for the past two months or so. I've got an old acoustic that I play, but I smashed it up a few weeks ago. Luckily Butch was able to fix it for me. He's handy like that. Just ask my Auntie Linda.'

'Why did you smash it?' Kelly asked.

'It's a long story,' Douglas said. 'I love your outfit. You went the whole hog and got the undercut too,' Douglas said, marvelling at the shaven left side of Kelly's colourful head. 'She was in that video from the Goonies, wasn't she? And she was at Wrestle Mania 2.'

'Well, you certainly know your stuff,' Kelly said. 'You gonna get me a drink then, birthday boy, or are we gonna stand here gassing all night.'

'Maybe we could do both?' Douglas said.

Kelly grinned back at him. 'Yeah, maybe we could,' she said, playing with his red school tie. 'You can tell me all about how you blew up that sheep. You're frigging wild, motherfucker!' she said, flipping the tie up in his face. 'Come on.'

'I guess I'll leave you two to it then,' Daisy said as Kelly made her way towards the bar with Douglas following on gingerly behind. Daisy pulled at the bottom of Douglas's jacket and he stopped where he was. 'Told you she liked you,' she said with a wink, turning away.

'Daisy,' Douglas called out as the material girl made off to mingle. 'You look great too, Daisy, really. Thanks for coming.'

Daisy leaned in and gave Douglas a peck on the cheek. 'Happy birthday, Douglas,' she said, before sashaying off towards the dance floor.

38

Bertie had experienced his fair share of phantom knocks on the front door of the bungalow since he came back in August. He sincerely hoped that this was another, but the feeling in the pit of his stomach, combined with the two dark shapes he could see through the door's frosted glass outlined by the porch light, told him otherwise. He opened the front door, knowing exactly who he was going to see standing there. Behind him towards the end of the hallway, Bertie heard the kitchen door creaking open.

'Evening, sweet'art,' Rhonda said. She was wearing a white leather biker jacket with frayed tassels hanging from the sleeves. She crushed out a cigarette on the doormat of the front step with the toe of her black high-heeled boot and pointed a skinny finger at him. 'You make a terrible breakfast in bed, d'you know that?'

Bertie gave her a humourless smile as he surveyed his visitors. Glancing to his right he could see Graham peeking out from behind the curtains in the living room.

'All right, champ?' Dai said, standing beside Rhonda, chewing gum with a menacing intensity.

'So this is where you've been hiding out, is it?' Rhonda asked.

Bertie said nothing. He was thinking about slamming the door in their faces, but knew it would be pointless to do so. Not now they were here. Instead he simply turned and walked back down the hallway leaving the front door standing open.

'Charming,' he heard Rhonda say as he re-entered the living room.

'Who is it, mate?' Graham said with a broad grin of mock surprise.

'You arsehole,' Bertie said, sitting back down in the armchair beside the hi-fi as Rhonda and Dai came in.

'This is nice and cosy, isn't it, boys?' she said in a broad Welsh accent, taking a seat on the sofa between the two men. Dai sat on the arm of the sofa closest to Bertie, staring intently at him.

'Oh, you've been watching a film, have you?' Rhonda said, nodding at the freeze-framed image on the TV screen. 'I think I've seen this one.'

'Yeah, I bet you have,' Bertie said.

'Where's the money, Bert?' Dai said.

'Blimey, you don't mess about, do you?' Bertie said.

'Wasn't enough that you fucked off with the prize money...'

'That I won fair and square, eh, Dai?' Bertie said, cutting in. 'And let's not forget my nice little nine-dart bonus!' Bertie added with a wink and a smile.

'Fuck off, wanker,' Dai said, taking his eyes off Bertie for the first time and turning his attention to the dartboard on the wall.

'You looking at that tricky double 8 are you, Dai?' Bertie said, grinning at the Welshman. 'All that time behind bars that you had to practise, and you still couldn't beat me,' Bertie said, shaking his head. Dai turned back, staring a hole through Bertie, his chest rising and falling with the growing intensity of his breathing.

'Taking the prize money is one thing,' Rhonda said, 'but pissing off with the takings is, well, taking the piss.'

Bertie laughed. 'Just call it compensation for all the fraudulent maintenance money you took me for over the years. And having to put up with you and your antics.'

'Ha! Speak for yourself,' Rhonda said, 'You were a bloody embarrassment to me. I stood by you watching as your game fell apart. You become the bloody laughing stock of the town.'

'Yeah, coz your karaoke went down so well, didn't it?' Bertie said. 'That was really good for business.'

'No wonder I banished you to the kitchen then, is it?' Rhonda said, ignoring Bertie. 'Or why I started looking elsewhere,' she said, rubbing Dai's muscular shoulder beside her.

255

'Yeah, and you didn't have to look very far, did you?' Bertie said. 'Going off with lover boy, just coz he's got a better average. Mind you, we all know you lot like to keep it among yourselves, don't we?'

'There's nothing average about me, Bert, I promise you,' Dai said.

Bertie laughed. 'You never were gonna get back with me after the tournament anyway, were you?' he said, now looking at Rhonda. 'You had two horses in the race. It was win win for you, wasn't it? I just complicated things for you both by winning it myself. I'd bet my entire winnings that you were planning on doing the exact same thing to me if I'd stayed on, like you thought I was going to. You'd've had that money off me by the time *Songs of Praise* came on Sunday night. We were both stringing each other along with the exact same idea; I just beat you to the punch.'

Rhonda smiled, showing a crooked row of nicotine-stained teeth. 'You're not as stupid as you look, are you?' she said.

Bertie laughed. 'You are.'

Rhonda's smile morphed into a sneer. 'Still got the old caravan, I see,' she said. 'That brings back memories, eh, Bert? Me and Shirley. You and Mr You've Been Framed over there,' she said, nodding at Graham, who was being unusually quiet watching the drama unfold. 'Between us we pretty much took 'em for all they was worth, issenit? A bit like you did to me,' she said, levelling an icy gaze at Bertie.

'Yeah, except Jim Bowen never tracked me down afterwards, asking for it all back like you two clowns.'

'Where is it?' Rhonda asked.

'Where's what?' Bertie said, shaking his head.

'Come on, Bert, don't make this any harder than it needs to be,' Rhonda said. 'I wouldn't want Dai here to get upset.'

'Oh no, we wouldn't want that, would we? We all know what a bad loser he is,' Bertie said, sitting up in his chair, warming to the charade.

'Just give 'em the money, Bert,' Graham said from over by the window.

'Oh, the prat out of hell's finally found his voice again. Yeah, you'd like that, wouldn't you, Graham?' Bertie said. 'Love to see me get what's coming to me finally, wouldn't you? Is that why you got these two jokers involved, is it? Because you're too pig shit ignorant to do it by yourself?'

'You're a flash bastard, aren't you?' Graham snapped. 'You always were. Better on the board, better with the birds. I would say a better dad, but that's debatable, isn't it, given how things are between you and Douglas.'

Bertie smiled. 'And this coming from the man who can't remember where his own son is buried. No wonder Edna can't wait to get shot of you. And besides, it's thanks to you and your big mouth that things are the way they are between me and Douglas. Let's not forget that.'

'Yeah,' Graham said sitting up in his chair, 'and I can make them a damn sight worse for you 'n' all if I wanted to, couldn't I?' he said, nodding at the TV.

Out in the hallway a door slammed and the kitchen light came on. Everyone except Bertie turned towards it.

'Who's that?' Rhonda asked.

'That?' Bertie said casually. 'That's my wife.'

Dai got up, pulling Bertie's darts out of the board. He walked back to the red strip of the oche marker on the carpet and started to throw. 'Your wife's dead, boyo. Fatty here told us all about it. Shocking,' he said, shaking his head with a smirk on his face, 'and if you don't go and get that money pretty bloody sharpish, you'll be getting reunited with her.'

'That money is for my son,' Bertie said, looking at Rhonda. 'My real son. Not some foster son of a two-bit jailbird loser.'

'You think I'd've 'ad an 'alf English kid running about the place?' Rhonda said. 'Not a chance. Now, one more time, where is the money?'

Bertie remained silent as Dai continued to throw his darts, the Welshman looking on in quiet amazement as each dart he threw fell to the ground before it made contact with the board, as if being swatted away by an unseen hand which, as Bertie knew, was most probably the case.

'Having a bit of trouble, are we?' Bertie said.

Dai picked up the darts and threw again. The same thing happened. 'Fuck this,' he said, turning and grabbing Bertie by the scruff of the neck. 'Where is it?' he shouted.

Graham shifted uncomfortably in his chair. 'Just give 'em the money, Bert,' he said with beads of perspiration popping on his forehead. 'Come on, you don't want any trouble, do you?'

'It's a bit late for you to start giving a shit, isn't it, mate?' Bertie said, his voice constricted by the strangulating neckline of his T-shirt that Dai was twisting. 'Anyway, I've told you, the money isn't here, so you two clowns can do your worst for all I care.'

Dai released his grip on Bertie's shirt and sat back down on the arm of the chair, eyeing Bertie with seething intensity, his chest rising and falling with each angered breath. Beside him Rhonda shook her head. 'Looks like it's gonna have to be plan B then, issenit?' she said, looking up at Dai.

'What's plan B?' Graham tentatively asked.

'Bully's star prize,' Rhonda said.

39

'I like a lad with a good sense of humour,' Kelly said to Douglas, as the pair of them stood on the Pressed Fruitbowl's makeshift dance floor in front of a focused Tony Gables' DJ rig.

The pair had been chatting virtually non-stop since Daisy had introduced them. Douglas had regaled her with tales of his wild antics back in August: smashing the windows; taking Moses for a 'walk' on the railway (something, he was quick to point out, that he was not at all proud of); then the fete itself and all the subsequent carnage that that day had brought. That day had been different, though. He was secretly quite pleased with how things had turned out that day (minus the accident that had landed him in the wheelchair, of course). He'd even confided in Kelly about his dad. Talking to her felt so easy and so natural. Despite her lively personality and lairy image, she was a sympathetic and understanding listener. Other than making a bit of casual chitchat with his guests, again mostly about his antics back in August, he'd broken away from Kelly's side just once for a quick pep talk with Butch, then to Tony's DJ booth for the musical request he hoped would help him seal the deal. It was a request for the song he had sung along to at Butch's on the day they had made his outfit and painted his guitar, though that day he thought it was going to be Daisy he was going to have to try to impress.

As it was, when Tony Gables put on Crowded House's 'Fall at Your Feet', it was Kelly's colourful, fingerless-gloved hand that Douglas had requested on the dance floor: a hand she was only too happy to give. Douglas took it and led her to the middle of the dance floor. It wasn't really dancing, as Douglas still relied heavily on his crutches for balance, but he could shuffle round on his false legs, and with Kelly's arms wrapped tightly around him as Butch Ransom's hero Neil Finn serenaded them, Douglas was in dreamland. Butch was watching the germination of his step-nephew's first proper shot at romance from the sidelines with obvious enthusiasm and quiet pride. Linda beside him smiled at the young pair shuffling around on the dance floor. It was all going perfectly to plan until a moment of unforeseen embarrassment threatened to sabotage all of Douglas's previous hard work.

'Douglas, how many crutches do you have?' Kelly said. 'Coz it feels like there's a third one digging into my hip.'

Douglas felt his insides constrict and his face flush with an embarrassment that, were it not for the multi-coloured lights of the dance floor, would have been as red as his outfit. For a moment he contemplated breaking away from Kelly's embrace, until she pulled him closer and smiled.

'It's OK,' she said, with a little laugh. It wasn't a laugh designed to illicit shame; it was warm and understanding. 'In fact I take it as a compliment,' she added, looking into the pair of downcast eyes, semi-hidden by the peak of his red velvet cap. She flipped up the peak of the cap and kissed him on the cheek.

'I'm sorry,' Douglas said as the pair continued slowly rotating.

'Don't be daft, you silly sausage,' Kelly said, raising Douglas's hand to her lips and giving it a kiss. 'Maybe it's just your brain's way of compensating in case you over-balance?'

'That's one way of looking at it, I suppose,' Douglas said, feeling his spirits lift.

'What happened to your hand?' Kelly asked, examining Douglas's scarred palm in the multi-coloured illumination of Tony Gables' disco lights.

'I cut it on some broken glass,' he said. 'Both hands. It was from a picture of my mum. It got broken.'

'Oh, that's sad,' Kelly said. 'How did it get broken?'

Douglas hesitated a little. 'It went flying out of my lap when I jumped out of my wheelchair to punch my dad in the bollocks,' he blurted out.

Kelly held a hand of her own to her mouth. 'Sorry,' she said, unable to suppress her giggling, 'I know I shouldn't laugh, but...'

'It's OK,' Douglas said, smiling himself. 'It's ridiculous, I know it is. If it makes it any funnier, this was before I had these things,' he said, tapping his false leg. 'I was airborne for about a second. I also pulled Graham

Glass's trousers down, trying to pull myself up. It was at my mum's wake. It happened just over there,' Douglas said, nodding towards the jukebox.

'Shit, man, you sure have got some stories, haven't you?' Kelly said, this time kissing Douglas's scarred palm. 'And I must admit, you dance quite well for a guy with no legs,' Kelly said, moving her hands down from Douglas's hips to his backside, giving his cheeks a little squeeze.

Douglas smiled, nuzzling his chin into the comforting warmth of Kelly's neck, enjoying the fruity scent of her colourful hair. It then occurred to him how, after finally succeeding in winning the affections of someone of the opposite sex, and not just anyone but someone as beautiful and exotic, as wild and wonderful as Kelly, now the person he wanted to tell most, apart from Butch who smiled and raised a pint glass at him, was his dad.

40

Dai kicked the television over with considerable and unnerving force. It fell backwards in a flash of sparks and a puff of smoke. The freeze frame of Bertie and Edna went with it. Graham, sitting closest to it, watched on with genuine fear now evident on his face. Bertie just watched the Welshman's tantrum impassively from the comfort of his own armchair.

'As you can see, Dai is beginning to lose his patience,' Rhonda casually remarked just as the lights in the living room began to flicker. Then the door slammed shut. It opened and closed three more times. Dai marched across the lounge and behind the armchair where Bertie was grinning and shaking his head. The Welshman wrapped a muscular arm around Bertie's neck.

'I'm not fucking about any more, Bert,' Dai hissed. 'Now, where's the money!?'

Bertie's face was quickly turning red as he struggled to breathe.

'Just tell 'em, Bert, for God's sake!' Graham shouted in clipped, panicky tones, his face now a glistening sheen of sweat.

Unable to breathe, let alone speak, Bertie tapped Dai's beefy shoulder and the Welshman eased up his grip, but did not let go entirely. 'Right, you got something you want to say to me, Englishman?'

Bertie took in a gulp of air and his face returned to a slightly more normal colour. He looked at Rhonda, then up at Dai. 'What money?' he said with a perplexed shake of the head.

'Right, I've 'ad enough of this shit,' Dai said, releasing his grip on Bertie and going towards the closed living room door. He turned the handle but the door would not open. 'Unlock the fuckin' door!' he bellowed.

'There isn't a lock on it, you berk,' Bertie said. 'Maybe you're just not as strong as you thought you were, Dai. Need to go back inside and start lifting them weights with the big boyos again.'

'Bertie, come on,' Graham said. 'Enough's enough. They're bloody serious. Stop mucking about. Give them the money and they'll be out of here!'

Dai finally opened the door and left the bungalow.

'Is that what you expected when you were planning this, was it, Graham?' Bertie said. 'For these two bozos to rock up and for me just to roll over and give them the cash? Are things not quite going how you all planned?'

Dai was back in the living room with a roll of gaffer tape, a green and red bar towel and a small brown bottle of liquid.

'Did you remember to shut the front door?' Bertie said. 'You'll let the heating out. I'm not made of money, you know.'

'One more time, you English wanker,' Dai said, breathing deeply in and out, standing over Bertie, his muscular frame rising and falling with each seething breath. 'Cash!'

The plastic lid of the hi-fi's record player started opening and closing like the maniacal mouth of some demented robot. Dai, wearing the roll of gaffer tape on his fist like an oversized knuckle duster, slammed it down on the turntable, smashing the lid and bringing Thin Lizzy to a premature end. The Irish rockers were replaced by a low humming noise. The broken lid continued to open and close spasmodically, so Dai brought his gaffer-taped fist down on top of it again and again until finally it stopped. He then turned his attention to the Blouse family photo on the wall above the fireplace.

'Ahhh, happy fuckin' families,' he said with a disingenuous smile, before smashing his gaffer-taped fist into that too, sending a spray of shattered glass tinkling to the floor as the photo fell from the wall to join the glinting shards on the carpet.

As Dai sneered, admiring his handiwork, the speaker on the left side of the stereo flew through the air towards the grinning Welshman, its sharp wooden point catching him flush on the temple, immediately drawing blood before clattering to the floor and landing at his feet. Dazed and disorientated, Dai fell to one knee clutching the side of his head, and for a few seconds nothing happened and nothing was said, until Rhonda lit a cigarette.

'Looks like it's definitely plan B then,' she said, exhaling a cloud of smoke.

'Sorry, did I say you could smoke in here?' Bertie asked. 'I've actually given up. I don't like that sort of thing in the house.'

Still on one knee, Dai shook his head, blinking away the pain. He looked at Bertie, got to his feet and charged over, wrestling Bertie out of his armchair, cinching his hands behind his back and wrapping them together with the gaffer tape. 'Any last words before we say night night, Bert?' Dai said, pouring the liquid from the brown bottle on to the green and red 'Allbright Bitter' bar towel.

'Yeah. I hope that shit'ole pub of yours closes its doors for good. It's no wonder you're going out of business if you're still selling that piss 'n' all!' he said, looking at the now sodden bar towel. Bertie then turned his attention to Graham. 'She's gonna leave you, mate,' he said. 'Regardless of what these two nob 'eads have in store for me. If she can't be mine, at least I know that she won't be yours. Tell Douglas I love him and that I said happy birthday.'

'Very sweet,' Dai said, grabbing Bertie in another strong headlock and smothering his twisting, turning face with the wet bar towel. Bertie kicked and struggled, but his gaffer-taped hands made it impossible for him to escape. Dai held the towel over his face, watching as Bertie's movements slowed, before going completely limp as he lost consciousness. Dai pulled off a strip of gaffer tape and stuck it over Bertie's mouth before wrapping his ankles together as well for good measure.

'Right you, fuck off,' Dai said to an ashen-faced Graham who had been watching the whole thing in abject terror. 'And don't you breathe a word of this to anyone, or else we'll be back for you 'n' all, right?'

'What are you gonna do?' Graham asked in a trembling voice.

'None of your fuckin' business,' Dai said, grabbing Bertie under the arms.

Graham struggled to his feet, watching as Bertie was dragged out of the living room and down the hall towards the open front door. He was a few feet short of it when all the lights in the house went out and the front door slammed shut.

'Looks like your old lady doesn't want to let you go,' Rhonda said to an unconscious Bertie as she grappled with the front door handle. 'Don't worry, love,' she shouted into the darkness, 'he'll be with you soon enough.'

'Out the way,' Dai said, dropping Bertie back down to the floor with a thump before kicking the front door open. 'Right fatty, out!' he said.

Graham squeezed past them all in the hallway on his way to the front door, stepping out into the cold night air.

'And oi, remember, not a word about this to anyone,' Dai said, pointing his finger at Graham. 'You just go and have a nice time at that party and keep that big fuckin' mouth of yours shut, right?'

Graham nodded, his mouth agape but remaining deathly silent, looking from the front step into the darkened hallway. He made his way down the garden path and through the open garden gate, slowly putting distance between himself and the bungalow. He allowed himself one last furtive look over his shoulder. Dai was bundling Bertie's limp body into the caravan. Rhonda was walking towards the Sierra.

41

Douglas had his cut-out guitar slung back over his shoulder and was leaning on one of his crutches at the bar with Billy Idol, Johnny Rotten and Elvis. His red blazer was slung over a nearby bar stool, his white shirt sticking to his back with sweat. In his free hand he was holding a cold pint of lager, his eyes focused on Kelly on the dance floor: she was nose to nose with Daisy as the two of them belted out the chorus of T'Pau's 'China in Your Hand'. He was a bit tipsy from the alcohol, but by no means drunk. His feelings for Kelly as he watched her pirouetting were far more intoxicating than any amount of booze he'd consumed. As he watched the girl who had been hanging on his every word almost all night, he felt a comfort and a serenity that he hadn't felt in such a long time, if ever.

The feelings of anger and frustration he'd felt since the accident; the painful frustration of rehab; the isolation; the wheelchair; even all the emotional baggage he'd been carrying around with him since before his mum had died – those feelings felt like they had been gently washed away. A few hours in Kelly's company had proven to be far more effective than any amount of counselling he'd had to endure over the past couple of months. Now, standing once again on what he would have to accept as his own two feet, he felt a strange but very real sense of contentment.

'You smooth little rascal!' Butch said, putting his arm around Douglas. 'Told you it'd do the trick, eh?' Butch held up what was left of his pint. 'Cheers!' he said.

Douglas smiled. 'Cheers, Butch,' he said, for once not prefixing his name with the usual antagonistic familial association. Butch grinned and departed, heading over to Tony Gables' DJ booth. Moments later, the music faded away to silence and the multi-coloured lights surrounding Tony's disco booth went out. Only the soft lighting behind the bar and the disco ball rotating overhead remained on, ensuring the pub was not left in total darkness. An ethereal glow emanated from behind the kitchen's porthole window; a moment later it opened as Linda came in holding the birthday cake, her face illuminated by the eighteen candles dotted around the base of the pyramid. The pub burst into a rousing rendition of Happy Birthday and Kelly came to Douglas's side, putting her arm around his waist and leading him over to a strategically positioned single table in the middle of the pub.

Douglas smiled as Linda set the cake down in front of him, and he gazed in awe and wonderment at the heavy metal baking creation. As the singing came to an end, he looked around the pub at all the smiling faces. He felt a sizable lump in his throat as it really hit home that for the first time ever, neither of his parents were here to share in the experience.

'Go on then,' Kelly said, nodding at the cake. 'And don't forget to make a wish,' she added, flashing Douglas one of the sweetest smiles he had ever seen.

Douglas took a deep intake of breath and gazed into Kelly's eyes, winking at her before doing what was required of him, extinguishing all eighteen candles in one cheek-expanding blow. Tony's disco lights came back on, flashing and rotating once again in multi-coloured splendour as everyone gave Douglas a round of applause.

'Speech!' Butch shouted.

For a brief moment the old feelings of awkwardness and embarrassment threatened to sabotage Douglas's moment as he struggled to find his voice. But he only had to gaze round the pub at the people surrounding him – at Linda, Butch, Daisy, Kelly, and all the other assembled guests – for that uncomfortable moment to pass. He smiled, thinking back to previous birthdays when his mum had made cakes just as impressive as the one before him. A tear rolled down his cheek and a brief giggling fit was overcome as Douglas cleared his throat.

'I never thought I needed anyone,' he croaked, clearing his throat for the second time in the silence. 'And I never had too many friends. When I think about it, after the things I've done, I don't blame people for not wanting anything to do with me. After the accident, my Auntie Linda kept telling me that I needed people, and I thought she was talking rubbish. I thought that after everything that's happened to me and after everything I'd put people through, they wouldn't want to know, and that they probably thought I deserved what had happened to me,' he said, tapping his right false leg with the tip of his crutch. 'But she said this one thing, and despite what I thought then, it's always stuck with me. She said, "Don't give up on them and they won't give up on you".' Douglas smiled, looking at his auntie who smiled back with a tear in her eye. 'So I'm glad that you're all here. And I'm glad that you haven't given up on me.'

There was a collective 'Ahhhh' from the pub and another ripple of applause.

'I wish my mum was here,' he continued, the words only just making it past the resurgent lump in his throat. 'She'd be well chuffed with all this, that's for sure. Still, it goes to show that her skills run in the family,' he said, looking at Linda.

At the back of the room the pub doors clattered open and Graham Glass walked in. Briefly, everyone turned in his direction.

'Sorry,' Graham said, looking a touch embarrassed. He remained where he was and all eyes once again returned to Douglas.

'I guess what I'm saying is that my Auntie Linda was right. You do need people. And the more the merrier!' he added, raising his pint glass to the assembled congregation, and feeling Kelly's arm tighten around his waist. 'Here's to you all!'

Everyone clapped as Linda handed Douglas the large knife beside the cake. He took it from her, smiling as Graham quietly made his way towards the end of the bar. A few moments later, a fresh pint and a whisky chaser were placed in front of him.

'You got some skills, haven't you, Linda?' Douglas said, brandishing the knife.

'I'm afraid I can't take credit for it, Douglas,' she said.

'No?' he said, his brow crumpled, the knife hovering above the pyramid's iced golden capstone.

'No,' she said, 'your dad made it.'

268

Douglas's eyes widened and his mouth hung open a little. 'He made that?'

'Very, very cool,' Kelly said beside him.

Douglas looked at the cake, smiling and shaking his head. 'That bloody bloke,' he said chuckling away.

'Maybe he might like a piece?' Kelly said, looking up into Douglas's eyes. He stared back, still not believing that this beautiful girl had come into his life.

'Yeah,' he said, placing the knife back down beside the cake. 'I suppose he might.'

42

'That was a lovely speech, dear,' Reverend Bowen said. 'Your mum would be so proud of you.'

'Thanks, Hilda,' Douglas said, gingerly making his way back to the bar, though this time not to order a drink. 'You've been gone a while, haven't you, Meatloaf?' he said to Graham who was cutting a sizable but lonely figure at the end of the bar. 'You seen my dad?'

'Err, yeah,' Graham stuttered, wiping sweat from his brow with his shirt sleeve. 'Yeah, I saw him.'

'How was he?' Douglas asked, retrieving his red school blazer from off the bar stool.

'Well, he was a bit worse for wear when I left him, to be honest,' Graham said, stumbling with his words. 'We had a couple of drinks.'

'Oh yeah? You don't look too good yourself. Maybe a piece of cake and some fireworks will sort the old sod out, eh?' Douglas said as Linda helped him to negotiate his arms into the sleeves of his jacket while he tried to maintain his balance on one of his crutches.

'I wouldn't bother, mate, honestly,' Graham said.

Douglas laughed. 'Well, given your recent track record, you'll forgive me if I don't believe a bloody word you say, pal.'

'Amen to that,' Edna said, standing nearby.

'Why did you say he'd gone back to Bridgend?' Douglas asked, now successfully back in his jacket. 'Edna said you all knew he was coming back, so why did you tell me he'd gone off again?'

Graham stared silently at his pint.

'Well, whatever,' Douglas said casually, emboldened by drink and high on romance. 'It doesn't matter now, does it? I'm going down there to get him. He can still make it for the fireworks, can't he?'

Refusing company for the short walk down to Pugsden Lane, Douglas left the pub. Within seconds the warm sweat on his back turned to a chilly sheet of ice as he gingerly walked with the aid of his crutches towards the orange sodium streetlight glowing above the street sign of his old road, and his old home beyond. As he rounded the bend with his old house coming into view, Douglas noticed an unfamiliar car parked out in front of the caravan. As he got closer, he could see that it was a red Ford Sierra. Around him he heard fireworks going off in the village.

He drew level with the house, to see a large man in a black leather jacket locking the door of the caravan. He could also see now that there was a woman sitting in the passenger seat of the Sierra.

'Who the bloody hell are you?' Douglas asked.

The large man, clearly a little startled by Douglas's sudden appearance, turned to face him.

'All right?' the man said. 'I'm, err, just picking up the caravan. I'm a friend of your dad's.'

Douglas detected the Welsh accent straight away and, though he'd had a few drinks, it was not enough to silence the alarm bells now ringing in his head, nor quell the churning in his stomach. He also noticed that the caravan was hooked onto the Sierra's towbar.

'I didn't know he was selling it,' Douglas said, leaning on his crutches, partially taking the weight off his aching stumps. He looked over at the bungalow. The front door was standing wide open. His heart beat fast beneath his shirt and blazer. 'Where's my dad?' he said.

The man squared up to him. 'I'd get lost if I was you, boy,' he snarled.

Douglas looked down at the woman smoking a cigarette in the passenger seat of the Sierra. Her face was partially clouded by smoke but exposed by the half-wound-down window.

'All right, Rhonda?' Douglas said.

The woman looked up instinctively at the sound of her name, telling Douglas all he needed to know. Her sour-looking face was the last thing he saw before Dai knocked him out.

Rhonda got out of the car and flicked away her cigarette, looking down at Douglas who was now lying unconscious on the driveway, his crutches either side of him. 'What the bloody hell are we gonna do with him?' she asked.

'I'll tell you what we're gonna do,' Dai said, grabbing Douglas under the arms, in much the same way he had his father ten minutes earlier. 'We're gonna give these two wankers a nice bit of family bonding time. That's what we're gonna do.'

Dai dragged Douglas towards the caravan door, his false legs leaving a trail in the gravel. Dai unlocked the door with his free hand as the other held up Douglas. 'I brought you some company, Bert,' he said, dragging Douglas into the caravan's gloomy interior. Bertie, still unconscious, was in no fit state to hear him. 'Little unexpected visit from the birthday boy. Wrong place, wrong time, unfortunately. Shame really, but there you are,' he said, making to leave the caravan. 'I'm just gonna take a couple of little souvenirs, if it's all right with you,' he said, turning back and grabbing Douglas's left leg, sticking his hand up Douglas's shorts, fumbling about for a moment as he blindly negotiated Douglas's artificial hardware. Eventually Dai succeeded in pulling down the black rubber sleeve that went from Douglas's upper thigh and down over his socket joint, the black sleeve that had until now kept his artificial limb in place. Dai then succeeded in removing the leg altogether, exposing Douglas's stump which was wrapped in a smaller black sleeve of its own. He then repeated the process with Douglas's right leg. 'Well, we'll just drop you two off; then me and the missus are gonna leg it back to Wales. Sorry we got off on the wrong foot,' Dai said to a now legless Douglas, lying as silent and motionless as his father at the other end of the caravan. 'Well, better run!'

Dai stepped out of the caravan, opened the boot of the Sierra and threw in Douglas's false legs, along with his crutches. He closed it back down, locked the caravan once again and got into the driver's side of the car. He started it up and put his foot on the accelerator. The car resisted a little at first under its newly acquired payload. Dai gently increased the pressure on the pedal and slowly both vehicles began to move.

43

The music was still pumping out at the Pressed Fruitbowl and the dance floor was full as revellers hoo hoo'd their way through the opening bars of Deacon Blue's 'Real Gone Kid'. The pyramid Powerslave cake remained fully intact on the single table, the clean knife lying beside it.

'That was a lovely speech he gave, wasn't it?' Linda said to Butch, raising her voice in order to be heard over the music. 'I didn't know he had it in him. Alice would've been so proud.'

'Yeah, he did great,' Butch shouted back. 'And who'd've thought it, eh? Him and Kelly. The girl can't seem to get enough of him. I knew he'd come good in the end.'

'Thank you,' Linda said. 'You've been great for him. With all his problems around his dad, it's been brilliant having you around to help him with the boys' stuff. I really am very grateful.'

'No sweat,' Butch said, drawing Linda close and giving her a big kiss on the lips.

'Pah!' she said, pulling a long dark hair from her mouth. 'Your bloody wig!'

'Sorry, sweetheart. Just trying to Cher the love,' Butch said, grinning.

'Appalling,' Linda said, though she was also smiling.

Linda craned her neck to look at the clock by the bar. 'What time did Douglas go? He's been gone a while now, hasn't he?' Linda scanned the pub. Kelly and Daisy were dancing. Reverend Bowen and the Bumstead twins along with their father Eric were also throwing shapes on the crowded dance floor.

The pub doors swung open. Linda turned, expecting to see Douglas and Bertie walking in. Instead she saw a policeman.

'Hey up, the stripper's arrived!' Butch shouted as Sergeant Frisk made his way towards the bar. 'How goes it, Alan? Not sure if you'd be Douglas's first choice, mate, but we'll be sure to run it past him when he gets back.'

'Butch, shhh,' Linda said, slapping Butch's arm.

Over at the bar, Graham Glass was sweating profusely and still sitting alone; he ordered another double whisky, occasionally looking over to take fearful glances at Sergeant Frisk. Edna, polishing glasses at the other end of the bar, was watching her husband with a keen eye.

'The birthday boy not around?' Frisk asked as Linda steered him to a quieter corner of the pub.

'He went down to get Bertie about twenty minutes ago,' Linda said. 'What's wrong?'

'He went down to get his dad?' Frisk asked. 'Down Pugsden Lane?'

'Yes,' Linda said, not liking the expression of concern burgeoning on the policeman's face. 'Alan, what is it?'

'Has Bertie sold the caravan, d'you know?' Frisk asked.

'Not that I'm aware of,' Linda said. 'Why?' Edna left the end of the bar to join them.

'Well, it's just that I was pulling into the station a minute ago when I saw it going down the High street. You're sure he hasn't sold it?'

'I'm not a hundred per cent, but I think it highly unlikely. He certainly hasn't mentioned anything of the sort to me. Are you sure it was the same caravan?'

'Yes, I'm sure,' Frisk said with a little smile. 'I've seen that caravan enough over the years; though I've never seen it in motion. It was definitely a Marauder 500. It was being towed by a red Ford Sierra. I don't know if that rings any bells with anyone?' Frisk said, his question receiving only blank expressions and shakes of the head. 'The other thing I thought strange about it was that it turned down the causeway. I didn't recognise the car as belonging to anyone local. Also, there was a little Welsh flag on the back of it. Now if anyone from Wales was buying it, then going down the causeway certainly isn't the quickest way back there; not unless they'd taken a wrong turn.'

Edna looked over at her husband. Graham's pale face was staring back at them all, the sweat teeming from under his Meatloaf wig.

'What have you done?' Edna said, moving towards her husband. Linda, Butch and Frisk followed behind her. 'I asked you a question,' Edna said as they all gathered around Graham.

He began to mumble to himself, his eyes glassy with tears and his bottom lip trembling. 'I told him to give 'em the money,' he finally blurted out. 'They said if he gave them the cash, there wouldn't be any trouble. But he wouldn't have any of it.' Tears were now rolling down his chubby cheeks. 'He wouldn't give 'em it so they...'

'Who did, Graham?' Frisk asked.

'You told them, didn't you?' Edna said. 'You treacherous bastard, you told Rhonda and that thug boyfriend of hers, and now they've come up here, haven't they?'

'I thought they'd just take the money and go,' Graham said, his voice faltering.

'You're pathetic,' Edna said. 'A pathetic fucking Judas.'

'Bertie and Douglas still haven't come back, Sergeant,' Linda said, her voice rising with concern and audible to the rest of the pub over the top of the music, now turned down to a much lower volume. Everyone, including DJ Tony Gables, was now looking over towards Sergeant Frisk and the others.

'I never meant it to happen,' Graham stuttered.

'Bit late for all that,' Edna said, looking disdainfully at her husband.

'Sergeant, please, we must go and look for them,' Linda said. 'You said they were heading down the causeway. What d'you think they could be up to?'

'I wouldn't like to speculate,' he said, 'but it's probably best we go and find out.'

44

Fireworks were going off all over the village as Dai drove the Sierra and the caravan towards the Stocks Lane level crossing. Its barriers were raised, its warning lights dull and inactive.

'Are you sure about this?' Rhonda said beside him.

'Bit late for that now, love,' Dai said. 'And anyway fuck 'em. Fuck Bertie and fuck that spazzy little cripple kid of his. That money was our last chance at keeping the pub open, you realise that, yeah? Well you can kiss that goodbye now, love. Fuckin' goodbye, Red Dragon,' he said with a little wave of his hand as they crested the incline of the level crossing, coming to a halt on the railway line.

Dai inched the car forward, checking his mirrors. He got out to appraise the caravan's position. Satisfied with his parking, he unhooked it from the Sierra's towbar. The caravan was now parked right across the up line, where services heading to London passed through the village, more often than not at very high speed.

'You wanna stay and watch?' he asked Rhonda casually as he got back into the Sierra's driver's seat.

Rhonda silently shook her head and Dai drove off the crossing and away from the caravan.

45

Douglas came to, holding the side of his head, wondering what the hell had happened to cause such a throbbing pain. Having already suffered one serious concussion, he remembered how the doctors at the hospital had told him that another blow to the head could have serious implications for his long-term recovery.

As his surroundings fuzzily began coming into focus, he then wondered what the bloody hell he was doing in the caravan. He'd not set foot in it since he'd last had an actual foot to set in it. And that was the third alarming question that he posed himself. He now had neither real nor artificial feet. His new legs had gone. Only the sore and aching black-sleeved stumps were visible in the poor light of the caravan. He'd fully intended to get completely legless at the party, but this was definitely not what he had in mind. He looked around him towards the windows, wondering where the lights were coming from. After spending so much time in the crappy old thing over the years, he had become accustomed to its permanent positioning on the driveway of his former home, and to its surrounding geography. He couldn't see the familiar lone orange street light that had stood sentry over the old thing for the past six years. Now there was a soft orange glow coming from all directions. 'I don't think we're in Kansas any more, Toto,' he said to himself, still a bit woozily, rubbing his head. As his vision became clear and his eyesight gradually adjusted to the light, he looked down the caravan towards where the two single beds were, the channel between the two beds being his former oche. In that channel he now saw the dark outline of something ... or someone. His heart rate increased as he pulled himself towards the shape barely illuminated by the soft orange light. His mind went back to that terrible night in August when he had found his mum by the trembling light of his battery-powered torch on the kitchen floor.

He almost passed out as it became apparent that history might very well be repeating itself.

Instinctively he tried the door handle of the caravan as he dragged himself towards the dark, immobile shape. The door was locked. Despite this disconcerting revelation, a little laugh escaped him. Douglas made it to the dark shape at the opposite end of the caravan. It was his father, just as he knew it would be. Douglas felt his dad's neck for a pulse, feeling a weak but definitely present beat. He was alive at least. He shook him, doing his best to rouse him, but it appeared to be of little use. He saw now that his dad's legs were taped together, as were his hands behind his back. Another piece of black gaffer tape also covered his mouth.

'Fuckin' 'ell,' he said, looking from his father to where his new legs used to be. Douglas pulled himself up and on to the left-hand single bed, frustrated by the awkwardness of his progress. He pulled back the tatty net curtain, drawing in breath and not believing what he saw. The rails glowed orange from the four lights overhead that illuminated the level crossing. 'Oooofff,' Douglas said as he realised with growing anxiety where the caravan was parked. There was no signal box, though, he realised, leading Douglas to deduce that they were on the Stocks Lane crossing. His head still pounded as his memory returned. He recalled talking to the Welshman outside his old house, and seeing the sour face of his dad's ex. Then he woke up here. Douglas looked down at his father, who was still not moving. Gracelessly he threw himself down to the floor, wincing at the pain from his stumps as they banged on the floor. He pulled himself back over to the door, frantically pulling at the handle, but getting the same results as before. The door wouldn't budge. Despite this he tried again, beginning to giggle as his mind became increasingly frantic. He could hear fireworks going off and wished so much to be back at the party in Kelly's arms, eating cake and watching fireworks of his own. Then came the sound that filled him with dread. The crossing's alarm began to sound, accompanied by the illumination of the flashing red warning lights either side of it. The barriers descended, with the caravan trapped between them. As quick as he could physically manage, Douglas pulled himself up and over the prone figure of his father, back on to the single bed. Again he pulled back the curtain, laughing as he looked down the railway line into the darkness towards the west, where in the very far distance a twinkling white light was growing increasingly brighter.

46

After divulging the events of what had happened down at the bungalow, Graham cut a sad and lonely figure at the end of the bar of the Pressed Fruitbowl: full of free alcohol, but stone cold sober with the terror of what might be happening elsewhere in the village.

Frisk had radioed out an APB to police stations in the surrounding area, giving his colleagues the registration number and description of the car he had seen towing the caravan.

'With any luck they'll still be around,' he said. 'They can't have gone far.'

'I'll do a circuit on my trike, see what I can see,' Reverend Bowen said, fishing her keys out of her black jeans. 'It's all right, Alan, no need to get the breathaliser out, I've been on the ginger beer.'

'Hilda, if you do see them, please don't try to apprehend them yourself,' Frisk warned her. 'Come and find me. From what Graham's told us, they are clearly desperate and potentially very dangerous individuals. Who knows what they're capable of.'

'God help them if I do find them, Sergeant,' Bowen said as she left the pub with Frisk following on behind her.

'If anything has happened to those two, I'm holding you responsible,' Edna hissed, pointing a finger at her silent, soon to be ex-husband.

'Oh and Graham,' Frisk said, turning round, 'I'll be wanting a word with you about some bootlegged videotapes that have been doing the rounds. Your name's come up on more than one occasion during the course of my enquiries, so don't go too far, will you?'

'Linda, is Douglas going to be all right?' Kelly asked nervously, twirling a strand of multi-coloured hair. Daisy had her arm around her friend.

'I'm sure they'll be fine,' Linda said, trying her best to sound convincing.

'I'm going out to look for them too,' Butch said.

Despite the seriousness of the situation, Linda could not help but laugh looking at Butch in his stockings and suspenders. 'Dressed like that?' she said. 'God, you'll be the one getting arrested if you go out looking like that! That's if you don't freeze to death first.'

Butch smiled, kissed Linda warmly on the lips and headed out the door.

Over at the bar, in between swigs of beer, Graham was mumbling away to himself. 'I'm sorry,' he said, looking round at Linda. 'I didn't ... I ... I wasn't ... I never...I mean, I never...'

'Yeah, that'll be your epitaph, Graham,' Edna said, frantically polishing an already clean pint glass. 'You bloody never.'

47

After being confronted by the barriers and flashing red lights of Steventon's second level crossing, Dai reversed away in frustration. He had intended to go back the way he had come, over Stocks Lane and back out of the village that way. The only problem being that by the time he had spun the Sierra round in the car park of a converted barn at the bottom of Stocks Lane, the barriers had come down, sabotaging the plan entirely. In frustration, they had sped around the village in an attempt to make an escape, only to be halted by the village's second set of barriers at the causeway level crossing.

'I told you we should've scoped this fuckin' place out properly, didn'I?' he said, running a sweaty palm over his shorn head. 'How are we meant to get out of here now if the fuckin' railway's blockin' us off at every pissin' turn? Them bastard barriers aren't gonna go back up after the train's smashed through that piece of shit caravan neither. Driver'll radio it in. We gotta find another way out of yur.' They set off down Castle Street, back the way they'd come, back towards the Stocks Lane crossing. As Dai rounded the bend back into Stocks Lane, the caravan came back into view.

'Fuckin' 'ell!' Dai shouted, sticking the car in reverse and backing away at speed. 'What's up yur?' he said, reversing back into the car park of the converted barn and taking a right up the farm track that ran alongside it.

'This don't feel right to me,' Rhonda said, bumping around in the passenger seat as the car rattled over the potholes and rough terrain of the farm track.

'Well, we haven't got us much fuckin' choice now, 'ave we?' Dai shouted as up ahead in the beam of the car's headlights a gate came into view. It was a five-barred gate but it appeared to be shut.

'Fuckin' 'ell!' he shouted again, hastily jumping out of the car to inspect the gate. He found a chain and rattled it, testing its security. The chain in turn rattled a rusty padlock: old but secure. The gate was firmly locked.

'Fuckin' thing's locked,' Dai said, getting back into the car.

In the still of the night came the sound of a distant horn. Rhonda looked at Dai, though in the darkness he couldn't see the look of concern on her face.

'We gotta get out of this fuckin' place, sharpish,' Dai said. Rhonda nodded but remained silent, the sound of the horn getting closer and louder, being sounded almost continuously now as it competed with the sound of the fireworks going off all round the village.

48

Douglas was beginning to giggle as he again heaved himself off the single bed, back over his dad and towards the door of the caravan, trying the handle one more time. He slammed his fist into it. He even tried head-butting it, but it was no good. His giggling was turning into full on laughter now as he pulled himself round so his black-socked stumps were facing the door, his hands holding on to the units either side of it for purchase. 'Come on,' he said, as he rolled back, pulling back a stump and kicking at the door. Though there was seemingly nothing but empty space between his stump and the door, Douglas definitely heard a dull thud and saw the door move and indent just a little. He tried again, laughing loudly now as the phantom limb made a visible and permanent dent in the door. The feet he'd had interred with his mum felt as real to him now as they had at any time in his life when they had been part of his physical body, and the tickling sensation he was feeling in those feet was just as real and just as eye-wateringly funny too. He rolled back again, still holding on to the units, and this time pulling back both stumps and lunging at the door as the tickling sensation increased in conjunction with his laughter, which was now veering into hysterics, feeling invisible fingers on his phantom feet. He thought of his mum; and of his severed feet in the shoebox with the picture of Mr Tickle on the lid that he'd drawn from his hospital bed during those early post-feet days. He'd completed that through the pain and the grief and the drugs, then given it to Reverend Bowen who, after retrieving Douglas's feet from her freezer, passed the lot on to funeral director Roland Pollard. His final task, prior to screwing down Alice Blouse's coffin lid, was to place the shoebox in her hands, lacing her fingers over the smiling face of the orange, spaghetti-armed Mr Man character.

In between the thumps at the door and the fireworks going off around them, Douglas also heard his dad starting to groan where he lay between the beds. The other sound now dissonantly harmonising with them all was that of the train bearing down on them. He knew it would not be long until it was upon them, and that it would be going far too fast to stop. Douglas retracted his stumps one last time and manically kicked out at the caravan door with all his physical and non-physical might, feeling the thump on the soles of his invisible feet and the rush of cold air that charged through the caravan door as it swung open, revealing the long dark railway tracks that disappeared under the road bridge in the distance.

Douglas looked to his left, seeing now that his dad was attempting to move. The muffled noises he was making beneath the gaffer-tape gag were getting louder. Douglas dragged himself over to him. He had expended a lot of energy in getting the door open and the tickling sensation he had been feeling in his feet was now beginning to dissipate slightly, but still he felt the odd purchase that made his navigation through the darkened caravan a little easier. He reached his dad and began to pull him towards the door. After spending the last three months in the wheelchair, his upper body strength had increased significantly, and though his dad was by no means light he still managed to pull him towards the open door. Bertie was now beginning to aid his own movement, but was still hampered by the gaffer tape that secured his wrists and ankles. Still, he was able to make spasmodic lunges towards the door, like a large deranged caterpillar, while Douglas continued to do his bit by dragging him with all the strength he had left in him.

The train driver could obviously now see the caravan as he began manically sounding his horn in alarm. It merged with the clacking thrash of the engine that sounded even louder now through the open caravan door. The cacophonous combination was getting closer and more intense.

Douglas's heart was pounding and his muscles were burning, but amazingly both he and his father were now at the door. Douglas bumped himself down and out of the caravan. Reaching back in he grabbed his dad under the arms, trying not to think of the hundred odd tonnes of whatever it was that was careering towards them on the other side. He could hear the rails starting to hiss, bringing back memories of his mooning days. As the engine's horn became deafeningly loud and the ground began to rumble, Douglas summoned one last hysterical, ticklish surge of strength to pull both himself and his dad clear of the railway line and on to the ballast of the embankment, giving them a front row seat as the double-headed class 50 English electric diesel engines obliterated the caravan as if it were matchwood, sending debris flying in all directions under the orange lights of the level crossing. The seismic draught caused by the train was sufficient enough to blow Douglas's red velvet cap clean off his head. Instinctively he buried his face in the crook of his elbow, shielding himself as the rake of carriages hammered past just yards away. Bertie, who could do no such thing simply closed his eyes and turned his head. The carriages clattered over the level crossing and continued on towards the bridge. Cautiously, both Douglas and Bertie opened their eyes, turning their respective gazes back towards the diminishing train heading east, looking on breathlessly by the side of the railway.

Douglas watched the red glow of the train's rear carriage light recede and disappear into the night as the last pieces of debris – namely the caravan's net curtains – fell silently to the ground.

As he surveyed the scene of destruction before him, Douglas again began to laugh. Not a ticklish giggling fit, but a full-throated belly laugh, drinking in the sight of the Marauder 500's total annihilation.

Douglas helped his dad up into a sitting position against the barrier's mechanical control box at the edge of the crossing. He ripped off the gaffer tape that covered Bertie's mouth. Bertie gulped down huge breaths of cold night air as he stared in amazement at his son.

'You coming down for some cake then, or what?' Douglas said to his wide-eyed father, still a little out of breath.

Bertie's mouth hung open in disbelief. Eventually he closed it and smiled. Douglas smiled back.

'You saved my life, Dougie,' Bertie said. 'How? ... Why? ...' He trailed off, gently shaking his head.

Douglas looked at his dad, his breathing beginning to slow along with his heart rate. 'You might be a silly old sod,' Douglas said, 'but you're still my dad, aren't you?'

Bertie leaned in to Douglas, attempting an impossible hug, given that his hands were still gaffer-taped behind his back. Douglas put his arm round his father.

'I think that might've been a rail tour, you know,' Douglas said, looking in the direction of the departed train. 'Did you get the numbers?'

'Sorry, Dougie,' Bertie said, beginning to laugh, 'I missed them.'

Douglas was now laughing along with him. 'I didn't know you could bake,' he said.

Bertie looked up at his son. 'And I never knew that a boy with no feet could kick open a caravan door,' he replied.

Douglas laughed, giving his father a steady appraising stare. 'I guess there's probably still quite a lot that we don't know about each other, isn't there?' he said.

Bertie smiled. 'There's still plenty of time to find out, son,' he said.

'Yeah,' Douglas said with a little wry grin of his own. 'Yeah, I suppose there is.'

49

Dai could find nowhere to turn around, so instead he decided to reverse away from the five-barred gate in growing frustration and at high speed. The horn they had heard in the distance had grown louder, reaching its peak as it passed through the village. Then it ceased and was heard no more. As Dai reversed down the farm track and back onto the tarmac of Stocks Lane, the level crossing came into view in Dai's rear-view mirror once more. The barriers stayed down and the lights carried on flashing. The caravan, however, was now nowhere to be seen. But some of the wreckage had made it over the barrier and was now strewn across the road.

'Jesus,' Rhonda said as she looked over her shoulder towards the crossing.

'Good riddance,' Dai said, looking around to assess his options for escape. 'Pair of English wankers.' A thought suddenly struck him. 'Hang on. We come in over the bridge, didn't we?' Dai said. 'The railway bridge? The railway goes that way,' he said, nodding in the direction that the train had just gone. 'There's another track there, look. That must go up that way,' Dai pointed towards another farm track that went off to the left off Stocks Lane.

'Yeah, I guess so,' Rhonda said.

'Fuck it then,' Dai said, steering the car down the dark farm track. 'Haven't got much of a fuckin' choice now, have we?'

He motored on, shaking his head in frustration as the bumpy farm track abused the Sierra's already battered suspension. The track drew parallel with the railway as it rose in a gradual incline, and the orange street lights of the High Street came into view on their left.

'Look, there!' Rhonda said, pointing at the road ahead. 'That's it! That's where we came in.'

'Fuckin' right it is,' Dai said, gleefully applying more pressure to the accelerator pedal, now ignoring the banging and clunking coming from underneath the car.

Dai was just short of the road when a bright singular light dazzled him up ahead, temporarily blinding him. He put his hand over his eyes and his foot on the brake, and began winding his window down. As his eyes adjusted to the light, the outline of a vehicle came slowly into focus. It looked like a big motorbike, and it was completely blocking their escape route. Dai stuck his head out of the window, revving the accelerator in futile frustration. He could now see that the vehicle up ahead was a trike.

'Stop!' the rider of the vehicle said. 'In the name of the Lord!'

From the left, blue lights came flashing into view with a siren wailing aloud, drawing closer to the trike. The police car pulled up behind the trike, its doors flinging open. As Dai's mind played out the very real possibility of him returning to prison, all he could do was utter two simple words.

'Fuck it.'

50 *Saturday, November 6*

In the kitchen of Pugsden Lane, Bertie took a long knife out of the top drawer and placed it beside the pyramid cake. He re-lit the eighteen partially burned down candles standing around its base and turned off the light in the hall. In the living room, now adorned with Douglas's big birthday banner and balloons from the previous night, Linda did the same thing.

Butch and Linda, Daisy and Kelly, Bertie, Edna and Reverend Bowen began singing Happy Birthday to Douglas, who had just turned the volume down on the hi-fi with the smashed-in lid, reaching over from the armchair beside it in which he was sitting. Kelly was next to him on the arm of the chair. His smiling face was illuminated by the candles as Bertie entered the room and put the cake down on the coffee table in front of him.

'Before anyone asks, I'm not doing another bloody speech,' Douglas said after the singing and clapping had finished.

'But because you didn't cut the cake the first time round, you're entitled to make another wish,' Bertie said. 'It's the rules. But don't worry, it won't invalidate your first one.'

'Damn right it won't,' Douglas said, looking up at Kelly's candlelit face.

'Can it be for Graham to do five years for video piracy?' Edna said, sitting beside Reverend Bowen on the sofa. 'Bloody big-mouthed sod. I hope Alan throws the book at him.'

'And at those bloody caravan-pinching, telly smashing Krankie wankers,' Douglas said, nodding towards the empty space in the corner of the living room by the bay window where the television used to be.

'Oi, language,' Linda said from over by the bay window.

The Krankies were Scottish, mate,' Bertie said, sitting on the arm of the sofa next to Edna.

'Well, wherever they were from,' Douglas said with a dismissive wave of the hand, 'they were a pair of nob 'eads, whoever they were, weren't they?'

'Go on then,' Bertie said, nodding at the cake.

Douglas looked up at the re-framed family photo on the wall above the fireplace, and the mantelpiece now adorned with birthday cards, focusing on his mum's smile that beamed at him even through the candle-lit gloom of the living room, thinking back to the day it was taken. He could almost feel her fingers in his sides, making him laugh as the timer on the camera wound down in the back garden. The tickling that had brought the smile to his face in the photo was just as real then as the tickling he'd felt on his phantom feet the night before, as he'd kicked his way out of the caravan. Douglas looked around the room at the smiling, expectant faces shadowed by candlelight, silently contemplating his wish as he drew in breath. Holding it, he briefly turned to his father, who gave him a little wink. Douglas smiled, looked back up at the family photo on the wall, then extinguished the eighteen candles once again in one big blow.

Everybody clapped as Bertie got up to turn the living room lights back on. He sat back down on the arm of the sofa and put his arm around Edna.

'You gonna be staying here from now on then, Edna?' Douglas asked.

'Hey, don't be so nosy,' Linda said.

'I think it's sweet,' Kelly said, putting her arm around Douglas. 'Everyone needs someone, don't they?'

Bertie smiled. 'That might be the case,' he said, looking at Douglas.

'But only if you're OK with it,' Edna said.

Douglas smiled. 'You know what, if it had been anyone else, I might not have been. But you're like family to me anyway, Edna. Peter was like my brother. And you saved my life at the fete.'

'And you saved mine,' Bertie said, reaching out and putting his hand on Douglas's arm. 'This will always be your home. You'll always have your room here if you want it.'

'How on earth you got out of there, I'll never know,' Linda said, shaking her head. 'When I think what could've happened to you both, it makes my stomach churn. It certainly was some feat!'

Douglas grinned at Reverend Bowen, who smiled and winked back at him. Bertie smiled at the pair of them. Then they all began to laugh.

'What are you lot all looking so pleased with yourselves about?' Linda asked. None of them answered. They just kept on lauging.

'Oh, I was just thinking about something from yesterday,' Douglas eventually said, as his laughter subsided. 'It just tickled me that's all,' he added, with a grin.

Though the record player of the hi-fi was broken, the tape deck and CD player still worked. Douglas reached over and turned the volume back up. Playing in the left cassette deck was a copy of the compilation tape that Bertie and Edna had made up for Alice before the funeral. The song now playing was 'Every Time You Go Away' by Paul Young. Douglas silently mouthed the song's chorus to himself, looking again at the family photo and smiling.

'Anyway,' Douglas said, 'I like it at the vicarage. It's much bigger. And it's good to be close to mum. You know, I think she'd approve of you two,' he said, looking at Bertie and Edna, then again at the photo. 'I know she would.'

Everyone in the room was now either smiling at Douglas or at the photo he was looking at.

'And I'm gonna get a Mr Tickle tattoo on my arse,' Douglas boldly proclaimed. 'Now that I'm eighteen.'

'Really, Douglas?' Linda said. 'Do you honestly think that's a good idea?'

'Ahh, lighten up, girl,' Butch said beside her. 'After all, it's his arse.'

'Yeah, I wanna get those bloody dots covered up,' Douglas said. 'I think mum'd like it.'

Linda's frown dissolved and a smile spread across her face. 'Yes,' she said, 'you know, I think she probably would.'

'I wanna see your dots before any burly tattooist tickles your arse, young man,' Kelly said, prodding Douglas in the ribs.

Douglas smiled, looking up into Kelly's eyes, admiring her beauty. His first wish come true. In contrast to how she looked at the party, her hair was now devoid of hairspray and its subsequent volume. Though still colourful, it was now combed and tied up on one side, revealing the orange undercut on the other.

'Are you gonna cut that thing then or what?' Bertie said, nodding at the cake.

'It is so cool,' Kelly said, gazing at the pyramid. 'You got skills, Mr B!'

Bertie smiled and Douglas picked up the knife. 'I'll drop a piece round to everyone who came last night,' Douglas said. 'Annoying we had to go and give our statements, wasn't it? Didn't get to say 'bye to anyone. Still, I'm glad that Alan caught up with those nutter friends of yours.'

'Those people are not my friends, Douglas,' Bertie said. Edna gave his hand a little squeeze.

'And at least I got my legs back,' Douglas said, 'and my crutches. I don't think the people up at the hospital would have been too pleased if I'd lost my new legs after only having them a couple of weeks.'

'Dai couldn't win a leg off me at the tournament, so he decided to pinch yours instead,' Bertie said.

Everybody laughed.

'That was so cool what you did last night, Hilda,' Douglas said, beaming at Reverend Bowen. 'I bet they couldn't believe it when they saw you there in front of them. Or what you said to them! Classic.'

'Just a little divine intervention,' Bowen said with a smile.

'It didn't take your mum long to hear about what happened to the caravan, did it?' Butch said to Daisy, who was sitting on the floor up against the radiator.

'It never does,' she said.

'God, she completely freaked out when we got back, didn't she, Daisy!' Kelly said, sitting up straight on the arm of the chair. '"I told you, there's always trouble when that boy is around!"' Kelly said, mimicking Daisy's meddlesome mother. '"I told you, you shouldn't have gone to that party, didn't I?! I knew all along that there would be trouble! ... And after everything he's done to you!"'

Everybody laughed at Kelly's lively and highly accurate impersonation, Douglas included, sitting smiling up at her long after she'd finished talking.

'What did you wish for then, tin man?' Kelly said. 'A heart? Or legs that don't look like a pair of silver dildos?'

'My legs are badass, I'll have you know,' Douglas said. 'And I've got a heart, thank you very much.'

'I know you have, dear,' Kelly said, sliding off the arm of the chair into Douglas's lap, kissing him on the cheek. 'And it belongs to me now.'

There was a collective 'Ahhhh' from the living room. Douglas felt himself blush, but he didn't care. He just smiled and kissed Kelly back.

'Get a room, you two,' Daisy said.

'Good idea!' Douglas said. 'How does a night in a Marauder 500 caravan sound? It's in the back garden ... There's just one small problem.'

'Come on then, Douglas, are you ever going to cut that bloody thing?' Linda said, raising a hand to her mouth.

'Linda, language!' Douglas said, frowning as everybody laughed.

'If you don't mind?' Douglas said, now looking at Kelly, who dutifully retook her position on the arm of the chair. Douglas leaned forward, brandishing the knife. 'I kind of don't want to cut it up,' he said, looking at Bertie.

'Go on, get stuck in,' Bertie said. 'I can always make more. Could do a run of Iron Maiden cakes. Might revamp the menu down the Fruitbowl,' he said, looking at Edna. 'Start serving afternoon tea maybe?'

'Yeah, I'm sure that'd go down really well with the regulars, Bert,' Edna said with a sarcastic grin.

'Yeah, stick to your burgers, pop,' Douglas said. 'I'm bringing Kelly down for a Big Girl's Blouse burger tomorrow before she goes home. I'm gonna give it a go riding mum's bike down there. Take it for a spin. Daisy's coming 'n' all, as long as her mum doesn't find out.'

'"After everything he's done to you, you're going for a burger with him!"' Kelly said in hysterical tones, flying back into character. '"Who knows what might happen to you!?"'

Laughter filled the room as Douglas sliced into the cake, drawing the knife slowly down from the pyramid's capstone before the blade became

294

stuck about three inches from the cake stand. The blade had hit something solid.

'What the ffff?' Douglas said.

Linda tutted. Butch smiled.

Douglas drew the knife out towards him, tracing the blade over whatever it was that was lurking inside the pyramid. As it reached the edge of whatever it was, the knife sliced down through the last few inches of sponge pyramid.

'Interesting,' Douglas said with a rather bemused look on his face as he continued to cut slices of cake. Some cut clean, others were again impeded by the cake's unseen contents. As further pieces were removed a rectangular white chocolate box was revealed at the cake's centre, recessed into the layers of sponge. The box's exterior was covered in hieroglyphics, some genuine, some just silly squiggles and amusing random doodles. Douglas could make out a pair of false legs, an acoustic guitar and even Mr Bump in amongst the Egyptian doodles.

Linda was still carefully wrapping pieces of cake in serviettes for all the guests who had missed out the first time round, when Douglas had finally cut enough cake to be able to remove the white chocolate sarcophagus. He picked it up, feeling the weight of something else inside it. He gave it a gentle shake.

'Have I disturbed the pharaoh's tomb?' he said with a curious smile.

'Sooo cool,' Kelly said, resting her arm across Douglas's shoulders as she looked at the white chocolate box that Douglas had begun to nibble at.

'Why don't you crack it open and see what the gods have in store for you?' Bertie said.

Douglas picked up the knife, holding it vertically with the tip of the blade pointing into the middle of the top of the box. He drove it in and the box broke up into pieces. Inside it was another small sarcophagus that resembled a miniature Tutankhamun. This, however, was not made of chocolate. It was a small tin tomb about three inches long with two hinges on one side and a small latch on the other.

'Open it then,' Kelly said excitedly beside him.

Douglas did as he was told, opening up the tomb. Inside was a rolled up piece of paper tied up with red cotton. Douglas pulled the paper free from its constraints and unrolled it. It was a cheque made out to him for ten thousand pounds. He stared at it in wide-eyed wonder, then looked at his dad.

'Happy birthday, son,' Bertie said, smiling beside him.

*

It took a while for it to sink in, but eventually Douglas started to get his head around the idea. And having Kelly on hand to help him think of all the possibilities that ten grand could be used for certainly helped. Excitable chatter at the prospect of crowd surfing legless at next year's Monsters of Rock festival at Castle Donington was met with a cautious appeal for calm from a mildly concerned-looking Auntie Linda, and an enthusiastic nod of approval from a smiling Uncle Butch, who was also quick to suggest that Douglas could upgrade the 20 watt combo amplifier that Linda had bought him for his birthday – along with a cherry red Epiphone SG just like Angus Young's – for a twin 4 x 12 Marshall stack and head. Linda, however, was not amused.

After tea and cake, everyone put their coats on and headed out into the chilly night air of the back garden. The fireworks that had been intended for the previous night's party were all lined up, ready and waiting. Behind them was an enormous pile of wood that stood well over six feet tall.

'Now, about that night in the caravan,' Douglas said to Kelly on his arm, nodding towards the unlit pyre. They laughed, looking at the shattered remains of Bully's star prize. The jagged, splintered pieces of wreckage sat among chunks of broken-up wooden pallets, supplied by Butch, making up almost half of the towering pile. Not all of it, but enough.

'Good fuckin' riddance,' Douglas said, walking towards it with Edna's lighter in his hand. With Kelly's support he gingerly bent down and lit the kindling at the base of the bonfire. It didn't take long for it to catch, and within five minutes it had taken hold and was well ablaze.

Bertie brought out a tray of drinks to put on the plastic green table out on the back garden's small patio. He poured glasses of red wine and cracked open cans of beer as the blazing bonfire started to kick out more and more heat.

'Give us that then, step-nephew,' Butch said, setting his beer down and liberating Douglas of Edna's lighter, before walking towards the row of rockets. He crouched down and lit the fuses of the first two. After a sparkling moment of anticipation, the rockets hissed and whooshed their way skyward, exploding in a bomb burst of pink and green. These were swiftly followed by a third and fourth burst.

Unbeknown to everyone around him, Douglas had started to feel a mild tickling sensation. He started to giggle, looking up at the fireworks. Beside him Kelly smiled, oblivious to the source of his amusement.

There was another explosion of pink in the sky as Bertie handed Douglas one of the two cans of beer he was holding. Douglas was still giggling a little as he opened it, though there was also now a sizable lump in his throat and a tear in his eye.

'Cheers, Dougie,' Bertie said, holding up his can.

'Cheers, dad,' he replied, clinking cans with his father, sensing an unseen presence nearby. Just as he had done during some of his darkest days over the past few months, knowing that she had been with him through it all. Every step of the way.

All eyes were on the fireworks exploding overhead into the cold night air. All except Douglas's. He was looking past the remaining rockets lined up in front of him, towards the bonfire; staring just beyond the crackling, rippling flames and straight into the eyes of his mum. Her smiling face was lit in shadow by the bonfire's orange glow, watching on as he shared a drink with his dad. Above them another rocket exploded into colour, fully illuminating Alice for the briefest of moments. Douglas smiled and held up a hand to his mum, a tear rolling down his cheek. In the time it took him to wipe it away she was gone, but by then Douglas was pretty sure that his second wish had also come true.

Acknowledgements

Thank you to everyone who bought, read, enjoyed and said such nice things about the first book. (That almost certainly means you, oh dearest returning reader). Your kind words gave me the confidence and encouragement to see this story through to the end.

Super-Smashing-Great thanks to Jason Cripps, Neil Frame, Emily Stannard, Alison Busby, Ray Hunt, Karen Farley and Nigel Mitchell and his wonderful team at Biddles Books.

Last but by no means least thank you to the magical village of Steventon - My spiritual home. Without you there would be no story.